## The Urbana Free Library

To renew: call 217-367-4057
or go to *"urbanafreelibrary.org"*
and select "Renew/Request Items"

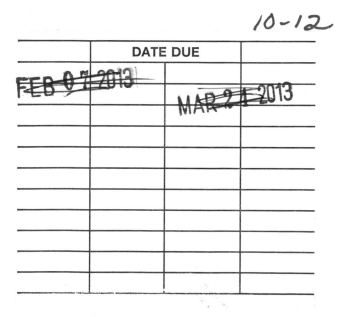

# BLACK FLOWER

## ALSO BY YOUNG-HA KIM

I HAVE THE RIGHT TO DESTROY MYSELF

YOUR REPUBLIC IS CALLING YOU

# BLACK FLOWER

## YOUNG-HA KIM

Translated from the Korean by Charles La Shure

HOUGHTON MIFFLIN HARCOURT

BOSTON · NEW YORK

2012

www.hmhbooks.com

*Library of Congress Cataloging-in-Publication Data*
Kim, Young-ha, date. [Kŏmŭn kkot. English]
Black flower / Young-ha Kim ; translated from the Korean
by Charles La Shure.
p. cm.
ISBN 978-0-547-69113-8
I. La Shure, Charles. II. Title.
PL992.415.Y5863K6613 2012
895.7'34—dc23      2012014220

*Book design by Melissa Lotfy*

Printed in the United States of America
DOC 10 9 8 7 6 5 4 3 2 1

*If death is death,*

*what then of poets*

*and the hibernating things*

*no one remembers?*

— FEDERICO GARCÍA LORCA,
"Autumn Song," translated by Martin Sorrell

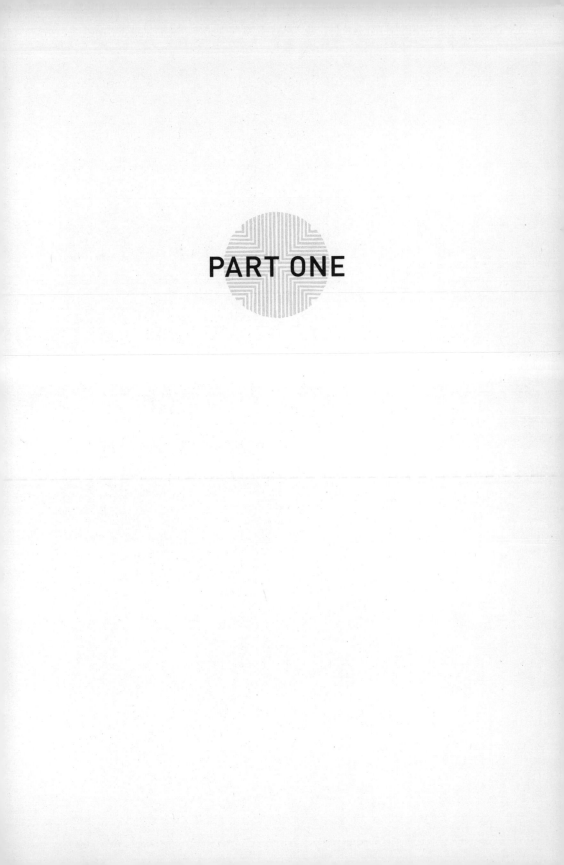

PART ONE

# 1

WITH HIS HEAD THRUST into the swamp filled with swaying weeds, many things swarmed before Ijeong's eyes. All were pieces of the scenery of Jemulpo that he thought he had long ago forgotten. Nothing had disappeared: the flute-playing eunuch, the fugitive priest, the spirit-possessed shaman with the turned-in teeth, the girl who smelled of roe deer blood, the poor members of the royal family, the starving discharged soldiers, even the revolutionary's barber — they all waited for Ijeong with smiling faces in front of the Japanese-style building on the hill in Jemulpo.

How could all these things be so vivid with closed eyes? Ijeong was mystified. He opened his eyes and everything disappeared. A booted foot pushed on the nape of his neck, shoving his head deep into the bottom of the swamp. Foul water and plankton rushed into his lungs.

# 2

FEBRUARY 1904. Japan declared war on Russia. Japanese troops landed in Korea and seized Seoul, attacking the Russian fleet at Port

Arthur. In March of 1905, 250,000 Japanese troops fought at Feng-tian in Manchuria, losing 70,000 men but winning the battle.

Admiral Togo Heihachiro's Japanese combined fleet held its breath and waited for the Baltic Fleet under Admiral Rozhestven-sky, which had rounded the Cape of Good Hope and was heading for the Far East, unaware of its fate.

In the spring of that year, people flocked to Jemulpo Harbor. The crowd included everyone from beggars to short-haired men, women in skirts and Korean jackets, and runny-nosed children. Short hair had been in fashion since ten years before, when the king, Gojong, had cut off his topknot due to pressure from the Japanese and issued the Hair Cutting Edict in 1895. In that same year, he also lost his queen to assassins sent by his father and by Japan, her body ruthlessly stabbed, then burned by Japanese thugs. In one stroke, he lost the hair that he had grown from his youth and the queen who had long been by his side; the king fled to the Russian legation and attempted to stage a comeback, but it came to nothing. A few years later, in 1897, the kingdom became an empire and the king became an emperor, but he was impotent. It was in that year that America won its war with Spain and gained the Philippines. There was no end to the ambitions of the powers that surged toward Asia. The powerless emperor was plagued by insomnia.

But in 1905 Jemulpo was a desolate harbor. With the exception of the Japanese settlement and the Japanese consulate, which had been built magnificently in the Renaissance style, it was hard to find even a single decent building on the sloping hill. The coastal islands and inland mountains were treeless; they looked like piles of peat. There were quite a few private houses. Their thatched roofs, though, squatted round and low to the ground, so they weren't very noticeable. The Korean burden bearers, wearing white cotton head-bands, walked along in single file, barefoot children running along behind them. Near the Japanese consulate a group of Japanese women walked with mincing steps. The spring sunshine was dazzling, but the women walked with their eyes on the ground, as Japanese soldiers in black uniforms stood guard. Holding rifles with fixed bayonets, they glanced sidelong at the procession of women. The kimono parade passed in front of a European-style wooden building. On the front of the building hung a wooden sign on which were written the words "British Consulate." A Westerner came out of the building and went down to the pier.

The Japanese imperial fleet, which had participated in the siege of Port Arthur, could be seen heading south, flying high the flag of the rising sun. The black guns on the sides of the ships glistened with oil.

# 3

THE BOY TOOK A SPOT in the cabin in the bottom of the boat; there was room for him in a corner. He curled up as much as he could and covered himself with the clothes he had brought. Then he looked around the cabin, gloomy as a cave. Those who boarded as families gathered in circles. Men with buxom daughters were on edge, the whites of their eyes bloodshot. There seemed to be five times as many men as women. Whenever the women went anywhere, the eyes of the men followed them secretly and persistently. Four years. That's how long they would stay together, these people. If a girl reached marrying age, might she not become a wife? This is what the single men thought. The boy didn't think that far ahead, but he was at a hot-blooded age and sensitive to everything. For several days his dreams had been troubled. Girls would appear and set his head spinning. Dreams where a girl caressed his earlobes and disheveled his hair with her delicate hands were fine, but sometimes a girl would rush at him naked and wake him from his slumber. After nights like those, his chest pounded even when he was awake, and he had to pick his way between the sleeping people and go out onto the deck to get a breath of the dawn's cold sea air. The SS *Ilford* was stuck in the harbor like an island. How far would they have to go to reach that warm country? No one knew for sure. There were those who said that, surprisingly enough, it would take a half year, and there were those who said they would arrive in ten days at most. No one aboard had ever made the journey before, so confusion was natural. Everyone swung back and forth like pendulums between vague hope and unease.

Leaning on the side of the ship, the boy carved the three characters of "Kim I Jeong" into the oaken railing with a knife from his pocket. He had gained those three characters here in Jemulpo, right at this pier. A strapping man with a long scar on his wrist asked, "What's your family name?" The boy hesitated. The man nodded as if he understood. "Your name?" "People just called me Jangsoe," the boy said. The man asked him where his parents were. The boy didn't exactly know. He didn't know if it was the Military Mutiny of 1882 or the Donghak Rebellion, but his father had been caught up in one of them and killed, and his mother had gone off somewhere as soon as his father died. He was taken in and raised by a peddler. The only thing the peddler ever gave him was the name Jangsoe. When they stopped near Seoul, the boy ran away while the peddler slept.

"What sort of land is Mexico?" This was at the Seoul Young Men's Christian Association. An American missionary spoke, his black beard covering his neck. "Mexico is far. Very far." The boy narrowed his eyes. "Then where is it close to?" The missionary laughed. "It's right below America. And it's very hot. But why are you asking about Mexico?" The boy showed him the advertisement in the *Capital Gazette*. But the missionary, who did not know Chinese characters, could not read the advertisement. Instead, another young Korean explained the contents of the advertisement in English. Only then did the missionary nod. The boy asked him, "If I were your son, would you tell me to go?" The missionary did not understand right away, so the boy asked again. The missionary's face grew grave and he slowly shook his head. "Then, if you were me, would you go?" The missionary was lost in deep thought. The boy hadn't been long at the school, but he was bright and unusually quick to understand. He had been raised as an orphan, but had not grown timid, and he stood out from the other students with similar stories.

The bearded missionary gave him some coffee and a muffin. The boy's mouth began to water. The peddler who had taken him around the country had taught him: "If someone gives you something to eat, count to one hundred before eating. And if someone wants to buy something of yours, double the price that comes to mind. That way no one will look down on you." The boy rarely had the opportunity to follow these instructions. No one gave him anything to eat, and no one wanted to buy anything he owned. The missionary opened his eyes wide. "Aren't you hungry?" The boy's lips moved slightly. Eighty-two, eighty-three, eighty-four. He couldn't bear it any longer. He took the sweet-smelling raisin muffin and began to stuff it into his mouth. When he had finished the muffin and coffee, the missionary brought him to a room with a lot of books and showed him a map of the world. On it was a country that looked like a sunken, empty belly. Mexico. The missionary asked him, "Do you really want to go? You've only been attending school for three months . . . How about studying more before you go?" The boy shook his head. "They say that chances like this do not come often. I heard that boys with no parents are welcome." The missionary could see that his heart was set. He gave the boy an English Bible. "Someday you will be able to read it. If you earn some money in Mexico, go to America. The Lord will guide you." Then he hugged the boy. The boy held the missionary tightly. His beard brushed the nape of the boy's neck.

The boy went to Jemulpo and stood at the end of the long line. In that line he met the strapping man who tousled the boy's hair. "A person must have a name. Forget childhood names like Jang-soe. Take Kim as your family name and Ijeong as your given name. It's easy to write — just the character *i* (二), meaning two, and the character *jeong* (正), meaning upright." As the line grew shorter he wrote the boy's name in Chinese characters. It was seven strokes in all. The man's name was Jo Jangyun. A staff sergeant engineer in the new-style army of the Korean Empire, he had set aside his uniform when the Russo-Japanese War broke out. There were a number of others in the same situation. Two hundred of these men, who had suited up together and trained in the new-style long rifles with the Russian advisory corps, had thronged to Jemulpo. There were enough of them to form an entire battalion. They had no land and no relatives. No nation needed an army more urgently than the feeble empire, but no rice could be found in the empire's storerooms to feed them. Above all, the Japanese were demanding a curtailment of Korean military expenditures and a reduction in force of arms. Soldiers on the frontiers left their barracks and wandered off, and when they saw the Continental Colonization Company's advertisement they raced to Jemulpo. They were the first to want to leave for Mexico, where work, money, and warm food were said to await them. Jo Jangyun was one of those men. His father, a hunter in Hwanghae province, had left for China; someone had seen him living with a Chinese woman in Shanghai. But Jo Jangyun did not go to Shanghai. Instead he chose Mexico, where they said the sun was warm year-round. And didn't they say his wages would be dozens of times higher than a soldier's pay? What did it matter where he went? There was no need to hesitate. Life in Mexico couldn't be any harder than it had been in the army.

The boy cast his gaze over the ocean once more. Three black-billed seagulls wheeled above his head. Someone had said that there was gold in Mexico. They said that yellow gold poured forth from the earth, making many suddenly rich. "No. That's America," insisted another, but he sounded uncertain too. The boy repeated his name. "Kim Ijeong. My name is Kim Ijeong. I am going to a far land. And I will return as an adult Kim Ijeong. I will return with my name and with money and I will buy land, and there I will plant rice." Those with land were respected. That was a simple truth the boy had learned on the road. It couldn't be Mexican land. It had to be Korean land, and a rice paddy. But another thought had raised its head in the boy's heart, the thought of another strange land, called America.

The seagulls fluttered above the surface of the water as if dancing. The quicker ones flew away with fairly large fish in their beaks. The wings of the gulls were tinged red. The sun was setting. The boy went down to the cabin and again wedged himself into the corner. The coarse, low voices of men could be heard between the cries of children. There was no strength in the voices of these men; they did not know their futures. Their words dissipated like the foam that washed against the prow of the ship. The boy closed his eyes. He hoped that he would not wake until breakfast.

# 4

THE NEXT DAY, John G. Meyers gathered everyone on deck and spoke to them in English with a strong Dutch accent. A short young man with sagging eyes interpreted.

"Our departure has been delayed. The British minister to Korea, Sir John Gordon, is not allowing the *Ilford* to depart. Because this ship is British territory, we must receive Sir John's permission to depart. We have quarantined the young children who have caught chickenpox, but there may be additional cases, so we have been ordered to stay at anchor here for two weeks. Wait just a little more. Once we reach Mexico, beautiful houses and hot food will be waiting for you."

After he finished his announcement, Meyers crossed over to the pier with the interpreter, Gwon Yongjun. Those left behind huddled together and grumbled. "We sailed all the way to Busan and were turned back because we didn't have proper passports, and now they say we have to wait two more weeks? At this rate we'll never get there this year."

# 5

EARLY IN THE MORNING, people began to gather at the entrance of Dangjin Town, a place filled with row upon row of thatched roofs. Old villagers with long pipes in their mouths and sniffling children, male and female, young and old — it seemed as if every villager with two legs to stand on had come. They were all staring at one tree. Said to be over three hundred years old, the tree was draped with red and blue cloth on each branch. Every year the villagers prepared offerings and presented them to this tree, especially women with no children or women whose husbands were far away. Everyone continued to stare at the tree. They were staring at the body of a woman, hanging like a piece of fruit. Her blue skirt flapped in the wind below her short white jacket. On the ground beneath her feet lay a hairpin. As soon as men climbed up the tree and cut the cotton cloth that was wrapped around her neck, the body fell. Dry dust rose up. Young women ran forward and tried to untie the cloth, but it wasn't easy. The men came down from the tree, brushed off their hands, and kept their distance from the body. The cloth was finally removed from the woman's neck. Someone took a few steps and threw the cloth into a fire.

Someone spread out a large straw bag and the woman's body was laid on top of it. The men tied up the bag with practiced motions. They cinched the bag tightly with straw ropes where they guessed the neck, waist, and ankles to be, then put it in an ox cart. "Hiya!" The ox began to walk. As the sounds of the whip on the ox's back grew fainter, the remaining men all headed in one direction. They walked slowly, but with strength. As the march continued, farming tools such as sticks and metal rakes were passed among the ranks. Before long the men stopped. They looked just like a historical painting of the start of a peasants' revolt.

White walls and a bell tower, out of place among the low thatched roofs of the village, rose before them. The wooden cross on the bell tower stood in curious contrast to the bladed metal implements in the hands of those crowded around it. One man rolled up his sleeves and walked toward the church. The man halted for a moment in the dark entrance, leaned the metal rake he was carrying against the white wall, and hesitantly disappeared into the church, empty-handed. After some time he emerged again and the men raced inside.

"He's gone!" someone shouted. "There's no one here!" Three men caught a cripple in the shed behind the church and brought him out, still holding a broom. He was the janitor who took care of all the chores around the church. He raised his hand and pointed toward the ocean. A man wearing a bamboo hat took out his wrath on the janitor by thrashing him across the back with a stick. A man with a long beard and a horsehair hat restrained him by clearing his throat. The janitor huddled over like a caterpillar thrown into the fire. "He has done nothing wrong," the man in the horsehair hat said feebly. "Let's burn it!" a large man said as he pointed at the church. The man in the horsehair hat hesitated for some time, as if to lend more dignity to his words, and then shook his head. "That's enough. Such is the virtue of the barbarians. They do not sacrifice to their ancestors, nor do they cry when their parents die, so what good is it to speak of the chastity of a married woman? Board up the barbarians' sanctuary so that no one may enter." The enraged men ran forward and nailed pieces of wood across the church door and windows. They did not have enough wood, so they tore the cross from the roof, broke it in two, and used it to board up a window.

After the men had eaten, they climbed up the hill behind the village, dug a shallow pit, and tossed in the woman's body wrapped in the straw sack. They filled in the pit with dirt and wordlessly climbed back down the hill. They could see the ocean from the squash patch between the village and the hill. They spit violently toward that ocean, hazy with shimmering heat waves.

# 6

FATHER PAUL BAK GWANGSU knelt before Bishop Simon Blanche. He lifted his head and saw the white clerical collar. The bishop looked into the young priest's eyes with a pained expression. "You must go back. That is your calling. Even if you are stoned or rolled up in a straw mat and beaten, you must reveal the truth and present the Church's position. Our Lord, who rules over all, will ultimately reveal all things."

The bishop knew more than anyone else just how difficult mission work was in Korea. He had landed on Baengnyeong Island in 1880 and was arrested for his mission work in Baekcheon, Hwanghae province, then freed, thanks to the open foreign policy of the Min clan oligarchy. He was then ordained as the eighth archbishop of Korea. Compared to many of the Western priests before him who had been beheaded at the execution ground outside the Lesser Western Gate, he was truly fortunate. He was also the one who had sent the young Bak Gwangsu to seminary in Penang, Malaysia, and the one who had made him a priest. The conflict with the natives that Father Paul now faced was a rite of passage, something he must inevitably endure. Surely he hadn't become a priest without knowing that, had he?

The young man lowered his head again. The bishop assured him once more: "I know it is difficult. But please tell me you will do it. That place is sacred ground that our Church has defended with blood. The Lord forgave the Roman governor Pilate and the crowds who shouted for Him to be nailed to the cross. Please do the same."

The priest made the sign of the cross and stood up. The old bishop embraced him. Father Paul left the bishop's office with a heavy tread. The sun was dazzling. He squinted. He saw the body of the woman hanging from the tree like a phantom. Father Paul covered his eyes with his hands. He murmured, "Lord, I have done no wrong. My Father, you know this."

He lowered the hands from his eyes. Then he shook his head fiercely. "I cannot go back there. No matter what you may do, Lord,

I will not go back to that land of demons. They will kill me, and it will be a meaningless death."

Then what do you plan to do? He heard the question coming from deep inside him. Do you plan to disobey the bishop's order? Are you not a priest who vowed to obey those above him? Father Paul buried his head in his hands. "Oh, I don't know! Why am I so weak? Should I have never become a priest?"

He walked away flustered. He wandered aimlessly for a while and then squatted down in front of a door to someone's house. The world looked different from down low. All he could see were feet and legs. He stared at these bodies devoid of character and suddenly fell asleep. He dreamed. He was walking in a place full of trees, flowers, and birds that he had never seen before. The leaves grew so thick that the day was as dark as night. His sweat fell like rain. When he passed this place he climbed up a steep hill, and there the land spread out flat before him for dozens of leagues in all directions. That strange hill, without a trace of human presence, seemed like a place where humanity could communicate directly with God. The place was filled with curious letters and sculptures, and a white horse descended from heaven and opened its mouth wide as if to swallow him.

# 7

THE JOSEON DYNASTY lasted for five hundred years. When it was founded, in 1392, the neighboring peoples were forced to take note of this new country, one born of a mighty military power forged in the north and the political order of Neo-Confucianism. Yet after two hundred years, Toyotomi Hideyoshi and his army crossed the ocean from Japan, and the kingdom reeled for six long years.

The samurai were driven off, but not long after, the Jurchen army attacked, and the Joseon king beat his head on the ground, begging for mercy. The blood that flowed from his forehead stained the pavement stones around him.

In the years to follow, members of the royal family continued to be born, grow up, and leave behind more royal descendants. Suppressed by the power of the Andong Kim clan and the Min clan, they could not hope to be restored to their former glory, but they were still the Jeonju Yi clan, the royal family. After Gojong was made emperor in 1897, they were elevated from royal family to imperial family, but some of them still went hungry. Their social status kept them from planting rice seedlings in the fields or entering the market as merchants. The emperor's concubines were forced to mend their own clothes. Their bloodline gave them nothing, but demanded much — a curse rather than an honor. They were thorns in the side of Japan, which would soon swallow up the Korean Empire. The Japanese minister did not rest in his watch of the emperor's close relatives, especially those who might accede to the throne. Russia and China had lost their influence and retreated; no one knew what Japan might do to those of noble blood. After all, the empress had been brutally stabbed by Japanese thugs not many years before.

Yi Jongdo, cousin of Emperor Gojong, called his family together: "Japan's victory is imminent. The emperor is unable to sleep." As soon as the title of the august ruler passed Jongdo's lips, the whole family bowed. "We are leaving." He wept. His son and daughter, who were not yet married, kept their heads bowed. Only his wife, Lady Yun of the Papyeong Yun clan, approached him. She sat down close to him. "Where do you intend to go?" His wife and children could think of only a few places in the southwest. They would flee to the countryside when a political crisis neared, raise the younger generation, and bide their time, as the officials of Joseon had done for the previous five hundred years. And then, when the political climate in the capital changed, the former rebels would return as loyal vassals — was that not the history of politics in Joseon? Yet from the lips of Yi Jongdo came instead a three-syllable word they had never heard. "Mexico? Where is that?" In reply to his wife's question, Yi Jongdo said that it was a far land, below America. He added in a grieved tone, "The empire will not last long. We cannot be dragged off to Japan to see our lives end there, can we? We must learn from the civilization of the West. We must build up our strength there. Before the break of day we will go to the royal ancestral shrines, bow to the deities of the nation, take the spirit tablets of our ancestors, and leave for Jemulpo. I pray you will accept your father's decision." Yi Jongdo shouted in a loud whisper: "Long live His Majesty the Emperor!" His family shouted in reply: "Long may he live, long may he live, long, long may he live!" But their shouts did not pass beyond the threshold. Yi Jongdo's young son, Jinu, could not help but cry. This was a difficult situation for such a young member of the imperial family, only fourteen years old, who was reading introductory Chinese classics like *The Analects of Confucius* and *Lesser Learning*. His elder sister, Yi Yeonsu, who was of marriageable age, showed no emotion. She knew that the tide was already changing. Even girls were cutting their hair and studying the new learning. A time was coming when they would learn English and geography, mathematics and law, and stand shoulder to shoulder with men. Of course, this was not true of respectable women. The missionaries first drew the socially ostracized women to their school. The daughters of butchers, gisaeng courtesans, and orphans with no one to turn to formed one class, and the school was their only choice. There they found clothes, books, and a place to sleep. Her mother reviled the female students who walked the streets in their short skirts, calling them "despicable girls," but Yeonsu, wrapped in her cloak, envied them. She did not know the land called Mexico, but she was familiar with America. If Mexico was a neighbor to America, then it must be fairly civilized, a place where women could learn and work and speak their minds, just like men, and more than anything else where they would not shackle people with the seemingly attractive yoke of imperial blood, as they did here. They would be enlightened there, wouldn't they? She shut her mouth tight and did not say a word. Her family took her silence as approval.

Within two days, they had abandoned their home, slung their ancestors' spirit tablets over their backs, and left for Jemulpo.

# 8

FATHER PAUL FELT hands groping him and opened his eyes. Right in front of his nose was a man's face. The moment he shouted, "What are you doing?" the man grabbed him by the throat and butted his face with his forehead. Then he used his fists to hit the priest repeatedly in the face. Father Paul fell over like a sheaf of straw. The man took the priest's belongings, ripped his money from his chest, and calmly walked away. Was that priest crazy? Sleeping laid out on the street like that when it's only barely spring?

The thief opened the silk pouch he had stolen. It was heavy in his hand. He reached in with his other hand and took its contents out one by one. Various and sundry items emerged, but the most curious was a silver cross. It was engraved with letters he did not recognize, and the surface was covered with a delicate pattern. It was not a product of Korea. It must have been from China or one of the Western countries. Why would they have made this shape out of silver? He tilted his head. It wasn't a ring, nor was it a woman's trinket.

A leather thong ran through a ring at the top of the cross, showing that it was used as a necklace. Still, it was silver, so he could melt it down and sell it. The thief put the cross necklace away. Also in the pouch were a few pennies, some documents written in foreign letters, and a small book. He took the money and threw the rest into the gutter. He gently shook his burning fists and continued walking. He could take care of food and lodging for a few days with this. He was humming as he turned into an alley, but ran right into someone. He sized up the other man out of habit. The other man bowed his head and apologized, though it wasn't necessarily his fault. The two exchanged glances but the priest did not recognize the thief, and the thief set his mind at ease. He stared after the priest's retreating figure. Dimwitted aristocrat. He trudged along with a scowl, following the priest at a distance. The priest went up the hill, asking people something and rubbing his bruised face as he went along. He passed the Chinese and Japanese neighborhoods, then stopped in front of a handsome two-story building. On the front of the building, in Chinese characters, was written "Continental Colonization Company." Several hundred people seemed to be waiting in line there. The thief asked what the line was for. After he heard their answer he went to a nearby marketplace, where he ate hot soup and rice. Then he went back to the Continental Colonization Company. The man who had lost everything to him was sitting at the end of the line. The thief took a seat behind the man. Their eyes met a few times, but only when he saw that the priest still did not recognize him did the thief speak. The priest introduced himself as a student from Chungcheong province. When the thief pointed to the bruises on his face, the priest said that he had been robbed. "Oh!" The thief slapped his knee. Then he said that there were many light-fingered fellows in such open ports as Jemulpo, and advised him to be careful. Yet the priest did not seem too concerned about the things he had lost. He just buried his face between his knees and waited for the line to grow shorter. The employees of the Continental Colonization Company worked diligently. They had to pack everyone in tight and weigh anchor before the imperial government and the Japanese minister changed their minds again. They wrote down names, number of family members, and hometowns. "Don't worry," they said. "The Mexican farm owners will pay for your passage, food, and clothing." At that time, they did not need to pay a single penny.

The thief, who would later be called Choe Seongil, robbed two people of their possessions that night. People who had come to the city for the first time or whose hearts were restless with thoughts of leaving for a distant place often failed to guard their belongings. Choe Seongil was excited, and pondered leaving for Mexico with these people. Once the thought entered his mind he could not find a reason why he shouldn't. Even if I only hit one mark, he told himself, it will be better than here. If it doesn't work out, I can always come back.

Choe Seongil boarded the *Ilford* with the priest, without having disposed of his stolen goods. The boat was more like the warships he had heard about rather than a passenger ship. Surely this was one of the Black Ships, the Kurofune, that had appeared in Japan and put the Tokugawa shogunate in its place. Choe Seongil's mouth dropped open. He liked the power, dignity, and authority of the West that the great steamship exuded. He got the vague feeling that these things would protect him from all ill fortune and threats. Even the strange new smell of coal tar was pleasantly fragrant. Choe Seongil walked boldly onto the ship, feeling as if he had already become a member of the West. The German, Japanese, and British crewmen were moving around the boat with purpose. It was a world unto itself and, as the minister Sir John Gordon had declared, British territory afloat on the ocean.

Choe raced ahead of the slow-moving family groups and quickly chose a good spot to lie down. Next to him lay a boy who still had pimple marks on his face, peering into every corner of the dark cabin with his deep-set eyes. The scaly rashes on his face betrayed his poverty. The thief immediately felt as snug as home in the cabin, which was like the innards of some mythical beast, and he took the blanket that had been given him by a German crewman, pulled it up to his eyebrows, and went to sleep.

# 9

YI JONGDO LED HIS family onto the *Ilford* and, as always, looked for someone in authority. But he met only crew members who spoke rough Western languages. Those who caught on quickly had gone below deck to find good spots early on, but Yi Jongdo stood firm on the cold deck swept by the sea winds, waiting for someone who could understand him. Before long, John Meyers and the interpreter Gwon Yongjun appeared. Gwon Yongjun asked him, "Why do you not go below?" Yi Jongdo knit his brows. He had intended to reveal that he was the descendant of such-and-such a prince, and thus blood kin to the emperor, but he saw Oba Kanichi, dispatched to Jemulpo by the Continental Colonization Company, standing next to the interpreter, and he swallowed his words. Instead, he merely asked for a cabin becoming of his status as a literati — a scholar-bureaucrat and member of the nobility. "I can't very well stay in the same place as them, can I?" Yi Jongdo pointed at the place where people had gone below. While Gwon Yongjun passed along Yi Jongdo's comment, several Koreans had gathered behind Yi Jongdo. They were not members of the imperial family, but judging by their clothing and the shape of their horsehair hats, they were clearly aristocrats. They were expecting similar treatment if Yi Jongdo's request was accepted. In the meantime, Yi Jongdo's wife and son felt an intense horror at the prospect of having to live with commoners, and even beggars. Lady Yun continuously wiped away tears with her sleeve. Yet Yeonsu, his only daughter, looked around with interest at the new people and scenery. From a little farther away, though, Yi Jongdo and his family were a sight to see. Two women wrapped in cloaks and a horsehair-hat-wearing aristocrat putting up a bold front stood in curious contrast to the Union Jack that fluttered from the mast.

Meyers finally spoke. "This boat was not originally a passenger ship but a cargo ship. Even the crew are sleeping in narrow bunk beds, so we cannot assign cabins to Koreans." Yi Jongdo was frustrated that Meyers did not understand him. "I'm not asking for rooms for everyone. I am asking for treatment becoming of our standing and status." Meyers made his final decision known through Gwon Yongjun. "I am sorry, but we don't have the space for that. If you do not like it, disembark. There are many people who want to go." Yi Jongdo's pride was wounded that such a natural request had been denied. "What an ignorant fellow," Yi Jongdo cursed at Meyers as the man went up to the bridge. Then he spoke to his family. "There will be people in Mexico who will understand me. I have heard that there are landowners and a powerful aristocracy there. Anyone who has ever had a man work for him knows that not all human beings are the same. We are not going as workers, we are going as representatives of the Korean Empire. We must not forget this. The eyes of the wicked Japanese are on us now, so we must persevere for the time being, but when we weigh anchor I will meet the captain and ask again."

Yi Yeonsu spoke. "It would be best if you did not. I think it would be more reasonable to go to Mexico and there meet with someone of high standing and explain our situation." Even as she spoke, she did not think such a thing would come to pass. Yet the other members of the family agreed with her. They knew all too well the usual results of Yi Jongdo's stubbornness. Resigned, Yi Jongdo went down to the cargo hold that was being used as a general cabin. It was already full of people. He stood among them and cleared his throat, but no one prepared a place for his family. Everyone covered themselves with their blankets and stretched out their legs. "If I had known it would be like this, I would have brought Myeongsik." Yi Jongdo regretted having left his servant behind. His family's dignity did not permit them to squeeze into any of the narrow spaces; they had to stand awkwardly for some time at the edge of the cabin. Lady Yun looked as if she were about to cry and gazed downward, and Yi Jongdo stared at the ceiling. After they had stood that way for an hour, a wailing was suddenly heard from a corner of the cabin. "Oh! Oh!" A man was holding a piece of white paper that had been brought to him by an employee of the Continental Colonization Company. He held it in front of him and his family bowed as one and wailed. It seemed that one of their relatives, an elderly one at that, had died. The dry, tearless mourning continued like a ritual, and then the family began to gather their belongings. They had received the message; they had no choice. They left the ship with sorrow-stricken faces. Yi Jinu ran to claim the empty spot. Yi Jongdo cleared his throat once, disapprovingly, and slowly walked to the place. It was only a few steps away, yet in the time it took him to cover the distance the area had already shrunk, but it had been occupied by five people and so was still not too small to seat four. It was not, of course, sufficient space to observe Confucian etiquette, but they were satisfied for the time being. As long as they could get to Mexico.

# 10

As the ILFORD'S DEPARTURE continued to be delayed, it began to feel as if the ship had been a permanent part of the scenery at Jemulpo. Panicked rumors spread among those who had come to send off their friends. But the rumor that the passengers were about to be wiped out by an epidemic was quashed when John Meyers allowed them to leave the ship. Then another rumor began to spread: they were all to be sold as slaves. They had signed a document of slavery, and they were going to a cotton plantation where blacks worked. This was the reason the *Ilford* was unable to leave Jemulpo harbor: the Korean Empire's Ministry of Foreign Affairs had belatedly discovered that its citizens were being sold as chattel and had called for an investigation into John Meyers and others at the Continental Colonization Company. Unconcerned about the panicked atmosphere brewing among the spectators, some belatedly joined the ranks of the passengers, even though they had not received permission to leave for Mexico. They calmly walked onto the ship, pretending to be officials, or swam to the ship at night and climbed aboard. Many of these stowaways were discovered and sent back, but many refused to give up and lingered around the harbor.

Did the rumor of the passengers being sold into slavery ever reach the ears of the empire's officials? Even if it did, the government had no interest in these 1,033 souls, at least at the time of their departure. On March 25, as they were traveling back and forth between Busan and Jemulpo because of the problems of passports and epidemics, Emperor Gojong was begging the Russian czar to contain Japan. No reply came. The czar's fate was also in peril. Russia had been in the maelstrom of revolution since January 22, the so-called Bloody Sunday incident. There was insurrection in the Russian military. And there was no prospect of victory in the war with Japan. The Baltic Fleet, which had passed through the Strait of Malacca and was heading for Asia, was the only hope for turning the tide of the war. If the fleet annihilated the Japanese navy and protected Russian dominance in Yongampo and Port Arthur, the problems facing the czar and Gojong would be solved. For the czar, it was an opportunity to raise Russian pride; to Gojong it was the chance to escape the brutal grasp of Japan. Of course, Nicholas II did not show his trump card to Gojong. Gojong knew only that, a fortnight before he had sent the personal appeal, Japan had defeated the Russian army, captured Fengtian in Manchuria, and occupied the island of Dokdo by force, renaming it Takeshima.

Seeking a way to survive in this shifting balance of world powers, the emperor secretly sent Yun Byeong and Syngman Rhee to present President Theodore Roosevelt with a declaration of independence, but this went unanswered as well. There was nothing but a succession of depressing news. On May 27, the emperor received breathless reports that a large convoy had been spotted by Mokpo fishermen in the sea off Chungmu. Russia's Baltic Fleet had indeed passed through the Korea Strait on May 26. Yet Britain, which in no way desired a Russian victory over Japan, was telegraphing the course of the Baltic Fleet moment by moment to Japan. But that was not all. The fleet had been tied up for months in places like Madagascar because British-owned ports refused to supply the ships with coal. The czar's weary fleet had not once been sufficiently supplied with fuel. At 4:45 in the morning on May 27, the combined

Japanese fleet launched a preemptive strike. The ensuing naval battle in the East Sea lasted for nearly twenty-four hours, and the Baltic Fleet was dealt a crushing blow. News of the Japanese victory dashed Gojong's faint hopes. There were no flukes in history. The death knell was tolling in the czarist establishment as well. Nicholas's primary enemy was no longer Japan but the young revolutionaries — Lenin, Trotsky, and Stalin — who silently sought his life.

Meanwhile, unaware that the world powers were engaged in a history-making struggle over the fate of East Asia, the 1,033 passengers of the *Ilford* remained mesmerized by sweet dreams of a land called Mexico. Finally, one spring day in April, when a breeze blowing off the South China Sea caused the deck to roll, the *Ilford* weighed anchor with a loud clamor. Passports had at last been issued for all passengers. When John Meyers couldn't gain the cooperation of the British minister Gordon, he sought out the French minister Victor Collin de Plancy and asked him to use his influence with the government of Korea. Mexico and the Korean Empire did not have diplomatic relations, and the Emigration Office, which had been established by the imperial government for emigration to Hawaii, prohibited contract labor, so Meyers's demand was seen as illegal. With the help of Collin de Plancy's efforts, though, the passports were issued, and the *Ilford*'s human cargo departed for Mexico, where there was not a single Korean resident, let alone a diplomat. It was April 4, 1905.

# 11

THE ANCHOR WENT UP. The deck was crowded all the way to the stairs with those who wanted to see Jemulpo one last time. It was a departure for which they had waited too long. Because of children who had caught chickenpox, because of passport difficulties, and because of the British minister's strict inspection, they had had to go back and forth between the ship and the harbor for some two months. But now, at least, there was no distinction between commoner and noble, man and woman, or young and old, and every face was bright. A ship slicing through the ocean wind and heading out into the vast ocean is a finer sight than a ship at anchor. Yi Jongdo's family, Kim Ijeong, Choe Seongil, and the others were all on deck and flooded with emotion. It was a clear day. The wind was somewhat strong, but the weather was beautiful, with white clouds sailing through the blue sky. The small boats that had been idling about next to the *Ilford* rowed in unison and backed away so they would not be swept up by the wake. Like a great dog shaking water off its body, the *Ilford* pushed aside everything around it and began to sail into the Yellow Sea. Korean laborers with towels wrapped around their heads waved to the emigrants on deck. There were those among them who had tried to board the *Ilford* up until the very last moment.

The British steamer's whistle was resonant. The black smoke that puffed from its stacks mixed with the sea winds and left a long trail in the blue sky. The German sailors in their striped shirts went about their work with blank faces. There was a unique, cold vitality to these men who began and ended their lives at sea. They had absolutely no interest in the social meaning of the work they did, but they attributed an absolute significance to its practical value and always worked energetically. Raising the anchor, letting down their fishing poles to catch fish for food, swabbing the deck, and inspecting the ropes — all these things were in this purposeful domain.

A short while later, as Jemulpo harbor gradually receded into the distance, the passengers lost interest in the surrounding scenery and went down to the cabin by ones and twos. Yi Jongdo stayed on deck for a while, following with his eyes the ocean and the jagged western coastline of Gyeonggi province. Many of the kings of Joseon, Yi Jongdo's ancestors, had never seen the ocean. A retainer who had been appointed an emissary and traveled to Japan gained an audience with the king upon his return, and the king asked him, "How did you travel to Japan?" "We went on Your Majesty's vessels." "How many people were on each ship?" "Each ship carried around thirty people, including soldiers and crew." Only then did the king ask quietly, "I still wonder. How is it that such a heavy ship carrying so many people does not sink but floats on the water?" There were countless kings who had never even been to the Han River, only six miles from the palace. The retainer searched for a way to make the king understand without exposing his ignorance. "Your humble subject does not yet fully comprehend the principle behind it, but Your Majesty's fishermen and navy discovered this principle early on and have made good use of it. I can only surmise that they are aided by light wood and tar." These were civil officials. Being unable to understand the principles behind tools was by no means a reason for shame. The king and his retainer exchanged curious looks and then forgot about the ocean and the ships. Now their descendant Yi Jongdo found that being on a ship was similar to riding a palanquin over a rough road. His stomach was already beginning to churn. He took a deep breath. Korean air filled his lungs. In the midst of this turmoil, Yi Jongdo recalled a poem by Du Fu, a Chinese poet, that sang of the sadness of leaving one's home: "The color of spring in the heavens hurries to fade, and my tears of parting are added to the distant silken waves." As he recited the verse, it seemed to be talking about the fate of the dynasty, and his heart grew troubled. His stomach began to churn more and more.

He may have been seasick, but he did not want to go down to the cabin. The aristocrats and beggars and peasants and the lower class kept sharp eyes on each other in the midst of the tension. As John Meyers had said, this was not the Korean Empire, it was British territory afloat on the seas. It was now an everyday occurrence for the common rabble to defiantly hold their heads high and stare at him and his family. No one lowered their head when he passed, nor did anyone step aside when they met in a corridor. The Korean status system, which was now only implicit even in Korea, had disappeared without a trace aboard the *Ilford*. Yi Jongdo raised his head to the sky with an aggrieved heart. I have sinned much against my ancestors. I am paying the price for that. The aristocrats hid their horsehair hats while the peasants stuck out their chests. Their speech and writing were different, so one could guess another's stock after only a few words. It didn't take long for Yi Jongdo to realize just how reckless it was for him to insist on his privileged position. Yet he firmly believed that this would not be so in Mexico. Things might not go so well, but then he would entreat the emperor in Seoul. The emperor would grind the ink imported from Beijing and write a letter in splendid calligraphy to the ruler of Mexico. He would very politely request that he save his unfortunate cousin and his family. As soon as Yi Jongdo thought this, his heart grew lighter. And the commoners on this ship would also keenly feel the need for people such as himself. When the landowners and officials inevitably mistreated the common people, who would stand up for them and rebuke their oppressors with stern words and letters? Who else among them had both the noble lineage and the learning to represent them? He had looked over every passenger but found not a single familiar face among them. "Ah, no one knows the depth of the common people's ignorance," Yi Jongdo lamented, then went down to the cabin. On his way he bumped shoulders with people at least three times. Such a thing would never have happened in Seoul. The last person he came into such unpleasant contact with was Choe Seongil. Choe looked around casually. The first thing a thief had to do was examine his surroundings. Thieves had to be more sensitive and diligent than any other type of criminal. They had to scout out the area, decide on the items they would steal, check the escape route, make sure that there was no one to witness that escape, and inspect their own demeanor. This attitude was second nature to Choe Seongil. No one had taught him; he knew these things by instinct.

He walked around the cabin and examined people. There was probably no one who could guess the former occupation and status of the passengers as well as he could. He could even estimate the amount of cash and gold the passengers carried without a great margin of error. Only the man who had drawn him here, the man who had carried the cross, was a riddle. But Choe had already stolen all of his goods, so he was no longer interested in him. As he strolled about the cabin, which had already begun to reek of something like rotten horseflesh, he discovered a number of fellows not unlike himself. Like beasts that recognized their own kind by the smell of their urine, they quickly became aware of each other's presence and exchanged glances, concluding a sort of nonaggression pact. Then they began to loosely divide up their domains. All without a single word.

Most of the passengers were plagued by seasickness. Lying on the floor with ashen faces, they had no idea how to deal with the rolling that they were experiencing for the first time in their lives. Strangely enough, Choe Seongil did not grow seasick. Had he been a sailor or a fish in a former life? Though he was rocked by the waves in the dark cabin beneath the waterline, Choe felt nothing. Rather, he whistled and enjoyed the rolling of the ship as he walked around and idly watched the others.

In his eyes, the passengers could be divided into a few general categories. First, the ruined aristocrats. These had lost their land or office in the violent changes that took place after the opening of harbors; their plight had grown so desperate that they couldn't even offer sacrifices to their ancestors. They took out books here and there around the ship and read them to relieve the boredom. Their hands were white and soft, and they usually tied their hair in a topknot and wore horsehair headbands. They apparently had no intention of getting along with the other classes in the cabin, and so they simply endured the situation without a word. These aristocrats were most agonized when it came time for meals, which consisted of a kimchi that was actually just salt sprinkled on wilted cabbage, watery miso soup, and rice mixed with other grains. Thinking that others would naturally allow them to be served first, they waited quietly, but the only thing they received was mockery. Yet they could not very well rush forward like pigs to the trough. Unable to bear it any longer, an aristocrat from Cheongju suggested that it would be fairest if they decided on an order, then began from the front one time and from the rear the next time. This idea was met with silence. The proposal itself was rational, but the commoners knew that once you started to listen to aristocrats, they would ultimately seize control. It may have been somewhat inconvenient, but standing in line at every meal was a way to give those loathsome aristocrats a hard time. With no other choice, the aristocrats stood in line as well. Their slow step, their way of walking with their toes pointed outward, soon disappeared of its own accord, and they began to walk more quickly like everyone else.

By number, the peasants were the largest group. They were characterized by rough hands, sun-blackened faces, and strong muscles and frames like Chinese coolies. More than any other class, they had no complaints with life on shipboard. A life where they did not have to work and yet food was still served when the time came was like a dream to them. On land they labored all year, but when a drought or a flood struck, everything came to nothing and they would starve until the spring barley harvest. Even if the next year saw an abundant harvest, there was never anything left after they repaid their debts to the landowners. Mexico, a country with no winter, where there was much land and no people, thus making people as precious as gold, was the land of their dreams. After all, the fatigue of farming was the same anywhere.

After the peasants were the former soldiers of the Korean Empire, like Jo Jangyun. These two hundred or so young, robust men were the pride of the Continental Colonization Company. At first glance they looked similar to the peasants, but most of them were city dwellers who had no experience in farming. Unlike the peasants, who were accustomed to disorder, the soldiers had grown up in an organization that loved order and discipline. They were used to meaningless waiting, hunger, and harsh environments, and they were sensitive to the vagaries of politics. A few of them had been members of the old-style army that had assaulted the palace and engaged in a brutal battle, but they did not make themselves known. They supported the isolationist policy of the Daewongun and burned with wrath against Japan and the Western powers, and it was for this reason that they had lost their jobs and were forced to leave the country.

The rest were city vagrants like Choe Seongil and Kim Ijeong. There were no women who boarded by themselves. It hadn't been permitted by the Continental Colonization Company, and in the social atmosphere of the time, for a woman to leave by herself for such a distant place was intolerable. The women boarded the ship as members of families. The company had not forgotten its experience with Hawaii, where only single men had been allowed, causing a massive imbalance in the ratio of men to women, which led to social problems. So this time they invited primarily families, and in response quite a few women put their fates in the hands of their husbands and fathers.

# 12

THE VOYAGE WAS LONG. The *Ilford* was completely lacking in material comforts, and not only were the passengers stored like baggage but they exceeded the optimum capacity of the ship by at least three times, making their suffering that much worse. They had heard the name of the ocean they had to cross and were envisioning in their own way a sea like a vast and tranquil lake. The Chinese had long ago called this ocean Taipingyang, combining the characters for "great" (太), "peaceful" (平), and "ocean" (洋). But the ocean, contrary to the wishes of the one who had christened it, was rough and unpredictable. Every time an enormous wave crashed against the side of the ship, the passengers in the cargo hold beneath the waterline were tangled together with no regard for decorum, etiquette, or Confucian morality. Embarrassing scenes were continually played out where men and women, aristocrats and commoners were thrust into one corner with their bodies tossed against one another. Chamber pots were overturned or broken, and the vomit and excrement within spilled out on the floor. Curses and sighs, criticism and fistfights were everyday occurrences, and the vile stench did not fade. No one dreamed of such extravagant notions as laundering or bathing. The passengers' only desire was that the boat would arrive quickly so they could stand on firm land.

The sailors did not descend to the cabin but called orders down from the top of the stairs, and the interpreter Gwon Yongjun conveyed their intent. He was the only authority figure among the 1,033 travelers. His father had been a member of the class of technical

officials – higher than the commoners but lower than the aristocrats – and an interpreter who traveled between Qing China and
Korea. The wealthy and those in authority bought from China most
of the luxury items needed for marrying off their daughters or pleas-
ing their concubines. Silk and jewels, tobacco and liquor came in
along that route, and the interpreters made a great profit mediat-
ing these transactions. Scholars coveted Chinese books. Not only
the classics but also books that introduced Western thought. Such
books, though they were prohibited in Korea – or rather *because*
they were prohibited in Korea – were extremely popular among the
scholars. Books about Catholicism, which said that all humanity
was equal before God; about the heliocentric theory, which stated
that a round earth revolved around the sun; about the histories of
the British Empire, France, Germany, and the United States, were
packed onto ships and sold the moment they arrived in Korea.

Korean ginseng, in particular red ginseng, was very popular in
China. The trade in women was not profitable, mainly because the
Chinese valued women who bound their feet, and there was no
such custom in Korea. Gwon Yongjun's father was born into an interpreter's family and learned Chinese at an early age. He passed
the interpreter's test with ease and went on to amass a great fortune,
but he also knew that China was falling into sharp decline because
of the Opium Wars. In Beijing, he saw with his own eyes the alarm-
ing arrival of the Western powers and the possibility that they might
soon swallow all of Asia.

Of his three sons, he taught the first two Chinese, but he hired
an English teacher for his youngest. The youngest son had been
slow to start talking, worrying his parents. He was particularly poor
at learning Chinese characters, and his skill did not develop beyond the elementary level. That being the case, his father felt it
would be best to teach him an entirely new language. The sounds

of a language that had not been heard for hundreds of years, even in the house of a storied interpreter, rang out. "I am a boy. I learn English. I am a student. I live in London." The youngest son's skill in English was not outstanding, but almost no one in Korea spoke English at the time. When America and England founded their legations in Seoul, his father's foresight paid off. His youngest son, Yongjun, went to the American legation and said that he wanted to work as an interpreter. The diplomats, who had lived half mute on a linguistic island for several months, hired him on the spot. Gwon Yongjun had not been working at the American legation long when his father and brothers set sail from Tianjin, China, on a boat laden with silk. Gentle waves and mild sunshine seemed to bless their voyage. His father had said that when a route was created that would connect China, America, and Britain with Korea, their family would be able to stand side by side with any distinguished family in the nation. "The class system is about to disappear. The age when one's status is determined by the size of one's hat is over. Look at your hair. Now the day has come when no one will know you are the children of an interpreter." His two sons awkwardly patted their oiled hair with both hands. They still felt that something was missing. There was nothing where there should have been a topknot. At a word from their father, after Gojong's Hair Cutting Edict, they had snipped off the hair that had been growing their whole lives. "This is a good thing for us. Our hair would just be crawling with lice anyway." With the characteristic decisiveness of a practical man, he had obeyed the Hair Cutting Edict before any other interpreter. Their heads did feel a little bare, but his two sons felt they had done the right thing in obeying their father's decision. After this, their business flourished and the great wooden floor in their house shone with oil. "When we return from this trip to China I will see you married," the father promised his eldest son. Perhaps that

was why the eldest son kept looking off toward the Ongjin Peninsula and smiling, and in doing so he spotted a ship rapidly approaching. Its bridge was low and its hull was wide, making it well suited
for sailing in shallow waters like the Yellow Sea. It was not a fishing
boat, seeing as it had no nets, nor was it a diplomatic ship carrying
officials.

The mysterious ship pulled alongside them and crewmen tossed
over ropes and tied the two ships together. From the interpreter's
side someone shouted, "What are you doing?" but he was struck
by several bullets and fell into the ocean. Ten or so sturdy men ran
across the ropes to the interpreter's ship, shouting. Armed guards
on the interpreter's ship met the invaders, but they had already lost
the advantage. The attackers, Cantonese-speaking men, skillfully
wielded their swords and began to take control of the ship. The interpreter calmly evaluated the situation, but it was hopeless. In less
than five minutes the wounded or dead guards had become food
for the fishes. Like expert fishmongers, the pirates carried out their
work with blank faces. The interpreter and his two sons fell to their
knees next to a Korean official on his way back from Beijing who lay
with blood flowing from his head. The pirates grinned and marched
the interpreter to the bow of the ship and then prodded him in the
back with the tips of their swords. He closed his eyes and fell into
the ocean. His two sons were taken to the pirates' ship and thrown
into the hold. The official who had been stabbed suffered the same
fate as the interpreter. The two ships changed direction and fled to
the south.

Gwon Yongjun heard the news a few days later, but he was not
greatly saddened. He held a magnificent funeral with the elders of
his family and greeted the guests. He, as the youngest son, had not
expected any inheritance, because the custom of primogeniture
had become firmly established, but suddenly he was rich. He was

only twenty years of age. When he opened the doors of the family's storehouses he found silks and rice piled up to a man's height. The books written in Chinese characters, which he had difficulty understanding, were the first things he sold off. Then he put the rest of the valuable goods on the market. Even had he not intended to do so, traders somehow found out and came to him and offered to do business. One day a military officer dressed in fine silks and a high and splendid horsehair hat came to Gwon Yongjun's house. The officer said that he kept three or four of the finest gisaeng in the city, and he requested the honor of offering the young nobleman a drink. There was no reason for Gwon Yongjun to refuse. The next day, the officer sent a palanquin for him. He sat haughtily atop the palanquin and was borne away to the gisaeng house at the foot of Mount Nam. There he enjoyed luxury like that of the emperor of China: white snake liquor and Chinese tobacco, the dancing of Pyongyang gisaeng who had been trained since the age of eight, musicians playing wind and string instruments who could easily surmise the next tune merely by exchanging glances, an old singer from Iksan in Jeolla province who was sightseeing in Seoul, and delicacies of land and sea on plates of Meissen porcelain. And when he grew tired of all that, the gisaeng offered him Shanghai opium. The days slipped by in a fog. After a while Gwon Yongjun didn't bother to go home; he stayed at the gisaeng house. Little by little his servants sold off the silk and rice from the family storehouse, and the clever officer slowly raised the price of food and lodging for his long-term guest. Only when the season came for farmers to reap what they had sown before the first frost did the palanquin that had brought Gwon Yongjun there take him back home. It was a final thoughtful gesture by the officer: when Yongjun later returned to the gisaeng house, the officer didn't even open the door. Gwon Yongjun's house was chilly after his long absence. The market and the connections his father had established were cold to the son who had squandered his entire inheritance at a gisaeng house. The young profligate fought with withdrawal from opium, the cold, and uncertainty about the future, until finally he had no choice but to admit that he was penniless. The only asset that the gisaeng and the officer and his servants had not taken was his fluency in English, but he did not want to return to the American legation, which he had quit rather haughtily. Then he saw the advertisement in the *Capital Gazette* and went to the Continental Colonization Company and decided to start a new life in Mexico, the land of gold, where nobody knew him. He met John Meyers at the company, where filthy people stood in line. "Your English is good enough, but you will have to learn Spanish," Meyers advised him. He gave Gwon Yongjun the Spanish textbook he had used. In a land without a single Spanish-speaker, Meyers had no other options.

# 13

KIM IJEONG OPENED his eyes. The ship was sailing without much pitching or rolling for the first time in a while. The *Ilford* had tossed and lurched violently for days due to continuous storms, and the cabin was filled with a sour stench. There were those who tried to bear it by drinking the ginseng juice they had brought with them, those who had stuck needles in their forehead and palms, and those who pricked the tips of each of their fingers to let blood flow. All endured the harsh life at sea with their own remedies. Kim Ijeong was not free from this suffering either. He had no knowledge of acupuncture, nor had he brought any ginseng juice with him. He went up onto the deck. There he watched the German crewmen moving around. Because of their sharp noses, angular chins, and great height, he could not think of them as humans like himself. Unable to speak to them, he watched them from afar and then went back down to the cabin. He found himself walking along the labyrinthine corridor that led to the quarters of the German crewmen, the captain, and the ship's mates. There was no one in the passageway, perhaps because they were all up on the bridge. He came to a flight of stairs and climbed down toward the savory aroma of food. The door was ajar, and he saw people working inside. It was, as he suspected, the galley. If there were a Christian hell, then surely it would look like this: the blazing fires, the cooking utensils that hung from the ceiling and clattered loudly, and the cooks shouting over the noise of the boiler room, their clothes filthy and their long hair hanging down in front of their eyes. The floor glistened with discarded food and grease, yet no one slipped. This was where the food had to be prepared for 1,033 passengers, the captain, the ship's mates, the crewmen, and the galley workers themselves.

The ship listed to one side and Ijeong tilted that way as well, slamming into the wall with a crash. The sound was drowned out by the galley noise, so no one had yet become aware of his presence. Even as he fell he watched the cooks. They kept their balance by cleverly holding on to straps with one hand. They did not let a single piece of vegetable fall out of their frying pans.

A fat, bearded man saw Ijeong and shouted in Japanese. He approached with a knife in his hand, and Ijeong cowered. The man's eyes flashed with unpleasant curiosity. He yelled the same thing again. But Ijeong could not understand him. Instead, he picked up a broom lying nearby and started sweeping up the cabbage leaves and potato peels that had fallen on the floor. The bearded Japanese shook his head. He didn't need him for that. Ijeong continued to work without looking at him. The Japanese thundered at him before giving up and returning to his comrades. The men carried on in Japanese. Ijeong had heard the language spoken in the Japanese concessions at open ports when he was with the peddler, but he had never learned it. At any rate, Ijeong helped out with the cleaning, though no one had asked him to, and he got to know the cooks. And those cooks who at first only cursed at him, not even deigning to look at him, began to put him to work doing odd jobs. He brought bags of onions from the hold and cleaned up the dining hall after meals. During brief breaks, the Japanese cooks went up on deck and smoked cigarettes. One of the cooks was tall for a Japanese. His hair was short like a soldier's and his body was slender. He taught Ijeong some Japanese after he was finished cleaning. He said his name was Yoshida. He first taught Ijeong the names of ingredients, like onions, potatoes, rice, and water, so that he could run errands for him. Whenever Ijeong forgot or confused a word, Yoshida rapped him on the head, but gradually that happened less and less often. Ijeong was a quick learner. After about three days, he at least did not confuse the names of food items. With that, Ijeong was given more work to do. The cooks shouted his name, like merchants at the market. He hurried back and forth from the hold, the deck, and the dining hall, and when night came he collapsed like a wet noodle. But now he no longer had to wait at the end of a long line for just a bowl of rice. Every night he returned to the cabin reeking of grease. Next to him, Choe Seongil pinched his nose shut. One night a young farmer from Pyongyang called Ijeong a Japanese dog and spit at him. Ijeong waited for him to fall asleep and then beat him with a club. "Owww!" The young farmer covered his head and curled up, but Ijeong wordlessly rained down blows on his body. Choe Seongil was the first to realize what was going on. As soon as he opened his eyes he grabbed Ijeong by the waist and pushed him up against the wall. A few more people who had been stepped on woke up and held Ijeong back. The farmer had been beaten nearly senseless. "How does it feel to be thrashed by a Japanese dog!" Ijeong screamed. "Haven't you been wolfing down the food this Japanese dog has cooked for you?" The others calmed him down. The Pyongyang farmer, bleeding from his head, picked up his blanket and ran far away from Ijeong.

The commotion soon died down. Life in the cramped cabin led to frequent quarrels. It was amazing that there hadn't been a knifing yet. The men brandished their fists over seating, over a spoonful of rice, over a pretty woman, or over an ugly look. "You're a dead man. I'm going to throw you into the ocean!" This was the most common threat, but it never happened. Kim Ijeong lay down flat, trying to calm himself. He had grown up on the streets; this was nothing to him. Strangely, though, his rage did not fade easily. Suddenly he felt as if all the men in the world were his enemies. Seized by this unfathomable hostility, he angrily squeezed his hand into a fist. And with that fist he wiped away a tear that welled up in the corner of his eye.

Early the next morning, he woke up before anyone else and quietly left the cabin to go to the galley. He walked along the passageway with his senses alert, just in case the Pyongyang farmer was hiding somewhere to jump him from behind. As he turned the corner to the stairs leading down to the kitchen, he sensed that someone was there, by the makeshift bathroom for the women. She must have been surprised, for she let out a soft gasp. Unable to cover her eyes with her cloak, the girl came face to face with Ijeong. It was only a brief moment, but it was enough time for the sixteen-year-old boy and the girl to become fully aware of each other. The girl, whose name was Yeonsu, moved aside and waited for Ijeong to pass. He walked by, then stopped and turned to steal a glance at Yeonsu as she turned the corner. The way she walked, lifting her heels ever so slightly, and her long skirt made it look as if she were floating in midair. And that strange scent . . .

There was no one in the galley. Ijeong was gathering his cleaning paraphernalia when he spotted a knife stuck in a cutting board. At any other time he would have passed it by, but he must have been possessed by something, because he took the knife in his hand. Japanese knives were much thinner and longer than Korean knives. It was a fillet knife and reeked of fish. Then he saw a square knife for chopping meat. The handle was covered with dried blood. He put down the fillet knife and picked up the cleaver. He liked the weight of it. Something sharp seemed to push up from deep inside him. He was overwhelmed, caught between his longing for the girl and the primal fascination with sharp things of steel, when he heard a voice like thunder behind him. He put down the knife. It was Yoshida. He ran toward Ijeong, cursing, and struck him on the cheek. He did not stop at that, but hit him dozens of times. Ijeong collapsed to his knees. The other cooks came running and asked what had happened. All they had to do was look at the knife in Yoshida's hand to understand. The knife was the most sacred of objects to a cook. The hierarchy among cooks was a fearsome thing, even if they were cooking things like pork porridge on a foreign cargo ship. Ijeong retreated from the galley and began cleaning just like any other day. "Have I really become a dog?" the sixteen-year-old boy cried. The chaotic morning meal was soon over. Yoshida took Ijeong up on deck and sat. Red clouds hung low over the horizon. Yoshida caressed Ijeong's red, swollen cheek and said, "I was once a soldier of Japan." Ijeong understood next to nothing of what he said. Still, Yoshida began to talk at length of his past, like an incantation. He had been in the Japanese navy, and one year earlier, when the Russo-Japanese War broke out and the fleet laid siege to Port Arthur, he had fled in the night. His face was sad when he said that his wife and two daughters in his hometown of Kagoshima must have been ashamed when they heard of his desertion. All Ijeong managed to grasp was that Yoshida had once been in the navy. If he is a Japanese sailor on a British ship, then he must be a deserter, Ijeong thought. Yoshida caressed Ijeong's cheek again. Yoshida's eyes were moist. His rough hands enveloped Ijeong's face, and his lips came closer, as if it were the next natural step. Ijeong wavered, his lips met Yoshida's lips, and then Yoshida's tongue was in Ijeong's mouth. Yoshida grabbed Ijeong tightly with both hands and the boy toppled over backward. Yoshida's body began to burn amid the thick ropes that curled like snake skins on the deck. Ijeong's heart pounded violently. This was the first time he had experienced such a thing with either a man or a woman. The man before his eyes who cried as he pushed his tongue into his mouth had been the kindest to him, yet he had also beaten him so hard that morning that his cheek swelled up. It would have been easier for him to decide how he felt if it had been only one thing or the other. In that moment of confusion, Yoshida's hand moved toward Ijeong's groin. Yoshida gently stroked the boy's erect penis. Then the morning sun, which had been hidden by the clouds on the horizon, showed its face. Like a sharp blade, the sunlight divided their two faces into darkness and light. Ijeong squinted. It was time for the Koreans who had finished eating breakfast to come out on deck to smoke their pipes. He shook off Yoshida's hand. Then he shook his head. With plaintive eyes, Yoshida begged for Ijeong's affection. When Ijeong shook his head again, breathing hard, Yoshida's face slowly returned to its usual gruff expression. He did not show any hostility. Like a snail that had briefly pushed its body out into the world, he was returning to the safety of his shell. Yoshida reached out a hand to Ijeong. Ijeong held out his hand hesitatingly and Yoshida's rough hand grabbed his and stood him up at one pull. When Yoshida let go of his hand, Ijeong brushed off the seat of his trousers. Without a word the two returned to the galley. With the severest expression he could muster, Yoshida spoke to Ijeong: "Follow me." Ijeong followed him down to the dark hold. Yoshida handed a fresh apple to the terrified boy. When Yoshida returned to the kitchen, Ijeong shut himself in the hold and ate the whole red apple, even the seeds.

When he had finished, Ijeong left the hold and went up on deck. For the first time in a long time, a gentle breeze was blowing. The Koreans, who tired of life in the cabin, filled the deck, basking in the sun and breathing the fresh air deep into their lungs. Someone tapped Ijeong. He turned around to find Jo Jangyun, the one who had given him his name. "Isn't it rough?" He was talking about life in the galley. Ijeong shook his head. He said that he was able to move around, so it was better because he wasn't as bored. Jo Jangyun agreed. "And there's probably a lot to eat, too." Ijeong only smiled broadly. "Being shut up in the belly of the ship like this, the aching in my legs is almost too much to bear." Jo Jangyun stretched himself. "What I wouldn't give to take just a few steps on solid ground, even if it were in hell!" He tapped the metal railing. "Who knew there was such a big ocean? My goodness, no matter how far we go there is no end. They say we still have a month to go . . . It's enough to drive you crazy." He seemed to be expecting some hopeful words from Ijeong, who spent his time with the crew. But Ijeong knew nothing more either. The ocean was vast, and at the end of that vast ocean was their destination. He had glanced at the world map on the wall when he brought breakfast to the captain, but he had no way of knowing where they were at that moment. They could do nothing but wait.

When Jo Jangyun's comrades from his military days came up, they stuffed tobacco into their pipes and lit them. The massive steel ship and their pipes seemed out of place on the tropical ocean. None of them spoke of the past. The only topic of conversation was the uncertain future. "When we arrive, let's not separate," someone suggested. "Of course, of course." Everyone agreed. "We can just ask them to keep us in one place." "Who will ask?" "The interpreter, of course." "He looks like a shameless fellow — I don't think we can trust him." "Still, it's his job to tell them what we say." "He'll do it, won't he?" They all nodded their heads uneasily. Ijeong walked away from them and went back down to the galley. It was already time to prepare for lunch. Yoshida was still silent. "Today's lunch is miso soup!" someone shouted. A large chunk of miso was thrown into the soup pot. The savory aroma filled the galley. The bearded cook who had first yelled at Ijeong clapped him on the back of the head. Ijeong hauled up a sack of onions. Sweat poured ceaselessly from the cooks' bodies because of the intense heat. Someone chugged Japanese liquor that they had stashed away, and someone else sang a plaintive Japanese melody at the top of his lungs. They could not all have been deserters, and if that was so, how did they all come to be here? Ijeong wondered. But he did not ask anyone. When he brought the wrong ingredient, Yoshida quietly cursed him — "Bakayarou!" — but his voice was weak. He may even have been cursing himself. Ijeong did not know much about men loving other men, but he sensed only that Yoshida's actions were born of affection. This sort of thing happened often enough among peddlers who lived long on the road, but Ijeong had left that world before he learned much of that side of it.

Ijeong thought that perhaps it might be best if he simply went down to the cabin and didn't hang around the galley anymore, but he couldn't do that. This lively hell was far better than being stuck in the foul-smelling cabin all day. He felt an attraction to this world

44

where only men worked side by side in the narrow space. They cursed each other and slapped each other on the cheeks, but that was a normal part of life. So every time they struck Ijeong on the head, he felt that he was being accepted just a little more into their world. To Ijeong, who had lived as a wanderer, the galley of the *Ilford* seemed like a cozy family. Even though he was being carried to a place farther than he had ever gone, it did not feel that way to Ijeong.

Yoshida continued to keep his distance from Ijeong, but at every opportunity, as if it were somehow his noble duty, Yoshida with his gloomy countenance would solemnly teach him Japanese and, when the morning chores were finished, take him down to the hold and give him an apple. This secret pleasure in the dark hold slowly brought back together these two who had been torn apart by Yoshida's unexpected actions. Ijeong smelled the sweet fragrance that wafted from the flesh of the apple. Then he polished it on his sleeve and bit into it. Yoshida gazed hungrily at Ijeong's mouth as he ate. That was all. When Ijeong had eaten the red apple down to its seeds, only then did Yoshida turn to his chores. He organized the hold and selected the ingredients necessary for preparing lunch, putting them into a sack. He did not ask Ijeong to do anything. Ijeong went up on deck and savored the sour taste that lingered on the tip of his tongue. In the following weeks, without a word from Yoshida, he would go down to the hold and wait. A few minutes later Yoshida would appear and silently hand him an apple. Ijeong also ate other fruit that he had never seen or heard of. Whatever they were, Ijeong enjoyed them. He gradually began to wonder if he should do something for Yoshida. And though the thought did occur to him, he did not know what it was he should do, so he shook his head violently, went up on deck, and abandoned himself to the strong winds.

# 14

YI YEONSU HADN'T worried about her body in their house in Sagan-dong, in the heart of Seoul. There had been no need to. Her
body was simply there, and she just used it. She was more interested
in ideological and abstract things. Where did I come from, what
do I live for, and what happens when I die? Her parents had taught
her that she came from her ancestors, that she should live for her
father and her future husband, and at the moment her life ended
she would become a spirit. But she could not easily accept what the
women in literati households were taught and convinced of. She
did not deny that she came from the flesh and bone of her ancestors.
Yet she had a different idea about what she was to live for. Deep in
her heart, the idea that was too dangerous for her to dare to say out
loud was: I live for myself. Gone were the days when women were
forced to commit suicide when their husbands died, to be rewarded
with gates erected by the king to commemorate their faithfulness,
but that didn't mean that anyone believed a woman could live for
herself. What's wrong with that? Is the joy of learning different for
men than for women? Though she sat quietly and embroidered an
image of the ten symbols of longevity, dangerous thoughts that the
times could not accept grew in the mind of this sixteen-year-old girl.
She had no concrete way to make these thoughts a reality, and that
just made her even stronger-willed, and thus she struggled to turn
a relatively blind eye to the changes taking place in her body. She
had her first period, her breasts swelled, and the baby fat began disappearing from her face. Yet the more she changed, the more she
clung to ideological issues.

But she could not do so on the ship. Her flesh did not leave her
mind for even one instant. The problems of eating and drinking and

defecating harassed the women in the cabin at every turn. There was a separate toilet for the women, but it was a shameful thing to weave their way among the men to get there. The men snickered openly. When she had to go with her mother, her demeanor was more imposing. In Sagan-dong there had been a convenient item called a brass bedpan, and the servants emptied it in the morning, but she could not expect such luxury here. So she ate and drank as little as possible, reducing the number of times she would have to go to the toilet. The rocking of the ship was as severe a burden. She vomited three times not long after the ship had set sail. Each time, she could not help but think of the obvious animal nature of her flesh. She was a creature plagued by hunger and nausea and the unbearable need to urinate. Most painful of all was the fact that her flesh was exposed to the eyes of all, with no walls between them. These eyes did not talk to her, nor did they laugh kindly. In fact, laughter was what she feared most of all. Every time those countless looks came and pierced her body, she realized anew that she was a weak and powerless creature trapped inside a prison called flesh. People watched everything as she woke and defecated and slept and ate. After a week passed like this, her agony gradually diminished. She was now able to withstand the furtive glances of the men and the jealous eyes of the women with some composure. For the first time in her life, she looked straight into the eyes of a man who gazed up and down her body. The experience made her heart sink, but she also felt as if she were opening a door that led to a new world. Before long, she decided she would not hide her face with her cloak when she was seated, and she expressed stubborn defiance when her mother rushed over to lecture her with a look of shock on her face. It was already far too late to be covering anything with a cloak. And she had also come face to face with a boy early one morning and been unable to move. Nothing happened between the two of them, but Yeonsu could not shake off the obvious eroticism that had been present in that brief moment. She, like other girls her age, cherished a sweet vision of romance that she had learned from classical novels. The idea that she herself could fall into a forbidden love, like Unyeong in *The Story of Unyeong,* was no longer strange. This boy was not from an aristocratic family, like the young Esquire Kim in the novel, so he was not the type of person who would understand poetry and be able to express his love through it, but there was a gentle and impressive intensity in his face that would make anyone stare long at him. She sometimes looked for him even when she was seated. Yet she rarely saw him.

As the voyage went on, the stench on the ship grew fouler and did not distinguish between aristocrat and commoner. In the cabin, where there were no wells or modern sanitary facilities, the horrible stink was only natural. People expressed their humanity through every hole and every pore in their bodies. Women smelled of women's odors and men smelled of men's odors. The distinction between the sexes became clearer than the distinction between classes, and that was wholly because of smell. Even when the men were trying to sleep, their eyes shot open if a woman passed by. A woman could smell a man coming up behind her. As more time passed without their being able to wash their bodies or clothes, the inside of the dark cabin became no different from a poultry coop. Even in that chaos, there were those who had peculiarly strong odors. These intense yet attractive odors spread far from their owners, and those who smelled them once could not easily forget them. The odor had nothing to do with the character or personality of its owner. Thus when people turned their heads toward the source of an approaching smell, they were often surprised at the unexpected conclusion.

Yi Yeonsu was one of these. After ten days aboard the ship, when the moon was full, there emanated from the girl an odor that everyone recognized. When she walked by, those who were sleeping awoke, and children stopped crying. Men who had not had an erection for years ejaculated in their sleep; young boys were roused from slumber. Women chattered and men turned their heads painfully. Her family knew as well, of course. Yi Jongdo often went up on deck. Yeonsu's mother, Lady Yun, changed her daughter's clothes behind the curtain put up for the women and sighed that she should have married her daughter off before leaving. Yeonsu's younger brother, Jinu, woke up early each morning and, the blood having rushed to his crotch, rubbed himself against the straw mat on the floor of the cabin. Only she herself was unaware. It wasn't only the smell. Her face began to shine as well. Her naturally noble manner and uncommon arrogance shone more brightly amid the filth. The men's lust and the women's jealousy were boiling over.

# 15

CHOE SEONGIL, THE THIEF of Jemulpo, was plagued by nightmares all that night. While he was caught between dreaming and waking, the boy lying next to him, Kim Ijeong, raised himself up. It was time to go to the galley, as always. Choe Seongil tried to say something to him, but no sound came out of his mouth, and suddenly Choe Seongil understood that his body would not move as he willed. His body shuddered involuntarily, and his legs were as heavy as if they were paralyzed. He wanted to lift his hand and grab Ijeong, but the boy, unaware of all of this, simply rose and left. After a long while had passed like this, Choe Seongil was seized by the fear of death. He could not die on this vast ocean with no family and no friends. The moment this thought entered his mind, his father's face appeared in midair. His father looked at ease, sitting beside a long, thin waterfall and enjoying something to drink. "Ah, that's delicious!" he said. Then, "The hardships of the world are ended, and this is paradise! Come quickly, son." Somewhere behind his father, someone was singing a song: "White dog, black dog, don't bark. White dog, black dog, don't bark." Sure enough, just then a white dog and a black dog appeared before his eyes and greeted him. In order to reach his father, he had to cross a river on a ferry that was tied up at the water's edge. The white dog and the black dog were happily wagging their tails on the boat. He had never in his life liked his father, but the vista there was so beautiful that all he could think of was going to him. It was a place of delicious food and drink and cool waters. As he approached the ferry, the white dog leaped down from the boat and walked along the riverside, while the black dog stayed on the boat with his tongue lolling from his mouth.

# 16

BY AFTERNOON, THE wailing that seeped out from between her clenched teeth became a scream like the tearing of a thousand yards of cloth at once. No one could be free from the sound. It was a woman from Seoul whose husband had pleaded and pleaded with his wife, who was nearing childbirth, to leave Korea. They had wanted to emigrate to Hawaii, but the Continental Colonization Company had urged them to go to Mexico instead. The company men claimed that Hawaii was already full. And Mexico was in no way inferior to Hawaii. And once someone makes up his mind to leave, he will find a way to leave. His heart already across the ocean, her husband went to her parents to help convince his wife. Her belly bulging, she protested. "I can't go. Father, Mother, please stop him." But in the end they could not overcome her husband's stubbornness. She had boarded the ship thinking it would be better than becoming a widow, and now her water had finally broken. Her husband just puffed away at his long pipe; there was nothing he could do. The interpreter went up and told Meyers's party that a woman was about to give birth. They called the Japanese doctor, but he had never delivered a child. Even more unfortunately, this young Japanese from Sizuoka was not really a doctor. He had merely studied veterinary medicine at an agricultural school, but he had been captivated by the company's attractive advertisement, so he lied and boarded the ship. All he had to do was accompany them on the comfortable British ship for its one-month journey to Mexico. Furthermore, they would give him two times the salary of a Tokyo doctor. He had thought he would encounter nothing more serious than seasickness, but as soon as he boarded the ship he realized his error. On a ship that was carrying three times its capacity, it would have been strange had there been no illness. Every night he opened his medical dictionary and studied the diseases that might occur at sea. Perhaps it was fortunate that his first task was to deliver a child. The most basic skill in veterinary medicine was delivering animal offspring.

He went down to the cabin. The horrid stench assaulted his nose. Despite her extreme pain, the pregnant woman expressed hostility toward the man who approached her open legs. The women gathered around her did not make way for him. And when he opened his mouth and Japanese came out, their anger increased. He told them he was a doctor, but it was no use. The woman's pain continued. The already filthy floor grew slippery with the amniotic fluid and sweat and blood that poured out of the woman's body. "Aaaahh!" The woman's screaming did not stop, and the old women who fancied themselves midwives began to cry out in unison. Children poked their heads through the gaps in the curtain to watch, and the veterinarian from Sizuoka waited nervously outside the curtain for the baby to come out. The midwives and the pregnant woman cried out as if they were fighting with each other, but the baby did not emerge. A sweaty midwife emerged from behind the curtain with a tearful face and pulled the Sizuoka veterinarian inside. The baby's foot was sticking out of the woman's vagina. He knelt down. It's a foal, it's a calf — he repeated these words to himself like some incantation and wiped the sweat from his face. Later, he would not remember exactly what had happened after that. Whatever the case, the baby's foot went back inside, the mother-to-be screamed in pain, and some time after that the baby's head appeared. He quickly grabbed the blue child. A woman brought a jar to hold the placenta and umbilical cord, and she took them outside. The child that had just come into the world did not breathe for several seconds, but with a slap to its buttocks it cried fiercely. The mother was spent and collapsed, and the women hustled the Sizuoka veterinarian back outside. "You did an excellent job, Dr. Tanabe," someone said to him. A number of baby names were discussed, but the father, Im Minsu, gave his son the name Taepyeong. It was the name of the ocean on which they were afloat and it was also an expression of hope. Im Taepyeong, who would have been thrown into the sea by his own father had he been born a girl, was thus born with the blessings of all the passengers.

# 17

ONE MONTH AFTER the *Ilford* had left, the last emigration ship, the *Mongolia*, left for Hawaii, carrying 288 passengers. The Emigration Protection Act, made law under pressure from Japan, prohibited Koreans from traveling abroad; Japan did not want the people who would pour out of Korea to compete with Japanese emigrants. The emigration companies were forced to close their doors. Brokers such as John Meyers were denied reentrance into the country. The brief history of emigration that the Hawaii sugar plantation laborers had begun to write in 1902 was turning its last page three years later. Then came the Protectorate Treaty of 1905. Diplomatic authority of the Korean Empire was transferred to Japan, and the diplomatic legations of the United States, Germany, and France withdrew from Seoul. In July of that year, U.S. Secretary of War William Howard Taft and Prime Minister Katsura Taro of Japan exchanged secret memorandums, yielding rule over Korea to the Japanese and the Philippines to the United States.

The country the *Ilford* had left was slowly fading, like a drop of ink fallen into the water.

# 18

THE NUMBER OF PEOPLE with diarrhea increased. Others suffered from high fevers, babbling incoherently and retching violently. The small toilets overflowed with feces. Those whose symptoms were most severe relieved themselves where they lay and shivered uncontrollably as they called to those who had already passed on to the next world.

The veterinarian from Sizuoka was called. He covered his mouth with a towel and plunged into the sickening stench. There was no doubt that these were the symptoms of dysentery. It was a highly contagious disease, so the patients must be quarantined, but there wasn't enough room. It was important to wash one's hands, but there wasn't enough water to do that. All they could do was divide those who had been infected from those who had not, and make sure that no one passed from one group to the other. The *Ilford* was not equipped with sufficient medicine to treat dysentery, so the patients' only hope lay in their own natural healing abilities.

The dysentery that had broken out in the cabin meant that Kim Ijeong was temporarily forbidden from entering the galley. Sitting in a corner and looking around, Ijeong leaped up in surprise as if he had been burned. Something wet had seeped into the spot where he had been sitting. Choe Seongil grabbed Ijeong's ankle. Ijeong shook his leg desperately but could not break free. "Help me," Choe Seongil said. Ijeong picked up his blanket and looked at Choe Seongil's face. His eyes were sunken and hollow and his face was nothing but skin. There were traces of vomit around his mouth, and his blanket reeked. Ijeong and some others combined their strength to move him to the patients' area. As he was carried off on the makeshift stretcher, he cried, "I don't want to die here!"

It was already deep into the night when the body was discovered. The first fatality. Two passengers wrapped the body in a sack and brought it up on deck. They stood there, not knowing what to do, and John Meyers held a towel over his mouth and repeatedly urged them to throw the body into the ocean. Four whalers from Pohang supported Meyers's words and explained to those passengers ignorant of customs at sea that this was the usual practice. But how could they just cast a person to the fishes, far from home, with no ceremony at all? The people formed a circle around the body and stood at a distance, unable to do anything. Flies had begun to gather on the body. When no one stepped forward to oversee the funeral proceedings, the whalers exchanged glances, picked up the sack with the body in it by the four corners, and threw it overboard. As the whalers sang their own peculiar song, neither a prayer nor a boat song, the victim disappeared beneath the screws of the ship. Four hours later, there was another fatality. The body was brought up on deck in the same way. The whalers stepped forward once more and lifted the sack, but some other passengers came forward. "They are not dogs or pigs. How can we do this?" cried one, a middle-aged farmer.

After a slight commotion, a man was pushed forward. His mouth shut tight, the man struggled to ignore the corpse at his feet, but when faced with the desperate stares of the crowd pleading for succor, he was shaken. "They say he's a shaman," some murmured. He retorted, "I am not a shaman!" As soon as he opened his mouth, his densely packed, in-turned teeth shone in the darkness. The crowd opened their eyes wide. "There is no one in all of Incheon who does not know that you are a shaman. Please put this man's soul to rest. At this rate we will all die. We have all watched with our own two eyes as you performed exorcisms to appease the souls of the dead." Someone found a long wooden staff and placed it in the shaman's hand. The staff was more than twice the height of an adult. Strips of white cloth had been attached to one end. It was a sacred staff. People believed that the deity would come down and inhabit it. The one said to be a shaman caressed the staff in resignation and then returned it. "I do not need this. Only the southern shamans who cannot call the spirits use this." The shaman closed his eyes and began to murmur a chant. A man pulled a flute from his pocket, as if he had been waiting for just this moment, wet the dry mouthpiece with his tongue, and put it in his mouth. A strong wind blew. The people listened to the shaman's song as their clothing flapped in the wind. The shaman was plunged once again into his painful destiny. He became another person entirely, shaking his body, grabbing the corpse and wailing as if he had forgotten that the person had died of a contagious disease, and he took out a handful of brass coins and flung them onto the deck. Seized by the fear of death, the crowd cried, laughed, sang, and became entangled in each of his words, and in a moment the deck was burning with a carnival-like fever. The sound of the flute, which awoke a sense of excitement deep within, strove against the sound of the smokestacks and the waves and the wind, and did not waver once until the ritual ended. The fair-skinned musician's cheeks puffed out like a frog's and his face grew red. The Japanese crewmen in the galley threw out a rooster, its legs tied. The shaman, lost in his own frenzy, bit down on the rooster's neck and then slit its throat with a knife and held it up. The blood drenched his sleeves and ran down to his armpits. A hot steam curled up from his forearm. The shaman shed tears. "Mother, mother, my mother! My cruel mother who gave me none of your food and never once held my hands or feet, let's see if you survive without your son whom you have sent away! No, no, I'm sorry! I was wrong, my mother. Live well, my mother. Live long and live well. Eat my food and live long and well. Oh, it's cold! Oh, it's cold! It's so cold that I can't go on living even if I wanted to! I came because I was hungry, and now I have died of this cursed disease!" The headless chicken thrashed about on the deck, hopped onto the belly of the corpse, and finally fell down. There were no offerings, no drums or gongs, so the ritual did not last long. The gas lamps lit by the German crewmen shone down faintly on the scene, so things looked crueler than they actually were. This dizzying festival, formed by blood and darkness, song and dance, and the corpse and the shaman, stirred the hearts of this agrarian people faced with an epidemic on the ocean. The rhythm pulsed through their veins. Tears streamed down their faces. Many cried and many fainted. The German crewmen on the bridge grinned and looked down on the commotion.

When the spirit had at last left the shaman and he collapsed on the spot to catch his breath, the whalers took the sack with the body in it by the edges. They swung it back and forth three times and then heaved it into the Pacific. They hoped that would be the end of it, but no one could be certain. The crowd looked down at the black ocean that had swallowed up the corpse.

# 19

NOT EVERYONE WATCHED the ritual for the dead. While the ritual was comforting the soul of the deceased who had become food for the fishes of the Pacific Ocean, Yi Jongdo's daughter, Yeonsu, sat with her cloak over her head and watched a boy who sat across from her. It was the boy she had come face to face with at dawn on that morning. The boy, who had claimed a seat early, was listening to the shaman's chanting with his chin on his knees. His lips were firmly pressed together and his large eyes gazed unwaveringly at something. He was not watching the shaman. Whenever a torch shone on the boy's face, it lit up like a shooting star and then faded again. It was the first time in her life that she had stared for so long at the face of a man whose name she did not know, made possible because the boy was paying attention only to the darkness inside himself. Her heart gradually grew more confused at the ritual, where the shaman's chants and the cries of the crowd, the dark night sky and the torches, and the song and the blood all mixed together. The cloak that covered all but her eyes made her feel even more confined. Finally the boy got up. Ijeong brushed off the seat of his pants and turned his back on the ritual. After all, he had not known the dead person. The burial grounds and afterlife the shaman sang of were just abstract words to him. He was still at an age when death did not feel real. Even if he were to leap into the ocean, it did not seem that he would die that easily. How could he imagine catching dysentery, suffering diarrhea, and dying? Rather, the things that moved his heart were Yoshida, Mexico — the land it seemed they would never reach — and the hot flame of love that burned within him. Having no skill in letters, he did not know how to express the agony that welled up in his heart.

As he rose from his place and walked away from the crowd, Ijeong was suddenly captivated by an odor and stopped on the spot. He had smelled it somewhere before, but he could not imagine what it could be. He had smelled all sorts of things in the galley, but nothing like this. Even if he mixed together all the spices he knew, he would not be able to re-create it. He looked around. Yeonsu was there. Her dark eyes flashed with light and then retreated into the darkness. The smell disappeared with her. Ijeong filled his lungs with the salty air. He heard a guttural voice. "Did someone slaughter a roe deer?" It was Jo Jangyun. "That's what it smells like when you cut the neck of a roe deer and drink its blood." He smacked his lips. "There was an unusually large number of hunters in our unit, and whenever they missed that taste they went into the mountains and bang, bang! Then they would cut the neck and catch the hot, steaming blood in a bowl and drink it right there." Ijeong tilted his head. "Doesn't it taste bad?" he asked. Jo Jangyun laughed and ruffled Ijeong's hair with his large hand. "I think I'll join the ritual." He disappeared into the crowd. There were 1,033 of them — no, two had died and one had been born, so there were 1,032 of them on the ship. The crowd pressed so thick around the ritual area that there was nowhere to set foot. After Jo Jangyun had gone, Ijeong turned to look around, but the girl had already disappeared. He could not find her. His heart had taken flight, and he could not stay still. He

went down to the cabin and saw the girl sitting with her family and
sewing.

# 20

THE ARGUMENT ON the deck was in full swing. Everyone was
talking agitatedly, some wanting to throw the seriously ill into the
ocean before the disease spread any further, others wanting to move
them to the deck during the day so they could get some sunshine,
and still others wanting to stop at the nearest land and let them off.
Yet they were unable to reach a conclusion. There seemed to be no
land anywhere nearby, and the weather was cloudy. Of course, they
could not throw into the sea those who were still alive – the families
of the ill would make sure of that. And they could not toss overboard
only those who had no family.

Father Paul walked past where the possessions of the dead were
being burned, then went down to the reeking cabin. At Penang they
had taught some medicine to the seminary students; there was nothing like Western medicine for gaining the trust of the natives and
strengthening ties. He did not think that he could fight this epidemic
with what little he knew, but he could be a small help. In the cabin
many suffered from dehydration and asked for water. He brought
them water. Yet he was more suited to consoling than offering physical treatment. He listened to what they had to say. Many people suffered delusions and could not speak properly. Perhaps there might
be Catholic believers. If so, would he have to perform the sacra-
ments? If someone recognized him and asked him to perform the last
rites, what was he supposed to do? Did a priest who had disobeyed
a bishop's order and abandoned his flock have such authority?

He somehow fell asleep amid the cries of the sick. He did not dream of anything. Morning came and a dim light shone into the cabin. He rose and took care of the sick again. It was better than spending time alone, in agony, wrapped in his blanket. Some awaited his aid, and in their pleading eyes he felt a secret pleasure. Even the demon of disease had passed him by.

A day passed.

Tanabe, the veterinarian, his mouth covered with cloth, went down and helped Father Paul. The two of them checked to see if one gravely ill man was still alive. He showed no sign of movement. If he was dead, they would have to throw him into the ocean. Paul pulled back the blanket from the man's face and his eyes narrowed. The face was familiar. The man had once told Paul to beware of thieves in an open port. He had grown quite gaunt, but Paul recognized him easily. He had thought the man, who went about humming merrily, was adapting well, and now he was hovering on the brink of death. Paul shook the man. His lips moved. He was alive. Paul nodded his head at Tanabe. He was about to cover the man with the blanket again when something fell from his chest to the floor with a clink. Tanabe picked it up. It was a necklace. He handed it to Paul. Tanabe looked at him to see what he wanted to do, but Paul only looked back and forth between the necklace and Choe Seongil. It was clearly the necklace of Bishop Simon Blanche. Paul closed his eyes. He handed the necklace back to Tanabe, and Tanabe retied the cord and put it around Choe Seongil's neck. Perhaps this disturbed the sick man, because he began to twist and turn.

Paul went up to the stern deck and stared blankly at the wake pushed back by the giant screws. The red sunset hung like laundry left out to dry in the western sky. His clothes quickly grew damp from the humid South Pacific wind.

# 21

A FEW DAYS LATER, Ijeong was allowed to return to the galley. He rose early in the morning and walked carefully along the slippery corridor. He reached the stairs and started down when his heart leaped. He did not know why. Yet he was convinced that if he went down the spiral stairs, that which he had been so desperately seeking would be waiting for him at the end. It was not just because of the smell. He did not go to the galley but turned toward the engine room. She was there.

The two of them stood facing each other. Without a word, they gazed at one another as fervently as their eyes and — as they had never been taught that they shouldn't — their hearts allowed, as much as their bodies could stand, and then without realizing it they were holding hands. Had they been in Korea, this would never have happened. But it was a different story in the middle of the ocean, where an epidemic was at its height. For the first time in his life, Kim Ijeong felt the touch of a woman's hand and, flustered, he hung his head. So did she. He didn't know what to do next, so he simply stuttered, "I am Kim Ijeong, the 'two' character for 'i' and the 'upright' character for 'jeong.'" Her head still bowed, the girl giggled. Then she lifted her head and revealed the face that had been hidden by her cloak. The gas lamp in the passageway shone on her. Upon closer inspection, her face glowed with a mysterious spirit that could not be hidden by any filth. Unlike her cheeks, stiff with anxiousness, her eyes smiled gently and welcomed a new love, and the smell of roe deer's blood was the same as always. Ijeong touched his own face. It burned like fire, and the muscles in his arms trembled as if he had just finished hard labor. "I am from the royal family," she said, "the Jeonju Yi clan, and my name is Yeonsu." They heard a clamor from the other end of the passageway. Finding no more words to say, they looked into each other's eyes and finally unclasped their hands. Yeonsu returned to the cabin. Ijeong stayed where he was and suppressed the feelings that welled up inside him. Having been raised with no mother or sisters, by the rough hand of a peddler, Ijeong found everything about her wonderful. He had no idea what to do next, but this only heightened his excitement.

# 22

PERHAPS IT WAS satisfied with two victims. The dysentery lost its strength. The diarrhea stopped and the fevers went down. Those who had gone all the way to the threshold of the next world before returning were still weak, partly from being unable to eat because of dehydration and high fever. Yet Choe Seongil was different. As soon as he woke from sleep in the morning his hand went to his crotch. His penis stuck straight up, red and stiff. His thigh was cold but his penis was hot. At that moment he knew that the demon of illness had retreated for good. His hand came up from his crotch, felt his sunken belly, and then moved on to his chest. He opened his eyes and peeked at what he held in his hand. It was the cross. He thought that perhaps it had protected him like a spirit pole standing at the entrance to a village, or maybe like a talisman.

With his left hand he held the cross to his chest and with his right hand he grabbed his hot penis and rubbed it against his thigh. A feeling of bliss rushed over him. I am alive. He shut his eyes tight and continued to masturbate furiously. Someone sitting next to him cleared his throat, but he paid no mind. Before long a few drops of semen shot out and wet his waistband. With his right sleeve he wiped away the semen, with his left sleeve he wiped away a tear, and then he heaved himself up. He felt slightly dizzy but soon regained his balance. He carried the blanket that had covered him for nearly a week out onto the deck. Father Paul followed him with his eyes. Choe Seongil spread the damp blanket out to dry. Then he sat down next to it and lit a cigarette. The blazing sun was warm and the wind tickled his earlobes. Some boys were shouting and spinning a top made from wrapped-up coins.

Father Paul drew near. "Thank goodness you are feeling better." He held out some bread. "It's the Westerners' rice cake, and it doesn't taste too bad. I saved some from yesterday. Try it." Choe chewed and swallowed the bread. At first it felt like eating cloth, but its flavor came out as he continued to chew it. The ill began to show themselves on deck by ones and twos. Many were still bedridden, but it was clear that the worst of it was over. "How many died?" Choe asked. "Two. There was a shamanic ritual, too. You must not have seen it." "Is there a shaman here?" "There is a fellow who has been possessed by a spirit, but he pretends to know nothing about it. He boarded the ship because he was tired of being a shaman, but once he had a wand in his hand he was willing enough." Choe looked uninterested and scratched his stomach. Father Paul saw the string that held the cross around his neck, but he said nothing. It was clear that the man was the thief. Yet what would he do with the cross if he got it back? Had he not turned his back on the Church and on God? Still, Paul circled around the cross as if it had some sort of pull on him. For his part, Choe was irritated with his loot's owner and deliberately cut off the conversation several times, but Paul did not go below; he stayed nearby without a word.

That night black clouds rushed in low. A tropical storm began to pour down rain, and lightning flashed the whole night. Choe Seongil deliberately went up on deck and stood in the downpour.

On a ship, where water was scarce, it was the easiest way to wash oneself. On the dark deck he cast off his clothes and gave himself over to the harsh rain. Lightning slithered out from between the dark clouds like a snake's tongue and the thunder roared, but he had returned from death and thought of it as a fireworks display to commemorate his recovery. He giggled and ran about the deck. I almost died in the wrong place! He draped his clothes over his wet body and headed for the galley. If Kim Ijeong was there he would get something to eat, and if not he would steal something. Since his return from the threshold of the next world, he had been plagued by a voracious hunger. He smacked his lips and went down the iron stairs, but a black shape blocked his path. He could not see the face, as if someone had blotted it out with ink. His body shook violently. "Who are you?" The black shape spoke in a low voice that sounded as if it came from a deep well. "I am the one who died in your stead." The black shape reached out a hand and squeezed Choe Seongil's neck. "I have come to claim the price for my life."

# 23

As always, Yoshida led Ijeong down to the hold. He gave him an apple and spoke. "We will soon arrive in Mexico. There are only lizards and cacti there. You can stay on the *Ilford*. The captain will allow it. After all, you don't have any family, do you? Learning to cook and wandering the globe is not such a bad life." Yoshida's eyes were earnest. Ijeong turned away. His whole being had been violently seized by the image of Yi Yeonsu; the affections of this deserter cook were a burden. Ijeong crouched down and bit into the apple. Silence fell. The potato box against which Ijeong was leaning fell over at an angle. As if that were his signal, Yoshida leaped up and grabbed Ijeong by the shoulders. Then he kissed him. Yoshida's tongue entered Ijeong's mouth and licked the root of his tongue. Of course, Yoshida was too strong for him, but Ijeong also didn't think there was any real need to resist. It was a strange feeling, but there was no reason for Ijeong to push him away. Taking Ijeong's lack of resistance as permission, Yoshida grew bolder. He caressed the boy's chest, penis, and buttocks as if mad. Ijeong closed his eyes. This is the last time. He wants this so badly, and it will only be a moment. After all, there was nothing else that he could give him, was there? Acid rushed up from his stomach. Ijeong swallowed. Yoshida had longed for this for over a month, and his body grew hot and was quickly boiling toward a climax. As Yoshida's tongue was licking Ijeong's earlobe, something hot pierced his rear. Ijeong shut his eyes tight. The stench of pig fat wafted up. Yoshida's slippery hands grabbed Ijeong's shoulders so tightly he thought they would be crushed.

When Yoshida broke away, Ijeong finished eating the apple he had been holding in his right hand. "I'm sorry," Yoshida said. Ijeong shook his head. Then he spoke. "I am going to get off in Mexico and go with the Koreans." Yoshida got down on his knees and grabbed Ijeong's hand. Ijeong coldly shook off those hands, slippery with pig fat. "Thank you for your help. But this is the end. When we reach the harbor I will go where I set off to go." Yoshida sank to the floor and held his head in his hands.

Ijeong looked down coldly at Yoshida. A moment later Yoshida regained his composure and picked himself up off the floor. Then he looked at Ijeong with the eyes of a wounded animal and left the hold without a word. Ijeong followed him to the galley. He worked like mad. In the blink of an eye, food for one thousand people was prepared. Ijeong forgot about everything. But as soon as the work ended, he thought of Yeonsu's shining black eyes and white skin beneath her cloak, and his heart leaped.

# 24

A FEW DAYS PASSED without anyone being born or dying. Other than one man who pestered another's woman and so received a slight knife wound, nothing happened. The weather gradually grew hotter. Someone spoke of the equator, but almost no one understood him. The concept of the globe was unfamiliar, let alone the idea of the equator. It was a tedious voyage that seemed as if it would never end. Then someone pointed up at the sky. A large bird with its wings spread wide was circling above the *Ilford*. Soon another bird appeared. Both had the red necks and black bodies of frigatebirds. People came up on deck to look at these strange beings. "Seeing birds," said the Pohang fishermen, "means that land is not far." People shaded their eyes with their hands and gazed around, but the coastline was nowhere to be seen. Yet the two frigatebirds breathed new life into the enervated people who had been lying about. The deck and cabin suddenly grew noisy. The passengers tirelessly watched the flight of the frigatebirds. "Their tails are like swallow tails." "They fly like hawks." Everyone had something to say. Then a flock of birds of another kind flew toward them from the west.

A day passed. More birds were spotted. Blue-footed cormorants flew by and landed on the flagpole, resting before flying off again, and brown pelicans with beaks shaped like gourds soared past them. All of these things were interpreted as signs of abundance. Ospreys dove into the water and caught fish the size of one's arm before flying back up again, and the cormorants continuously puffed up their throats and swallowed small fry. The passengers had eaten less and less for so long, but now they began to eat more. Having regained their appetites, they sat around in small groups and predicted the future.

Thanks to their chatter, down below the waterline Yi Yeonsu guessed what was happening. Yet the fire that burned deep in her heart burned not for the approaching unknown land, but for one boy. When she saw no sign of him for two days, Yeonsu's anxiety reached the breaking point. Where has he gone? Does he spend the whole day in the galley? All sorts of questions raced through her head. What kind of person is he? How much has he studied? Knowing nothing of him but his name, Yeonsu was anxious with suspense. I can't take it anymore. Yeonsu stood up from her seat. Next to her sat her younger brother, Yi Jinu, who had been depressed and silent for days. Even when his sister stood up, he did not react, as if he were lifeless. "Hey, why don't you go out and get some fresh air?" she said. Yi Jinu shook his head. "The sun hurts my eyes. And I get dizzy." As if she had been waiting for the moment, Yeonsu weaved through the narrow path between people's legs. After she passed by, her unique smell lingered. Those who were asleep opened their eyes, and those who were awake shut their eyes. As soon as she entered the passageway outside the cabin she could see two eyes sparkling in the darkness. He was there. Yeonsu walked toward him. But his eyes drew back as if teasing her. He ran and Yeonsu chased him. They changed direction a few times and went down two flights of stairs and there he was again. He opened a door with a key. Yeonsu followed him inside as if spellbound. He closed the door. She was not the least bit afraid. The air smelled of rotten fruit and vegetables. From above came the odor of garlic. "Did you just stand there? Until I came out?" He nodded. "I haven't moved for two days, ah . . ." Their lips met. It did not take long for their two filthy bodies to become one. Clunk, clunk. A few thick bulbs of garlic rolled off the shelf and hit Ijeong on the back of the head. Yeonsu only wondered at how familiar all of this was, and how alive all of her senses were. Pain flooded deep inside her body, but it was also sweet. In the dark hold, Yeonsu grabbed his face and let out a single long, sharp scream.

Lukewarm fluid dribbled down her thigh. She lay there and thought about the fate that had just brushed by her. She closed her spread legs. Her pelvis was stiff and her flesh prickled where it rubbed against the hem of her clothes. Ijeong said, "I am a wandering merchant and a lowly orphan. But in Mexico, where we will soon arrive, none of that will matter. Somehow I will earn money, and I will find you and marry you. Please wait for me." Yeonsu laughed weakly as she lay there. She was not laughing at him, yet laughter came out. "You could be killed. Though we may be dressed in filthy clothes and eat and live like pigs here, my family is royalty and my father is a blood relative of His Majesty. He is not one of those ruined aristocrats who do not have money for a proper hat. If it weren't for the wiles of Yi Haeung, my father might have ascended the throne. Such a person would never accept anyone as my husband, not just you."

Ijeong spoke. "Do you really think the distinction between high and low, old and young, and man and woman will be as severe as it is in Korea? Look at this ship we are on. Aristocrat or commoner, all must line up to eat." Ijeong pointed above his head. "In the eyes of those Westerners above us, we are all just the same — Koreans. They only count our heads, and they do not care about our family registers. There is no one on this ship who could stand side by side with you anyway." Ijeong held Yeonsu. The smell of roe deer blood washed over him. She did not argue. Her own foreboding was not that different: Life there will be vastly different from Korea.

I will go to school and to church. I will earn money with my own hands. I will be a woman who will rely on no one. When that time comes, my mother and father will have no hold on me. The two young people came together once again. In every way it was easier than the first time. This time they took all their clothes off and held each other. A rotten potato that was rolling around on the floor was crushed beneath their bodies.

# 25

CHOE SEONGIL WOKE UP in a strange place. It was not the corner where he always slept, but the middle of the cabin. What happened? As he stood up and brushed himself off, he heard something in his ear, his inner ear: "I have come to claim the price for my life." Who can it be? More than that, how did I come to be lying here? He looked around. There were no familiar faces. Then someone walked toward him. "You're awake." It was the fellow whose possessions he had taken. Choe Seongil furtively touched his chest to make sure that the cross necklace was still hanging there. Nothing was out of place. Father Paul gave him a dipper of water. "Drink this. They found you lying on the floor and brought you here. You're not fully well yet." Choe Seongil tilted his head. "No, that's not it. Maybe I was dreaming. Look here, my Chungcheong province friend, do you know anything about dreams?" Father Paul waved him off, but Choe Seongil did not stop. "I must have been dreaming, but I thought I met a strange person in that passageway. I could not see his face at all, as if someone had blotted it out with a brush, and he suddenly appeared and — I can still hear it as clearly as if he were talking right into my ear — he said, 'I am the one who died in your stead. I have come to claim the price for my life.' I couldn't tell if I was dreaming or awake, but who on this ship would say something like that to me?"

Father Paul knew who had died in this man's, and humanity's, stead. The man who had saved his own life, too, and for whom he had traveled all the way to Penang and back. He had made a vow to become like him; he had bowed down on the floor and received his ordination. When he had first heard the story of that man, in a coal village in the heart of the mountains, he was captivated at once by the birth myth of the mysterious religion. It was a truly strange tale, but he could understand how a god might be born into the body of a human. Such a thing was entirely natural in his hometown on the island of Wi, where the gods manifested themselves in human form dozens of times each year. Yet this was the first time he had heard of a god never leaving the human body, spending the rest of his life there. The cruelty of his execution — spikes driven through the hands and feet of a living person, then into a tree so that he could not move and only wait for death — was also nothing new. Yet Paul was amazed to hear that a god who had taken a human body finally died powerlessly. It was even harder to understand that this man had died for the sins of all humanity. And though he had gone to so much effort to die, after only three days he was resurrected and went up to heaven with his body again intact. Maybe the contradictions that filled the story were what fascinated him. He was a god and yet a man, omnipotent yet powerless, horrible yet wonderful. He said that he loved humanity, yet he made those humans whom he loved eternal sinners. And now the son of this lofty god had appeared before the eyes of this petty thief and said, "I am the one who died in your stead." Was this yet another of his contradictions? It couldn't be. It had to be some Korean who detested Jesus and his religion, a soldier who had once chopped off the heads of Catholics — now that he thought about it, wasn't this place teeming with soldiers? — and was pretending to be Jesus in order to play a trick on the weakened Choe Seongil. After all, Jesus wasn't the type to go around claiming a price for his life.

"It was just a silly dream." Paul patted Choe Seongil on the back. He stood up. Yet he did not feel at ease.

# 26

SOMEONE WAS POUNDING impatiently on the door of the hold. Ijeong straightened his clothes and opened it. Yoshida. The gas lamp cast a deep shadow over his face. While the two men stared at each other, Yi Yeonsu threw on her cloak and slipped out. Yoshida grimaced at the girl whose intense odor assaulted his nose. His lips trembled. "Bakayarou!" His voice shook like that of a teenage boy. The weak curse only annoyed Ijeong. "I did what I could for you, did I not? Make way." He took a step forward. Yoshida stepped back weakly. Worried that Yoshida might attack him from behind, Ijeong walked forward with anxiety in each step.

A short while later, he heard the sound of the hold door closing. Yoshida had gone inside. Ijeong went up to the cabin to lie down. It's over with the galley now — but didn't they say we would arrive in port tomorrow? As he thought this, he already missed the experience of life in the galley of a large ship. It had nothing to do with Yoshida; he missed the violent, hot atmosphere created by the kitchen crew's sweaty flesh so close together. It was a world of only men, and for that reason it was further outside reality. Nothing could intrude on it. Family troubles, regrets about the past, and worries for the future all had their place, even if it was far away. Why should Ijeong be any different? Why should he have no fear of the approaching New World? If his future were truly unknown, he might have hesitated a little, but his future was approaching with a distinct form and smell. The fog cleared and the western coast of Mexico showed itself faintly. Whitish cliffs like mold on wallpaper alternated with sandy beaches. The Koreans went up on deck to see the bewitching silhouette of the new continent. "There is absolutely no green to this land," someone said with tilted head. "That's because it's the seashore," someone else shot back.

Jo Jangyun and three other soldiers climbed up the crane in the bow and shaded their eyes as they looked at the coast. "Looks like we're almost there," Jo Jangyun said, and two of the soldiers, Kim Seokcheol and Seo Gijung, licked their lips. Kim Seokcheol, whose cheekbones stuck out and whose eyes seemed to be almost pasted onto his forehead (earning him the nickname of "Deva King") started talking about finding a wife: "If I can earn some money and return to Korea, the first thing I'll do is get married." Seo Gijung, who was a head shorter than Kim Seokcheol and had always been the brunt of jokes in the empire's military because of his small stature, teased: "After the five years that will take you, why settle for just getting married? You could take a concubine as well." Kim Seokcheol liked the sound of that and chuckled. "Even a short fellow like you got married, so what could stop me? What will you do with the money you earn?" Seo Gijung glanced toward the west, where his wife and children had remained, and spoke in a quiet, shy voice. "I'll buy a rice paddy." A brief silence followed, dampening their boisterous mood. "What, did someone die?" Jo Jangyun joked, but no one laughed. None of them would have boarded that ship had they had their own land. They had no land, so they became soldiers; they had no land, so they couldn't get married; they had no land, so they had no place to return to and had crawled into those awful barracks. "Now that our days in the garrison guard are over, I realize they were good times," Kim Seokcheol said dreamily. "What do you mean good times? They were hard times." The three of them had volunteered for the new army, reorganized according to the Russian model in 1896. Emperor Gojong, who had moved his residence to the Russian legation and resisted the Japanese, hired a drill instructor from Russia and poured forty percent of the yearly budget into cultivating the army. As soon as word spread that the empire was choosing new soldiers, more than one thousand young men from around the country applied, and there was a bustle in the garrison guard courtyard. Only about two hundred men were chosen, though. Two of them were stationed with the 5th Regiment's 2nd Battalion at the Bukcheong Garrison Guard. Jo Jangyun, Kim Seokcheol, and Seo Gijung had been engineers and staff sergeants. Seo Gijung had been trained with them, but he was stationed with the 3rd Battalion at the Chongseong Garrison Guard. Then, on October 18, 1904, the Japanese army marched into Hamgyeong province, which was strongly pro-Russian, and set up a military administration, disbanding both the Bukcheong and the Chongseong garrisons. The Japanese would not leave the untrustworthy army of the Korean Empire in Hamgyeong, their front line with Russia.

"Things worked out for the best. After all, we only ever chased around the righteous armies who refused the emperor's order to cut their hair." "Why did you have to bring that up?" "Well it's the truth, isn't it? Damn, cutting someone's throat because he refuses to cut his hair." "I never did that." "Me neither." But all of them felt a twinge of regret.

The fourth soldier, Bak Jeonghun, had been silent up until then. He was a man of so few words that he was called the Stone Buddha. He was an expert marksman, shooting perfect scores even with the old Japanese-style rifles. There were rumors that he had killed a tiger on Mount Guwol and a bear on Mount Baekdu, but he remained silent on the matter. Bak Jeonghun had served as an infantryman in the central army that defended Seoul and the royal palace. He had such a strong sense of responsibility and drew such a clear distinction between public and private life that when his wife grew ill and died, he wrapped her in a straw sack with his own hands and carried her up the hill behind his village to bury her before returning to his post. Yet this only earned him the ire of the corrupt officers. When Hasegawa Yoshimichi, the commander of the Japanese army, proposed the reformation of the Korean imperial military system on December 26, 1904, Bak Jeonghun was the first to lay aside his uniform. Three months after that, he boarded the ship at Jemulpo. He was normally a quiet person, but he was also given to sudden fits of depression, and he had hardly spoken since the *Ilford* had sailed. So when he made as if to say something, everyone paid attention. Having seen the coastline, Bak Jeonghun suddenly opened his mouth. "Me, I don't plan on going back." Their eyes grew wide and they stared at him. It was the first time anyone had said anything like that since the journey started. "That pitiful country, what has it done for us that we should go back? Did it not starve us when we were young, beat us when we grew up, and abandon us when life was finally bearable? The Chinese bastards above us, the damned Russians on our backs, and the cursed Japanese below us, kicking us with their military boots and then making us fawn before them. The Koreans treating their own people as coldly as the winter frost and cowering before another nation's army like a dog in summer. That country has no nerve or backbone. No, I don't plan to go back there. As long as I don't starve, I plan to somehow find a way to survive here. I'll buy some land" — here he swallowed hard, whether from tears or just saliva they did not know, before continuing — "and of course get married. And have children too."

The three other soldiers had little to say, knowing all too well what had happened to his wife and children. Only Kim Seokcheol mumbled softly, "Still, we have to go back . . . our ancestors are there." As the coastline began to show itself more clearly, the possibility that they might not be able to go back — a possibility that they did not dare put into words — began to come closer to reality. Rather than continue a discussion with no conclusion, they chose instead to fix their eyes on the silhouette of the land where they had to go. In anticipation, their palms were clammy. And if they opened their eyes a little wider, they could count the number of fishermen working on their boats at anchor along the coast.

# 27

THE SHIP CONTINUED SOUTH at a fixed distance from the coast-line. Before the passengers knew it, night had fallen, and, tired of waiting, they fell asleep by ones and twos. The once troublesome Pacific lapped gently at the *Ilford*'s hull. Before sunrise, a cold, salty dew covered the ship as if it had been wiped down with a wet rag. On the deck, Ijeong gazed at the dark surroundings. There was no reason for him to be up this early, but as soon as dawn broke his eyes shot open out of habit. It's only proper to say my farewells, he told himself. If it hadn't been for Yoshida, and if he hadn't worked in the galley, the voyage probably would have seemed endless. The cooks were a rough group, but after they accepted him as one of their own, they showed him a tenacious affection. He missed the taste of sake drunk straight from the bottle, too. Yoshida's hands, slippery with pig's fat, were unpleasant, but even so, he could not ignore the compassion he felt for him. Yoshida, the deserter who wandered the vast ocean with no family, no country, and no friends. He showed all the signs of one who had fought with life and lost early. Ijeong feared, however vaguely, that Yoshida's misfortune might rub off on him. The peddler had taught him how to discern the signs of the unfortunate and how to repel them: "If you meet a cripple, a lame person, a blind man, or a deaf person before a meal, sprinkle salt on them generously. If they come closer, hit them. If they ask for food, kick their rice dish hard. Don't think of this as being cruel. If a fellow with sores comes close, you will get sores, and if a fellow who has soiled his pants comes close, then you will smell of dung. He who touches pitch will be stained. Half of all merchants are sailors. That means that half of success is pure luck. What is this market we're at now? It's a five-day market, right? If we're unlucky for a day we starve for five. If we're unlucky for two days we starve for ten, and then what happens? We'll die."

Ijeong got dressed and started to go down to the galley, but then wondered if it might not be better just to leave, and he went back on deck, leaned against the railing, and stared at the Mexican coastline. The sun rose over the bow of the ship and shone on the deck. It hurt his eyes. The sun rose further, between the ship's bridge and a lifeboat, and slowly began to shine on Ijeong's face. Ijeong narrowed his eyes and peered at the Mexican sun. The angle of the sun and the ship gradually shifted. The *Ilford* was turning in an arc and changing course. Ijeong climbed to the upper deck. The boat was now heading toward the coast. Finally, the port, a real port bustling with cargo ships, warships, and passenger vessels, spread out before his eyes. Even this early in the morning, it overflowed with a vitality that far exceeded that of Jemulpo. Smaller boats went back and forth between the larger ships, carrying goods and people. The boats shook like autumn leaves each time the lithe, dark-skinned men pulled the oars. Before Ijeong realized it, passengers were gathering at his side, shouting excitedly. Someone approached Ijeong from behind and squeezed his hand. Ijeong turned around with a smile on his face. An unfamiliar man was standing there. Dressed smartly in a gray suit with his short hair slicked back, this gentleman led Ijeong through the crowd, and only when they neared the lifeboat did the man turn around. Yoshida. Completely changed, he stood at a comfortable distance from Ijeong. Then he spoke in proper Japanese. "I am much indebted to you. I am sorry if it was unpleasant for you. But I am glad I was able to spend time with you. I shall not forget this voyage." He held out his hand to shake in the Western style. Ijeong took his hand, then bowed his head low in the Japanese style and replied in Japanese. "It is I who am indebted. Farewell, Yoshida-san." The corners of Yoshida's mouth turned upward in a smile. "My contract as a crew member ends today. I am free to choose whether or not to renew it. First I will go ashore. Then I plan to go to the consulate in Mexico, turn myself in, and await my punishment. I will not live like this anymore."

Ijeong had always thought of Yoshida as simply a cook, but now that he was properly dressed in a suit he looked like a navy officer on leave. Ijeong examined the startlingly transformed Yoshida. It was more than just the fact that he was clean and well dressed; he seemed to have become someone else.

Yoshida shook Ijeong's hand once more and then they parted. The Koreans were already collecting their luggage and coming up on deck. Ijeong went down and picked up his sack, though it could hardly be called luggage. Yi Yeonsu's family had already gone up on deck.

The *Ilford* had arrived at the southern Mexican port of Salina Cruz after six weeks at sea. The date was May 15, 1905. John Meyers and Gwon Yongjun directed the disembarking. The ship was too large to approach the landing piers. Eventually, small boats approached to carry the people and luggage to shore. With flushed faces, the Koreans took the hands held out by an unfamiliar race, boarded the boats, and headed for the unknown continent. Ijeong climbed aboard a boat with a group of soldiers. When they reached the coast he discovered Yi Yeonsu and her family, but he did not go to them. When all the Koreans had disembarked, they gathered in an empty spot. Mexican customs officials approached Meyers and Gwon Yongjun, took their papers, and began to examine the immigrants' passports. The mood was friendly and there was no trouble. Cigars were provided for the Koreans. The men naturally sat down in small groups, smoking their cigars and chatting noisily.

Food was delivered from somewhere — rice balls, probably prepared in advance on the ship. When the officials finished their examination, John Meyers set out at the head of the throng of some one thousand people, like Moses leading the Hebrews out of Sinai. Before long a railroad station appeared. There was no train in sight. Gwon Yongjun announced that the train would arrive tomorrow, so they would have to spend the night here. The port at which they had just arrived was not their final destination. They had to take a train across the Isthmus of Tehuantepec, where the North American continent narrowed to a thin strip of land like an ant's waist, to the port of Coatzacoalcos, and from there they had to take another ship to the port of Progreso, the gateway to the Yucatán Peninsula. From there they had a journey of several hours to Mérida, the Yucatán's central city. This land that they had traveled halfway around the world to reach felt somehow familiar to them. May on the west coast of Mexico was mild and gentle, and the day they arrived happened to be particularly warm and fair. At night the temperature barely dropped, and they could make do without shelter. Compared to the cramped, dark *Ilford*, it was heaven. Excited at the feel of solid earth beneath them after so long, boys stamped their feet and leaped around. Children chased each other and the adults stretched out their legs.

# 28

THE TRAIN ARRIVED early in the morning. After it was loaded with cargo, the Koreans boarded. Many were riding a train for the first time. Some stuck their heads out the window and watched the scenery; some tried to fall asleep. At about the time they began to grow hungry, the train stopped at a secluded village. They got off and ate lunch in this village, which was so quiet it seemed that even the birds must be sleeping. Dark-skinned Mayans gathered around and watched them. When the meal ended, the Koreans boarded the train again and it departed. When night fell, the train stopped. Gwon Yongjun told everyone to get off. The Koreans formed a line next to the train station. The wind had a salty tang. It was too dark to see their surroundings, but they soon figured out that they were at a port. Far away, dim lamps bobbed up and down. Black dogs barked. Everyone moved to a field and settled there for the night. It was the second night they spent without a roof over their heads. Now that the excitement of landing had faded, the dew of dawn felt colder. People began to sneeze. "What are we, animals?" someone complained, but it did not spread far. Hairless dogs ran here and there, sniffing at the travelers.

Breakfast was pickled cabbage and rice. Afterward they lined up and boarded a cargo ship that awaited them. The voyage took three days and two nights, longer than they had expected. Those who had stayed on deck, thinking that they would soon disembark again, all went below to the cargo hold at night and found places to lie down. The ship cut across the Gulf of Campeche and arrived at the port of Progreso. The harbor was too shallow to bring the ship close to land, so it dropped anchor four miles from the coast, and small lighters streamed to the ship like a column of ants after something sweet. The lighters unceasingly carried passengers to shore. When they reached land, the Koreans looked around. Progreso was a sleepy port. No people were visible, and the village itself looked small. A lighthouse could be seen from afar, but it was not very high. The waters that flowed in on the Gulf Stream were turbid, and they could not see the ocean floor. Tropical trees they had never seen before lined the coast, and those who landed first waited in their shade for the rest.

Suddenly they heard a commotion, and everyone turned in that direction. Sparkling instruments were playing music — a welcoming party organized by the local government. The theme from Dvořák's *New World Symphony* rang out, but to the Koreans it was only a loud din. The immigrants wondered if the tubas and trombones and other brass instruments were made of gold; they saw the uniforms of the band and surmised that they must be soldiers, and judging by the splendor of the event, they thought that these must surely be people of high standing. The appearance of the band momentarily breathed new life into their tedious journey, and gave rise to a misunderstanding about the Yucatán Peninsula and the prosperity of Mexico. A fat Mexican took the podium and delivered a speech in Spanish; the immigrants clapped without having the slightest idea what he had said. For one reason or another, the Mexicans had also been eagerly awaiting the coming of the Korean laborers. Another fanfare played and the brief welcoming party was over. The immigrants began to move.

A black freight train awaited them at the end of the road that stretched all the way out to the piers. After an hour they arrived in the city of Mérida. They headed for a vast field. Tents, erected by the Mérida association of hacendados, were lined up in rows, waiting for them. The tents had no walls, and a dry wind blew through them. There they were provided with corn, flour, and a small portion of beans, a steel pot and firewood. The men built the fires and the women cooked the food. Sand kept getting into their mouths. People began to talk less. A few days passed without event. Anxiety wandered among the tents. John Meyers and Gwon Yongjun were spotted speaking with serious faces to a few Mexicans. Mosquitoes swarmed viciously night and day, sucking the blood of the strangers and laying their eggs in pits between the tents. Ants bit them on their buttocks. Unlike their original destination, Salina Cruz, the heat of Mérida was like embracing a ball of fire. Their lips dried and cracked. May was the hottest month of the year. The heat was far worse than the humid summers of Korea. If it hadn't been for the shade from the tents, some would surely have died of sunstroke.

As dusk fell, the sky turned red in an instant like an ill-tempered child. The Yucatán sun lowered its rear to the horizon rather late and then suddenly disappeared. There was not a mountain in sight. The vastness of the plain was felt strongly by the Koreans, who had never in their lives seen the horizon on land. They realized they had been born between the mountains, had grown up looking at the mountains, and went to sleep when the sun fell behind the mountains. This endless plain, with no Arirang Hill of their folk songs, was a truly strange sight, and they tossed and turned not so much because the ground was hard but because of the boundlessness and emptiness around them.

No one had seen anything like the rice paddies and fields of Korea, so their anxiety increased. "Is there no rice in Mexico?" For several days they were provided with boiled corn and tasteless corn tortillas. On the way to Mérida from Progreso, wherever they looked they saw strange plants arranged in evenly spaced rows on the dry earth, like upside-down demons' toenails, or flames, or even overgrown orchids. From the train they had occasionally seen Indians, dressed in white, cutting the leaves from these plants with scythes. A few of the quicker ones wondered if perhaps this was the work they would be doing. The Mayan Indians lifted their scythes slowly beneath a sun that beat down as if to vaporize everything. At first glance, the work did not appear difficult but more like a carefree pastoral afternoon walk. They cut the branches, tied them, and moved them to carts, and on occasion a man on horseback would say something, but they didn't seem to be talking about anything serious. Some thought it odd that not a single cow could be seen in the fields. "They're not going to use us as beasts of burden, are they?" There was all sorts of speculation.

On the fourth day, a two-horse carriage appeared, kicking up dust. The driver holding the reins and two servants escorted the master, who was dressed in white and had a black mustache. When the carriage stopped, the man in white got down and approached the Koreans. But the Koreans thought he was a servant because the uniforms of the driver and servants were far more extravagant and decorative. Several more carriages followed. As before, the drivers in their extravagant clothes sat in the carriages while their masters got down and greeted each other. They looked bright and cheerful. They must have been happy about something, as they repeatedly burst into laughter. Finally the six masters, the hacienda owners, gathered together. The Continental Colonization Company had the Koreans stand up and form themselves into lines. The hacendados walked around and pointed at people with their canes. They singled out those who looked strong and healthy first. Unconsciously, the Koreans straightened their backs. The hacendado who had arrived first took around one hundred people, while the others took slightly fewer. Apparently the one who hired the most had the right to choose first. The hacendados signed documents and handed them to John Meyers. That day, about half of the people traveled to haciendas from the three train stations situated around Mérida.

More hacendados continued to arrive into the next day. They did not comment on the workers, but simply chose the first ones they saw and took them to their haciendas. The Koreans from the *Ilford* were scattered among twenty-two haciendas in the Yucatán. It took a week for all 1,032 to be chosen. The last hacendado to arrive, a mestizo, appeared alone on a horse pulling a cart with no driver and no servants. He ran a hacienda near the Guatemala border. The representative of the Mérida association of hacendados pulled aside the tent flap, flashed him a smile, and went out to greet him. He brought with him a Korean man who had been squatting in the shade of a carriage to avoid the sun. "All the others have been taken, and only this one is left." The representative smiled broadly, showing his teeth. The young mestizo had no choice, so he signed the document and looked at the last Korean. It looks like it's time to hear a new song. The singing never ceased at his hacienda. He heard African songs from the blacks he had bought from Belize. He had Mayans, once the rulers of the Yucatán, singing Mayan songs. He had coolies singing the boat songs of Guangzhou. The mulattos from across the channel in Cuba were skilled in dancing and drumming. Now he would be able to hear strange new songs from this man who came from a place called Korea. The man's neck was long and he looked like he had a good voice. The hacendado was fortunate. The Korean was, in fact, the owner of a unique voice. He hesitated when the interpreter urged him to sing a song, and then he began to sing in a trembling voice: "Like the heart of a hen pheasant chased by a falcon on a hill with no trees, no boulders, no stones; like a sailor in the midst of the vast ocean on a boat carrying a thousand sacks of rice, having lost its oars, lost its anchor, broken its masts, snapped its rigging, and dropped its rudder, and the wind blows and the waves crash and the fog is thick, yet there are still a thousand miles, ten thousand miles to go, and the sky is dark and he is alone in heaven and earth and the sea shines red with the setting sun, and then he meets a pirate . . ." It was a song meant to be sung by a woman with a male voice. The melody was endlessly slow and mysterious, and the young hacendado was amazed. The man's voice was like a boy's before puberty, but also like the voice of a woman lost in sadness. The representative of the association of hacendados approached and raised his hand to stop the singing. Then he smiled broadly and squeezed the crotch of the last remaining Korean with his right hand. With a face that said "No wonder," he whispered something to the young mestizo. The Korean grimaced with shame, and the hacendado put him in his cart. With a discount of 50 pesos, as compensation for the testicles he had no use for, there was no reason not to take him.

His name was Kim Okseon. It was not until he was seven years old that he realized he was missing something. His family told the boy that a dog had bitten off his testicles when he was relieving himself. He was young, but he didn't believe them. It was not long before he learned that his father had tied off his testicles with a leather strap, so tight that the blood did not flow, and then cut them off. And before he was ten years old, he entered the palace and began to wait on the eunuchs. "It's a way to make a living, isn't it?" his father said. "What would you do with those balls anyway?" His father clapped him viciously on the back of the head as the boy left, crying. That was the last he saw of his family. Kim Okseon became a musician. He learned to play stringed instruments and the flute and he memorized songs. When the royal family held an event, he sang and sometimes danced. He once received a fan from Gojong himself during the festivities to celebrate the rebuilding of Gyeongbok

Palace. When the empress was stabbed to death, Gojong fled to the Russian legation, and the Coup of 1884 and the Reform of 1894 shook the world both inside and outside the palace. The fate of the eunuchs also flickered like a candle in the wind. They took sides, dividing themselves into enlightenment and conservative factions. The days when they weren't paid grew more frequent, so the musician eunuchs stopped going to the palace. Some of them taught music and dance to gisaeng. Others returned to their hometowns to farm, but their families did not welcome the eunuchs, and they found it difficult to bear the gossip. Kim Okseon and two other eunuchs wanted to leave for a place where no one knew them. One of them read the *Capital Gazette* and contacted the others, and a few days later they packed up all they owned and headed for Jemulpo. During their long voyage they spoke less and less to the other passengers, mostly keeping to themselves. Almost no one realized that they had once been palace musicians.

# 29

IN THE TENT VILLAGE on the outskirts of Mérida, Ijeong was interested in one thing alone. Who would be going to the hacienda with him? When it became clear that they were not all going to the same hacienda, Ijeong hoped that he could go to the same one as Yi Yeonsu and her family. If he could have one more wish, it would be to go with the former soldiers he had come to know on the ship. But everything was decided by the hacendados' canes. One by one, those he knew were chosen. Still a boy, Ijeong was called out much later than Jo Jangyun and his comrades. As he left, Jo Jangyun clapped Ijeong on the shoulder. "Don't be afraid. We'll see each other again soon."

It was sad for Ijeong to part with the person he had relied on like a father. "Farewell," Ijeong said, bobbing his head in a bow. He also said goodbye to Bak Jeonghun, who stood silently at Jo Jangyun's side. Bak Jeonghun squeezed Ijeong's hand. "We'll see each other again. The world is not nearly as large as you might think."

Yi Jongdo and his family were in a similar situation, and it was hard to find a hacendado who would choose a middle-aged man with a wife, a young boy, and a girl. What if they break up the families? Yi Jongdo was extremely nervous. He had long since given up any thought of boldly approaching a Mexican aristocrat and demanding a position appropriate to someone of his status. He was not a fool. On the way to Mérida, packed like luggage on the train, he realized just how impetuous his decision to leave had been, and he regretted it. Neither rank nor learning mattered in this place. The only thing left was his family. While he, thoroughly discouraged, read *The Analects of Confucius*, the only book he had brought with him, his wife and daughter surprisingly drew water, cooked their meals, and made an effort to get to know the women around them. Had they not, they wouldn't have been able to survive even a day. Yet the more they adapted, the more he was discouraged by his own powerlessness, which forced his family to mingle with those of lowly standing.

A hacendado who arrived late that day, at around sunset, must have had something in mind, for he began to choose mainly those immigrants who had families. Yi Yeonsu obediently followed her father and stood in a line in front of the hacendado who had chosen them. Among those who had not yet been chosen, she spied Ijeong's handsome forehead and eyes. Their eyes met. Yeonsu felt the strength leave her body, and she had to grab her mother's hand as she walked on ahead. Then another carriage arrived, and this hacendado, short and pudgy, chose mostly single men. He poked

Ijeong in the stomach with his cane. Yeonsu buried her face in her baggage. Tears gushed out. Once she started crying, she could not stop. Her father cleared his throat and her mother jabbed her in her side and scolded her. "Quiet!" Mucus ran from her nose, past her dirty lips, and into her mouth.

John Meyers look satisfied with himself. Taking into account the passengers' fare on the *Ilford* and the food and cigarettes they had consumed, even after splitting the profits with the Continental Colonization Company he would still be left with a large sum for which he would have had to work three years back home. The owners of the Yucatán's henequen haciendas, which suffered from a severe labor shortage, paid a relatively dear price for the Korean immigrants, who could not speak Spanish and thus were no risk of flight, and who did not have a diplomat stationed here who would interfere in the landowners' affairs. Henequen, the raw material for shipping rope, had become a precious commodity as shipping tonnage increased with imperial competition for colonies and the rapid development of Western capitalism. Rope made from the fiber of the henequen plant was durable and sturdy. The world rope market was divided between henequen fiber and the Manila hemp of the Philippines. "Put ghosts to work for all we care," said the hacendados of the Yucatán. They had much to do.

Henequen is native to Mexico and grows to about the height of a person. Leaves grow out from the short trunk, which is as sturdy as a tree. The thick, fleshy leaves measure between three and six feet in length, with sharp, white tips, and are four to six inches wide in the center. The leaves grow thick on the short trunk. After ten or fifteen years, a stalk about nine feet high emerges and flowers bloom. After the flowers fade, the stalk dries up and dies. A plant produces about thirty leaves a year, and anywhere from two to three hundred leaves in its lifetime. The edges of the leaves are studded with countless hard, pointy spikes, like a cactus. The Koreans said the leaves resembled dragon tongues, and so called the plant "dragon tongue orchid." It is not an orchid but a single-seed leaf plant that belongs to the class Liliopsida. It is similar in appearance to aloe, so many people confuse the two, but their uses are entirely different. A liquor called pulque is fermented from henequen. It is a very useful plant — for its fiber, for making alcohol, and for making dye. It is hardy in dry climates, so it is well suited to the Yucatán. Henequen and sisal hemp became the primary products of the Yucatán in the latter half of the nineteenth century.

The Yucatán Peninsula is roughly the size of South Dakota. To the east, it is separated from Cuba by the Yucatán Channel, which joins the Caribbean Sea and the Gulf of Mexico, and the Gulf Stream flows rapidly northwest. Joining Mexico on the Yucatán Peninsula are Guatemala to the south and Belize to the southeast, and with the exception of Belize, which was under the influence of the British navy and pirates, nearly the entire area had originally been ruled as a colony of Spain. But when the 1,032 Koreans arrived, most of the population of the Yucatán was Mayan. Hundreds of years had passed since the Mayan Empire had fallen, but the native people still used the Mayan language and lived according to the Mayan calendar. The descendants of the empire that had left behind great pyramids, the Mayans fought with the federal government of Mexico and the landowners of the haciendas. Their war for independence reached its zenith in 1847. Tens of thousands of Mayans fled to British-controlled Belize to avoid oppression, and those who were captured before reaching the border were sold as slaves to Cuba and the Dominican Republic. As many as thirty-three additional uprisings broke out between 1858 and 1864, and at one point the main Mayan force captured the central Yucatán city of Mérida. The Yucatán

Mayans, who bought weapons from the English pirates in Belize, attacked white-controlled areas using guerrilla tactics, on occasion winning major victories. Yet they were unorganized, and they each returned to their own cornfields whenever it rained, so they failed to secure a decisive victory. Such were the limitations of the peasantry. In the end, mercenaries from Cuba and one hundred military advisers sent from the United States landed, and a massacre began. Federal forces, supported by the United States, completely suppressed the Mayans in 1901. At the end of the long and arduous war, the Mayan population had been drastically reduced, but the demand for henequen fibers exploded. The hacendados had no choice but to import laborers from abroad. Four years later, the Koreans arrived.

The Yucatán is famous for having no rivers. Most of the peninsula's land is low and flat limestone, so even when rain falls no water gathers. There are few large trees; the land is covered in only short trees and brush. Water must be drawn from deep wells, and for this reason, great wells — underground ponds that go dozens of feet straight into the earth — are occasionally found near ancient Mayan ruins. People climb down ladders, past the limestone strata, to bring the water up. A small minority of the haciendas were fortunate enough to have these wells, called cenotes, nearby, but the rest did not. Cenotes were usually located at least a mile away. And the air was so hot that water either evaporated or was absorbed the moment it hit the ground. The very first thing to torment the Koreans, who came from a land with abundant water and firm earth, was precisely this lack of water. These were people who referred to the space between heaven and earth as "mountains and rivers." They could never have imagined a world without mountains or rivers. The Yucatán had neither.

# 30

IJEONG WAS TAKEN to Chunchucmil hacienda. A unique, flame-shaped white arch adorned the entrance. Once inside, a number of narrow rail tracks branched off and disappeared into the interior, winding into a building that looked like a large storehouse and then emerging and disappearing in the vast fields. The large storehouse Ijeong had seen was the mill where the workers extracted the fiber from the henequen. Mayans dressed in white loaded bundles of henequen into carts, which they continuously pushed into the storehouse. They stared at the newly arrived Koreans with blank faces. Ijeong realized he would soon be doing what they were doing. He watched them closely even as they walked into the hacienda.

From within the mill came the regular click-clack, click-clack of machinery, but he did not know what was happening or how. He only saw people in clean clothes counting the bundles of henequen in the carts at the entrance to the factory and then giving the workers chits. Under a sun that blazed down so fiercely it seemed it would burn their flesh, Ijeong and thirty-five Koreans continued to walk along the tracks and into the hacienda.

The hacienda was not like the plantations of Cuba or Hawaii. Unlike these slave plantations, designed according to the spirit of capitalist mass production, the haciendas of the conquistadors were for the most part feudal. The conquistadors from the mainland of Spain wanted to carry themselves like the aristocrats of their native land. To build beautiful houses and surround them with high walls, reigning like kings over their servants and slaves — these were their goals. Their children studied in Europe, while they, the hacendados, enjoyed living in the pleasant villages near Mérida or Mexico City, dropping in on occasion to play king.

Ijeong's group stopped in front of a great house. A man, perhaps the hacendado himself or just an overseer, appeared wearing a broad-brimmed hat, said something briefly in Spanish, and went back inside. The house was magnificent. The façade, decorated with marble and whitewash, was a vivid example of the wealth that the hacendados had accumulated. Red flowers bloomed in the splendidly decorated windows and verandas, and here and there around the building gilded angels blew trumpets. The group of Koreans began to march again. Every time they moved their feet, clouds of dry dust rose up. Finally they stopped in front of the casas de paja — which the Koreans shortened, incorrectly but conveniently, to "paja" — traditional Mayan housing that brought to mind the straw-thatched houses of Korea. They were huts with palm frond roofs, log frames, and walls plastered with mud and grass. The floor was slightly below the surface of the ground, so it was cool at night, but there were no windows and the huts were very small. The Koreans went inside and found dirt floors. When the first family entered, a squealing piglet leaped out. The Mayans cooked their meals, slept, and even raised livestock inside these huts.

One paja was provided for each family, and one paja was allotted for every four single men. Some had no problem adjusting to the pajas, but this was not the case for everyone. Many men sat outside their houses and gloomily smoked their pipes. Ijeong found a bed in the corner of his paja. It was a net bed, called a "hamaca" by the Mayans. Ijeong successfully strung up his hamaca while his bewildered comrades watched. And after a few tries, he was able to climb into it. His three comrades followed his lead and strung up their beds. Then they introduced themselves and talked about what would become of them.

"Aren't they going to give us something to eat?" one of the men asked. They had just started to get hungry. He stuck his head out the door to see what was happening and spied a Mayan walking around and handing out something to everyone. Corn. Another Mayan brought water. The Koreans built a fire, boiled the water, dropped the corn in, and cooked it. They munched on the steaming kernels until only the cobs were left. As Ijeong chewed his corn, he realized that this was their final destination, that this was where he would spend the next four years until his contract with the Continental Colonization Company ended, in May 1909, without seeing anything like a school or a market or a city. Had he come all the way across that great, fearsome ocean just to arrive here, a place that was even worse than Jemulpo? With a gloomy spirit, Ijeong looked up at the sky and thought of Yeonsu. Will we not see each other for four years? No, surely we will see each other. This is an enlightened land, is it not? There will be days off. And what country does not have holidays? When the time comes, there will be days when the Koreans scattered here and there will gather together.

The four men climbed into their hamacas and tried to sleep. It had been a tiring day, but none of them could fall asleep easily. "It won't be that bad." A pimpled, eighteen-year-old bachelor from Suwon, who pretended to be unconcerned but was twisting about in his unfamiliar bed, tried to comfort them all. "Farming is the same wherever you go." No one answered him. One boy thought of all the foods he had eaten at home. Stew, noodles, kimchi, red pepper paste, cabbage . . . food captivated him more fiercely than any other memory. Another young man thought of the bride he had left at home. Her parents stubbornly refused to send her, saying she was too young. So he asked her to wait four years, and left. Now, no matter how hard he tried, he could not remember anything about the girl except that her cheeks were ruddy. Would they recognize each other when he returned? He was suddenly worried. But he soon fell into a deep sleep, and a still silence covered the Korean workers' paja village.

Before they knew it, it was four o'clock the next morning. The whole hacienda began to stir to a clamor that sounded like someone banging on a pot lid. Some of the Koreans asleep in their hamacas were startled by the sound and floundered about before they flipped over and fell to the ground with a crash. Amid the chaos, the quicker ones had put on their shoes, gone outside, and were looking around. Men on horseback were cracking leather whips in the air and shouting. Over by the pajas where the Mayans lived, workers had already picked up their tools and formed a line.

Shortly thereafter, a man pushing a wheelbarrow tossed some long knives on the ground in front of the Koreans' pajas as he passed by. They were machetes, used to cut the henequen leaves. The women and children stayed in the pajas and the men grabbed the machetes with stern faces. The air was tense. The men's hearts grew warm with the excitement and fear of starting a new job. And as soon as they grabbed the hafts of their knives, they felt as if they were going to war, and the adrenaline began to flow through their bodies. Having done nothing even resembling work for nearly two months, the men felt that they could handle whatever was before them, and their bodies burned with the desire to show these Mexicans, with whom they could not speak, what excellent workers they were.

Before long, a man who looked like an overseer appeared on horseback carrying a torch, and he took command of the people. The Mayans went first and the Koreans followed behind them. The sky was still dark. After they had walked for about ten minutes, a vast field spread out before them, filled with the henequen they had seen on the train, looking like demons' toenails. Torches burned here and there, and the Mayans began to work. The Koreans stood by and watched. The Mayans cut the henequen leaves at their base with their machetes; when they had gathered fifty leaves, they tied them into a bundle and placed it to the side. That was all; it was very similar to harvesting rice. The machetes were like scythes, and the henequen plants were rice stalks. A few of the newcomers wanted to start working so badly they were licking their lips. When the Mayans' short demonstration was over, the Koreans entered the henequen field. Ijeong rushed in vigorously and grabbed a henequen trunk in order to cut the leaves. "Agh!" Sharp thorns stuck in his hand. Blood trickled down and wet the dry earth. It was not only Ijeong. Nearly all of the barehanded Koreans had injured their hands and were in pain. Henequen was no plant to be trifled with. Unlike rice, which had been carefully bred over thousands of years, henequen was practically a wild plant. Now Ijeong gingerly took hold of the trunk with his left hand and brandished the machete with his right. He failed to cut the leaf in one stroke, and so his left hand ended up scraping the thorns. With the next stroke of the machete he cut the leaf, but this time the leaf scraped his leg and left a scratch. It was still early morning and he was already sweating. A man on horseback approached, grinned, and kicked Ijeong in the back. "Hey, chales!" It was Spanish for sluggard, but Ijeong didn't understand him. He knew, though, that the man was telling him that he had to work faster. This was why the Mayans they had seen on the train from Progreso to Mérida had been working so slowly. The sharp and pointy thorns of the henequen made it utterly impossible to work faster.

Their bodies covered with wounds and sweating profusely, the Koreans cut the henequen leaves like the Mayans, and time did not pass quickly. They all spoke much less. At midday, the sunshine was more unbearable than the henequen. Sweat poured down and soaked their filthy clothes and seeped into their wounds, doubling their pain. There was no shade in the field. In that regard, it was far crueler than the sugar cane plantations of Hawaii or the orange orchards of California. At four in the afternoon, the Mayans pushed their carts filled with henequen bundles back to the hacienda. Only then did the Koreans realize how much work they were expected to do: thirty bundles of henequen, at fifty leaves per bundle, which made at least 1,500 leaves they had to cut each day. Yet by four o'clock they had each cut no more than five hundred leaves. The overseers picked up their whips, and cries of "Chales! Chales!" could be heard here and there. The whips flew toward their sweat-drenched backs. Ijeong turned his head. A man on horseback was leering and laughing. The whip flew again. Most of the workers were baptized by the whip that day. To the Koreans, who had no culture of whipping, this was a surprise before it was a disgrace. That is, it took a while for them to realize the shame of it. If the Mexicans had spit in their faces, they might have brandished their machetes on the spot. But none of them knew how to cope with this; whips used on horses and cows were being used on people.

The Koreans continued working until the sun set. That day, they barely managed to cut an average of seven hundred henequen leaves. They could not tie the bundles properly, and there were those who did not know that there should be fifty leaves to a bundle and so tied them up however they wished, so it took even longer to finish. As the Mayans had done, they loaded the bundles into carts and walked back along the rail tracks to the henequen storehouse. They were so hungry that their legs buckled. They had finished working so late that they had missed dinner.

In front of the storehouse sat a man who appeared to be a paymaster. He inspected the bundles, and when he finished, he gave the workers wooden chits according to the number of leaves they had cut. The men took the chits to the hacienda store, where they exchanged them for food. One thing soon became obvious: if they continued to work like this, not only would they not be able to earn money and return to Korea, they would end up starving here. Men without families were a little better off. The family men bought food that wouldn't have been enough to feed just themselves, and returned to their waiting families. Children were on the verge of tears when they saw their fathers with cuts and scrapes all over their bodies. The women boiled kernels of corn and made gruel. The men ate the thin gruel and lay down in their hamacas without a word. They were so very tired, but their wounds ached and they could not sleep. The wounds that the henequen juice had dripped into hurt even more. The men had no choice but to talk to their families. "At this rate, we'll all die. Tomorrow, everyone will have to go out to the fields."

Ijeong filled his stomach with the food he had bought from the store and lay down to sleep. In the beginning, Meyers had said that adults would be given 35 centavos a day, bigger children 25 centavos a day, and smaller children 12 centavos a day. Yet it cost 25 centavos alone to buy food for one person for one day at the store. That meant that most of what they earned went toward food. If someone grew ill and bought on credit at the store, he would be bound to repay the hacienda no matter how long it took. Any fool would soon realize that this was unjust. The uprising of Emiliano Zapata, a hero of the Mexican Revolution, would be sparked by this exploitation in the haciendas. The hacendados were working the peasants as bond slaves and would exploit them forever. If two peasants got married, the hacendado presided over the ceremony and demanded a large sum of money for his services. If a family member grew ill and required treatment, if someone died and a funeral was held, or if a peasant was caught up in a criminal case and needed money, he borrowed it from the hacendado and became further indebted.

There were differences from place to place, but before long the Koreans scattered among the twenty-two haciendas realized the injustice of the system in which they worked. They had been thoroughly deceived by John Meyers and the Continental Colonization Company. The promise that they would be able to work freely, earn lots of money, and go back home wealthy was just candy coating. This was the reality that all the weak people of Mexico faced; the hacienda system had been making serfs of the natives for hundreds of years. The Koreans were stuck here, cut off from communication or traffic, their eyes darting back and forth like frightened mice, desperately trying to think of a way out of a horrible situation.

# 31

YI JONGDO COULD NOT sleep. At Yazche hacienda, where he had been taken, the immigrants were accommodated not in the Mayan pajas but in spare communal housing with tin roofs and walls of thin, hollow, brittle bricks. They were easy to build, but during the day they were as hot as a kettle lid. Beneath the corrugated iron roof, built so low that one could barely stand up straight, Yi Jongdo had shut his mouth tight and agonized over how to escape from the nightmarish reality he had witnessed over the past few days. Farm work was impossible for the soft-skinned Yi Jongdo. His whole life he had done nothing but read books and write. Of course, some of his friends' families had come to ruin and had no choice but to dirty their hands in the earth, but even so, it had not been such uncouth work as this. And then the unique stubbornness of a Korean scholar came to the surface. On the first day, when everyone began cutting the henequen leaves, however awkwardly, he stood there with his mouth shut tight and did no work at all. "Look at the aristocrat! Look at him!" the immigrants whispered among themselves and mocked him, but he stood rigid, not even trying to avoid the blazing sun. The interpreter Gwon Yongjun was also at Yazche hacienda. He approached and asked him, "Why are you not working?" Yi Jongdo kept his lips shut tight and did not reply. Gwon Yongjun had figured out Yi Jongdo on the ship. Even now he insists that he's an aristocrat, so he should be treated like an aristocrat, right? Gwon Yongjun stuck his face right in Yi Jongdo's and asked again, "You don't want to work?" Yi Jongdo still did not reply. Guards on horseback gathered around them. Yi Jongdo stiffly lifted his chin and spoke to Gwon Yongjun. "There must be a governor or magistrate here. Take me to him." Gwon Yongjun grinned at this. "Fine, let's go." In a strange mixture of English and Spanish, Gwon Yongjun conveyed Yi Jongdo's wishes to a guard. The guard nodded and the two of them got into a carriage and headed toward the great house near the hacienda entrance. The manager, who was acting as the hacendado, was sitting in the shade of the house drinking liquor. "What's the matter?" Gwon Yongjun conveyed Yi Jongdo's words in stuttering Spanish: "Big man in Korea, does not want to work, he has something to say." The manager made a reluctant face. Then he mumbled in Spanish, "If he doesn't want to work, why did he come?" Yi Jongdo stepped forward and spoke. "I am a member of the royal family of the Korean Empire and a literati. I have not come to work but to lead the immigrants and be their representative in the emperor's stead. Please convey my words to the emperor of Mexico and let the emperor of Korea know that I am here. I will write you the proper letter. And our current residence is not fit for myself and my family, so please move us."

Gwon Yongjun translated this into English, and then someone translated that into Spanish for the manager. The manager looked mildly amused. He asked Gwon Yongjun, "Is what he says true?"

Gwon Yongjun smiled obsequiously and said, "Who knows? If that's what he says, then that's all I know." The manager looked at Yi Jongdo's shabby clothes and then took something out of a drawer and waved it before Yi Jongdo's eyes. "This is a called a contract. You came here on the condition that you would work for four years." The manager pointed at the name written on the document. "I paid John Meyers for you and your family, therefore no matter what happens in the next four years, you have to harvest henequen. If you break this contract, I will report you directly to the Mexican police. Emperor? There is no emperor in Mexico. It would be best for you to forget about all this, go back, and pick henequen leaves." The manager stroked his mustache and gulped down the tequila that sat in front of him.

Gwon Yongjun translated his words for Yi Jongdo. It was not as if Yi Jongdo had expected any other reply. As he returned to the dusty fields, he had already given up hope. Yet he still could not work in the henequen fields with the others. It was not a matter of pride, but of ability. So he returned to his dwelling. Lady Yun, who had been lying in the hemp bed, Yeonsu, and Jinu jumped to their feet and greeted him. "What happened?" Yi Jongdo shut his mouth tight, sat down on the floor with his legs crossed, and opened his book. That meant he did not want to talk. Gwon Yongjun poked his head in and glanced at the family. Then his eyes met Yeonsu's. The corners of his mouth turned up in a sly smile. Only when Lady Yun, who had fallen ill from fatigue, saw the interpreter did she guess what had taken place. Gwon Yongjun told her what had happened at the hacendado's house. And he added a warning: "If you continue to not work, it will be considered a breach of contract. There are limits to your employer's patience. He may pity the loss of his investment, but he will end up driving you away. Then what will happen to your family, unable to speak a word of Spanish? You'll be food for the vultures, that's what. I'm saying this as a fellow countryman – come to your senses. I don't know why you got on that ship, but this is not Korea, this is Mexico. One wrong move and you could easily starve."

After Gwon Yongjun left, Lady Yun grabbed Yi Jongdo and said coolly, "Shouldn't you try to do something? We've starved for two days already." Yi Jongdo had nothing to say and remained silent. Yi Yeonsu got up from her seat and went outside. All the men had gone off to work, leaving only the women and children. Women with towels wrapped around their heads glared at Yi Yeonsu as she stared blankly at the sky. It had been the same on the ship, with only Yi Jongdo's family being shunned. No one spoke to them. It was already widely known that they didn't work, so everyone was wary that they might come to beg for corn. Furthermore, whenever the men caught a glimpse of Yeonsu's face, at dawn or in the evening, they grew so flushed that they did not know what to do, and this did not go unnoticed by their women.

Yi Jinu, who was often so depressed that he would speak to no one, stood up. "I will go out to work." Lady Yun shushed her son. Then she pleaded with Yi Jongdo once again. "Dear, let's go back to Korea. That would be better." Yi Jongdo thundered, "They said we signed a contract, did they not? How do you propose that we return now? And who do you think will take paupers like us by train and boat so far a distance?" Lady Yun was breathless. It felt as if someone had stuffed her throat with paper. There was no way. Yet the young Jinu was far more realistic than his mother or father. And when he got over his depressions he often became manic, and this was one of those times. He felt that he could do anything, and he wondered why his parents were so worried. Whether they worked or not, they had to stay alive, did they not? That was his thinking. And no matter how hard he thought, he saw no other way to survive. He was also displeased with his father, who didn't know how to do anything and stayed at home like a snail. Yi Jongdo was like his declining nation: he didn't want to work, he was lazy, he was irresponsible. Having led his family to this end, it was only right for him to take responsibility.

The next morning, Yi Jongdo awoke early but did not move. Instead, Jinu boarded the carriage and went out to the fields with the rest. Lady Yun cried as her son left to do manual labor before the sun had even risen. "What on earth kind of place is this?" But Yi Jinu looked cheerful. He bowed his head in greeting to everyone who appeared older than him, and he found a spot at the front, next to Gwon Yongjun.

The only one who did not work in the henequen fields was the interpreter. The Spanish he had learned while on the ship was poor, but it was enough to act as a go-between. Everyone curried favor with Gwon Yongjun. After only a few days, he was being treated like a midlevel overseer. The Spanish hacendado also gave Gwon Yongjun special treatment. His pay was many times more than that of the others, and his house was a fine brick building. It was enough for a decent life, with a proper bed and an attached bathroom.

Yi Jinu wanted to be like Gwon Yongjun. At any rate, each hacienda would need an interpreter. Gwon Yongjun could not go around to all twenty-two haciendas, so if Yi Jinu learned even a little Spanish, he would be able to serve as an interpreter at another hacienda, where he would swagger like Gwon Yongjun and receive much higher pay. Yi Jinu was quickly growing accustomed to life on the hacienda. He followed Gwon Yongjun around, picked up the Spanish that he used, and practiced it diligently.

Of course, the work was not easy. On the first day Yi Jinu bled, and on the second day his sores oozed. After a week, calluses formed on his hands. For days on end he collapsed as soon as he got home, and fell asleep on the spot. As always, Yi Jongdo did not budge, but sat in his place and read *The Analects of Confucius*. Father and son no longer spoke to each other. Yi Yeonsu rubbed a salve they had brought from Korea on her brother's arms and legs. "It's rough, isn't it?" Yi Jinu shook his head. His eyes were dark. "It's not all that bad, it's fun. I'm going to be an interpreter. Then I'll go to another hacienda." "An interpreter?" "Yeah, I'm learning from Mr. Gwon. The first thing you need to learn are the numbers. Uno, dos, tres, cuatro." As he recited, he counted on his fingers. "Does he teach you well?" Yi Yeonsu patted her brother's shoulders. "The sages said there is no shame in learning." Yi Yeonsu had her doubts about her brother's studying. The interpreter's authority came from owning language, so why would he want to teach others?

When Saturday came, Yi Jinu took his wooden chits to the pay-master and received his pay. Then he went to the store and bought food for the week. It was nowhere near enough for a family of four. The days stretched on when they thought they would starve. Despite this, Yi Jongdo did not budge. Yet he still ate first, and he still ate the most. As if it were somehow his noble duty, at each meal he sat in the best spot, albeit on a dirt floor, and was the first to lift his spoon. He said not a single word of encouragement to his son, nor a single word of apology to his wife and daughter. He was a descendant of the royal line, where it was common for an entire family to be slaughtered because the patriarch fell out of favor. It might have been better for him had he been sentenced to death and forced to drink poison. No exile was as cruel as this. Even if the head of the family was banished to a lonely island in a distant sea, his family could wait for the king's pardon with their relatives and servants in their hometown. But here it was impossible for a literati to maintain the least shred of dignity. Yi Jongdo's tragedy lay in the fact that all these things were his own fault, as he had been needlessly pessimistic about the situation in Korea, and that there was no one with whom he could share the blame. He had thought that at least he would be able to use his writing to communicate, as he had in Beijing, where men like himself could make their thoughts known through the great Chinese characters, even if they could not understand each other's speech. He felt his error to the very marrow of his bones, yet he had to maintain his authority as the father. Not authority, but duty. He could not teach his children servility. This was the failing of the literati. If the head of the family bowed his head and admitted his error, who would forgive his family members when they were in error? Yi Jongdo slowly drank the thin corn gruel and spoke to his son.

"There is no shame in pulling a plow to cultivate a field. But why must you cling to this interpreter official and learn the speech of the barbarians?" His tone was stern. Yi Jinu looked into the eyes of his mother and sister, as if asking for their support, and then he answered his father. He had not yet passed puberty, and his voice trembled. "Then what would you have me do, Father?" He showed his father the scratches and welts on his hands and arms. "Look. After only three days, this is what the hands and feet of all our people look like. It is not because they are dull-witted, but because there is no other way. We must learn. Only by learning the ways of the barbarian can we survive."

They all thought that Yi Jongdo would fly into a thunderous rage. But, rather unexpectedly, that rage simmered down. As boiling foam subsides when the lid is lifted off a pot, so did every part of Yi Jongdo's being — his eyelids, his shoulders, his wrinkled cheeks, his waist — seem to suddenly succumb to the force of gravity and sink toward the earth. He closed his eyes. He turned his back. Then he called his son: "Jinu." This descendant of an ill-favored dynasty pricked up his ears at his father's voice. "You may be right. I don't know anymore. I just don't know." His family was speechless. His son and daughter, who had never learned how to comfort their father, went outside and sat down against the wall. And they said nothing. Yi Jinu felt burdened by his father's collapse. Was he going to leave everything to him? Here? At fourteen years old, his pay was less than that of an adult, and it was absurd to entrust the family to him.

"Jinu," his sister said, "don't worry. Surely we won't go on living like this. There will be a way." Seeing the profile of her younger brother, about to slip into depression again, Yeonsu thought of Ijeong. He would be bearing it with all his strength, like her younger brother. Cutting, binding, and loading the henequen leaves, with cuts on his hands and feet, and then collapsing at night and falling asleep. Is he thinking of me? Her body shook, longing for the warmth of his hand that had touched her breast. Jinu patted her shoulder as she sat there trembling, her eyes closed. "I must learn the language of this land and put food on the table," he said. "And it's not really that bad. It was much worse while we were on the ship. It felt like I was completely worthless; I was afraid of what lay ahead. I did not go up on deck because I was afraid I would throw myself into the ocean. But this is much better. I feel like I can handle anything."

The two of them went back inside the house and fell asleep with their mother between them. At this hacienda, they were not even supplied with hamacas. Yet their sleep was sweet. Their bodies, steeped in exhaustion, took no notice of the humid air or the vicious mosquitoes. At four in the morning, the noisy bell rang, starting the sound of men whispering as they rose and went outside. And the sound of women, too. Some women were now going out to the henequen fields with the men. Once they learned that women could earn money too, there was no reason for them to stay at home. Even the more traditional men had no choice. If the women didn't work, there was no way they could earn enough money to escape the hacienda. The Koreans, who were not yet used to the work, couldn't do half as much as the Mayans, though they worked from four in the morning to seven in the evening. Thus they received less than half of what they had been promised. The women wrapped their small children in blankets, tied them to their backs, and went to work. They spread out blankets between the rows of henequen plants and laid their children in the shade beneath them. The children cried from heat rashes and the ants, but they grew tired of even that, and fell asleep.

When the women returned from the fields, they had to cook food, look after the children, and mend the tattered clothes and shoes. The men made leggings so that their shins would not be scraped by the thorns, and gloves so that their hands would not be pricked. Now that they had some tools to help them, their work efficiency improved significantly.

Yi Jinu grew closer to Gwon Yongjun, who was pleased that the son of an aristocratic family was trying to get on his good side. He taught Jinu a few words of Spanish, as if he were doing him a kindness. As the sweat poured off his body, Jinu moved his lips and memorized the words he was taught. Every time the hacienda overseers exchanged greetings, like Buenos días, Buenos noches, and Hasta luego, he pricked up his ears and memorized them.

One day, Gwon Yongjun brought Jinu home with him after he had finished working. He poured a glass of tequila and offered it to him. Jinu took the glass and gulped down the strong drink. Gwon Yongjun taught him a few more words of Spanish. When he grew drunk he spoke in English, too. Yi Jinu looked at him with rapture in his eyes. He wanted most to become not some senior minister, but someone like this interpreter. He was not unaware of Gwon Yongjun's obstinate and harsh nature. He also knew of his vice of looking down on others and using them meanly with his modicum of authority. But that was how strongly Jinu wanted to become like him. Gwon Yongjun read in Jinu's eyes that uneasy fascination unique to young men. They were easily charmed by men older than them. They were completely taken in by power, freedom, and bluster, unable to keep their senses and then readily, willingly submitting. Gwon Yongjun drank the liquor left in his glass.

"Do you know why I came to this tiny Mexican village?" Jinu looked at him with curiosity. Gwon Yongjun wove the splendid tale of his father's and brothers' deaths and of his life of debauchery at the gisaeng house. The sadness of losing one's family and the memories of a magnificent fall moved the young man even more. Jinu was shaken by the fact that the world was far crueler than he had known. He looked with awe at Gwon Yongjun, who spoke of these things as if they were nothing. Maybe it was the burning tequila on an empty stomach. Gwon Yongjun mixed in some lies and made his comeback even more magnificent. He spoke dreamily of the past, then looked at Jinu with a forlorn face. The young Jinu was captivated by the loneliness, the glorious fall of a man who had experienced everything. It was at that moment that Gwon Yongjun revealed the desire he had kept hidden deep in his heart.

"There is not a gisaeng in the eight provinces of Korea whom I have not held in my arms, but I have never seen a woman like your sister." He glanced casually at Jinu. The young boy's face grew slightly darker, but he did not show open displeasure. Rather, he seemed pleased that Gwon Yongjun had put his trust in him. "Arrange a meeting for me with her." He reached into his pocket and took out a 5-peso bill. With that money, the family would not have to eat the thin corn gruel they had grown so tired of the past few days. They could buy cabbage and mix it with chili peppers to make something like kimchi. It would take Jinu twenty days to earn that much. This was the boy's first experience of the power of money. Gwon Yongjun had not mentioned a specific price, but his intention was clear. Ah, no, this is wrong. Jinu closed his eyes. No, she might understand. Could she not make that sacrifice for her family? I pick henequen leaves from early morning to night, pricked by the thorns, for my inept father and my family, so my sister should be able to just stop by this man's home in the middle of the night. He hasn't actually said he would do anything to her. And maybe it wouldn't even be a sacrifice. Though he knew it was wrong, Jinu did not stop thinking: All for 5 pesos. Did not the women of Korea cut flesh from their own thighs to feed to their sick fathers, and did they not cut and sell their own hair to send their children off to study? Wouldn't this be easier than that? Ah, no. It would not even be human. To sell my own sister. Not even a beast would do that. And if she should tell Father or Mother, I would not escape death. But would she tell them? Knowing that I would die at Father's hand, would she really tell them? She would just scold me fiercely, and it would end at that.

Gwon Yongjun saw the struggle in Jinu's heart as clearly as he saw the back of his own hand, and he took another 5-peso bill out of his pocket and laid it on top of the first. The fourteen-year-old boy swigged the last of his tequila. Then he took the 10 pesos and put them in his pocket. Thus a new contract was formed. He staggered out of Gwon Yongjun's house and ran to the hacienda store, where he bought cabbage, a little beef, tortillas, and chili pepper flakes, and then trudged home. He stopped a few steps before reaching the house and reflected on what he had done. The milk was already spilled. He went into the house and showed his family what he had bought. They had gone hungry while waiting for him, and their faces brightened. Even Yi Jongdo cheered. Yeonsu crouched down, built a fire, and put a pot of water on to boil. Things that he had never noticed before jumped out at him. Her hips certainly were large. As she fanned the flames, he caught glimpses of her breasts through the armhole of her blouse. He closed his eyes and let out a sigh, and his mother tapped him on the back. He turned around in surprise. "You've been drinking." Lady Yun narrowed her eyes. "Mother, I have committed an even greater sin. But I had no choice. If Sister makes a sacrifice, we can all live easily. You would have done the same thing." He left the house and looked up at the sky. A spotless full moon looked down on him, clear and bright.

## 32

IN 1883, THE 5,800-ton cruiser *Dmitri Donskoi* was built in the shipyards of St. Petersburg, Russia. It was named for the legendary king who had attacked the Tatars and liberated Russia from Mongolian rule. Befitting its name, this cruiser was the mightiest war vessel of its time and ruled the Baltic Sea. Some twenty years later, on May 27, 1905, as part of the Baltic fleet, it could not withstand concentrated fire from the Japanese navy in the East Sea and fled toward Ulleung Island. On May 29, Captain Lebedev ordered the crew into lifeboats and landed on Ulleung, and then decided to scuttle the ship. The first mate took the captain's place and, along with the young officers, stayed on the *Donskoi* and shared its fate. The 350 crew members were taken prisoner on Ulleung Island, but they were treated with respect by the Japanese navy, which admired their heroic actions.

But it was the end of the Baltic fleet.

# 33

ON THE SAME DAY, with no idea what had happened in the sea
near his homeland on the other side of the earth, a fisherman from
Ulleung Island was struggling with a life-and-death decision. "The
guards will come with their guns – do you really think we'll be OK
with our bare fists?" This old bachelor, Choe Chuntaek, his face
creased with wrinkles, rubbed his hands together and watched for
the retired soldiers' reactions. His skin was dark and rough from the
sea winds, and his thick hands were strong and hard. He was only
thirty-three years old, but he looked fifty.

The former soldiers were laying out a concrete strategy. They
would make their way around the houses at night, to convey to
the others what had been decided upon, and the next morning at
four, when it came time to wake up, the men would gather at Jo
Jangyun's paja. The women and children would stay indoors, just
in case. When the armed guards approached, the men would face
them with rocks and machetes. Deserters would be dealt with severely.

The night before the strike, the men could not sleep. Choe
Chuntaek met with the Pohang fishermen and talked about the
next day's revolt. "We have no choice. At this rate, we'll all die. A
month has passed, so we have grown somewhat accustomed to the
work, but at no more than 35 centavos a day, when will we be able
to escape those nightmarish jute fields?" At some point they had begun to call henequen jute. There were those who called it aenik-
kaeng. The workers at each hacienda called it something different.

The fishermen were ready for a fight. There were more than one
hundred Koreans at Chenché hacienda, where they had been sent.

Of the twenty-two haciendas, this one had the most immigrants. For this reason, the hacendado had been able to choose the healthiest men, but this was a double-edged sword. The hacendado did not know that a significant number of them had been soldiers, and so could organize and take up arms at any time. Furthermore, he had spent a large sum of money in his desire to secure as many laborers as he could, and had no cash in hand. Knowing his master's situation, the overseer solved the problem in the same way they always had. He raised the price of food at the hacienda store and cut the wages that had been promised. The Koreans had at first been unaware of this and were obedient, but after about ten days they began to grow enraged at the overseer's unjust actions. "Does he want us to work on empty stomachs? At this rate, we'll become ghosts of the Yucatán."

The soldiers followed their training and first scouted out the hacienda's forces. There were five guards who carried guns and rode horses. Beneath the hacendado was an overseer who carried a gun, and there were a few other men at the store and the factory, but they were unarmed and would only look on or flee if there was a conflict. Ultimately, the problem was the hacendado and the six armed men. At these odds, it was a risk worth taking. As long as the police or army did not come. The men of Chenché hacienda resolved to strike.

The next day the clamorous bell rang, but the men did not climb into the carriage going out to the fields. Instead, they met at Jo Jangyun's house and raised their morale, banging on pot lids like gongs. At first the women stayed in their pajas, but one by one they joined the men and shouted with them. It was a sight that would have been unthinkable in Korea, but in the Yucatán it seemed only natural. Before they knew it, the Confucian distinction between men and women had disappeared. Someone shouted, "Let's go to the hacendado's place!" Their morale high, they all ran toward the landowner's house. The clamor gradually grew louder. An armed guard with a rifle rode in and loitered nearby, and a fisherman got ready to throw a rock at him. The Korean soldiers restrained him. The armed guard turned his horse around and fled the area. When they arrived at the hacendado's house, the immigrants dropped to the ground and started shouting. None of them knew Spanish, so they were unable to properly convey their demands. The hacendado, Don Carlos Menem, showed himself on the second-story balcony, wearing a dazzling white shirt. He looked down on the Koreans with indifference and called his paymaster. "Where is their interpreter?" "I think he is at Yazche hacienda." The hacendado scrawled something on a piece of paper. "Send a telegram and have him sent here."

The sun had already risen halfway in the sky. May in the Yucatán was the hottest, driest, and cruelest month. Yet the strikers sat in their places and endured the waiting. When Gwon Yongjun arrived, their faces brightened. Finally someone who could speak for them. The interpreter got down from the carriage looking tired, and he listened to what Jo Jangyun and Kim Seokcheol had to say. Their demands were simple: Lower the cost of food. Don't whip us; we are not cows or horses. And supply us with corn. All sorts of demands came pouring out, but ultimately they were narrowed down to two: Treat us like human beings. And the hacendado should bear the burden for such staples as corn and tortillas. As they listed this demand and that, Gwon Yongjun's mind was elsewhere. Jo Jangyun and Kim Seokcheol, these men are the problem. They will without a doubt cause a problem again. Now he took the hacendado's side and asked a question that he then answered. "Do you know what the problem with Koreans is? They are lazy and unskilled, yet all they do is complain. Look." He looked around Chenché hacienda.

"The surroundings here are much better than at the other haciendas, aren't they? The walls are brick and the roads are clean and orderly. So what is the problem?" The ignorant fools, trusting in their own strength and running riot. He was ashamed that he belonged to the same race as them. They were all dressed in filthy clothes and their heads swarmed with lice. There were even a few fellows who hadn't cut off their topknots.

Gwon Yongjun went with their representatives to meet the hacendado. Don Carlos Menem came out to the entrance of his house to greet Gwon Yongjun, Jo Jangyun, and the others. Then he brought them into his home. As soon as they were inside the front door, they were greeted by a garden filled with all sorts of trees and flowers. A small rainbow glistened in the streams of water that gushed out of a fountain. Though they had merely passed through a single gate, the sunlight felt completely different. Outside, it seemed as if it would burn the flesh off of a man, but the light that fell on the fountain and trees was warm and gave a feeling of opulence. Although it had not been his original intention, inviting the representatives of the strikers into his home was a very successful move. Jo Jangyun and the others, who had never before set foot in a Spanish-style building, were overwhelmed by the grandeur of the place. Built in the Latin American architectural style, the building was surrounded by a high wall that prevented anyone on the outside from looking in. Within the wall, colonnades and rooms faced each other across a pleasant square garden. Continuing past the colonnades, one came to an arch, and through that was a separate building. Thus the houses of Latin America were far bigger on the inside than they appeared to be from the outside.

Menem sat down in a mahogany chair in a colonnade and put a Cuban Monte Cristo cigar into his mouth. "Well, what are their demands?" Gwon Yongjun conveyed their demands. Menem lit the cigar, took one puff, and spouted the smoke into the air. The smoke dispersed in an instant. "Is that all?" He began to scribble something on a piece of paper, as if he had forgotten about those before him. It was a scrawl that could not even be called letters. After some time he folded the piece of paper and stood up. "I spent a lot of money to bring you here," he said, "but I do not want to be called a stingy master." The overseer who stood next to Menem whispered something in his ear. Menem grimaced and shook his head. "There is no need for that. We will give you corn and tortillas for free. In return, those who refuse to work, and those who break their contract and flee, causing me loss, will be punished. What do you say?"

Jo Jangyun and his comrades listened to Gwon Yongjun and could not believe their ears. Just getting the corn for free would make life a lot easier. If that was the case, there was no real need to lower the prices of other goods. Menem opened the door of a bird-cage and poured water into a small Chinese porcelain dish. The parrot inside clucked in greeting to its owner. Jo Jangyun agreed. He promised that they would go immediately to the fields. When they had gone, Menem called the overseer and instructed him to distribute food once a week. The overseer quietly protested that he was being far too charitable. Menem relit his cigar, which had gone out. "We must increase output. And teaching them a lesson once will be enough. After all, we have to live together for the next four years."

Menem's father had been a vagabond from the Basque country. He spent his youth wandering around, taking up with a number of women along the way, and he became an officer in the French army under the rule of Napoleon III.

Napoleon III strove to re-create the glory of his uncle, Napoleon Bonaparte, and he particularly wanted to achieve something great in military terms. As a result, the army of Napoleon III never had a moment's rest. The same went for Menem's father, George. Napoleon III, being the meddler he was, became involved in the various problems in the New World. When the American Civil War broke out, he supported the South and stood against Lincoln and the North. The feudal nature of the South's cotton plantations were more suited to his temperament.

In Mexico, Benito Juárez had become the minister of justice and devoted himself to confiscating the idle lands owned by the Catholic Church and establishing a new civil law, a law that would apply equally to all citizens. The Church, landowners, and aristocracy banded together. Civil war erupted. After three years, when their defeat became certain, the conservatives requested the aid of Napoleon III. Flush with his recent conquest of Indochina, and hearing his Spanish wife, Eugénie, urge him to build a Latin American empire every time she opened her mouth, he was elated when the conservatives of Mexico came to him. He named Archduke Maximilian as his representative; the Mexican aristocrats begged Maximilian to become emperor of Mexico, and so he traveled across the Atlantic with the army of Napoleon III and landed at the port of Veracruz. Menem's father, George, sailed with them.

As soon as he arrived in the Mexican capital, Maximilian forgot who had invited him. To be precise, he realized that the conservatives were not very popular with the citizenry. He unexpectedly declared his support for Juárez's liberalist policies. The wrath of the betrayed conservatives rent the heavens. And yet Juárez had no love for him either.

These were trying times for Menem's father George as well. The Mexican peasant fighters seemed to lurk everywhere. They would appear suddenly, attack the French troops, and vanish again like ghosts. The massive cannons that the French had brought from west of the Alps were of no use in such guerrilla warfare. George's only goal was to stay alive, though he began to realize that this new nation of Mexico was a fine place for white people such as himself. Mexico welcomed Latino immigrants, so if he settled down, he could build a house like a fortress on a vast hacienda, work the Indio slaves, and live like a king. If he returned to France, he would have no other choice but to live out his life as a career soldier. Furthermore, Napoleon III was nearing the end of his fortune. Having at last grown weary of the antiwar sentiment in France, he decided to withdraw his troops. The final days of his puppet Maximilian were approaching.

Standing before his troops as they wearily retreated to the port of Veracruz, George delivered a speech: "We may retreat now, but this is because of the powerlessness of Maximilian and the Mexican aristocracy. Emperor Napoleon will not forget the New World. The day will surely come when the Tricolore will fly from Quebec to Panama. Soldiers, we are not defeated. Let us return with our heads held high."

When he finished his speech the troops erupted in thunderous applause. Some of them were so excited that they began to sing *La Marseillaise*. That night, George calmly packed the gold ingots that had been kept in the regimental headquarters and quietly left. The money had been offered to France as war funds by the privileged classes of Mexico, so he felt no guilt about taking it. He made the sign of the cross and prayed a short prayer: "Lord, gold is too precious a metal to be used for killing people." Do not the thieves of Mexico give thanks to the Blessed Mother every time they take their cut? He took off his uniform, buried it, and disguised himself as a Mexican. Wearing a poncho and a broad-brimmed sombrero, he returned to Mexico City, where he took a train to the Yucatán. He changed his name to Don Carlos Giorgio. With his Spanish name he bought a house in Mérida and then married a mestizo woman who was one-sixteenth Spanish, and she bore him a son. This son was Menem.

Giorgio first tried his hand at raising chicle before branching out into henequen also. The main ingredient of gum, chicle was a specialty of the Yucatán. He spent all of his days among his chicle trees, and one day before his sixtieth birthday, he was struck by a poison arrow shot by a disgruntled Mayan perched in a chicle tree, and died. As his mouth succumbed to paralysis, he called out to his son and made two dying wishes. First, Menem was not to give up the henequen hacienda, and second, he was to bury Giorgio in Nice, next to his first wife. The first request was relatively easy. He couldn't have sold the hacienda even if he wanted to. But the request to bury his father in Nice was troublesome. What will become of the hacienda while I go all the way to Nice to dig a hole in the ground? Menem simply ignored the second request.

Instead of searching for Giorgio's murderer, Menem drove off almost all of the Mayan Indios. In their place he hired the Koreans, who had just arrived in Mérida. The contract was for four years, and they came at a much cheaper price than the Indios. They also had no ill will toward him, so he wouldn't have to worry about uprisings or revolts. Yet now that he had met them himself, he found that they had fierce eyes and were rebellious, contrary to what he had heard. They were also much larger than the Mayans. So Menem determined to compromise. Providing them with corn and tortillas would not hurt him badly. And he had absolutely no desire to be struck dead by a poison arrow shot by a serf. The golden age of haciendas was over. He was more interested in the world of politics. Juárez's successor, Porfirio Díaz, who had shot Emperor Maximilian to death and ascended to power, was an ignorant and uncouth man. This former guerrilla had transformed himself into a pro-American dictator who supported the elite and the landowning class. It was Díaz who turned all the farmlands into haciendas, stealing property from the petty farmers and giving it to the great landowners. As a result, a single hacienda owned by the famed Teresa family in the state of Chihuahua was larger than Belgium and the Netherlands put together, and it took a full day by train to cross it. Ninety-nine percent of Mexico's farmland became haciendas, and ninety-eight percent of the peasants were robbed of their lands. Of course, Menem had no complaint with the hacienda system itself. He was simply displeased that President Díaz and a few families controlled everything. How could they not hold democratic elections? If Díaz held elections, as he had publicly pledged that he would, Menem had a mind to try his luck and run for governor of the Yucatán. Who knew how far he could go from that springboard, but at the very least he did not went to spend his entire life in this dusty wasteland.

# 34

TWO MONTHS PASSED. It was now July. The Koreans had changed greatly in appearance. Now almost none stuck themselves on the thorns of the henequen and bled. The women made leggings and gloves from pieces of cloth and sticks. The speed at which they worked also gradually increased, and after only two months they had caught up with the Mayans. They cut the henequen in silence. Laughter had disappeared. The women and children went out to the fields and worked twelve hours a day. There were suicides at a few of the haciendas. No one was surprised to see that someone had hanged himself from the crossbeam in a bathroom. The henequen juice got into their wounds and their flesh rotted from a skin disease; they caught malaria and hovered on the brink of death. No one batted an eye. Doctors were stationed at the plantations of Hawaii, if only as a formality, but at the haciendas there was not a single decent drugstore, let alone a doctor. In the Koreans' minds, there was only one way to survive: to work like ants — even three-year-old children — save money like misers, and return to Korea when their contracts ended.

The Mayans occasionally gazed vacantly at the Koreans. They had no place to save money and return to. This was their home. One day, strange people barged in, drew lines in their land, and began to call those places haciendas. Then these people told the Mayans to come work for them if they wanted to make a living. The overseers lashed out ceaselessly with their whips at these people who could not find any reason to work.

When the day's work ended, the men drank. Even though they had worked just as hard as the men, the women could not rest after going home. They lit the fires and cooked the food. They mended clothing, cleaned the house, and prepared the tools they would take with them the next day. "What I wouldn't give to do laundry just once in a cold stream," said a woman from Chungcheong province as she looked to the west, and the other women cried. Laundry was just as much of a luxury as bathing. The well was far away and water was scarce. They had no choice but to wait for the rainy season to begin.

Occasionally the hacendado would slaughter a cow or a pig, and the women would race to the spot and quarrel with each other over the still warm intestines or tail. The Mexicans of the hacienda snickered and called these women pek — bitches. With blood on their hands, the women returned with their spoils and boiled soup, and the children were so intoxicated by the smell of meat they would not leave the kettle's side. Even on days above 90 degrees, the women could not take off their skirts or short jackets; their shirtless husbands drank and beat them. Some men had started gambling. Gambling and liquor were deep-rooted vices for Korean men and were not easily remedied. Bickering and crying, shrieking and yelling continued all night long. The Yucatán was hell for the men, but it was far worse for the women.

At Ijeong's hacienda a Korean man from Pyeongan province violated a Mayan woman, and in retaliation his throat was slit. The police did not come. Directly after this, a Mayan man was stabbed to death with a machete. The hacendado seized the two Koreans whom the Mayans pointed out as the culprits, stripped off their shirts, threw them on a pile of henequen, and whipped them. The thorns on the henequen stems were more painful than the whip, and the two murderers writhed like worms on a pile of salt. When the whipping was over they were imprisoned in the hacienda's jail. The henequen thorns lodged in their chests stung with every breath they took. They wanted to pull out the thorns, but no light came in, so it was not easy. Their wounds festered and vilely reeked. Only when ten days had passed did the door open and light shine in. Now that the jail was bright with dazzling tropical sunlight, they cleaned up their feces. The piles of dung were completely dry and crumbled like cookies to the touch. Worms wriggled and fell out of them.

The two murderers returned to their paja and lingered in illness. Ijeong, who shared the paja, gave them food and water, with kimchi made from chili peppers and Western cabbage on the side. It was a delectable feast, but neither of them could eat much. They wobbled with every step, as if they had lost their sense of direction and time during their dark imprisonment; one of them passed away after only three days. As soon as the one died, the other rose as if it had all been a dream. It was almost as if the two of them had made a bet and agreed that the loser would give his remaining life force to the winner and take his leave. As the survivor stuffed his swollen face with corn gruel, he said to Ijeong, "Somehow I feel as if I will meet my end here. It's just too hot."

Ijeong shut his mouth tight and said nothing. In the space of only a few days, two of the four men who had slept under his roof had died. Ijeong wondered if maybe he was alive merely because he was lucky. When the man from Pyeongan went to attack the Mayan woman, Ijeong had been next door playing chess with pieces carved from stone. When the man's body was discovered, Ijeong had just gone to the cenote to draw water. The two enraged men did not look for Ijeong but went straight to where the Mayans lived, doggedly pursued a man who fled, and stabbed him to death. While the Mayan's blood seeped into the ground, the two men stood in a daze and stared at each other. Only then did they realize the gravity of what they had done, and they raced back madly on weakened legs, were arrested by the hacienda guards, stripped of their clothes, and beaten on the pile of henequen.

The one who had survived was called Dolseok; he was the son of a government slave. After the Reform of 1894, this slave had risen in status to become a commoner and sent his son to Seoul to make him a soldier. Dolseok did not follow his father's will, but boarded the *Ilford* at Jemulpo. He did not know how to write, so he had left without sending his father a letter. And within two months he had killed a man. "What on earth happened?" he said, shaking violently. It felt as if the Mayan men were going to rush in and take his head. Ijeong told him not to worry and tried to calm him down, but it was no use. The next day, Ijeong went to the overseer and pointed to the money in his pocket, then at himself, and then at Dolseok. Then he pointed at the Mayan village and made a slicing motion with his hand across his neck. He could not speak the language, but his meaning was understood. The Mexican overseer decided to sell them, a source of trouble, to another hacienda. Dolseok's involvement in the murder would reduce their price, so it naturally remained a secret. They were bound hand and foot to a column on a carriage. The weather was unusually cool. From afar, Ijeong saw black storm clouds moving in. Finally it would rain. He stared at the sky to the east and fell into a deep sleep.

# 35

HO HUI, a Chinese living in Mérida, met a group of Korean immigrants not far from the city's downtown. He wrote an article about how shocked he was upon seeing them and sent it to the *Wenhsing Daily*, a Chinese newspaper published in San Francisco:

> Once, they deceived and bought people in China, but then rumors spread and there were no more applicants, so now they are purchasing slaves in Korea . . . They are all dressed in tattered clothing and wear straw sandals that are falling apart. During a heavy rain that lasted for days, the Koreans were scattered to various henequen farms. When they work, the women hold their children in their arms and carry them on their backs as they wander through the streets. The sight of them was so like cattle and beasts and I could not witness it without tears . . . If they do not work properly on the farms they are brought to their knees and beaten, their flesh torn from their bodies and blood spattered everywhere. I could not contain my lamentation at this hideous sight.

Two Korean exchange students living in the United States, Jo Yeongsun and Sin Jeonghwan, read the article and hurriedly sent a letter to the Young Men's Christian Association in Seoul. Jeong Seongyu, a young evangelist at the YMCA, reorganized this information and sent it on to the *Capital Gazette*, and on July 29, 1905, the article was published, with the title "Our People Have Become Slaves, So How Shall We Rescue Them?" In this roundabout way, the truth about the bond slaves in the Yucatán was made known to the Korean Empire.

Two days later the *Capital Gazette* urged that measures be taken, saying, "We cannot bear hearing about the plight of the emigrants to Mexico." Emperor Gojong issued an imperial mandate the very next day, August 1. "Why did the government not prevent this when the companies were soliciting emigrants in the very beginning? We must devise a way to swiftly bring these thousand or so people home." It was an extremely direct and forceful declaration for the emperor of a Confucian nation known for skirting all subjects. The one who had become their lord was shaking with shame. After this, the *Korea Daily News* attacked the government's emigration policy. Public opinion around the nation condemning the impotent government had reached a boiling point. But Mexico was too far away, and the two countries had no diplomatic relations. Yet Yi Hayeong, the Korean foreign minister, sent a telegram to the Mexican government: "Although we have never established friendly relations with your honored nation, we request that you protect our citizens until we dispatch an official."

The Mexican government sent this reply: "Stories of people being treated like slaves have been falsely reported. The Asian workers are in the Yucatán, but they are being treated very well, and an article on this was published in the *Beijing Times*, so please refer to this."

# 36

ON AUGUST 12, 1905, the Korean vice minister of foreign affairs, Yun Chiho, was drinking coffee in Tokyo's Imperial Hotel. A meeting had been arranged by the pro-Japanese Durham Stevens, an American who worked as an adviser for the Korean Empire. Stevens began with a word of condolence. "I am sorry I could not visit you during your time of sorrow." Yun Chiho observed etiquette and bowed his head. "There is no need for such a busy man to concern himself with every such matter, is there?" Yun Chiho had lost his Chinese wife, Ma Aifang, that February.

Stevens introduced the two Americans sitting next to him. One had a white face, and the other's face was tanned dark by the sun. The white one was Heywood and the dark one was Swinsy, a representative of the Hawaii Sugar Planters' Association. Swinsy had an affable personality and appeared to know much about Yun Chiho. "The Hawaiian plantation owners are very displeased with the measures the Korean Empire has taken. The owners say that Koreans are more than welcome there, as they work far harder than either the Japanese or the Chinese, and are well behaved, but if they are suddenly forbidden from going, where are the owners to find such a labor force?"

Yun Chiho replied, "Is that so?" Swinsy pulled his chair forward and asked, "Is there any possibility that this measure may be rescinded?" Yun Chiho pushed his glasses up. "Well, both government and public opinion on emigration is quite negative, so it will not be easy."

At this, the diplomatic adviser Stevens interrupted. "Why don't you visit Hawaii? If you go and see for yourself how the peasants are working, give them some encouragement, and put in a good word with His Majesty when you return, it will greatly help to foster friendly relations between Korea and the United States as well. The Hawaii Sugar Planters' Association has said they will cover your expenses." Swinsy nodded at this, suggesting that they had already agreed.

Yun Chiho was the ideal person for this job. He was a Christian who had studied in the United States, at Vanderbilt and Emory universities, and had an excellent command of three foreign languages: he spoke fluent English, was skilled in Chinese, and had learned Japanese when he had fled to Japan during the Coup of 1884. But he raised his hand and refused the offer to pay his expenses. "I cannot very well accept money privately while working for my country."

Yun Chiho had never been fond of Stevens, who worked for the Japanese yet received a salary from the Korean government. The empire's foreign ministry, which had no choice but to hire him, was in a pitiful situation. Stevens shook hands with Yun Chiho and rose from his seat. "Anyway, please think it over. After all, this is one of those things an official of the foreign ministry must do."

# 37

IJEONG WOKE UP from a light sleep as raindrops spattered on the bridge of his nose. It was a welcome rain on the dry land of the Yucatán. The horses whinnied, glad for the water that fell on their hot bodies. The scent of dust rose from the ground. The horizon to the west was still bright. Ijeong could just see the steeple of the Mérida cathedral in the distance.

Dolseok poked Ijeong. Someone was walking toward them from far off, and his face looked like a Korean's. The man must have thought it odd to see these two men tied up to a cart, for he stared piercingly at Ijeong and Dolseok as he approached. He wore a Western suit and carried a bundle on his back. When he finally reached them, he spoke first. "Are you Koreans?" He spoke Korean, but this was the first time they had ever seen him. The cart had stopped in the shade, as if the driver intended to rest.

"I heard that Koreans had arrived in Mérida, and I was on my way to find them." He gladly took their hands. "My name is Bak Manseok. I sell ginseng in San Francisco, but I also travel to wherever there are Chinese to sell it. How have you come to this?" Bak Manseok looked at their hands and feet, bound to the pillar, and clucked his tongue. Dolseok said, "We've been in Mexico for two months, but there was a problem at our hacienda, so we are being sold to another hacienda." Bak Manseok listened as Dolseok told him everything that had happened to them. Bak Manseok asked detailed questions, like how much they earned a day and how much of that they spent on food. Dolseok told him how one person had slept in a cave and been bitten by a poisonous snake, how the hacendado wielded his whip and yelled like he was driving cattle whenever he came out to the henequen fields . . .

Bak Manseok told them the situation at the other haciendas, having heard the news from the Chinese in Mérida. One hacienda had a Korean interpreter, but in an attempt to curry favor with the hacendado, he cursed the workers and whipped them; they said he was even crueler than the Mexican foremen. Ijeong and Dolseok could guess who that was. "He wasn't that bad on the ship," they said, and clucked their tongues. They were dressed in thin summer clothes and barefoot. Bak Manseok sympathized with their plight and took from his pocket two 1-peso bills and gave one each to Ijeong and Dolseok. "I will see that this news reaches Korea immediately. Hold on just a little longer."

Bak Manseok did actually report everything he saw in letters he wrote on November 17, 1905, to the *Mutual Assistance News* and to the *Korea Daily News*. The letters arrived in Korea in December and were printed in the newspapers. As luck would have it, the day that he wrote the letters was the day the Japan-Korea Protectorate Treaty was signed.

# 38

THE THIEF CHOE SEONGIL skillfully cut up a watermelon with his knife and handed pieces to Father Paul and the shaman. Weary of the heat, they gobbled down the watermelon's red flesh without a word. Days when the hacienda store stocked watermelons made them feel as if they were sitting in some lookout shed back in their hometowns. The watermelon didn't taste that different either. They took the green rinds that were left over, cut them into thin slices, and mixed them with chili pepper flakes to ferment. Some called this watermelon kimchi, and others called it watermelon greens. Either way, they did not throw away a single bit of the watermelon.

They had been sold to Buena Vista hacienda, about forty miles from Mérida. The shaman had originally been sold to another hacienda, but a month later he had been moved to this one. Their tales of woe from the henequen fields were no different from those of the other haciendas, though these three had never farmed before and so suffered from an even more severe fatigue. Three bachelors, they came to live together in one paja.

As soon as he arrived at Buena Vista, Choe Seongil understood the reality he faced. There was no way to make money on the hacienda. Everyone was broke. There wouldn't be anything for him to steal. Earn much, my brothers, Choe Seongil silently pleaded. Fortunately, his brothers worked hard. While the Mayans could gather no more than four thousand henequen leaves a day, after only a few months his Korean brothers cut more than ten thousand leaves a day. Though the blood flowed freely from their hands, they continued to work. The men cut the leaves and the women removed the thorns. The children took string and tied the henequen into bundles. When the men got drunk they whimpered, wondering whether this was the cost of their nation's sins, the sins of society, their own sins, or simply fate. Choe Seongil was not fond of such a sentimental attitude. What use was it to argue about whose sin it was? The important thing was that they were here in Mexico. Perhaps nostalgia made them forget: they had not lived well in Korea either. Life had always been rough. Droughts, floods, and famines were yearly events. And the landlords of Korea were no better than the landlords of Mexico. At least here, no one froze to death.

Choe Seongil worked slowly, so he did not earn much, but he made extra money for food by gambling, which was practically swindling for him. It was hard working under the blazing sun, but gradually he got the hang of it, and it was no longer so hard that his breath rasped in his dry throat, as it had at first. He was more bothered by the nightmares that had begun on the ship, though they were far too vivid to be called nightmares. On nights when they visited him, he could not sleep until early morning. They always played out the same. A black shape whose face he could not clearly see appeared and approached him. As on the ship, the shape said, "I have come to claim the price for my life." At other times the shape said nothing. Choe Seongil tried to flee with all his might, but his body was rooted fast to the ground like a tree and he couldn't move an inch. He tried to scream with a voice that made no sound, and when he awoke he often found himself lying in a strange place.

The shaman who lived with him only glanced at him, but said nothing. When Choe Seongil drew close and asked him about his nightmares, the shaman shook his head and said he didn't know, but it was clear that he had seen something, too. Finally, the shaman could no longer stand the sight of him nodding off in the fields because he couldn't sleep at night, and he said, "Your shoulders are heavy, aren't they? An old man is sitting on your shoulders. He has a long beard and no hair. He looks mischievous. He's a wicked fellow. It's the ghost of a drowned man. He's fretting now because he wants to go back to the water. It looks like he's been with you since Jemulpo. How long has this been going on?"

Choe Seongil did not believe him at first. But after listening to him, he thought that his shoulders did truly feel heavy. Why did some blasted old ghost have to go sitting on someone else's shoulders? "Shouldn't we have a ritual or something?" He glanced at the shaman. The shaman was drawing something strange on the dirt floor. "What's that?" Choe Seongil asked, and the shaman laughed and said it was nothing. "Just something I was drawing out of boredom." Choe Seongil spit on the floor. "Don't go drawing strange things, that's bad luck. My dreams are troubled enough as it is." The shaman used his foot to erase the shape he had been drawing. After he had erased it, Choe became even more curious as to what it had been. "Ah, damn it." Choe Seongil went outside where Father Paul was sitting on a stump and looking up at the stars. "What are you doing?" Choe Seongil asked, and Father Paul scratched his head. "Looking at the stars." Choe Seongil sucked on a cigarette. "If you look up at the stars, will they give you rice, or rice cakes? If you've got nothing to do, go to sleep. Don't get bitten by mosquitoes for no reason."

Father Paul laughed good-naturedly and stood up. "Now that you mention it, I was just thinking of doing that." Paul didn't usually go inside when the shaman was in the paja, particularly when he was performing some ceremony. When Paul did go inside, Choe

Seongil raised his arms and stretched. From far off he heard the murmuring of people at the hacendado's house. From what he had heard, there was to be some great event at the hacienda on Sunday. Noble guests were coming from somewhere, and it sounded like some special Mexican festival. There might even be something for him to steal. But armed guards stood watch, and one mistake could mean a trip to the afterworld. And anyway, if he stole something valuable, where would he sell it? He couldn't speak Spanish and didn't know his way around. Choe Seongil gave up right there and went back into the paja. The shaman was bowing before an altar he had made of straw and crude pieces of wood. Though he had tired of being a shaman, he was never lax in serving his god. The candlelight flickered and cast shadows on the ceiling. Maybe those shadows resembled the god he served. Now Choe Seongil wondered if it was the shaman who was tormenting his dreams, and he stared piercingly at the back of the shaman's head.

After he finished bowing, the shaman began to sketch a person in splendid attire on a piece of wood using red dye he had drawn from a cactus. "Say, that's enough!" Choe Seongil shouted at the shaman as he glanced over at Father Paul, who was already asleep. Poof, the candlelight went out. Suddenly he was afraid of the shaman, rustling about wordlessly as he searched for his bed. No, he was afraid of the world with which the shaman was related. Where is this netherworld he talks about? Does it even exist? As he wondered these things, Choe Seongil fell asleep. How much time had passed? Choe Seongil opened his eyes. He was thirsty, and he opened the door of the paja and went outside. The hacendado's house was brightly lit. A savory aroma wafted toward him. Choe Seongil walked in that direction. Countless people were gathered around the fountain inside the front gate of the house. Liquors and meats were spread out there, a veritable feast, and he saw servants in uniform as well. He was ashamed of his shabby appearance and hid behind a tree. He wanted to step forward and eat those delicious things, but he knew the guests would not tolerate him. The longer he stood there, the more he was tempted by the food. Finally he worked up his courage and calmed himself, and he slowly approached a table piled with roast chicken. Yet as soon as his hand reached out to grab that glistening chicken, it disappeared like smoke. The lords and ladies that had been talking around him also vanished. In their place, a black shape with a hat pressed down over his face stood before Choe Seongil. The black shape squeezed his neck with his rough arm. Then he spoke.

"The time has come."

Choe Seongil did not resist any longer. He closed his eyes and surrendered everything to the shape's will. When he did, an unbelievably happy feeling, spouting forth like the fountain, suddenly gushed out from inside him. He was shaken by an amazing ecstasy, by a perfect satisfaction. If this is how it is, I can die, he thought. And he felt as if this joy would continue forever.

# 39

THERE WAS A BOY. His hometown was Wi Island, the largest populated island in the West Sea. The islanders made their living from yellow corvina. When the corvina fisheries in the ocean off Chilsan were at their peak, the ship owners pooled their money and held a shamanic ritual, and at the beginning of the year they held a grass boat ritual, sending off a grass boat loaded with misfortune and praying for a good catch. They also held a ritual to the dragon king for those who had drowned at sea. When the time for the rituals neared, the village was filled with taboos. Men kept their distance from women, and women who bled were isolated. As the people took care in each word and each action, the festival began, and the shamaness and the men who were not unclean made sacrificial offerings to their unseen guests. The women and children could only watch from afar. The first festival guests were twelve tutelary deities and the dragon king god. The old shamaness tied together the heads of the men participating in the offerings with hemp and dragged them into the shrine. The men, tethered like yellow corvina, delightedly gave their offerings. Only when these rituals had ended could all the people in the village join the festival. While musicians struck gongs and drums and played flutes, everyone came out of the shrine and swarmed toward the ocean. The men added to the excitement by shouting cries of "Hoist the anchor! Unfurl the sails! Row the oars!" and climbing atop the mother ship and dancing. The grass boat, which was tied to the mother ship, was loaded with all of the village's misfortune and dragged out to sea. When the waves grew high, as if the god of the ocean were raising his body, they stopped the boat there and cut the cord that tied the grass boat, letting it drift into the distant sea. The misfortune on the grass boat was carried off to China, and with it all the taboos disappeared. Wi Island reveled all night with merry dancing, drinking, and song.

The boy grew up in this sort of place. It was a place where one was born the son of a fisherman, lived life as a fisherman, became the father of a fisherman, and then died. There was no other way. The boy's father and uncles spread out their nets in the yard and tied the knots, and his mother and sisters reeked of fish. If they had salt, they pickled the fish, and if not, they ate it raw on the spot, dipped in soybean paste. One day, the boy's father decided to go out to fish for yellow corvina. The owner of his boat attempted to dissuade him, but the father just laughed. He never came back. The next day, the fishermen who had gone out as one to fish in the sea off Chilsan sighted the debris of a shattered fishing boat. A few days later, the boy's mother called the village shamaness and asked her to hold a ritual to save the spirit of her drowned husband. His mother, sisters, and aunts sat down together without a word and prepared for the ritual. His mother caught his sister crying in the outhouse; she beat her and drove her out of the village. "Don't even think of coming back before the ritual is over, you father-tormenting wench!"

As the ritual was being held on the shore, the boy's sister stared at the sea from the mountain behind the village. While all the villagers gathered and clucked their tongues, the ritual was reaching its climax. The tide came in and the waves shifted direction. "How cold it must be!" his mother cried. The shamaness, caught up in her own excitement, shook her sacred staff as if mad and called to the deceased. And then a strange thing happened that would be talked about for years whenever a ritual was held in that village. Something approached rapidly, like lightning, and drew near the warped pier that bulged out like a woman's breast. Even if three or four men had been rowing a boat, it could not have traveled faster. The shape, at first glance resembling a log, made straight for the place where the ritual was being held, and it came to a stop on a sandbar. People screamed, "It's Geumdong!" It was one of the boy's uncles, who had been on the boat with his father. The uncle's body sloshed back and forth with the waves, his fish-bitten arms flapping. The waves repeatedly licked his body like a cow's tongue. Nothing like that had ever happened in the shamaness's life, or in her mother's time. The ritual was meant only to save the soul of the drowned, not to reclaim the body. Anyone could tell that this was not the work of the shamaness. Yet Uncle Geumdong had clearly appeared before their eyes, right in the middle of the ritual. They covered his body with a straw mat and carried it up the mountain. His eyeballs were missing and

one arm hung loosely from its socket. An eel slithered out from between the folds of the mat and was trampled underfoot. And someone took out a small octopus that had crawled into an empty eye
socket. At that point the shamaness called off the ritual – "I think
it's time to stop. The dragon king doesn't want to see my face" – and
hobbled back to her house. Not long after that, another shamaness
who lived at Gomso Ferry came and held a ritual for the soul of Uncle Geumdong, who had died before he could be married, but no
one was very interested. Soon the town shamaness succumbed to a
lingering illness and died, and her daughter performed the ritual for
her mother's soul to the beat of her father's drum.

When the shamaness from Gomso Ferry didn't receive all the
money promised to her, she was furious and returned to her home.
Sometime later, a strange woman appeared before the boy. "Let's
go to the mainland. I'll give you white rice and meat soup. Your
mother is already there waiting for you." The boy took the prettily
made-up woman's hand and boarded her boat. After an hour they
arrived at Gomso Ferry. Only after they walked for some time and
then entered a house fluttering with cloth, colorful clothing, and
military officers' robes, and decorated with idols, did the boy realize
who was waiting for him. It was the shamaness of Gomso Ferry. Of
course, his mother was not there. The shamaness did not say a word,
and locked the boy in a shed. Has my mother sold me off? The boy
shed tears of outrage. But a short while later, he lifted his head at the
thought that it couldn't be true. That shamaness is laying a curse on
us. Fear swept over him. It was said that some shamanesses seized
children and starved them to death. They did this after they had
been serving their god for a long time and their powers were failing.
Then the grieved spirit of the dead child would enter them. It was
said that shamanesses locked children up in chests and poked them

with metal rods so that they couldn't sleep, tormenting them cruelly until they died. That way, the grieved spirit of the dead child would be powerful.

Three days later, the shamaness of Gomso opened the shed door and led the boy out. Then she taught him to play the drum. Bum ba-ba dum ba-ba dum . . . clack! He was clumsy. If he made a mistake the shamaness hit him. She did not lock him up in a chest and poke him with a sharp rod, but he was just as vexed. Day in and day out, the foul-mouthed shamaness swore to kill him. The boy wanted to see his mother and sister. His body swelled from some illness or other. The shamaness stuck charms on his body and mumbled for some time. He shivered with cold. Strangely enough, in only a day the swelling went down. When he was better, the shamaness started teaching him to play the drum again. Every night the boy dreamed that his mother came to find him. He dreamed that his mother threw open the doors of the dark shed, rushed in and grabbed his wrist, and led him home. But when he woke up, he was still in the shamaness's shed.

One morning, the shamaness had gone out to perform a ritual nearby. The boy broke the shed window and climbed out. He stuffed the rice cakes on the shamaness's altar into his pocket and ran away. He climbed hill after nameless hill the whole night. The next day, the boy arrived at a sturdy fortress. Old-style Korean soldiers were watching people as they passed by the gate. The boy was ill at ease, for it seemed as if the squint-eyed Gomso shamaness had ordered the soldiers to find him. He stopped some people and asked where he was, and they told him he was in Haemi. They said there was a market there, and the city bustled with people. The boy stayed close behind some men going into the city and tried to slip past the gate, but he was discovered.

"What's this?" A soldier lifted the boy up. The boy spoke in a terrified voice, "Gomso shamaness, chest, poke, on Wi Island, my uncle, ritual, my father, the shamaness died, I'm hungry, bum da dum bum da dum to General Gwanun and General Choe Yeong."

When the boy came to his senses again, he was at the soldier's house. After eating some porridge boiled by the soldier's wife and regaining his strength, he began to play with the children of the house, who were younger than him. It was a surprisingly quiet house. At night the family all gathered together, closed their eyes, and mumbled something. Two pieces of wood were tied together in a cross and hung on the wall, and they spoke toward this. He grew afraid again. The soldier saw his fear and took his hand. He told the boy that he must believe in the God of heaven in order to go to heaven. In that place there were no kings or aristocrats, no hunger or tyranny, and it was filled only with eternal joy. Whatever the case, the boy liked the part about there being no hunger. "Does the God of heaven get angry?" he asked. The shamaness of Gomso had only ever taught him of the wrath of the gods. Her god was always angry. Whether the food was too little, or the shamaness wasn't sincere enough, or there was an unclean person, the god burned with anger. The soldier laughed. "Jesus died on the cross for our sins. He felt compassion for us and died in the body of a man." The boy tilted his head. "Are you saying that he died because of us and he still doesn't get angry?" The soldier laughed and tousled his hair. "That's right. He is the one who died for our sins."

The soldier told him not to tell anyone what he said, no matter what. Not long after, a blue-eyed man in mourning clothes and a wide-brimmed mourner's hat came to the soldier's house and took the boy deep into the mountains. There, people were making charcoal in furnaces. They spoke the same way as the soldier and knelt down morning and night and mumbled something. They spoke repeatedly about someone's death, and every time they did, they were sad. It was completely different from the shamaness's house. The boy was baptized. He lived at the blue-eyed priest's house. He learned the church doctrines and memorized the prayers. Then he was sent to Penang, Malaysia, where he attended a seminary. But wherever he went, when he closed his eyes he was tormented by the sight of Uncle Geumdong splitting the waves and heading toward the pier. That had changed everyone's fortunes. When a fellow seminary student who had gone to Penang with him asked, "Why don't you go back to Wi Island and see your family?" the young man said nothing. What would I do if my mother really did sell me off? Mother, the son you sold off has returned. Should I say this to her and then bow down? Of course, that might not have been what happened, but still . . .

After many years had passed, Bak Gwangsu Paul, called Mr. Bak by his fellow Koreans on the hacienda, was asleep in the same room as the shaman. One never knew what life would bring. Is this also God's will? The shaman's speech, his every action, the blue and red strips of cloth, the idols he made, everything reminded him of the Gomso shamaness and made him ill at ease. His journey to Penang, through Nagasaki and Hong Kong, and his becoming a Catholic priest had come about partly because of Uncle Geumdong and the Gomso shamaness. He wanted to flee far from that ominous, magical world. Yes, he had accepted the religion from Palestine because it was a faith from far away. And now he had fled from even that religion and had come all the way across the Pacific Ocean to Mexico.


# 40


IN 1521, THE SPANISH soldier Cortés led six hundred troops to lay siege to and capture the capital of the Aztecs. Mexico and the vast domains of the Indios nearby all fell to Spain. Ten years later, an ignorant and ordinary Indio living in Tepeyac, Juan Diego, converted to Catholicism. After finishing Mass early one morning, he heard someone calling his name from Tepeyac Hill. He went to the top of the hill, where beautiful music rang out and a woman in splendid clothes and radiating all the colors of the rainbow waited for him. This mysterious woman, with her brown skin and black hair, said to Juan Diego, "Build a church on this spot." Juan Diego did not doubt for one moment that this woman, the very image of an Aztec Indio, was the divine manifestation of the Blessed Mother Maria. He ran down the hill and conveyed the command of the Blessed Mother to Bishop Juan de Zumárraga. Yet the bishop refused to believe that what had appeared before the eyes of one of these unenlightened people, whom the Spaniards had conquered ten years earlier, and who up to that point had devoted themselves to human sacrifice — and a truly trivial person even among those people — could be the Blessed Mother. Not to mention her brown skin! Was the Blessed Mother an Indio, then? He ignored the report.

Disappointed, Juan Diego returned home, and on his way he met the same woman. When he told her of the bishop's disbelief, the Blessed Mother said that she would give him a definite sign and that he should to come to the hill the next day. Only, waiting at home was his uncle, dying of fever. The next morning, after much debate, this kindhearted man went to find a priest to perform the last rites for his uncle instead of going up the hill to meet the Blessed Mother. But the mysterious woman was waiting for Juan Diego in an alley. She told him not to worry, that his uncle would be healed, and that he should take her sign to the bishop. With that she filled Juan Diego's tilma (a traditional Indio garment similar to a shawl) with roses. There was not a single rosebush anywhere, and furthermore it was December. Excited, Juan Diego took the roses and ran to the bishop. When he gave the tilma full of roses to him, the bishop was shocked, and he fell to his knees and bowed. The image of the woman who had appeared before Juan Diego, the brown-skinned Blessed Mother, was imprinted on the tilma like a photograph.

While Juan Diego was with the bishop, the mysterious woman appeared before Juan Diego's uncle, healing him of his illness and instructing him that she be called the Blessed Mother of Guadalupe. The Indios were awed by this event, and during the next eight years, more than eight million Indios converted to Catholicism. The Indios called her Tonantzin — Our Mother. It was the appearance of a new goddess.

Three years after this miracle, Ignacio de Loyola, who had been a warmongering soldier in his youth and had become a zealous Counter-Reformationist after he was wounded in a battle against France, founded the Society of Jesus. In the eyes of this ambitious apostle, who had resolved to drive off the Protestants and expand the power of Catholicism by force, the New World was truly the place for him to realize his ideals. He trained as soldiers of the pope young men whose judgment was clouded by the gold and silver pouring in from the Americas, young men who had an abundance of energy and passion (those who most resembled him in his younger days), and young men who had no thought of revising the system of faith they had inherited from their parents. Ignacio sent these young men to Asia, Africa, and the New World.

José Velásquez was one of these. Having gone to Mexico as a Jesuit priest, he was not particularly moved by the appearance of the Blessed Mother of Guadalupe. In fact, he had not believed this miracle from the start. To think that the Blessed Mother would appear in the guise of a such a lowly Indio woman! The way he saw it, Bishop Juan de Zumárraga was a surprisingly realistic and clever person. The bishop had imitated the story of Thomas in the Bible, the apostle who was filled with disbelief. It was clearly a parody of the scene where Jesus told Thomas that if he so doubted his resurrection, he should put his hand into his, Jesus', side. The reversal of disbelief and belief and the miracle were indeed sufficient to delude the foolish Indios. This first bishop of Mexico had given the Indios their lost mother. The Blessed Mother of Guadalupe was also well suited to the tradition of goddess worship on the Iberian Peninsula. Miracles and icons — were not these truly the two pillars that supported Catholicism? If it were not for them, this ancient religion of the Old World would not have lasted long.

José Velásquez loved Mexico in a different way from the bishop. Mexico did not like his way of loving, but at least his love never cooled. He quickly realized that the Blessed Mother of Guadalupe, whom the Indios insisted on calling Tonantzin, differed greatly from the Blessed Mother he knew. Most of the Indios showed an interest in talk of the Blessed Mother, but they were not interested in core doctrines like the Trinity. They understood everything in a slightly different way. Thus they turned everything upside down. They were always seeing Jesus' disciples or the saints as gods in themselves. To them, the Blessed Mother was a goddess and Jesus was merely her son. And they placed too great a meaning on that son's death. They enjoyed carving images of him lying in a coffin or hanging on the cross and bleeding. They were always adding severe self-mutilation and horrific penances to the Church rituals, making the complex and solemn Gothic-style ceremonies similar to the ancient Aztec system of human sacrifice. José Velásquez spent far too much time trying to convince them that just because it was a day commemorating Jesus' carrying the cross up the hill, it didn't mean they needed to drive nails into their own hands and hang themselves on crosses. He could not help but admit that his calling was to fight the traditional shamanism of the Aztec Indios. When he became aware of this calling, he realized that there were far too many foes around him. In each tribe, magicians cured the sick and oversaw the rituals. Only on Sunday were the Indios under the influence of the Church, and most of them remained loyal to the village shamans. There were many idols and totems that José had to destroy. The atavistic custom of drinking intoxicants like the fly agaric mushroom, to plunge the whole tribe into a trance, was as strong as ever. First the magician would drink the infusion, and when he entered into a trance the next person would drink his urine and fall into a trance as well. The fly agaric drink became more potent after being filtered through the body. After passing through three bodies, it would lift the whole tribe into an intense ecstasy. In the process, the Indios claimed that they met the Father, the Son, and the Holy Spirit, but really they often saw a great dragon or worshiped a feathered serpent.

In order to effectively fight this ancient religion, José gave up his duties as a priest and organized a standing army that was stronger than the Jesuits. He invaded Indio villages, tearing down idols and burning them. He slaughtered those in ecstasy, powerless as they were, and raised red crosses. His name was one of terror on the plateaus of Mexico. Even amid countless battles and the threat of assassination, he lived to the age of ninety, and in the end he died peacefully in his own bed. He never officially married, but he left behind countless illegitimate children, who devoted themselves as one to the Counter-Reformation movement and to converting the Indios. They also had many offspring. As time went by, the violent zeal of José Velásquez was greatly diluted, but slaves to this fanatical faith still sometimes appeared.

Ignacio Velásquez could truly be called proof of atavism. The owner of both Buena Vista hacienda and a small bank, he rose at five o'clock in the morning and went to a small prayer room in a corner of his house. He knelt on a wooden board prepared for that purpose and, as always, offered up his earnest morning prayers. Then he carefully cleaned the rifles hanging in his living room with an oiled rag. This was the only thing he did not leave to his servants. These rifles were a sort of legacy that proved that Ignacio was the legitimate child of José Velásquez. He had fought with José's numerous descendants and claimed the rifles. They were a record of the history of his family's struggle against the aimless idol worship and Satanism of the Yucatán. His heart welled up when he cleaned the scar-pocked barrels, and he had to calm himself several times. When he had finished polishing the rifles, he got on his horse and circled the hacienda. It was a long time since he had done so. He headed toward the dwellings of the Koreans he had hired a half year ago. It had been two years since he had conquered with hoof and whip the Mayans in his hacienda, who had painted the heads of stone idols with sap and made a small circle of pebbles and then burned incense and spun around in that circle. When it was all over, not only did the Mayans go to church each Sunday and attend Mass, but they also stopped their suspicious nightly activities. Yet he had no idea what the fifty or so newly arrived Koreans might be doing. He had heard that a few of them were Protestants (of course, these too were targets of conversion), and one of them (thanks be to the Lord, let His mercy pour down even in this backcountry) was said to be a Catholic. The rest of them were unknowns. So it was only natural for this descendant of an apostate priest, who believed in his family's sacred duty to obliterate superstition, to decide to convert every one of the Koreans on his hacienda.

He looked around the pajas of the Koreans, who had gone out to the fields. At first glance, he saw no idols. Pots and kettles, filthy clothes, and a hideous stench were all he found. Still, they must have some religion. He held his nose and slowly searched the pajas one by one. Finally, in the last paja he found a small altar, inscribed with strange letters and a colored portrait of a man wearing a hat drawn on paper. He searched further but found nothing except a few carved wooden figures. Having discovered that some of them worshiped idols, Ignacio became lost in thought for a moment, but the odor was so bad that he could stay no longer and went straight back to his house. Their idols were completely different from those of the Mayans. The letters looked like those of the Chinese, and they were written in red, the color of the devil. Once again he heard the sound of his blood commanding him from within.

He called the overseer and the Korean interpreter and said: "From this Sunday, all Koreans must attend Mass. In return, there will be no work on Sunday. Mexico is a Catholic nation, so the act of privately serving and worshiping idols is forbidden." This was a lie. There were many Catholics in Mexico, but it was not a theocracy. "Accordingly, let it be known that if you keep idols in your homes or worship superstitions, you will be driven away without receiving a single peso. If you convert and are baptized, I will raise your pay." The interpreter Gwon Yongjun, who had been called to Buena Vista hacienda, conveyed the hacendado's intentions to the Koreans. Most of them welcomed the news. They would not have to work if they went to church and sat for a little while, and that was not such a hard thing to do. There were those who said they would study the doctrines and be baptized. Their pay would be raised by one tenth, and they might even be able to rest a bit while they were learning the doctrines. Yet only Father Paul understood exactly what the hacendado meant by not worshiping idols. When Father Paul heard what Gwon Yongjun had to say, he turned to the shaman and said bitterly, "I think you're going to have to clear out the things in our room." The shaman looked at him in surprise. "Mr. Bak, what do they have to do with the hacendado?" "The god of his religion is very jealous and does not like his followers believing in other gods." The shaman said, "My god and his god are different. What if I don't want to serve his god?" Father Paul scraped the ground with his foot. "Anyway, that's what he believes. His religion is one that does not look favorably on ancestor worship, and this hacendado seems to be a believer to the bone. Be careful." The shaman had looked worried at first but quickly adopted an indifferent attitude. "I'm not putting a curse on anyone, so what could go wrong? But say, weren't you a Catholic?"

On Sunday, the Koreans wore their cleanest clothes and went to Mass in a small place prepared on the hacienda. A priest from Mérida rode in on horseback and officiated at the Mass. The hacendado and the overseers sat on mahogany pews made in Belize, and the Korean and Mayan workers sat on the ground as they listened to the incomprehensible Latin. They stood up and sat down a few times and the Mass was over, and then the hacendado brought out watermelon. The children were excited to have watermelon after so long, and they ran around the hacienda.

Father Paul's heart ached at hearing the Latin and the hymns. Kyrie Eleison. Lord have mercy. He watched the white priest reciting the Latin prayers and remembered how he himself had performed Mass in Korea. I may never again stand up at an altar. I don't even remember much anymore. Yet when it came time to take the Eucharist, he felt a strong temptation to go forward and accept it. But he did not. There was likely no Mexican priest who would offer the Eucharist to a foreigner in filthy clothes. And they would find it hard to believe that he was a priest.

Choe Seongil had stared blankly and said nothing all morning, but he was unable to resist the urging of the overseers and foremen and had gone to where the Mass was being performed. He had stared wordlessly at the Mexican priest at the altar until the ceremony was almost finished, and then he shot up and ran forward. The neatly dressed Gwon Yongjun and a young Korean boy, Yi Jinu, also shot up. Gwon Yongjun and the overseers ran toward Choe Seongil, but he flew toward the platform. Then he knelt in front of the cross and beat his body and wailed as if mad. It was neither Korean nor Spanish but a strange language. The overseers, foremen, and Gwon Yongjun rushed in and tried to lift him up, but Choe Seongil resisted with a frightful strength. Tears flowed down his face and he screamed at the priest.

The hacendado stood and made the sign of the cross. Then he approached the priest and whispered something to him. He told the foremen and overseers to leave Choe Seongil alone and spoke: "Those who were possessed by demons approached our Lord and shouted, 'Son of God, why have you come to interfere with us? Have you come to torment us before the time has come?' And he sent them into a herd of swine. And this herd of swine ran down a slope and drowned themselves in the sea. This fellow is just such a one." When the hacendado glanced at the priest, the priest wet his brush with holy water and sprinkled it on Choe Seongil. Choe Seongil writhed as if he were splashed with acid, then he foamed at the mouth and collapsed. "Isn't that epilepsy?" the Koreans said, tilting their heads, but the hacendado and the priest looked solemn. "In the name of Jesus you shall be saved!" The priest continued to splash him with holy water. Then he poured whole glasses of holy water over him. Only then did Choe Seongil open his swollen eyes, as if he had just woken from sleep. He looked around as if to figure out where he was. Ignacio embraced him in an exaggerated fashion.

Ignacio, who believed that they had driven out the demon with holy water and prayer, was once more aware of the noble calling with which he had been entrusted. After the Mass, Choe Seongil ate lunch with the hacendado in his house. It was a sumptuous feast that seemed like a dream. Pork boiled in the Yucatán fashion, with black beans, cilantro, onions, and tomatoes, and sopa de lima, cooked with lime and onion, awaited him. He ate like a glutton. Gwon Yongjun, who sat next to him, relayed the hacendado's words. "Mr. Choe. The hacendado thinks that he drove a spirit out of you." Choe Seongil bobbed his head and expressed his thanks. "Now that you mention it, I was told that some old man had been sitting on my shoulders." But these words, when translated, were embellished and conveyed as: "He says thank you for driving out Satan." The hacendado urged Choe Seongil to join the army of Jesus and fight Satan with him. Choe Seongil agreed unconditionally.

Gwon Yongjun and Choe Seongil got into a carriage and left the house. From that day forward, Choe Seongil's destiny was changed. He diligently wrote down the Latin prayers phonetically in Korean and memorized them, though he did not know what they meant. He diligently attended Mass. He gave those who didn't want to go a hard time. "If we suffer because of you, you'll be sorry. All you have to do is go and sit still. What's so hard about that?" People began to avoid Choe Seongil, who was always muttering something, but he was not concerned.

One night, Choe Seongil went to the paja of Father Paul. "Mr. Bak, wake up." Father Paul opened his eyes. Choe Seongil beckoned him outside. It was nearly a full moon. In the bright moonlight Choe Seongil took Father Paul's cross out from his bosom. "Have you seen this before?" Father Paul glanced sidelong at Choe Seongil. "Look, I'm sorry. I was ignorant and always wondered what this was, but now I finally know. This is a cross, and it has something to do with the Catholicism the hacendado carries on about, so the joke is on me. Here, take it."

He held out the cross so sincerely that Paul could not readily reach out his hand. "Can't you take what is yours?" Choe Seongil put the cross in Paul's hand. "I was hungry then, that's all. But I always meant to give it back to you someday." Choe Seongil sat on a stump and put a cigarette in his mouth. It did not light easily, and his flint sparked several times in the darkness. When he had taken a puff, he asked Father Paul, who stood there awkwardly, "So what are you, anyway? Are you just a Catholic, or . . ." Father Paul didn't say a word. "Fine. Whatever may have happened in your past, help me out. In simple Korean, explain to me what on earth this Catholicism is, and what's so great about it that the hacendado is so excited."

"I can't do that." Father Paul shook his head. "I don't know anything about it. And this cross isn't mine." Choe Seongil got up from the stump and drew close to Father Paul. "Let's help each other out. It shouldn't be that difficult. I gave you back your cross, didn't I?" Father Paul spoke in a soft voice. "I knew about it on the ship. When you were sick with dysentery — " Choe Seongil grabbed Father Paul by the throat. "What? You mean you were fishing around the trousers of a fellow so sick he couldn't move?" Father Paul could not breathe and gasped for air, and Choe Seongil had mercy on him and let go of his throat. "You seem to know just fine, telling that shaman fellow all about Catholicism. Show me a little kindness. If you don't, I don't know what happened that you would hide so, but I will go to the hacendado and tell him: Here is one of those Catholics you like so much!" Choe Seongil cackled and went inside the paja. Father Paul was disturbed by his words, which brought back memories of Korea's suppression of Catholicism. Here it was the opposite: Catholics were rewarded. But he had no wish to be dragged before the hacendado to testify to his apostasy, and he did not want to feign a false faith like the thief. Father Paul tilted the cross in the moonlight. The sapphire encrusted in the center shone with an eerie blue light.

# 41

YI JINU'S SPANISH grew better day by day. It was good enough that, given a little more time, he would be able to act as an interpreter on his own. After all, the Spanish used in the henequen fields was simple, and if he happened to misinterpret something, no one would ever know.

Gwon Yongjun sat next to Yi Jinu in the shade of a tree and lightly prodded him. "Have you talked to your sister?" Yi Jinu mumbled, "Well, I . . ." Gwon Yongjun erupted: "How long has it been since I asked you about that, and now I hear that you are roasting quail these days! You are of no use to me. You always take what you need and yet can't even grant that little request. This is why they say never to work with aristocrats. They gulp down what they like and then wash their mouths clean." Gwon Yongjun did not give Yi Jinu a chance to defend himself, but shot up and walked away. Yi Jinu grew anxious. He went home and sat down next to his sister. Yi Yeonsu stopped her sewing and looked at her brother's face. "What is it?" Her younger brother, who had once been such a child, now carried himself like a proper man after only a few months of work in the fields.

He said that he had a request. When Yeonsu asked what it was, he hesitated and could not bear to bring it up. But he had come this far, and it was the same as going all the way. Yeonsu kept urging him on. "What is it?" Yi Jinu hesitated, and then finally opened his mouth. "The interpreter . . . Mr. Gwon." Yeonsu nodded, but her face had hardened. "He keeps bothering me because he wants to meet you." Yeonsu turned her gaze back to her sewing. "So you learn Spanish from him and he keeps asking you about this?" Yi Jinu licked his lips and nodded. "Can't you meet him just once? All you have to do is go and tell him you don't want to come again. He may be low in status, but he seems to be a decent person." Yeonsu twisted the sides of her mouth into a smile. "What is status here?" The young man edged closer. "That's right. That's right, isn't it?" Yi Yeonsu looked straight into her brother's eyes and spoke resolutely. "Don't ever mention this to me again. If you do, I will be very angry. It is not because he is low in status. I just can't do it."

"But he has a lot of money!" Jinu spit out sullenly. "He not only speaks English well, he speaks Spanish well, too, and he won't starve no matter what he does. Do you think we will be able to go back? In the end we will die here. Four years from now, when our contracts with the hacienda end, you will be twenty, so you'll have to find someone to marry here anyway, won't you?" With every word that her brother spit out, Yeonsu's heart stung as if it were being stuck with needles. She knew better than anyone that her dream of studying, getting a job, and going out into the world to realize her dreams like a man was already gone. The henequen haciendas of the Yucatán were a far cry from such dreams. She would have to live with a man here. She would have to wake at half past three in the morning, prepare clothing and food for her man going out to the fields, feed her children, then go out to the fields herself and cut the henequen leaves, tie them up, and pile them in the storehouse, then go back to their barracks, prepare dinner, do the laundry, clean the house, and go to bed. She did not want to live like that. Once more, she thought ardently of Ijeong. Where is he? Perhaps he has met another woman. At Yazche hacienda, some of the men were already living with Mayan women, and some had taken concubines. The single men snooped around the Mayan dwellings at night. If a man caught a woman's eye, he would begin living with her right away. Perhaps Ijeong, too, had already . . . ? She took out the calendar she had made and looked at it. Three months had passed. It would be impossible to ever see him again, wouldn't it? Even if they were to meet, they would not be able to come together, to madly entwine their bodies. The desire that welled up suddenly shook her body. This is hell. A horrible man drools over me, my brother would sell his own sister to him, and I cannot see my beloved. Father is a walking corpse and Mother has stopped speaking. I cannot live like this. Maybe I should just flee into Gwon Yongjun's arms. No one would say anything now. Not Father or Mother. They might even think to themselves that it would be better that way. That was such a horrible thought that Yeonsu bit down hard on her lip.

Just then, a clamor came from the entrance of Yazche hacienda, and the Koreans rushed in that direction. Jinu, who had been sitting dejectedly, left the house as well and headed toward the noise. What was it now? The clamor slowly grew closer. It was not the sound of people getting angry or fighting; it was the sound of voices buoyed by gladness. Out of curiosity, Yeonsu opened the door a crack and looked out. Two men were walking toward her, surrounded by others. As those in love often do, Yeonsu overestimated the significance of this amazing good fortune, this meeting that she would savor for the rest of her life. There was nothing else to call this but destiny. He had come. Except for a slight limp, he looked healthy. Where was he coming from? Why was he coming? Was he coming to stay, or was he going to leave her again? There were many things she wanted to ask him, but she could not bear to go outside, so she simply watched him walk toward her from within the dark house.

From the moment he had entered Yazche hacienda, Ijeong had been thinking of Yeonsu as well, hoping she might be here. When he was handed over to the overseer and unshackled, and a crowd of Koreans pressed close to him on all sides, his longing became even stronger. Yazche was a larger hacienda than he had imagined. He and Dolseok were greeted warmly. The residents asked for news of the hacienda where Ijeong had been, and of their friends and relatives who might still be there. Ijeong saw among the adults a boy watching him and pretending to be dignified. It was Yeonsu's younger brother, Jinu. With this he knew for certain that she was at Yazche. Ijeong quickened his steps. The Koreans followed close behind Ijeong and Dolseok and asked endless questions about the situation at the other haciendas, the price of food, wages, mistreatment, the overseers, the foremen, the interpreter. Ijeong replied abstractedly and walked toward the house where he would be staying. His legs, which had been shackled for a long time, ached, but he soon forgot the pain.

Yet no matter how much he searched, she was not to be found. A few women were coming out to draw water or hang their laundry, but Yeonsu was not there. When he passed by a certain house his heart pounded fiercely in his chest. He did not know exactly why, but he looked into the dark house. From inside, a covered face peered out at him and then hid. The excitement rose in his chest until he thought he would go wild, but he passed by that house and went into the house where he would live. Though he had not clearly seen her face, he knew for certain that it was her. He felt her unique energy, a power that infused everything around her with a mysterious mood.

When they reached their house, Ijeong and Dolseok lay down on the rough floor. The people who had followed them continued to ask them questions. One of them was Jinu. "What hacienda did you come from?" "Chunchucmil." "Is there an interpreter there?" "Of course there isn't." "How do you work without an interpreter?" Ijeong looked at Jinu, who was a few years younger than him, and flashed him a smile. "Do you speak when driving cattle or horses? Everyone understands." Jinu's eyes sparkled as he listened to Ijeong speak. "How are the people at Chunchucmil?" Dolseok rubbed his eyes and spoke. "Already three have died. One stabbed, one by the whip, and one suicide. Has anyone died here yet?" They all shook their heads. Dolseok's words were a comfort to the people of Yazche hacienda. At least everyone here is still alive.

In spite of their fatigue, Yeonsu and Ijeong tossed and turned all night. The past three months had been too long a parting for hot-blooded young people.

# 42

"FIND ME A BRUSH and some paper." Early one morning when the others were going out to work, Yi Jongdo opened his mouth for the first time in what seemed like weeks as he lay in his bed. Lady Yun, who was busy preparing to leave for the fields, at first pretended not to hear him. Yi Jongdo said again, "Find me a brush and some paper." Lady Yun replied curtly, "And what are you going to do with them?" Yi Jongdo did not reply. Instead, his son said, "I don't think there are any brushes, but I will see if I can find something similar." Yi Jinu put on his leggings and gloves and went outside. The weather had grown a little cooler since May, when they had first arrived. Lady Yun gently grasped her son's shoulder as he went out. "Don't go to too much trouble."

On his way back, Jinu asked Gwon Yongjun to find a brush and some paper, but the interpreter didn't seem interested in listening to him. With no other choice, Jinu went to the store and asked if he could buy some paper and a writing instrument. Unexpectedly, they readily gave him the notebook, pen, and ink that they used and told him that they would take the price out of his pay.

Yi Jongdo tore the notebook paper a few times with the unfamiliar pen as he diligently began to write something. He rose in the morning and washed his face with the water that Lady Yun had drawn, then sat down before a discarded wooden box and slowly wrote one character after another. He devoted his entire day to the effort. At times he stared into space as if trying to jog his memory, and at others he took deep breaths as if emotions were welling up inside him. At lunchtime, Lady Yun offered him a tortilla, but he refused and wrote with glittering eyes.

In the evening, people began to gather at Yi Jongdo's house. The rumor must have spread that he had spent all day writing something. No one dared to speak to him, but many of them peeked into the house and murmured. Jinu made his way past them and went inside. Yeonsu couldn't budge within the prison of gazes. When the chattering outside grew louder, Yi Jongdo opened the door and looked out. The eyes of those who could not write pleaded with him: You are writing a letter, aren't you? We won't get in your way, so please write the letter. We will just wait. Let His Majesty and the government know what has really happened to us. We don't need money or fields, so ask them to please take us back. And when you have finished writing that letter, when you have written a letter to your kinfolk, to your flesh and blood, please write letters for us as well. Tell our brothers, our families, that all is not well, but we are fine. This is what their eyes said to him. It was a shock to Yi Jongdo. As a member of the royal family and a literati in Seoul, he had not once seen such pathetic gazes directed toward him. They stepped back and bowed their heads when he walked by, but they did not hide their hostility and scorn. Aristocrats were filthy and disgraceful creatures to be avoided. In a way, an aristocrat was like a brigand to them. It was best to live without meeting one.

Yi Jongdo spoke. "I am writing a letter to His Majesty. I have seen with my own two eyes the blood and tears you have shed in this land, so I know them well. Here in Mexico there must be a postal system. If someone goes as far as Mérida and sends this, within a month His Majesty will conceive a plan. Even dogs and pigs are treated better than this." At Yi Jongdo's words, the pain of the past three months — no, counting from the day they boarded the ship, it was closer to half a year — came to mind, and the eyes of some were growing red. One of them dug around in his pocket, took out a coin, and awkwardly gave it to Jinu, who stood at Yi Jongdo's side. "You are doing this for us, so please do not refuse this." At that, everyone began taking out money. Some people went home and brought back rice. Jinu politely declined them all. Yi Jongdo went back inside and sat down before the wooden box. For the first time he felt that his having learned to write had been worthwhile. From his youth, he had never once felt the simple pleasure of reading or writing. It was always merely a duty. Now it was different. Countless phrases that he had completely forgotten poured into his head like a column of ants.

"Father, did you not say that if we returned we would be dragged off to Japan and die a miserable death?" Yi Jongdo answered boldly, "It can't be any worse than this. Surely they won't make you work so that your palms are split like the teeth of a saw. I was wrong."

When the people who had been gathered around went back to their homes, Yeonsu left the house with a water jar and walked slowly in the direction where Ijeong had gone the day before. She glanced furtively about her but could not see him. Outside the hacienda's boundary and toward the cenote was a thick tangle of bushes. Yeonsu headed for the well. She was about halfway there. There was no sign of anyone in the brilliant moonlight. It was too late; had she come in vain? As Yeonsu was regretting her decision, someone approached her from behind and grabbed her jar. It was Ijeong. The two of them went wordlessly into the bushes. Ijeong set the jar down gently and held Yeonsu from behind. "I thought it would be four years before I would see you." Ijeong squeezed her harder. Yeonsu gasped. "I know, I thought so too, I thought so too. But it's OK, since you're here. No, I hate you. Why did you wait so long?" They kissed. Ijeong lifted Yeonsu's skirt and jacket and threw himself at her. The branches of the bushes scratched their arms and legs. "I don't believe it. It's like a dream. Three months. I'm sorry — who would have thought that I would see your body after only three months?"

After their passions had passed, Yeonsu and Ijeong lay side by side and looked at the moon. Ants crawled over their thighs and stomachs, but their dulled flesh could not feel them. "Father is writing a letter to His Majesty." Ijeong plucked grass and tore it apart. "I heard. Do you think we'll be going back, then?" Yeonsu sighed and rested her head on Ijeong's chest. "I don't want to. It is horrible here, but Korea is even worse." Ijeong ran his hand through her hair. "Shall we run away?" Yeonsu put a hand on the ground, raised herself, and looked down at Ijeong. "Really? But we don't know the language. Where will we go, how will we live?" Ijeong held her. "Wait a little while. I learned Japanese on the ship, so the language here won't be too difficult. Once I learn Spanish I am going to run far away. I will not be trapped here for the whole four years. They say that if you head north you can go to the United States. I met a ginseng merchant, and he said that the United States and Mexico are as different as heaven and earth. Let's go together. I'll work and you will go to school." She pushed her thumb into her lover's lips. "Ah, it would be so nice, even if it were only a dream." But then her face grew dark. "What if we all go back to Korea because of Father's letter?" Ijeong squeezed her nipple. "Then we'll really run away. It takes a few months for letters to come and go, and by that time we will be ready."

The young man and woman, unable to distinguish between the promise of adventure and sexual excitement, once again brought their warm bodies furiously together. The Yucatán moon shone down on flesh as pale as itself. Yi Yeonsu's buttocks shone with a blue light.

# 43

CHOE SEONGIL LEARNED the basic doctrines of Catholicism from Father Paul. He could not understand concepts like the Trinity, but he accurately grasped the core doctrines. "So there's one God, that's simple. There's heaven, that's good too. All you have to do is believe. He doesn't like people serving other gods but him. He sent down his son, named Jesus, but mankind killed him, so he got angry — what do you mean that's not it? Of course it is. And then there's his mother, and she's the Blessed Mother, and she went up to heaven too . . . Then what sort of relationship does she have with this God we're talking about? . . . Anyway, I understand. The Ten Commandments? What, things like 'Thou shalt not steal'? They put such an obvious thing in the Ten Commandments? Stealing is bad. Why are you staring at me like that? I said I was sorry about that, didn't I? You think people steal because they want to? Say, what are you, anyway? What were you? Did you kill someone or something? Why did you have to run away and come all the way here? No? What do you mean no, it's written all over your face. Did you commit a crime? You don't have to tell me if you don't want to. But I will find out. You wait and see."

When Choe Seongil grew sleepy, he went to bed. After a while he sensed someone moving about. He opened his eyes and looked around. He could vaguely make out a black shadow opening the door and going outside. Judging by the way he moved, it was the shaman. Is he going out to relieve himself? Choe Seongil also suddenly had the urge to urinate. He got up from his bed, put on his straw shoes, and went outside. He saw no sign of the shaman near the ditch where they urinated. Instead, he saw him walking down a path some distance away from the paja. The shaman went to a tree and knelt beneath it. He looked around for a moment, then began to dig with his hands. After busying himself with his back turned, he stood up again and returned to the paja. In the meantime, Choe Seongil had returned to his bed and lay down. He heard the faint rustling of the shaman coming in. The shaman let out a brief sigh and immediately fell asleep. When Choe Seongil was certain that he was sound asleep, he got up and went outside. He of course headed to the tree beneath which the shaman had been digging. He dug into the earth with a tree branch. Not far down he found a small box. He opened the box and found about 10 pesos inside. He took the money out, tucked it in his waistband, and buried the box again. On the way back, he hid the money in a pile of straw beneath the eaves of their paja. Then he calmly went back to bed. He was stimulated by the criminal tension he had felt for the first time in a long time, so sleep did not come easily. Choe Seongil did not trouble himself over the matter: It's all public money anyway. It must be the money that people bring when they come to have the shaman tell their fortunes. He can't have made that much money working in the fields. So what if he shares the money he got from the spirits?

But the shaman thought differently. On the hacienda, 10 pesos was more than enough money to kill for. One would have to work for an entire month in the scorching sun, from before dawn to after dusk, stuck by the henequen thorns, in order to see that amount of money. And, of course, that was only if one did not use any of it for food or living expenses.

A few days later, the shaman discovered that someone had stolen his money. He returned to the paja and confessed this to Father Paul, who was always silent. "What should I do? I worked so hard to save that money." Father Paul immediately suspected Choe Seongil. But he could not report a fellow roommate without any proof. The shaman asked for Choe Seongil's help as well, but the Jemulpo thief maintained his composure and scolded the shaman: "See, how could you bury something so important outside?"

"How did you know that my money was buried?" Choe Seongil winced. "Ah . . ." He poked Father Paul. "Oh, Mr. Bak told me a little while ago." "He couldn't have. He just found out himself." The shaman's eyes narrowed. Choe Seongil grew angry. "This shaman fellow would harm an innocent man!" The shaman was undaunted and grabbed him by the throat. But when it came to violence, Choe Seongil was better equipped. He kicked the shaman in the groin and butted his forehead against the bridge of his nose. "Ow!" The shaman collapsed on the spot, beside himself with pain. Father Paul held Choe Seongil back. "That's enough." "Oh-ho, so you told him! Why don't you drop dead!" yelled Choe Seongil. The shaman sat there crying and cursing. "Let's see how long you live!" Choe Seongil rushed at him and stomped on him.

The shaman, who never did find his money, went around voicing his grievance to the Koreans of Buena Vista hacienda. No one came forward because of the lack of evidence, but everyone was saying, "The shaman wouldn't try to frame an innocent man, would he?" So Choe Seongil, who obviously knew the truth, could not be at ease. Yet he could not follow the shaman around and stomp on him; he could only grin and bear it. Even Mr. Bak, who had been a victim of Choe's thievery, kept both eyes peeled. If the money happened to be found under the eaves of their paja, he would be rolled up in a straw mat and beaten by the Koreans of the hacienda. Yet Choe Seongil was not one to take things sitting down.

About ten days before the harvest moon festival, a man grew seriously ill with a skin disease called pellagra. The disease was thought to have been caused by the henequen juice that had seeped into his skin. The juice could cause one to go blind if it got into one's eye. Not only that, but the man's whole body grew as heavy as a lump of lead, making it impossible to go to the fields and meet the quota. The man burned with fever and his skin was rotting. Finally, his wife went to the shaman and asked him to perform a ritual. The shaman refused a number of times, but in the end he could not ignore her tenacious pleas. The man's family and neighbors agreed to donate the food and money necessary for the ritual. On the day of the ritual, the shaman and a few other men came back early from the fields, claiming to be ill, and prepared. Someone brought a pig's head that the hacienda's cook was going to throw away, and this was added to Mexican food such as tortillas and tamales, as well as watermelon kimchi, cabbage kimchi, and vegetable patties, set out on a table covered with white paper. When word of the ritual spread, nearly all of the Koreans at Buena Vista hacienda gathered. The healing ritual, which began in the sick man's front yard, involved the recitation of various scriptures and written prayers. The shaman went into the house, brought out a piece of clothing and a pair of shoes and burned them, and then he wrapped the sick man's head in a blanket, led him out to the yard, and had him kneel down. Then he performed the ritual in order to chase out the spirits of sickness that plagued him. If the shaman had had a chicken, he would have chased the spirits into the chicken and killed it, but it was too difficult to find a live chicken, so he omitted that part.

The ritual gradually grew more boisterous, though not so loud as to be heard beyond the paja village. The crowd beat pot lids together like gongs, but naturally they weren't as loud as the real thing. Yet right about when the ritual reached its climax, the sound of horses' hooves was heard. Riding in on a brown horse, the hacendado Ignacio Velásquez closed in on the shaman, who was lost in an ecstatic trance. Ignacio was so startled at the spectacle before his eyes that he nearly fell off his horse. Startled first and foremost by the 1-peso bills sticking out of the nose and ears of the pig's head, and shocked by the shaman's gaudy dress and what was clearly idol worship taking place around the shaman, he grabbed the long rifle that was stuck in his saddle and fired it into the air. The horse, startled by the noise, reared up on its hind legs and whinnied; the Koreans scattered in all directions. The hacienda overseers who rushed in from behind the hacendado began to destroy everything on the table. Ignacio chased the shaman, who managed to get away. The sound of screaming women and children rang throughout the paja village. They ran in all directions like rabbits, not even knowing what they had done wrong. The ritual soon became chaos, and the sick man with the blanket around his head was struck by an overseer's whip and collapsed.

Father Paul, who was in his house, looked outside when he heard the shooting. The thunder of horses' hooves and the crack of gunfire reminded him of a battlefield. A few children fled into Father Paul's house. "What's going on?" "The hacendado attacked the ritual." Father Paul rushed out. There he witnessed a shocking human hunt taking place. Fire burned in Ignacio's eyes at not having captured the shaman from right under his nose, and he searched throughout the paja village. At that moment, someone appeared before Ignacio and kindly directed him to the residence of Father Paul, which was also where the shaman lived. Choe Seongil. It was only then that Father Paul realized who had caused all of this commotion. Ignacio Velásquez approached Father Paul's paja, stuck out his chin, and spoke to him in Spanish. "Is that shaman of yours inside?" Paul could not understand the words, but he knew the hacendado was looking for the shaman. His ominous premonition had been on target. When Father Paul did not reply, Ignacio took his long rifle and got down from his horse. Then, pulling back and pushing forward the bolt of his gun, he approached the paja. Father Paul did not resist and stepped aside. Ignacio pushed open the flimsy door and went in. It was so dark inside that he had to wait a while before he could make out anything. The multicolored thread and cloth that were left over from the ritual were scattered about, and the small altar was still there. With his booted foot, Ignacio destroyed the altar. "Father, forgive them, for they know not what they do." With every kick, he recited that verse from the Gospel of Luke. The joy and conviction that came from doing the Lord's work welled up from deep within his heart. When the shabby altar was crushed, Ignacio looked carefully around the room. The shaman was not there. He caught his breath, left the room, and once more asked Father Paul about the shaman's whereabouts. When he still did not reply, Ignacio struck the priest's belly with the butt of his rifle, spit at him, and cursed.

"You filthy and ignorant children of the devil!"

Paul doubled over and fell to the ground. Back on his horse, Ignacio galloped off toward the road that led to the henequen fields. Blood backed up in the priest's gullet. As he spit up blood on the ground, the priest saw many things. From the boat ritual of Wi Island to the healing ritual of the Yucatán, everything played out in his mind like a film. Paul was thinking of the same verse as Ignacio: "Father, forgive them, for they know not what they do." To this prayer, offered up at the same time in the same place by the fanatic of the Yucatán and the priest of Korea, God made no reply at all.

Ignacio met the overseer Joaquín at the entrance to the henequen fields. Joaquín told him that he had captured the fleeing shaman and that he was being held in the storehouse. Ignacio ordered a telegram sent, calling for the interpreter at Yazche hacienda.

Yazche and Buena Vista were not far apart, only thirty minutes by horse. Then Ignacio galloped to the storehouse. The shaman was sitting inside, unexpectedly composed. Ignacio was surprised at how ordinary the shaman looked. He was no different from the other Korean workers. The overseers had reported that he worked more diligently than anyone else in the henequen fields. In this he was different from the Mayan and Aztec shamans, who never worked. They always seemed to be high on some mushroom concoction. Thus Ignacio was intrigued. A short while later, Gwon Yongjun arrived in a carriage. He looked confused: to be called so late at night meant that something urgent had come up, but now that he had come, he saw that it was only the shaman, tied up in the storehouse. He had been imagining a strike, a riot, or a mass escape, and now he felt deflated. "What is the matter?" Ignacio offered Gwon Yongjun a glass of tequila. "Do you believe in God?" Gwon Yongjun shook his head. Ignacio frowned. "You must believe in God! You and your family will be saved." Gwon Yongjun laughed bitterly. "My family is all dead. They were thrown into the ocean as food for the fishes, the work of Chinese pirates." Ignacio comforted him with exaggerated motions. "That is precisely why you must rely on the Lord." Gwon Yongjun did not understand what he meant. He simply laughed. "But what is the matter?" "I made a simple rule. I gave the workers the freedom to rest on Sunday and the privilege to attend Mass. I asked only one thing in return, that they not serve idols on my hacienda, that they not serve any other god but our Lord, and your Koreans promised me that they would do so. I even promised to raise by ten percent the wages of those who were baptized and converted. And yet" — Ignacio pointed at the shaman — "that deceitful man gathered my sheep in the night and worshiped a pig's head. The head of a pig. Why did it have to be a pig, into which our Lord drove the demons? Right in the middle of my hacienda, he made my virtuous people, who attend Mass on Sundays, lower their heads and bow."

Gwon Yongjun cut him off. He turned to the shaman and asked, "Did you perform a ritual?" The shaman nodded his head. "Yes." "Why?" "Someone was ill, so I performed a healing ritual. Are such rituals forbidden by law in this land?" "I don't think so. But this hacendado hates them. Didn't you know this?" "Yes, I knew. But I didn't think that he would make such a fuss. Look here, Mr. Interpreter. Ask the master. Ask him what I must do to calm his anger."

Gwon Yongjun conveyed these words. Ignacio Velásquez flashed a smile and said, "Leave your idols and accept our Lord Jesus Christ. Be baptized and convert. Then let all the others know of your conversion. That is all I ask. The price for a false conversion is death. I swear on my family's honor that I will kill you. You were caught fleeing the hacienda in the night, so you are considered an escapee. If I kill you, I will be tried in court according to the laws of the Yucatán. But know this. In the Yucatán the judges are hacendados, the prosecutors are hacendados, and the lawyers are hacendados. There is nothing in this world that hacendados hate more than workers who break their contracts and flee."

Frightened, the shaman closed his eyes and trembled. Gwon Yongjun encouraged him to convert. "You got on that ship because you were tired of being a shaman, didn't you? Now is your chance to give it up." The shaman shook his head. "I cannot do that. It is not for me to decide. It would be better for me to die." Frustrated, Gwon Yongjun strongly urged him one more time. "Just pretend to convert. Who says you have to believe for real? All you have to do is endure it for four years." The shaman looked at Gwon Yongjun impatiently. "It is impossible to disobey my god. Unless he leaves, I cannot send him away or take anyone else in of my own free will. If I could, do you think I would be here?"

"Then that god is still with you?" The shaman nodded his head. Unable to understand their conversation, Ignacio asked Gwon Yongjun, "What did he say?" "He says that he will not convert. Not because he doesn't want to, but because it is impossible. He says that the god that is with him must let him go." Ignacio asked him, "What does this god do?" "He says that he cures disease, and he prophesies. He also calls the spirits of the dead and speaks with them." Ignacio tilted his head. "Why would a god do something like that?" Gwon Yongjun answered with a mix of Spanish and English. "He says that he must do these things to entertain the god. That is what is called a ritual, and only if he performs rituals can the god be entertained. If the shaman says that he is tired, or if he says that no one asks him to perform a ritual and he does nothing, then the god gets bored and grows angry. He pesters the shaman to play with him. Then the shaman grows very ill."

"This god is obviously Satan," Ignacio concluded. Had it been a few hundred years ago, he would have had to call a clergyman specializing in exorcism from Mexico City. But it was no longer that age. One last time, Ignacio urged the shaman to convert. He held out a cross and a Bible and told him to swear on them. The shaman shook his head in frustration. "Did I not tell you that I cannot do that?" Ignacio took a whip from the overseer Joaquín. Gwon Yongjun received his fee from the overseer and left the storehouse. As he lingered outside, he heard the sound of the wet whip striking the shaman's bare body as he lay on a pile of henequen leaves, and he heard the hacendado shout. Gwon Yongjun thought, I am sick of those dimwitted people! He gave some of the money he had received to his Mayan driver. The driver's mouth dropped open. The carriage sped off toward Yazche hacienda. Of course Gwon Yongjun knew that just as it was no sin to be born a man, so it was no sin to live as a shaman. The shaman's only sin was that he had landed in this hacienda. And now the shaman was tied hand and foot in the storehouse and beaten nearly to death. The trunks and thorns of the henequen kept him conscious whenever he was about to pass out. Finally, as his spirit was about to leave him, those who were hitting him grew tired, and when they stopped to rest the shaman's eyes rolled back in his head and he began to mutter at Ignacio. "When the wind blows from the west, the sun will be hidden even at midday. When the flames move and the sound of thunder is heard, death will come quick. Death!"

That was both a curse and a prophecy. Yet there was not a single person in the storehouse who understood it. When this Cassandra of the Yucatán foamed at the mouth and passed out, Ignacio and the overseers locked the doors of the storehouse, went home, and threw themselves on their beds.

# 44

A FORTNIGHT AFTER meeting with the diplomat Durham Stevens, Yun Chiho, the Korean vice minister of foreign affairs, found a telegram from Seoul awaiting him at the front desk of the Imperial Hotel: "Depart for Hawaii and Mexico. 1,000 yen sent to the Bank of Japan. Seoul." He began to prepare for his trip, but Stevens, who came to visit him at the hotel, told him 1,000 yen was only $500 — barely enough to travel to Hawaii, let alone Mexico. Yun Chiho's face turned red from shame at his government's miserable funds, but he was not deeply troubled. "They'll surely send more."

Two days later, Yun Chiho boarded the *Manchuria* in Yokohama. His heart fluttered at the thought of a new journey, but it was also heavy. Hawaii, Mexico . . . it was his first time traveling to both, and this was not a lighthearted trip but a mission to check on the immigrants and resolve their problems. At four in the afternoon, the ship's whistle sounded. Oba Kanichi, of the Continental Colonization Company, came up on deck and tried to curry favor with Yun Chiho. Though Yun Chiho had always disliked Oba, a typical peddler, he had no choice but to deal with him. Oba launched into a defense of his company. "The reports concerning Mexico are all mistaken. The immigrants are doing fine. The Continental Company is opposed to Korean emigration to Hawaii, but we welcome emigration to Mexico. We have Japanese already working in Hawaii, which might make things difficult, but there are almost no Japanese in Mexico, so we foresee no problems there. If you can correct the erroneous rumors about what has happened in the Yucatán, the company will take care of all your travel expenses."

Yun Chiho bristled: Does everyone want to pay the travel expenses of an official of a poor nation? Yet there was clearly some truth hidden in Oba Kanichi's words: even though emigration to Mexico was extremely profitable, the company did not send Japanese there. This alone was enough for him to know that conditions in Mexico were much worse than in Hawaii. Oba was offering a trade: if Yun Chiho returned from Hawaii and Mexico and spoke well of them to the emperor, he would resume sending laborers.

On September 8, 1905, Yun Chiho arrived at the port of Honolulu and met with Governor Robert Carter and Japanese consul Saito Miki. At eight o'clock that evening he met eighty Koreans in a Baptist church. They all cried: they could not have imagined that such a high-ranking official would come to see them. A few days later, Saito met with Yun Chiho again, requesting that he pick up the $242 that had arrived for him at the bank. This was for his travel expenses for the trip to the Yucatán, sent from Seoul. The travel agency told him that the round-trip boat fare was $360. Yun Chiho went to the post office himself and sent a telegram to Seoul. The telegram read: "$300 more needed to go to Mexico." The telegram cost $18.48. That afternoon, he left Honolulu to meet with the Koreans who were spread out among the various islands.

For twenty-five days, until October 3 of that year, he visited thirty-two sugar plantations and gave forty-one speeches before some five thousand Koreans. He vigorously threw himself at the task. He scolded the lazy, soothed the diligent, and preached to them to believe in Christ. The conditions on the Hawaiian plantations he visited were relatively good; when Hawaii was incorporated into the United States in 1898, the bond slavery system was abolished, so Koreans could move freely between plantations. Many Christians and intellectuals could be found among the immigrants, though they did not adjust well to plantation life. Those who had never farmed went to the cities, like Honolulu, to start businesses and study. Young women back home had agreed to marry men based only on their photographs, and boarded ships to become the brides of men they were meeting for the first time in their lives. From what Yun Chiho saw, there were few problems with the Hawaiian plantations. The work was tiring and difficult, but as a Baptist, he considered labor a blessing from God. The only problems were with those Koreans who had fallen into a debauched life of alcohol and gambling. Here was an opportunity for Yun Chiho to strengthen his convictions about enlightenment. He firmly believed it was his duty to awaken these ignorant and immoral people. The Hawaiian plantation owners enthusiastically welcomed this attitude. They fought with each other to bring Yun Chiho to their plantations, and as time went on he began to seem like a hired lecturer. After his speeches, in which he told the Koreans to work hard, have faith, never fight, never gamble, and never drink, a sudden change would come for a few days. But the non-Christian Koreans quickly went back to their old ways, and the laborers grew derisive of Yun Chiho, who came wearing his black suit and white shirt with empty hands, only to scold them as he rode around all day in the plantation owners' carriages. "He should work like us for a day," some Koreans muttered. They had no reason to be pleased to see him.

Yun Chiho returned to Honolulu and checked for messages from Seoul, but there were none. Did he really have to go all the way to Mexico? He was already tired in both body and spirit from touring the Hawaiian plantations, which were all quite similar. And he didn't have the money. So Yun Chiho boarded the *Manchuria* and headed back to Yokohama.

In Tokyo, he received an imperial grant of 600 yen from the Korean legation. The emperor still wanted him to go to Mexico. Yun Chiho sent a telegram to the Ministry of Foreign Affairs: "Round-trip fare from Japan to Mexico will be 1,164 yen, a hotel will be 400 yen, for a total of 1,564 yen, but the 490 yen I received previously and the grant of 600 yen total 1,090, leaving me 474 short." He was depressed about having to do petty arithmetic with the imperial grant.

The next day, October 19, Yun Chiho met a slightly haggard Durham Stevens in the lobby of the Imperial Hotel. Stevens bit down on a cigarette and looked around. "There are a lot of Koreans who are threatening to kill me. But I am not concerned. Koreans don't have the courage." Everyone now knew that Stevens was actively supporting the interests of Japan, openly declaring that Koreans did not have the ability to rule themselves.

Yun Chiho emphasized the importance of his going to Mexico, but Stevens showed a completely different attitude from when they had last met. He spoke candidly: "I sent a telegram to Seoul saying that you must not be sent to Mexico." Yun Chiho asked why. Stevens flashed a smile. "The Japanese minister Hayashi and I distrust the emperor. Do you think he is trying to send you to Mexico because he pities his people? Hardly. The emperor wants to let everyone know that he wields independent diplomatic authority. If you were to act as the Korean consul to Mexico while you were there" — he smiled quickly again — "that would be a problem."

Yun Chiho made no reply. Perhaps Stevens was right: it had been a long time since Korea had been treated as a nation anywhere. The Straight-Forward Society was constantly urging the government to hand over full diplomatic authority to Japan. Yun Chiho sent another telegram: "Fare to Mexico has not arrived. Request permission to return to Korea."

On November 2, Yun Chiho left Tokyo. After four days at sea, he arrived at the port of Busan; from there he took the newly opened Seoul–Busan Railway. He arrived in Seoul shortly before midnight. On November 8, he had an audience with the emperor. The emperor asked his minister how far he had traveled and where he was living, but there was no strength in his voice. The emperor looked fatigued. Yun Chiho didn't mention Hawaii, let alone Mexico. Disappointed, he withdrew. The next day, the Japanese ambassador extraordinary, Ito Hirobumi, arrived in Korea. With the fate of the nation and the dynasty in Ito's hands, the Mexico problem was the least of the emperor's concerns.

On November 17, Minister of Foreign Affairs Bak Jesun and the Japanese minister Hayashi Gonsuke signed the Second Korea-Japan Treaty, also known as the Protectorate Treaty of 1905, which handed over diplomatic authority to Japan and reduced the Korean Empire to a Japanese tributary. Yun Chiho resigned his position as vice minister of foreign affairs.

# 45

FATHER PAUL WAITED for the shaman all night, but he did not return. When dawn broke, a number of people gathered at Father Paul's paja. Choe Seongil calmly lay in bed, pretending not to notice. Children ran in and said that the shaman was locked in the storehouse and had been whipped all night until he had passed out. "What did that interpreter son of a bitch do, anyway?" someone shouted, enraged. "They said he just took his money, got into the carriage, and went back to his hacienda." "Son of a bitch!" The men clenched their fists. The women began to denounce the hacendado, who had trampled on their ritual. "At this rate, we won't be able to perform any rituals at all. It's bad enough that we were deceived into coming here. Are they going to beat us senseless as well?" Several women fell to the ground and wailed. The gathering soon turned into a strike.

Choe Seongil got up, lit a cigarette, and quietly left the paja. Father Paul spoke to the group, haltingly at first, but once he started he grew so impassioned that he surprised even himself. It was almost as if someone were borrowing his body to speak through him. "We came to this place to earn money, not to be whipped. We came to this place because we were hungry, not because we wanted to become the dogs of some mad hacendado. He *is* mad — mad for religion and starving for blood. Let us go and teach him a lesson!"

People armed themselves with machetes and stones. The overseers, who had approached on their horses, figured out what was going on and fled. Now everyone gathered, including the women and children, and ran first to the storehouse where the shaman was. When stones flew and the storehouse windows broke, those who had been guarding the building fled. The men thrust open the doors and ran in. The shaman was asleep, still in chains. When they woke him up he stared at them in wonder. His face was empty, as if he had no idea what had happened. His naked body, striped with wounds like snakes, looked like a captured wild boar.

The crowd grew aggressive. Like a genie released from its lamp, they sought a victim. "Let's beat those overseers to death!" someone shouted. They went to an overseer's house nearby. Dozens of stones rained down noisily, breaking the windows. Joaquín, infamous as an evil overseer, more hot-tempered and rough than any of the others though merely twenty years old, boarded up the doors and windows and stayed inside his house. As the baptism of stones continued, he was so seized by fear that he dared not even breathe loudly. "He might have a gun," someone said, but the fear this conjured up only stoked the men's belligerence. To hide the fact that they were scared, the men attacked Joaquín's brick house like fiends. A few young men ran forward and kicked the front door. "Come out, you bastard!" The heavy door didn't budge. A few more climbed up onto the roof and began to tear off the roof tiles. When a hole appeared in the ceiling, the men shouted and threw the roof tiles into the house. A scream followed, and then Joaquín unbolted the door and ran from the house like a badger from his burrow. With every ounce of his strength, he fled to the hacendado's house. A stone hit him square on the back of the head, but he seemed not to notice. The massive door of the great house did not open to his pathetic cries, so he ran toward the front gate of the hacienda.

Seventy Koreans had congregated before the hacendado's house, which, having endured one hundred years of Mayan riots, stood more like a castle.

Rifle barrels poked out of the loopholes near the top of the wall. Shots rang out. "Sons of bitches!" The Koreans cowered and ran in all directions like a pack of rats. The sound of gunfire pierced the dawn, echoing through the hacienda. A short while later, mounted police raced through the front gate in a clamor of horses' hooves. At that moment, the hacendado's front door opened and the overseers rode out firing their guns, with Ignacio Velásquez in the lead. The mounted police struck the fleeing people with their clubs, seeking their next prey as soon as one had fallen. The hacendado and his overseers sealed the entrance of the hacienda and cut off the Koreans' escape. Those who had fled to the pajas were eventually surrounded and dragged out one by one. Those who had been struck on the shoulders or back by the clubs of the police were the lucky ones, though they bled from where they were hit. Father Paul was one. Unable to open his eyes from the blood that ran down into them, he was dragged before Ignacio. "This is wrong!" he cried to the hacendado, making the sign of the cross. "This is wrong! Has the God you believe in not taught that we should side with those who are most shabbily clothed, those who are poorest, those who are most oppressed? Has he not?" The only reply he received was a clubbing. No one at Buena Vista hacienda understood Father Paul's words that dawn. Even the Koreans did not understand. To them, Father Paul had been Mr. Bak. This Mr. Bak did not bend beneath the clubs but stood up with indignation and began to pray before Ignacio and his overseers in the Latin he had learned at the seminary in Penang: the Lord's Prayer, the Doxology, the Hail Mary, and the Apostles' Creed. He thought he had forgotten them long ago, but they all flowed freely from his lips. If there was a God, he would grant him dignity as his priest. Now more than ever, he needed God's power and miracles. A strange Mass began. A few of the overseers unconsciously made the sign of the cross every time Paul shouted "amen." But the hacendado resolved the confusion: "Look, Satan defiles the words of the Lord! The power of demons borrows his mouth to recite sacred prayers!"

In Ignacio's eyes, this man — from a savage land in the Far East, wearing torn clothes that showed his knees and shabby straw shoes, his hair unwashed for a month and seething with lice, fluently reciting prayers in Latin and pretending to be a priest — truly appeared to be the soldier of Satan. At Ignacio's words, a baptism of clubs poured down on Paul. He fell, catching a glimpse of Choe Seongil, who stood behind Ignacio, pointing directly at Paul.

In that moment, Paul realized that his God was without doubt a jealous God. God had shown no power whatsoever in this fight, which had begun with a shaman. Though he knew that these people suffered for all the sins committed by Korea, Japan, and Mexico, God was as jealous as a sulky little girl. Father Paul closed his eyes. No one would ever again call him Paul. He was no longer Father Paul. He was Mr. Bak, Bak Gwangsu.

# 46

AFTER EVERYTHING HAD calmed down, Ignacio Velásquez returned to his study, knelt on a satin floor cushion, and prayed. "Lord, why do you give me such trials? How can I bring your gospel to those ignorant people? Father, give me the strength and the courage to not submit to pain, and give me the wisdom to not fall to the temptations and wiles of Satan." In no time at all, hot tears flowed from Ignacio's eyes. His sympathy and compassion welled up for those poor people, those who refused to see his heart's desire to lead them to heaven.

When his fervent prayer ended, a servant brought him coffee. Ignacio smoked a Monte Cristo. When the servant held a spittoon in front of his face, he spit out thick phlegm with a practiced motion. Usually, the coffee and cigar — the former made by the Mayans of Guatemala and the latter by the blacks of Cuba — brought him joy. But the excitement at dawn had not yet faded. In particular, the sight of the one who had challenged him, and recited through madness those sacred Latin prayers, remained strong in his mind. He had never heard a single story like this from his grandmother, his grandfather, or all his many aunts. It was certainly difficult to fathom the mysterious powers of Satan. He shivered and crossed himself.

# 47

AT YAZCHE HACIENDA, they had no idea a riot had taken place at Buena Vista. Gwon Yongjun kept his mouth closed; he did not want any trouble at Yazche until the day he returned to Korea. During the harvest moon festival, the Koreans of Yazche assembled and performed their ancestral rituals. Yi Jongdo transcribed the written prayer and offered an interpretation of the complex rites. The festival was a traditional farmers' holiday, so Yi Jongdo, who came from an old family of Seoul aristocrats, had no particular interest in it, but he was the first to bow in greeting as a representative of all. This was the natural duty of a Confucian scholar, and no one was as well versed in complicated Confucian procedures as he. His face brightened slightly for the first time in weeks at being able to confirm that his existence had some meaning. The ancestral rituals stirred up nostalgia. Those from peasant families, who placed great importance on the harvest moon festival, were already growing red at the corners of their eyes after a few glasses of ceremonial liquor.

Gwon Yongjun did not participate in these rituals. He had separated himself as far from the hacienda's Koreans as possible. The way he saw it, the Koreans would lounge around as soon as the overseers looked the other way, so there was no choice but the whip. He was thinking like a hacendado and acting like the aristocrats of Korea. They didn't like to work but they liked to give orders, and they struck and scorned the weak as if it were second nature. But they bowed their heads without delay to the strong. The aristocrats who had swaggered down Seoul's Bell Street, going in and out of the gisaeng houses, were the only example he had, so it was natural for him to act like this. He had received the hacendado's permission and brought in a Mayan woman to keep his house, but at every opportunity he pestered other women. He lay down on his bed and fondled the Mayan woman's breasts, thinking of Yeonsu and eating corn.

When the ancestral rituals were over, the topic of conversation among the people shifted to Yi Jongdo's letter. Yi Jongdo cleared his throat a few times and said that he had finished the letter and it would be sent soon. He added that they should not expect much of it, but he could not prevent their hopes from taking wing and soaring to the heavens. "A reply should come in three or four months, shouldn't it?" someone said. "Maybe the government has already sent an official." Hope spread rapidly through Yazche hacienda, the hope that this letter would be sent and a diplomatic official would be dispatched who, after seeing their situation, would strongly protest to the Mexican government and the governor of Yucatán. It would be revealed that the contract was not binding, and the workers would be sent home. Some expressed the hope that Japan would handle the matter instead of the Korean Empire, but they were reproached by the others and immediately withdrew their opinions.

Yi Jongdo returned home and gave the sealed letter to Jinu. "There are three letters. I wrote more than one because one might be misplaced. Give these to the interpreter and have him go to Mérida and send them." Yi Jinu took the letters and went to Gwon

Yongjun's house. The Mayan woman stared blankly at him; she was naked. Gwon Yongjun took the letters. "Is this that letter?" The boy nodded, but his eyes strayed to the woman's breasts. "Very well, I will go to Mérida and mail these myself. Life on the hacienda was too much for an aristocrat of such high status as your father anyway. And the hacendados of the Yucatán will have gotten their money's worth from the Koreans by now, so they shouldn't have too much to complain about. Don't worry, you can go back now."

The next day, Gwon Yongjun rode a carriage into Mérida. He ate a pork dish at a Chinese restaurant in an alley in Mérida's southern market. His stomach full and his spirits high, he enjoyed the sunshine in the park that faced city hall and the cathedral. He looked around the cathedral. He admired the Baroque façade, which was completely different from the architecture he had seen in Seoul, and then went inside. Begun in 1561 and completed in 1598, the cathedral was built on a Mayan ruin, with stones taken from Mayan temples, but Gwon Yongjun had no way of knowing this. He was only impressed by the walls, so thick and strong that he wondered if it had once been a fortress. The stained-glass windows turned the intense Yucatán sunlight into brilliant colors and lit the dark interior. The cathedral, built during the colonial period, expressed the abnormal lust for power of Spanish politicians and clergy; it was far too large for the city of Mérida. Gwon Yongjun was exposed to that lust for power without any filters whatsoever. To him, the cathedral's majestic size and splendid height were its clearest aesthetic message. The feminine charm of Korean temples that bowed low on mountain slopes felt like a symbol of weakness and servility.

He walked north along the city's central road and found himself in front of another church. It was a Jesuit church built in 1618 for the order's missionary and educational work in the Yucatán. Ignacio Velásquez's ancestor José Velásquez had met his comrades here. Yet he drew a line between himself and the Jesuits, who had turned toward their peaceful work as he waged war on the native religions of the Mayans. Gwon Yongjun sat on a bench in Hidalgo Park, across from the Jesuit church. The Grand Hotel, along the south end of the park, tempted travelers with its magnificent exterior. On the hotel's sign was written in large letters that it had opened in 1902. Gwon Yongjun counted on his fingers. It was a brand-new hotel, only three years old. Being a hotelier in Mérida wouldn't be bad. If one had the money.

A university and high school were located next to the Jesuit church, and dozens of students were chattering in the small school-yard. When one of them stepped up on a raised platform and began to speak, applause poured out. With his limited Spanish, Gwon Yongjun had difficulty following the speech, but because he heard the name of President Porfirio Díaz a number of times, and because of the heated tone of the speaker, he had no doubt that the subject was politics. People flocked to the square, and the usually dull city center of Mérida was suddenly transformed into something like a market swarming with hundreds of people. The speaker did not seem to be of the lower class — judging by his speech, his sharp suit, and his hairstyle. He looked like a successful bourgeois or a hacendado. His polished shoes shone dazzlingly in the sunlight. Students and citizens listened attentively to his words and shouted and clapped with every sentence.

As the speech reached it climax, mounted police galloped past the bench where the interpreter sat. A few carriages followed, clattering over the cobblestones. Decorated with gold and jewels, these magnificent carriages turned north and the mounted police split into two groups, one continuing to escort the carriages and the other swooping down on the meeting. The square soon became bedlam. The crowd, comprised primarily of men, scattered into the web-like alleys of Mérida. The mounted police blew their whistles and secured the area, but they did not pursue the crowd any further.

Gwon Yongjun approached a street vendor and asked, "What on earth is going on?" The vendor replied indifferently as he swept the ground: "According to the new law, it is illegal for ten or more people to assemble. Going to church is the only exception. Isn't that ridiculous? The old dictator is shaking. What does he think would happen in this backwater town?" Gwon Yongjun asked, "What were those carriages?" "Those were the carriages of the governor of Yucatán. He's scared stiff as well."

Gwon Yongjun had an ominous premonition about the future of Mexico — from the mounted police's uneasiness as they suppressed the crowd, from the sarcastic shouts of the students, and from the faces of those who took part, so full of conviction. No, this country might not last long. He returned to the bench and drew from his leather bag the letters that Yi Jongdo had taken such pains to write over a number of days. He read them slowly. After the formal salutations, including apologies for being such a dull-witted fellow to trouble the emperor's spirit, there followed tale after tale of the woes his people suffered in Mexico. Yi Jongdo wrote that he would gladly take responsibility for his mistaken judgment. But he could not bear to look upon the suffering of ignorant people. He begged the emperor to have mercy on them and rescue them. Gwon Yongjun snorted. Aristocrats like this were precisely the reason that Korea had fallen. This Yi Jongdo had never once lifted a machete with his own hand, yet when he opened his mouth he was quite convincing. How much did he really know of suffering? All he did was sit in his house and recite the sayings of Confucius and Mencius!

Gwon Yongjun took out a match and set the three letters on fire. The flames leaped up and swallowed the paper in an instant. The ashes scattered with the wind around Hidalgo Park. He returned to the hacienda with a refreshed spirit, telling Yi Jinu that he had sent the letters, so he should not worry. He didn't forget to warn him that it might take a full three months for a reply to arrive, given Mexico's inferior postal system.

# 48

IJEONG AND YEONSU'S MEETINGS continued night after night. Perhaps they believed that the darkness of the lightless fields would hide them. Their trysts grew bolder. The first person to notice was Lady Yun, who was suspicious when her daughter came in each night drenched with dew. "Where on earth have you been?" Yeonsu shut her mouth tight and made no reply. Lady Yun did not directly tell her daughter what to do. "You can't get married here, you know. It is most important to exercise restraint. The life of a woman is to endure, to endure, and to endure some more." For the first time in her life, Yeonsu opened her eyes, looked straight at her mother, and asked, "Then what will you do, Mother? Will you keep me here in this house and make me a kitchen ghost?" Lady Yun spoke firmly. "We must go back." "Where?" "What do you mean, where? Korea, of course. We will go back to Korea and have a proper wedding for you." Yeonsu scoffed, "Do you really think we will be able to go back?" Lady Yun did not waver. "If I know nothing else, it is that the royal palace will do everything possible."

"Do you know whom I meet every night?" Yeonsu struck back boldly. Lady Yun covered her ears and shook her head. "I don't want to hear it. So please, don't say anything. Just be ready to go back." Yeonsu got up and paced back and forth in the house. "Think," her mother said. "If you want to be scorned by even the lowly people of the hacienda, then you do as you wish. But, my daughter, you cannot hide anywhere. Everyone is watching you."

This was the truth. Yeonsu was far too conspicuous to hide quietly and enjoy a secret affair. She was the tallest of the Korean women, and her round, thick cheeks, her high nose, and her neat eyebrows left such a deep impression that even when she appeared to draw water from the hacienda cenote, all eyes were focused on her. And the scent of roe deer blood emanating from her left a far more powerful impression than her looks. So there was no way that the acts of two young people in the brush every night would not be found out.

Jinu was also aware of his elder sister's trysts. The rumor went around and around and finally reached him. He noticed his sister's jar when she returned from the cenote. It should have been sloshing with water, but it was empty. Why did it have to be an orphan, who was no different from a beggar? Why couldn't it have been Gwon Yongjun? Then everyone would have been happy. He stood in his sister's way as she tried to slip out of the house at night. Yi Jongdo, who had no idea what was going on, opened his eyes wide. "What is going on?" Jinu stepped aside. "It's nothing." Yi Jongdo cleared his throat and lectured him. "Even between siblings there must be a separation between the sexes." Yeonsu gave up on going to draw water and sat sewing in the stuffy house, kept under watch in turn by Lady Yun and by Jinu. Her needle pierced her flesh a few times. Dark red drops of blood fell on her sleeve.

The overseer Fernando and Gwon Yongjun followed Ijeong after he finished the day's work. Pushing his cart along the rail tracks and suffering from too little sleep after waiting all night for Yeonsu in the brush, he looked haggard. When he had handed over his bundles of henequen to the paymaster in front of the storehouse,

Gwon Yongjun asked Ijeong to come to the office. "The work seems to be too hard for you," Gwon Yongjun said to him. Ijeong told him that it was not. Fernando stared intently at Ijeong and said something in Spanish that Ijeong could not understand. He did hear the word "hacienda" a few times and had a bad feeling about it. Gwon Yongjun smiled and interpreted Fernando's words. "Don't worry. You're going to a better place. Although it is a bit far from here."

"That makes no sense. I haven't been here for that long, have I?" Gwon Yongjun took the contract that Fernando was holding and showed it to him. Of course, Ijeong could not read a document crammed with Spanish. "That is up to the hacendado for at least four years. Have a nice trip. A carriage is waiting outside, so you can board it immediately." Ijeong glanced outside and saw a driver stroking the mane of a gray horse. "I need to stop by my house to get my things." Gwon Yongjun shook his head. "What things? Just get in the carriage. You'll have everything you need where you're going. Those clothes of yours that even a beggar wouldn't wear? We'll send them later."

"Am I going alone?" Gwon Yongjun nodded. Ijeong shot up from his seat and tried to dash outside, but Fernando, who had been waiting by the door, caught him by the waist. A few foremen and overseers put Ijeong in the carriage and bound his legs with shackles. Ijeong continued to struggle after he was caught; his arms and legs were scraped. "Young people have no manners." Gwon Yongjun struck Ijeong on the back with a club. The workers who had submitted their henequen bundles for inspection by the paymaster and were returning to their houses could only stare blankly. One of them remarked, coldly and resentfully, "Serves him right for chasing women when he's still wet behind the ears."

Just as the carriage with Ijeong aboard was passing the boundary of the hacienda, Dolseok let out a shout and ran toward it. In his hand was a wrapping cloth that held Ijeong's clothes and belongings. "I came to give you this." Ijeong took the bundle and gave Dolseok a firm handshake. Who knew when they would see each other again? Ijeong said, "You must tell her. Wherever I go, I will surely return, and I will take her with me."

Dolseok, who could not pass beyond the edge of the hacienda, stood beneath the limestone arch that served as a front gate and waved until Ijeong disappeared from sight. The carriage rattled for two hours and let Ijeong off at the entrance to another hacienda. A few workers had come out to greet Ijeong and take him in. They told him where he was. The name of the hacienda was Chenché, and the hacendado was Don Carlos Menem.

# 49

DON CARLOS MENEM was not at the hacienda. He was meeting with his friends in Mexico City, talking about the political situation. What had begun as a denunciation of the so-called Científicos, who talked only of science whenever they opened their mouths, had led to criticism of President Porfirio Díaz's excessively pro-American policies. Menem shook the ashes from his pipe into an ashtray and raised his voice. "Those fellows mention Auguste Comte at the end of every statement, but what would that blasted old man know about the reality of Mexico? They are all busy feeding their bellies, those cunning fiends. Only conscientious people like us suffer."

A young man who stood by with a cup of Darjeeling tea in his hand smiled down at Menem and said sarcastically, "Will the laborers at your henequen hacienda feel the same way?" Menem did not hesitate for a second before replying. "Of course! There is no hacendado in the Yucatán as benevolent as I. And what about your sugar cane hacienda?" The young man shrugged. "No matter how well we treat them, there are limits. We are not Spanish aristocracy, we are but Mexican businessmen. If we cannot make a profit, we must close up shop. Thus we cannot help but urge on lazy workers. Think about it: the neighboring haciendas bring in Chinese coolies no different from beggars, work them, and then sell their products at a low price in the United States, so what hacendado in his right mind would not do the same? In the end it is all about competition, is it not? And we must also compete with the darkies of Cuba and Dominica."

"That is precisely the logic of Díaz, of his Científicos! Competition, competition, competition!" A middle-aged gentleman with a red beard leaped into the fray, his face turning red, too. The young man gave the English porcelain cup with the Darjeeling tea to a servant and smiled at him. "So what of it? We are all hacendados. We all want to bring in cheap laborers from the Philippines or Canton if we have the chance. No, this has nothing at all to do with our preferences. Even if we don't want to, we have to. Like getting our hair cut!" No one laughed.

"Your premise itself is flawed." A woman who until then had sat quietly and listened carefully to the men speak opened her mouth. "Porfirio Díaz tells us to cultivate sugar cane, henequen, and chicle, even if we have to import laborers. As you all know well, he draws in foreign capital and allows foreigners to manage the haciendas." Menem agreed. "That's right. American hacendados have entered the Yucatán as well. Those damned Yankees!" The woman continued: "He says that haciendas are vital to Mexico, but that is a lie. Sure, the Americans are in favor of them. They grow cheap agricultural products in Mexico, pack them up at the port of Veracruz, and sell them at a higher price in Europe. And in the process, owners of vast haciendas as large as the Netherlands or Belgium, and the Científicos of Mexico City, earn a fortune. In the end, only America and Díaz's people earn money while the rest of us gasp for breath. What Mexico needs is not haciendas, it is democracy."

Menem was fascinated by both her charm and her speaking ability. Who knew that such a powerful poison could come from those beautiful lips? But such poison was sweet to him. "That's right, Lady Elvira. What we need is not haciendas, it is democracy. But this is impossible with Díaz. You would all agree to that?" Those seated around the study all nodded. But their gazes were filled with distrust for each other. Democracy instead of haciendas? They knew better than anyone else that there was not a single person in Mexico who could achieve this. It was either more haciendas or more power!

"Hmm, very well." Lady Elvira rose from her seat. "Then there are some people I would like to introduce to you. You can all come here next week, no?"

Groups opposing the dictator gradually began to appear.

# 50

WHILE MENEM WAS FREQUENTING the anti-government salons of Mexico City, taking care of both his love life and politics at once, the Chenché overseer Álvaro took the place of the graceful hacendado and played the role of the villain. He confined the Ulleung Island fisherman Choe Chuntaek, who had been caught trying to escape, in the hacienda jail and had him whipped. He referred to the agreement between Menem and the Koreans that he would provide corn and tortillas free of charge yet deal severely with escapees, but the flogging inflicted on Choe Chuntaek was overly cruel. The last riot erupted because of the hacienda store, but this time it was because of the whipping. The working conditions worsened drastically while the hacendado was gone. Before, all work had ended when the sun set, but now they had to work overtime at the henequen hemp mill until late in the evening — and for the same pay.

No one knew why the cowardly old bachelor Choe Chuntaek had tried to escape. No one knew where he would have gone if he had escaped. He did not know a single word of Spanish. He had insisted that his fellow Koreans must not learn Spanish, that if they learned Spanish they would not be able to return to their homeland. When asked why, he repeated the same words, as if frustrated with the questioner. "I'm telling you we just can't. If we learn Spanish we will forget our own language, and then how will we go back?" He carried on continuously in the Ulleung Island dialect, which other Koreans had a hard time understanding, and if a foreman called his name, he pretended not to hear. When his work was finished and the paymaster asked him, "Cuántos son?," how many henequen leaves he had cut, he merely held up his fingers to indicate the number, never letting the Spanish numbers that he knew pass his lips. He chose a moonless night, waited until everyone was fast asleep, took the small amount of money he had saved, and climbed over the hacienda fence. He was discovered by a sharp-eared Mayan guard and caught before he could get far.

The retired soldiers met once again. Jo Jangyun, the Deva King Kim Seokcheol, the half-pint Seo Gijung, and the reticent sharpshooter Bak Jeonghun called the men together one day before the break of dawn. The whalers and peasants from Pohang made up the main force. There was also Ijeong, who had arrived the night before. He was not in the mood to participate in any struggle, but he was also not the type to hide at home sizing up a situation. He was glad to have finally been reunited with Jo Jangyun and the soldiers, and the talk of the fight they were planning to carry out stirred his hot blood. His rage at the hacendados, selling them all like dogs and pigs, suppressed his desire to give in to despair and plunged him into this new situation. Once again, the men armed themselves with machetes and picked up stones and put them in their pockets in advance. Ijeong was given a machete as well. Just in case, they decided to divide themselves into three groups, each led by experienced soldiers. The aristocrats, who did not want to fight, were left out. Women and children were told to stay at home. With a great cry, the men ran toward the hacienda jail where Choe Chuntaek was being held. The guards out front were demoralized and fled. The men broke down the door and rescued Choe Chuntaek, but he had already lost his senses and collapsed. Enraged even more at seeing him this way, they thronged toward Don Carlos Menem's house, as they had done the last time. Yet the overseers and foremen who were gathered at the house were not as yielding as they had been the last time. They immediately went on the counterattack, firing their long rifles. Bullets grazed a few of the Koreans' arms and thighs. It was still before sunrise, so they could not tell exactly where the bullets came from. The other side aimed at the torches the men carried, until they had no choice but to douse the torches and retreat. A few of them threw stones, but there was no way they could storm the high wall of the house. As soon as the Koreans began to retreat, the foremen and Mayan guards led by Álvaro all leaped out with a shout. The sound of gunfire, like corn popping, rang in their ears. With their escape cut off a number of times, the mob fled toward the storehouse and jail where Choe Chuntaek had been confined. "Damn it, we're completely trapped!" Jo Jangyun and Kim Seokcheol blocked the storehouse door with the chairs and desks from inside and put wooden boards up over the windows, building a barricade. Jo Jangyun said, "Since it has come to this, let us make our stand here. If they kill us, it will only be their loss as our buyers, so I don't think they will fire at us indiscriminately. We're better off here. If we hold out for only a few days, their loss will be great, so they will ultimately try to negotiate with us."

The standoff began uneasily. Outside, Álvaro continued to fire his gun into the air and threaten them. It was best for him to resolve the situation before his master returned. In his eyes, Menem was nothing more than a political aspirant who knew nothing of the ways of the world. Thanks to his attempt to curry favor last time by promising to provide corn and tortillas free of charge, the hacienda's finances were already leaning toward the red. This time, before Menem returned from Mexico City, Álvaro had to break the spirit of those Koreans. Yet the Koreans had barricaded themselves in the storehouse and were preparing for a long fight. Of course they had no food or water, so they were not likely to last long. Still, Álvaro became anxious. Fatigue washed over him and his body grew hot. He asked the foremen for their opinions. "Shall we go in?" They all shook their heads. Despite the fact that they were armed, no one wanted to raid a storehouse teeming with eighty men wielding machetes.

# 51

THREE DAYS PASSED. A few of Álvaro's bullets pierced the barricade, and the enraged soldiers threw stones out the windows, managing to hit one of the foremen on the shin, but both sides grew weary of the long standoff. Thirst was the biggest problem for the Koreans trapped inside. The soldiers urged the men on in order to prevent desertion, but a few of them had said they were seeing things and waved their hands about. Their annoyance with each other was causing dissension in their ranks. The sunshine was cruelly hot, and the inside of the limestone storehouse was above 100 degrees. They began to show signs of dehydration, and some of them were already in a serious state. Outside, Álvaro guzzled cool water to provoke them. "Should we surrender?" A group of peasants in a corner were tearing their clothes. When Jo Jangyun asked what they were doing, they did not reply. When he asked again, they said curtly that they were making a white flag.

Just then someone shouted for quiet. Everyone stopped talking. Then came the rumbling sound of thunder followed by the patter of raindrops. It was a rainstorm, a rare sight in the Yucatán. The storm poured down in buckets. The sound of cheering rang out in the storehouse. Men climbed up onto the rafters on the shoulders of others and tore away the roof. The rain soaked them through the wide-open hole. They held their mouths open to the torrent. Ijeong thought of a secret meeting on a rainy day and Yeonsu's body as steam rose from it. Some thought of Korea's wet season, others thought of a neighbor's melons on a rainy day, and still others thought of their mothers. All of them were things they would never find in the Yucatán.

When their thirst was quenched, the Koreans laughed and joked with each other. "Hey, this is even better, since we don't have to work and can just relax!" someone shouted. There were those who chimed in, "That's right, that's right, this is better." Yet behind that hearty laughter, they were all uneasy. "What if," said a whaler from Pohang, "they send all of us away?" All of their faces stiffened. There were those who tried to comfort him, saying that such a thing would never happen. But what would they do if the angry hacendado really did say, "I don't need any of you, go away"? Someone else asked, "How much is it to get back to Korea?" No one knew. Ijeong said, "I heard at another hacienda; they said it was about one hundred pesos."

Silence filled the storehouse. One hundred pesos? No one had so much as ten pesos, let alone a hundred. Even if they had the money, the thought of going back to Jemulpo empty-handed was dreadful. After all the suffering since February, were they supposed to go back with only their cracked hands, their diseased skin, and their sun-blackened faces?

"Let's get out of here." The farmers stood up. The soldiers blocked their way. "If we go out now, we are finished. We only have to hold on a little longer." "Did you not see what happened to Choe Chuntaek?" said a middle-aged farmer. "All we have to do is not run away." Kim Seokcheol grabbed the farmer by his throat. The others pulled him off the man. "If we do not show strength, they will despise us! Now they only beat those who run away, but later the whip will fly if we are even the slightest bit lazy." The argument grew threatening. "You bastards!" The farmers raised their machetes high. The soldiers aimed their blades low. Those between them screeched like startled monkeys. The mood was so ugly that it would not have been the least bit strange had something horrible happened right then.

A single mosquito relieved the tension. A few weeks before the incident, this mosquito, which had hatched in a puddle near the cenote, followed the scent of humans and flew toward the hacienda. She drank the blood of a few people, laid her eggs, and died. One of those people was Álvaro. The overseer was pacing back and forth with his rifle raised high, watching the movements of the enemy, when he suddenly began to waver and then collapsed with a thud. Ijeong had been watching these events through a crack in the window and reported this to the others. The foremen ran over to Álvaro and carried him away. "It's heat stroke," someone said. "I don't think so," said another. "It's not like he's never seen this sunshine before. And he was wearing a hat, too." There were a number of opinions, but no one knew the exact reason. The siege had been ended, and when night came the Koreans went back to their homes. Jo Jangyun suggested that they take turns standing guard, and the others agreed. Yet there was no movement that night. And when four o'clock in the morning came, no bell was rung. The men, who had starved for three days, wolfed down tortillas all night long. Only when the sun had risen halfway into the sky did they hear from the Mayans that Álvaro had caught malaria, had a high fever, and was on the brink of death.

Ijeong sought out Jo Jangyun as he stood guard at the break of dawn. Ijeong's expression was dark, but his body was fully tense, like a gamecock preparing to fight. "I have something to say." Jo Jangyun asked, "What is it?" Ijeong said, "I plan to escape from this place tonight." Jo Jangyun opened his eyes wide in surprise.

"The work is hard for all of us," he said. "It's not because the work is hard," Ijeong said. "Then what is it?" "I do not like being sold here and there like a dog or a pig." "So you will run away? What if you are shot? Didn't you see Choe Chuntaek?" "They are confused as well, so they will not know what is going on. Now is the best time." "What will you do after you've run away? You don't speak Spanish." "I will learn. I learned Japanese, so why shouldn't I be able to learn Spanish?" "You'll learn it — you'll learn it and do what?" Jo Jangyun said. "I will go far away and start a business." "With what money? And you know that when they find out that you have run away, things will go badly for us. The hacendado will bring it up in his negotiations." "Still, you have to help me," said Ijeong. "Why?" "You gave me my name, didn't you?" "Fine, but if you are caught, I will claim to know nothing of this. If you don't think you can make it out there, come back. We'll speak to the hacendado for you. You can work to make up for the time that you ran away."

Ijeong went back to his room and plotted his escape. Jo Jangyun gave him 5 pesos and said, "Pay me back if your business is suc-

cessful." Álvaro was taken to the hospital in Mérida that afternoon.
Then Menem returned, almost as if a baton had been passed. The
Koreans continued to refuse to go out to work. They saved up food
and prepared for a long fight. This time as well, Menem trusted far
too much in his own diplomatic abilities and proposed negotiations.
He called Gwon Yongjun from Yazche hacienda and met with Jo
Jangyun and the other strike representatives. Menem promised to
stop the whipping, which had been the start of the problem. But
he vowed that if someone escaped, the remaining Koreans would
have to pay damages for the breach of contract. The Koreans readily agreed. But Jo Jangyun, Kim Seokcheol, Seo Gijung, and the
other retired soldiers brought up another issue. "How much do we
have to pay if we want to leave the hacienda before our contract is
up? Please tell us the precise amount." This was a new negotiating
condition that the Koreans had thought of during the several days
they were trapped inside the storehouse. Menem left to consult with
his lawyer and then returned. "Under no circumstances will you be
able to leave the hacienda before two years is up. But after that, you
will be able to leave if you pay one hundred pesos. I promise."

The strikers insisted that one hundred pesos was too much. After persistent negotiations, the amount was decided upon: eighty
pesos. They readily agreed to the two-year minimum because they
knew that it would not be easy to save eighty pesos in two years. Kim
Seokcheol mumbled, "Eighty pesos to be free, another one hundred pesos for boat fare back to Korea — when are we supposed to
earn that?" But at any rate, the reduction of four years to two was
hopeful. They were buoyed by the thought that they might be free
of this henequen hacienda more quickly if they did well. The promise of early freedom was not a losing prospect for Menem either, because it raised their desire to work. Furthermore, it was not such a
bad deal to work them for two years and receive eighty pesos; there

was no guarantee that he would receive more than that if he were to sell them to another hacienda at that time.

Thus ended the strike that had kept the hacienda tense for several days. A few days later, Álvaro's body was returned to the hacienda. The Koreans all lined up and attended his funeral. A few of the men shed tears in front of the body of the overseer who had tormented them nearly to death. To Menem, this was truly a strange sight. Even spitting on his grave would not have been enough to ease their bitterness, yet the Koreans had showed him the ultimate respect. Menem called to Jo Jangyun and asked him, "Why are you crying?" Jo Jangyun answered quietly, "That is our custom. We cry when someone dies. Then we drink liquor and eat pork and watch over the corpse all night long. This is because we believe that only then will the ghost not seek to do us harm." Gwon Yongjun interpreted "to do harm" as "to take revenge." Menem shrugged and said, "How is a dead person going to take revenge?" On that day, he gave the Koreans liquor and pork for the first time. In no time, two pigs were reduced to bones. The Koreans laughed and chattered and drank next to the coffin of the wicked overseer Álvaro, and a few of them gambled. The solemn funeral was transformed into a raucous, party-like atmosphere. A few of the Koreans got drunk, some scuffled with each other, someone sang a folk song.

Late that night, Menem came out and saw this. He thought he had been duped and was displeased. "No, this is normal," said Gwon Yongjun. "In Korea, this is also part of a funeral. They make a clamor so that the deceased and the surviving relatives are not too grieved. They sing and play silly games. They did not like Álvaro, but these are the only funeral customs they know, so they are just playing them out. Please let them be, at least for today."

As the watch on the hacienda relaxed with the settlement of the strike and the mood grew chaotic with Álvaro's funeral, Ijeong climbed over the hacienda's steel fence. He looked at the stars and headed northwest toward Mérida. The rough bushes repeatedly scraped his calves. He stumbled in a deep hole and fell over. He did not rest but kept walking, knowing that he had to flee as far as possible before the sun rose. He had not gone far when he grew thirsty, but he had no way of finding water. Only two hours after he left, regret began to rise. The morning star, which stood a handbreadth above the horizon, was telling him that this was his last chance to turn back. Ijeong paced back and forth for a while, and when the sun rose faintly in the distance he began to walk northwest again. It's already too late. Just as when he had boarded the *Ilford* at Jemulpo, he felt both unease and excitement.

# 52

No flowers were seen for two months. Yi Yeonsu chewed her fingernails. Her father was waiting for Emperor Gojong's letter, and her younger brother studied Spanish unceasingly. Jinu followed the overseers around and picked up a word here and a word there. Lady Yun was focused on the problem of how to hang herself. She had entered menopause in Mexico. Perhaps it had been the rapid change of climate. Their reasons were different, but the two women of that one household stopped regular ovulation at nearly the same time, and they suffered for it. Lady Yun lost her appetite and thought only of suicide. The depression triggered by the change in her hormones seriously shook her being. Yet suicide would not be easy. There were days when she went as far as thinking that if she were raped, at least there would be no place where she could hide from the shame and no possibility of recovery, so it would be easier to make the decision.

Yeonsu never considered anything like suicide. She believed that Ijeong would return. But before he returned, her stomach would swell and the child would be born. How could he be there and not here? She put aside her grief, calmly soothed her mind, and set about finding a way to contact him. Yet no matter how hard she thought, there was no way except through that disgusting interpreter. And there was no way that she could venture an escape to Chenché hacienda by herself without knowing the way.

When it becomes known that I am pregnant, Mother may end her own life out of shame. Before that happens, Father and my brother will give me a knife and urge me to commit suicide. "End it cleanly. Aside from this, there is no other way to wash away the dishonor." Jinu himself might stab me in the heart with a knife and then claim it was suicide. The others would accept his words as they have always done. That would be the easiest solution for everyone.

One night, when those who had returned from the henequen fields were asleep and the small groups who had been drinking hard liquor were snoring, she quietly got up from her bed and went to Gwon Yongjun's house. A Mayan woman sat outside the door smoking a cigarette. Yeonsu smiled obsequiously at this woman who did not speak her language, to let her know that she had no intention of taking her man away. The woman absent-mindedly avoided her gaze, as if she were not concerned with anything like that, and looked only at the stars strewn across the sky. From her cigarette wafted a strong fragrance like burning sagebrush.

Yeonsu opened the door and went inside. Gwon Yongjun shot up in his bed in surprise. Without even dressing himself properly, he hastily pushed aside the mosquito net and got down from the bed. Unlike the way she had dealt with the Mayan woman, Yeonsu faced him standing straight. Thus she seemed much taller than Gwon Yongjun, and she overwhelmed him psychologically as well.

From that dignified pose, which she had learned growing up, it was difficult to imagine her as a girl who would roll around in the brush with a young man her own age. "What is it?" Yeonsu bit her lip. Her lips opened only enough for a single ant to crawl through them. She had made a difficult decision, but now that she had come to it, it was not easy. The words that would say she was pregnant and needed to find the father, the words that would ask for help, refused to pass her lips. Gwon Yongjun himself was desperately trying to think of why she had come to see him. Could it be because of money? It could be. That thoughtless young man alone earns the money, yet there are four of them. Are not her once plump cheeks sunken, her once pretty skin pale? He took the lead and asked this girl, who had straightened her back and pulled in her chin but could not bear to bring up what she had to say, "Is it money?" She said nothing. Myriad thoughts flew through his head. He suddenly realized why she was here, why she had approached him in the middle of the night, standing so aloof and yet so restless. He waited until she said it for herself. After a long silence, after deliberating for a long time in confusion, she finally opened her mouth.

"If you help me, I will not forget your kindness."

# PART TWO

*A year passed.*

*Then two years passed.*

*Some died, some escaped.*

# 53

IT WAS MAY AGAIN, three years that month since they had first set foot in Mexico, but not many people talked about that. The labor went quietly and simply, like a closed monastery where a vow of silence had been taken. After a number of strikes and riots, the hacendados and the immigrants learned how to get what they wanted from each other without resorting to serious threats. The hacendados accepted that the Koreans were different from the Mayans. From the Rio Grande to Cape Horn, they were the only Koreans in all of Latin America, so their solidarity had to be strong. Furthermore, their core was comprised of soldiers, intellectuals, and city dwellers, so they had a relatively high level of literacy and knowledge. Whipping did not work with them. For their part, the immigrants no longer antagonized those who ran the haciendas. This was not because they understood what it meant for hundreds of small and medium-size haciendas to be jumbled together, but because they knew there was nothing more to be gained from the hacendados. It was also because they had come to the painful realization, through a number of attempted lawsuits, that all the institutions and laws of the Yucatán were favorable to the hacendados. For this reason, the immigrants worked like seasoned soldiers about to be discharged.

They counted each and every day, but they obediently did all that was required of them, dreaming of the outside world.

Some of the more restless workers had already paid the hacendados eighty to one hundred pesos and walked away. Most of these went to Mérida or Mexico City and found manual labor, but a few of them were determined to return to Korea. Gwon Yongjun was one of them. More and more people were learning Spanish, decreasing his value as an interpreter, and since he had earned enough money, he did not particularly want to stay in the sweltering Yucatán.

"Look here, I have to go back," Gwon Yongjun said as he ate a tortilla laden with cabbage kimchi. A girl who was gently rocking a baby in a hamaca turned to look at him as if she had just been burned. "How could you do that?" Gwon Yongjun's expression showed that he had expected this reaction from Yi Yeonsu. "How? Even a fox dies with its head turned toward the place where it was born, so what is so strange about saying I'm going back to my native land? Come with me if you want." Gwon Yongjun pushed the kimchi tortilla into his mouth.

"Ijeong will come back. He'll come back and be a proper father," Gwon Yongjun said slyly. The Mayan woman came in and neatly folded the laundry she had taken off the clothesline. A brief silence fell. Yeonsu had known that such a day would come, but she had not known it would come this fast. She lifted the child from the hamaca. The netting left checkered marks on his bare bottom. He looked at Yeonsu and his lips moved slightly. "Omma." Yeonsu held him to her. Gwon Yongjun lay down with his head on the Mayan woman's thigh and said, "You have no cause to scowl at me. I'm not the one who did you wrong, am I? He'll come back next year. If he can avoid the police, the bandits, and the hacendados, that is." He smacked his lips. "Ah, there are so many things I want to eat, I can't bear it. I'm going back."

"I can't go." Yeonsu hugged the child hard. Gwon Yongjun flashed a smile. "You have to go. Do you plan on starving to death here? Who will feed you? Your parents? Your brother?"

Yeonsu took the child and went outside. She could not think. After she had had relations with Gwon Yongjun, she had not been terribly surprised or flustered by anything again, but this was different. It seemed as if she had aged many years at once. The Gwon Yongjun she had known until now could not be called an evil person, but neither could he be called a good person. At first he liked her, and he treated her more luxuriously than was necessary for the privilege of embracing a young daughter of the royal family. When her stomach swelled, he even told a lie for her that no one would believe. No one openly contradicted it.

"He's sleeping with two women," people would mutter behind his back. The women at the cenote expressed their open scorn for the girl who had fallen from being the only daughter of a literati to being the concubine of an interpreter. If she picked up an item of clothing that had fallen from a woman's laundry basket and returned it, the woman would wash it again. Her child did not get along with the other children. It was her first child, so her milk did not come easily, but when she went looking for a wet nurse, they turned their heads. Only the Mayan woman with whom she lived, Maria, offered her breast. A strange friendship grew between these two women who lived with one man. Maria's mammary glands swelled on the day Yeonsu gave birth. Before Yeonsu's first milk came out, Maria happily fed her milk to the newborn, who had a distinct Mongolian spot on his buttocks. She might have been thinking of her own two children, who died young. They, too, were born with spots on their buttocks, proving that they were the descendants of those who had crossed the frozen Bering Strait so long ago. Maria handed the child over to Yeonsu whenever she wanted him, even if Maria was feeding him. If Yeonsu handled the child clumsily, she brusquely took the child and cared for him.

Yeonsu brought the child to her parents' house. The door to the house was open. Lady Yun, in a dragging skirt, was fanning herself out front. "Mother," Yeonsu said. Without replying, Lady Yun turned on her heel, went inside, and pulled the door shut by its flimsy handle. From inside came the sound of Yi Jongdo reading aloud, then stopping, apparently wondering why the door had been closed. Perhaps he realized why, for he began to read again right away. Mother, Father, I may be going back. Her lips moved slightly, but she could not say the words.

Her family had no intention of accepting her. One year after they had arrived at the hacienda, her younger brother was recognized for his fluency in Spanish and sold to a hacienda with no interpreter. Lady Yun's depression grew worse, and she attempted suicide regularly, but she failed every time. Yi Jongdo had given up all hope of being rescued. It had been two years since the hacienda managers had begun visiting Mérida once a month and bringing back bundles of letters from Korea in their carriages, but there was no word from his noble cousin who sat on the throne. Instead, he heard the news that Yi Jun, the emperor's secret envoy, had applied for a seat at the International Peace Conference in The Hague, but was rejected and committed hara-kiri. He learned that Prime Minister Yi Wanyong, acting for Japan, forced Gojong to abdicate the throne, and at this the people set fire to Yi Wanyong's house. He learned that the army of the Korean Empire had its last disbanding ceremony at its training center. He learned that Gojong yielded his throne to his son. At all this news, Yi Jongdo dressed himself in clean clothes, bowed toward the west, and wept in sorrow. He blamed himself for having so rashly resented the powerless emperor. Thoughts of his daughter, pregnant out of wedlock and now concubine to an interpreter, never once entered his mind. He lamented the plight of the native land he had left behind on the other side of the world and confined himself to his house, agonizing over how to drive off Japan and build a strong and prosperous nation. Then he began to write down the results of this agonizing on paper. Of course, these were nothing more than idealistic arguments that had little relation to reality. There was no one who did not ridicule him as he bowed toward the west in the morning and shut himself in to establish the framework for a new nation in the evening. The immigrants had hung a shadow of hope on his letter to Gojong, and now they lamented their stupidity, counted the days, and thought only of living from one week to the next.

Without another word to her family, Yeonsu returned to Gwon Yongjun's house. She said, "I will go with you." Gwon Yongjun nodded, as if he had known she would come around. "You made the right decision. There is no other way." He was already packing his things. "But I will leave the child behind," she added. Gwon Yongjun was stuffing something into a bundle and he opened his eyes wide. "What? Leave the child? Why?"

She spoke boldly. "I want to start anew. When we return to Korea, send me to school. We have the money, don't we? The child is a nuisance." Gwon Yongjun didn't seem to object to the idea. "Then what shall we do with the child?" She answered as if she had been waiting for the question, "We will leave him with Maria. She likes Seobi." Gwon Yongjun grinned. "Well, we can do that if you like."

He called to Maria, who was hanging laundry outside. He told her that they were leaving the child to her and gave her money. Maria stared blankly at Yeonsu and simply nodded her head. She did not seem sad, but then she did not seem particularly happy either. Yeonsu took Maria's large hand and expressed her thanks. Then she caressed her toddler son Seobi's forehead and cried.

"So now I only have to pay off your contract." As if to once again establish his ownership of her, Gwon Yongjun grabbed Yeonsu's waist as she cried. She turned away from him and he pressed his lower body against her. Maria got up, took Seobi, and went outside. Yeonsu grabbed the oak table with both hands, and received him as he slowly pushed into her flesh. Though it was their first coupling in a long time, her body opened surprisingly easily. He glanced down absent-mindedly at his genitals, going in and out between the folds of her skirt, and continued his mechanical, repetitive motion. A short while later, Seobi toddled into the room and stared vacantly at his stepfather's face. Maria followed him in, embraced Seobi, and looked at the man and woman bent over the table. Yeonsu smiled at Maria; Maria smiled back. Then she went out again. Gwon Yongjun made a serene face and ejaculated. In the moment that his penis slipped out and his semen trickled out of her, she felt as if everything over the past few years were pouring out of her. This daydream made her careless, and before she knew it, she farted very loudly. Both of them were startled by this unexpected commotion. Gwon Yongjun giggled and fell down on the bed, and Yeonsu fell on top of him and covered her face. Gwon Yongjun slapped Yeonsu's buttocks. At that, she farted again. It put her strangely at ease. Her wearisome relationship with him felt like a farce. Something that had been pulled so tight inside that it felt as if she would snap had now loosened. For the first time, she giggled and fully enjoyed the comedy of her own flesh. Gwon Yongjun called to Maria. She lay down between them and fondled Gwon Yongjun's limp penis. The three of them looked like an affectionate family.

# 54

THE MEXICAN DICTATOR Díaz, during a press conference with the American *Pearson's Magazine,* announced that he had made sufficient efforts for the modernization and economic growth of Mexico, and it was now time to hand his position over to a successor, if only because of physical debility. "I welcome the emergence of an opposition party in the Republic of Mexico. If an opposition party emerges, I will not consider it a sin but a blessing . . . I have no plans to continue my presidency . . . I am seventy-seven years old, and this is enough."

He expected that when he made the announcement that he would not seek reelection, cries of "Please reconsider!" would sweep the whole of Mexico like wildfire. Yet the result was the exact opposite. He had opened a Pandora's box. Liberals around the nation rallied around Francisco Madero. In no time, Madero emerged as a political opponent of Díaz. There were even those in the ruling party who took Díaz's words at face value. The fight for succession grew fierce. Díaz reflected on his error of trusting too much in the people and immediately went into action. He ordered his henchmen to organize a movement to oppose his decision not to seek reelection. Then he cruelly oppressed any and all attempts to make good on his announcement not to run for the presidency.

People soon figured out the dictator's intentions, but political ambitions had already been set free. Politicians like Aquiles Serdán were not cowed by this oppression. Serdán led the way in the struggle to oppose Díaz's reelection. He organized a liberal club called Light and Reform, basing his activities in his hometown of Puebla. He attended the joint party convention of the Anti-Reelectionists, gladly casting a vote to nominate Francisco Madero as a presidential candidate.

## 55

AMONG THE RETIRED soldiers at Chenché hacienda, Kim Seokcheol and Seo Gijung paid to be released. As soon as they had enough money, they went to Don Carlos Menem, handed over their 80 pesos, and became free men. They went to Mérida and rented a small house together. The house was much smaller than their paja at Chenché, but it was incomparably more comfortable. They could wander about as they pleased, and there was a market nearby that was far cheaper than the hacienda store. They were particularly delighted to discover a Chinese restaurant and grocery, where they bought soy sauce and other ingredients so they could cook dishes similar to those in Korea.

"I feel strange," said Kim Seokcheol as he loafed around in their room. "We could sleep for the whole day and there is no one to say anything." Seo Gijung chided him: "Surely you don't miss the hacienda, do you?" Kim Seokcheol waved his hand. "No, of course not."

But their bodies were far too familiar with the rhythm of a henequen hacienda to easily deny it. In Mérida they still woke up at four o'clock. When they dressed and went outside, the light in the cathedral's belfry was looking down on them. The money they brought with them gradually dwindled, and there weren't that many ways to earn more in Mérida. "Maybe we should just go back to Korea." But they didn't have the money to do that. Even if they had had enough to travel, they would be just as hard-pressed to make a living when they returned.

Jo Jangyun stayed at the hacienda for the time being. During the

course of a few strikes, he lived up to his reputation as the workers'
representative of Chenché. "I can't leave," he would say, but the
truth was that something was writhing inside him. He already understood that many Koreans would ultimately have no choice but to
remain in Mexico. If that was so, there would be a need for an organization to rally the Koreans scattered across the country. Now we
may be contract laborers at the haciendas, shackled as bond slaves,
but next year will be different. Jo Jangyun naturally began to imagine himself as the head of this organization. Is not this a place where
there is no discrimination between high and low? It had been long
since the few aristocrats at each hacienda had been reduced to pari-
ahs. There was no way that those who could not properly handle a
single task entrusted to them could secure political hegemony. Unlike them, Jo Jangyun had learned how to organize groups and had
acquired leadership skills and a strong will in the Russian-style new
military. Or maybe he was born that way: when his mother carried
him in her womb, she dreamt that a tiger with two heads had leaped
into the folds of her skirt. When he thought of it like that, his plans
grew bigger. Why should I not be able to form a righteous army organization here that would cross the border between Manchuria
and Hamgyeong province to attack and harass the Japanese army?
Our nation has long revered culture and scorned the military, so we
have come to this state of affairs. Mexico, where there were some
two hundred retired soldiers, was the perfect place to establish a
new independence army. Furthermore, there was no Japanese sur-
veillance here, so attempting this task would be even easier.

From then on, Jo Jangyun began to spread the philosophy of
"revering the military," which he himself had devised, to those
around him. The new nation that he imagined on that Yucatán hacienda would be ruled by a charismatic soldier or retired soldier,
and it would pour all its strength into building independent military

power. Under a universal conscription system, all citizens would have a duty to national defense. The press — he thought of those young scholars who wrote appeals to the emperor — would have to be subject to appropriate limitations. First, the military had to marshal all its strength to repel the surrounding strong nations, represented by Japan and Russia. Gojong's followers, who had relied on diplomacy, were utterly naïve.

The number of people who sympathized with Jo Jangyun's ideas grew. "When our contracts are finished and we leave the haciendas, let us collect money and found a school, one that reveres the military. And we will have to create an army." "And weapons?" "For the time being, we concentrate on an organization; the weapons will gradually come about somehow. Might not a war break out between the United States and Japan? If Japan is fighting Russia, there is no reason why they might not fight the United States. If that happens, the United States will give us weapons. Who knows the mountains and rivers of Hamgyeong and Pyeongan better than we do? We will return with dignity to our homeland as part of the American army and crush the Japanese. If we are to do this, however, we must organize the army in advance."

Jo Jangyun began to write down these ideas. Great beads of sweat dropped from his forehead and soaked the paper.

# 56

CHOE SEONGIL WAS in a good mood as he swayed on his horse and headed toward the henequen fields. He wore a stylish, broad-brimmed sombrero, and a leather whip was tucked in his saddle. The cross that he had snatched from Father Paul sparkled in the light on his exposed chest. Seen from afar, he looked every inch a native Mexican overseer. When he arrived at the henequen fields, the Koreans greeted him. He slowly circled the fields, barely acknowledging their greetings. The henequen leaves cut by the machetes helplessly fell to the ground. The women and children bound them. Everything looked peaceful.

From afar, Choe Seongil saw the shaman moving about with difficulty. He lightly prodded the horse's flanks with his spurs and trotted over to him. "Hey!" At Choe Seongil's call, the shaman took off his hat and looked up. His eyes were blinded by the sunlight and his face scrunched up as he squinted. "How are you doing? Are you handling it?" The shaman nodded his head. "Well, do a good job, otherwise you'll end up like Bak Gwangsu."

When Choe Seongil had gone, the shaman spit violently. Mr. Lee, who had been working beside him, came up to him and sympathized: "That bastard thief. That hacendado's bitch." The shaman looked up resentfully at the sky, empty of even a single speck of cloud. "I wonder if Mr. Bak has died," said Mr. Lee to no one in particular, as if talking to himself. "Well, whether he died from sickness or starved to death, one way or another he must be gone." Mr. Lee struck a henequen leaf hard in his rage. "They keep saying believe, believe, but that hacendado and that bastard thief shut him up in that hut just because he's sick, so who would want to believe what they believe? Even the grandmother goddess from our old neighborhood wouldn't do something like that."

When the day's work had ended and it grew dark, the shaman packed some corn pancakes and cabbage kimchi and secretly climbed over the hacienda wall. He walked thirty minutes to a ramshackle hut that was used for quarantining the sick. A stench wafted out from the hut, which was barely sturdy enough to withstand a stiff wind. "Hey, Mr. Bak." He went inside to find Bak Gwangsu Paul lying on a mat, sunken-eyed. The shaman slowly raised him, offered him food, and said, "Do you intend to die in a foreign land?" Bak Gwangsu shook his head to say that he wasn't hungry, but then he ate a bit of the cabbage kimchi. "What's that?" The shaman pointed at a small mound of earth in the field, and Bak Gwangsu laughed, saying, "Do you know what I did for the first time since I came here?" The shaman narrowed his eyes. "So you buried a dead body. But with what?" Bak Gwangsu lifted his hands and laughed weakly.

"You had no choice," the shaman said. "You couldn't very well sleep among rotting corpses." He looked blankly at Bak Gwangsu. "Still the same as always?" "Yes. I cannot do anything because I have no strength in my hands, and there is not a spot on my body that doesn't hurt, but then again it's not a fatal illness. I can't sleep at night. I see too many things. When I close my eyes, everything turns white. It feels like someone is gnawing away at my bones."

The shaman grimaced and closed his eyes. "That's why you need to listen to me. There is no other choice. I don't do this because I want to either. But there is no other way." Bak Gwangsu shook his head. "I cannot do that." But the shaman pressed him: "Why on earth can't you?" After a long silence, Bak Gwangsu opened his mouth. "I was a Catholic priest." There was little change in the shaman's expression; he didn't understand what difference that made. That put Bak Gwangsu at ease. The shaman said, "No one knows. The spirit just comes. You cannot resist him. You'll die. You have no choice but to receive him. The spirit says he wants to come in, so you have no choice, do you?"

The shaman left and Bak Gwangsu's suffering continued. When night fell, a woman came. She was not from Buena Vista hacienda. "Who are you?" The woman wordlessly prepared a table for him. She fried a yellow corvina and laid it on white rice. Next to that she put crunchy cabbage kimchi, red chili pepper paste, unripe chili peppers, pickled oysters, pickled clams, and steamed crab. Bak

Gwangsu glanced at the woman as he wolfed down the food. It was a table of which he could only have dreamt. He dug into the yellow corvina and grabbed a large, steaming chunk of its white flesh with his chopsticks. The woman went outside to boil water in the rice pot. He called out to her, "Mom?" The woman laughed and shook her head. "Do you not know me?" Bak Gwangsu, now full, slowly examined the woman's face. She set down the tray with the boiled rice water on it and sat quietly next to him. He gripped the woman's wrist; it was warm and comfortable, an indescribably pleasant feeling. He closed his eyes. Far away, he saw a single tree. "Let us meet there." He ran with all his might. From the great spirit tree, which grew clearer in the early dawn mist, something large hung and swayed, like a branch that had been struck and split by lightning. He realized what it was. Suddenly a pain like a squeezing of his limbs washed over him. Here was the woman who had hanged herself, the woman who had become a young widow at the age of twenty and who whirled about him every night. He did not understand. Early one morning, she had invited him to the entrance of a foggy village and showed him her corpse, though he had done nothing wrong. Had she waited, weaving her web, just to show him that? The absurdity of it took his breath away. It was like a trap that God had prepared to test and punish him. The judgment had already been handed down when he had succumbed to temptation. Perhaps everything that had happened after that was the tedious process of carrying out the judgment that had been handed down.

Time passed by again in a flash, and twelve spirits galloped on horseback into his hut, waving swords and flags. On another day, an old man appeared and fed him, but when he received the food he went up to heaven and shared it with the birds and beasts. Finally, the horrible shamaness from Gomso Ferry appeared, thundering, "It is no use to run away. I chose you not because I liked you, but

because I needed your body. Now I have come for it!" The religion
that had saved him when he fled from Gomso Ferry had no satis-
fying reply to a situation like this. At last, his eyes met those of the
woman who had hung like a fruit. He recoiled in fright and opened
his eyes. There was nothing in the dank and gloomy hut. No yellow
corvina, no beautiful woman.

A few days later, the shaman, with a few dozen others, came to
see Bak Gwangsu. To avoid being seen, they arrived after midnight.
They took a great risk to witness the curious sight of the shaman pre-
siding over the initiation ritual of another shaman. They had bribed
the Mayan guards and made sure that Choe Seongil was asleep.
They had also found out that Ignacio Velásquez had gone to Mérida
and was not returning that night. Many people from nearby haciendas, including several musicians, had heard about the ritual and
flocked to the hut. Among them was the eunuch Kim Okseon, who
had grown very gaunt over the past three years. He said he would
play the flute. Made from some unknown Mexican grass, his flute
produced a sound similar to that of a Korean flute. If one listened
closely, the high notes brought to mind a Korean small horn. Someone else brought a double-headed Mexican drum made of cowhide,
so it was a proper ritual to a certain extent.

The initiation took place in the yard in front of the hut, in the
middle of an abandoned wasteland where even henequen did not
grow. The land stretched out in all directions, with no mountains or
rivers, and the ritual lasted for over five hours. The musicians and
the shaman had never practiced together in their lives, but they performed in time with each other as if they had been a team all along.
The palace eunuch, the spirit-possessed shaman from Incheon,
and the leader of a folk percussion troupe from a mountain village
played the flute, danced, and beat the drum for the former priest.
The women, tired from their hard labor, surrendered themselves to

the familiar melody that ran through their veins and to the rhythm that was engraved on their bones. In an instant, the yard was swept up in a carnival-like frenzy that transcended nationality. Laughing and crying as if mad, the women danced and the men drank for the whole five hours. Bak Gwangsu lost his senses. Like one in a trance, he did what the shaman said, undressing if he was told to undress and dressing if he was told to dress, standing up when he was told to stand up and sitting down when he was told to sit down. At the end, the vision that came to Bak Gwangsu was, strangely enough, a white horse. The white horse galloped toward him from the distant horizon and swallowed him. He immediately came out again and rode the white horse, carrying a red flag and a white flag. And he shouted, "I am the white horse general!"

This was the spirit that the shamaness of Gomso Ferry had served. Suddenly, between visions, the groundless certainty that the shamaness of Gomso Ferry had finally died flashed into Bak Gwangsu's mind and then disappeared.

# 57

IT WAS LATE AT NIGHT by the time Gwon Yongjun and Yi Yeonsu arrived at the port of Veracruz. They found a room in an inn near the train station. Gwon Yongjun, who had so much luggage that he had to hire a porter, felt good at the thought of leaving this loathsome land. He was also happy to be taking Yeonsu with him. He went down to the bar on the first floor of the inn and drank rum. He offered some to Yeonsu, but she refused. He drank one glass after another. When the sailors next to him sang a song from their hometown, Gwon Yongjun sang a song from his. He bought them a bottle of rum and they applauded him.

Yeonsu helped him back to their room and he fell fast asleep. Yeonsu took off his clothes. She neatly folded his shirt and pants and put them in her pack, then threw his socks and shoes out the window. She took about 50 pesos from his pocket. The rest of the money he kept in a money belt strapped to his waist, so she couldn't take any of that. Still, Yeonsu had enough to return to Mérida and pay for her son Seobi's release. She quietly opened the door and went downstairs, going out through the side door of the bar where the sailors were chattering. She made her way down a dark alley and walked in a daze to the piers. She did not know when Gwon Yongjun might come after her. Her clothes were sure to catch people's eyes. And she didn't speak any Spanish.

Yeonsu sat down on a bench by the street. Her legs hurt. She felt dizzy and hungry. A night watchman carrying a lamp glared at the first woman from Korea he had ever seen. She forced her sore body to rise and continued to walk toward the nearest pier. A savory aroma flowed out of a small alley nearby. It was a familiar smell. She turned her head. A red lantern hung in front of a restaurant. On the lantern were written familiar characters: "Cantonese Restaurant." She pushed aside the red curtain before the door. Inside, an old Chinese man who looked as if he had once worn his hair in a pigtail, in the style of the Manchus, stared at her. Yeonsu could not understand his Chinese. In Chinese characters she wrote, "I'm hungry. Can I get something to eat?" They wrote back and forth for a moment and he disappeared. Soon he returned and served her hot rice and egg soup. She ate quickly, then a sudden fatigue washed over her. It was far too strong for her to resist. As soon as the owner came and cleared away the dishes, her head dropped onto the table.

As if in a dream, she saw a man moving violently on top of her. But she could not lift a finger. Then everything went black again.

Gwon Yongjun only realized what had happened when morning came. He was seized by rage and cursed his foolishness. She would go back to Yazche hacienda to find her son. Gwon Yongjun paid the innkeeper and called a tailor. When his suit was finished a few days later, he went to the train station and demanded a refund for his ticket. He was denied a refund. He hesitated for a moment. What good would it do to go back and kill her? He would spend the rest of his life in jail. And he wouldn't be able to drag her back with him. That vicious woman. He poured out every curse he knew, and then he carefully searched the piers and the area around the station, just in case she was still in Veracruz. A few people said they had seen an Asian woman walking about alone. But no one knew where she had gone. A few days later, Gwon Yongjun boarded the train alone.

He arrived in San Francisco and stayed a week. Boats to Yokohama were not frequent. A week was too long a time to spend in a harbor inn. Gwon Yongjun went to Chinatown. It looked as if one of the Chinese markets he had heard of from his father and older brothers had been transplanted to San Francisco. The streets were filled to the brim with old men who practiced augury based on birds, acupuncturists, vendors selling the feet of brown bears and the teeth of Siberian tigers, ducks tottering about with their legs tied to fire hydrants, and the smell of stir-fried vegetables and meat, the fragrant aroma of licorice root wafting from herb sellers' stands, and the nauseating scent of incense. As Gwon Yongjun ventured deeper into the alleyways, a feeling of tranquility seized him. A woman approached and grabbed his arm. She wore a fragrance that he had inhaled long ago. Men lay in rows, sucking on pipes with their heads turned languidly to the side. Opium. Gwon Yongjun took off his clothes. A woman washed him with hot water and laid him on a bed. Then she lit the opium and handed it to him. It was truly a simple affair. Without taking a boat to Yokohama, he could immediately return to his homeland. He met his father and mother, and he met his older brothers too. He could see Yeonsu slowly sucking on his penis, reassuring him that they made the right choice in leaving.

When he came to his senses, a toothless Chinese woman was kneeling and pouring tea. "Will you be going now?" she asked. Gwon Yongjun shook his head. Then he took a fistful of money from his pocket and gave it to her. "Let's do it again." The woman, whose feet had been bound when she was young, hurriedly shuffled out and returned with more opium. When Gwon Yongjun came to his senses again, the ship had departed. But he didn't mind. This type of life was as comfortable to him as an old shoe. For the first time in a long while he thought of the cruel military officer in his uniform and smiled vaguely.

When Yeonsu woke up she was not in the Chinese restaurant but in a large house. An old Chinese man she had never seen before took out a piece of paper and wrote that he needed a concubine to bear him a son. Yeonsu calmly wrote that she already had a husband and a son and was on her way to find them. The Chinese took out a document and showed it to her: it recorded in Chinese characters the sale of one woman, Yeonsu. The old man pushed some silk clothes toward her. But Yeonsu stubbornly shook her head.

The old man forced himself on Yeonsu every night. But not once did he succeed in taking her. On some nights, two women would come in and hold down Yeonsu's arms and legs. Even then the old Chinese could not enter her, and would collapse to the floor. The women beat Yeonsu until she was bruised and gave her tea when she woke. When Yeonsu drank the tea, she lost consciousness. It was like one long nightmare.

When she opened her eyes again she was in another Chinese

restaurant near the Veracruz piers. Her head hurt. The baggage she had brought with her was gone. A short, fat man stared at her when she woke. He laughed smugly and gave her Chinese women's clothing to wear. Then he held out another document. Unbeknownst to her, she had become indebted to this man for 100 pesos, and so would have to work for him. "What sort of country buys and sells people like this?" she wrote. "You must have been sold here like me once. This is not fair." At that, they took away the paper and pen and never gave her another. From that day on, Yeonsu worked all day in the kitchen and served food. It was a large restaurant. The owner's sons watched her so that she would not escape, and when night fell they locked the door to her room.

Most of the customers were Cantonese, and whenever they came they brought news. Through them, Yeonsu gradually learned about what was going on in the world. Her Cantonese improved more quickly than her Spanish. Seobi appeared before her eyes every night. She also wondered about Ijeong. Where might he be? She would have to return to the hacienda to find him, but she could come up with no way of leaving Veracruz. Gwon Yongjun was right: perhaps following him would have been the best thing to do. There were many days when she regretted her escape.

From time to time she even missed her younger brother, who had made a name for himself as a talented interpreter; her powerless father, who had spent years with his hand to his brow; and her mother, who suffered from depression and dreamed only of suicide. Thankfully, the restaurant owner, Jien, had no designs on her body. He seemed to have bought her without that in mind. But his wife, who had borne him many sons, never took her eyes off the attractive nineteen-year-old Korean maiden. Yeonsu made several failed attempts to escape. The Veracruz police caught her a number of times and returned her to Jien.

# 58

WAITING FOR IJEONG after his escape were heat, thirst, and yet more haciendas. It was a long way to the United States. It took money to get from the Yucatán to the northern border. He worked at haciendas here and there to earn money, and used that money to move forward. Contracts were for at least six months, and the conditions were better than they had been in the Yucatán. This was because there was no money to be paid in advance to brokers. Ijeong worked on chicle and sugar cane haciendas, and sometimes on henequen haciendas.

A few years later, he spread out a map of Mexico and calculated the speed at which he was advancing north. From Mérida to Ciudad Juárez, on the northern border, over four years he had gone 2,100 miles, which made it almost a mile and a half a day. During that time he met countless Mexicans. Life was pretty much the same everywhere: his people had been deluded to think that only the Koreans of the Yucatán were suffering. Petty farmers all across Mexico shared the same plight.

Every time he arrived at a hacienda he sent letters. Jo Jangyun at Chenché sent a reply from time to time. But there were no replies from Yeonsu. Dolseok, who was still living at Yazche, didn't know how to read. The amount of time that Ijeong spent writing letters gradually decreased. He began to wonder if his love had been betrayed. His doubts consumed him and he became a more cynical person.

Having finally reached Ciudad Juárez, across the Rio Grande from El Paso, he came up with a plan to cross into the United States. He was nothing more than a Mexican migrant worker with no entry visa. Crossing the border would be no easy task. He had to make doubly sure of everything. At one point he had procured from Jo Jangyun the address of an organization in Los Angeles called the Korean National Association of North America. As soon as he reached the border city, he sent a letter to them. A reply arrived immediately. They said that since the contracts for the Koreans in Mexico were nearing their end, they had been about to send two representatives to help resolve any legal problems. They would go straight to Ciudad Juárez, so he should wait there.

A month later, two men came to see Ijeong. One of them was Hwang Sayong and the other was Bang Hwajung. The two wore black suits and had their hair cut short, parted neatly and oiled. Bang Hwajung was an evangelist, and Hwang Sayong was in charge of affairs for the Korean National Association.

"The contracts end in one month, right?" asked Hwang Sayong. Ijeong was momentarily stunned. Had it been that long? "What is the situation like in the Yucatán?" asked Bang Hwajung.

"It's been over three years since I left, so I don't know what the situation is like now, but when we first arrived it was horrible beyond compare." Ijeong showed them his cracked hands. "This is life on the haciendas. It is not only a problem in the Yucatán. There is no hope in Mexico. Only the hacendados fill their bellies, while the rest of the citizens suffer from hunger and hard labor. The citizens of this country are suffering, so there is no room for foreigners like us to squeeze in. We came to the wrong place."

Ijeong looked at the map they had spread out. He marked Chenché hacienda, where Jo Jangyun was, and the haciendas where he himself had worked on his journey north. "You should meet Jo Jangyun first. Chenché hacienda is the biggest, and everyone follows him. But what is the United States like?"

Bang Hwajung said, "I don't think it is as bad as here. There is a shortage of workers in California, so the wages have gone up a lot.

But you will still have to live as a day laborer. A few of our brethren have opened small shops, but these are exceptions to the rule. If you have nothing special to do, how about returning with us to the Yucatán?"

"No. I must go to the United States." The twenty-year-old Ijeong spoke resolutely and offered them a drink. But they declined, being faithful Baptists. The next day, they set out on the long road to the Yucatán.

# 59

JO JANGYUN RECEIVED news from Kim Seokcheol and Seo Gijung, who had been released early and gone to Mérida, that the representatives of the Korean National Association had arrived in the port of Progreso. That day happened to be Sunday. As the representative of the Protestants on the hacienda, Jo Jangyun asked the overseer for permission for them to leave. The overseer secured his assurance that he would take responsibility for their return and then gave his permission. This was the normal weekly procedure when the Protestants gathered at a house in Mérida for worship, and at times as many as seventy or eighty of them attended from various haciendas. Ignacio Velásquez hated Protestantism as much as he hated shamanism, but since their contracts were about to expire anyway, he and the other hacendados allowed the Protestants to go out on Sunday as long as there was nothing else happening.

When Jo Jangyun went to Mérida, he found that Bang Hwajung and Hwang Sayong had already arrived. The people gathered there were glad to see the visitors, grabbing their hands and bemoaning their own plight. In their neat black suits, the two men looked strong, unlike the Koreans of the Yucatán. They left a deep impression when they spoke in fluent English with the American Baptist missionary who had come out to greet them. The Yucatán Koreans felt pitiful compared to them. Their faces were so blackened that they looked like Jamaican slaves, and their cracked hands looked like wood that had been sawed.

"What is the most pressing matter?" Bang Hwajung asked Jo Jangyun. Jo Jangyun spoke without hesitation: "First, that we receive the one hundred pesos in compensation that is due when our contracts expire." Hwang Sayong cut in, "Let's see the contract." Jo Jangyun and Kim Seokcheol handed him copies of their own contracts. It was only after some time that Hwang Sayong was able to find the sentence, written in small print, that said they would be paid one hundred pesos. "Good, let's give it a try. We will need to hire a lawyer." Jo Jangyun said, "We don't have that kind of money." Hwang Sayong laughed. "The money will come from the Korean National Association. In return, when you are released, you will all have to join and pay your dues." Everyone's faces grew brighter.

The next day, Bang Hwajung and Hwang Sayong went to the city hall, across the street from the cathedral, secured a list of registered lawyers, and hired one from a nearby office. With this lawyer, they sought out each of the hacendados who were trying to avoid paying the one hundred pesos and negotiated the matter.

A few days later, after Jo Jangyun had gone back to the hacienda, the Deva King, Kim Seokcheol, said, "There is another important problem." "What is that?" asked Bang Hwajung. Kim Seokcheol brought two Koreans to them. They called themselves Shin Bonggwon and Yang Gunbo. They had married Mayan women and had children; they asked to be able to bring their wives and children out from the haciendas with them. They said that there were many others in a similar position. Shin Bonggwon's wife had had three children during those four years. "My, you've been prolific," joked

Bang Hwajung, but they did not laugh. Bang Hwajung and Hwang Sayong never once thought the matter would be difficult or serious. They couldn't imagine that anyone would not be allowed to bring his family. They made up their minds to meet with the hacendados and settle the matter. "Who would be best to visit first?" Those who knew the situation in the Yucatán recommended Don Carlos Menem of Chenché hacienda.

Yet Don Carlos Menem was unexpectedly obstinate on the issue. It was not so much that his attitude was resolute; he just did not believe there was any need to discuss it. He simply laughed. "Children born on a hacienda belong to the hacendado. To whom does the woman belong? To me, the hacendado. Now this woman has a child. So to whom does it belong?" Bang Hwajung said, "In our country, we consider the child to belong to the father." Menem lit his cigar. "This is not your country. And would you be able to prove that he is really the father of that child? Do you know why a child is given the father's family name in all the countries of the world? Because only then will fathers believe that the children are theirs and feed, house, and raise them. The family name is the social answer to a father's mistrust. The only thing that is certain is that the mother gave birth to the child. On the haciendas here, the identity of the father is uncertain, unclear, and unnecessary. Go back and ask in Mérida. The law is on my side. The law does not like such vagaries."

Menem felt good about having driven off the unwanted guests, and the Koreans and their lawyer understood that there was no defeating the hacendados, at least not on this matter. The laws of the Yucatán and Mexico strongly supported Menem's claims. Furthermore, there was no hope in lodging a lawsuit in a place where all lawyers were hacendados. And on top of that, there was a special law known as the Hacienda Autonomy Act that granted hacendados broad discretionary power concerning anything that happened on their land. The married men had no choice but to part with the Mayan women; the children would be left behind on the hacienda and become the property of the hacendado.

Finally May arrived, and the contracts that had shackled the Koreans became meaningless scraps of paper. Three days before their release, a local branch of the Korean National Association of North America was established in Mérida. At that point the contract had not yet expired, so the various haciendas sent only about seventy representatives to Mérida. Those who had already been released and the hacienda representatives tearfully celebrated the birth of an organization it had taken four years to establish.

Jo Jangyun, who was chosen as the first president, stepped up onto a hastily built platform and gave a speech he had written long before. Considering the time he had spent preparing it, the speech was a little disappointing. He was interrupted a number of times, overcome with emotion, and he kept losing his place. But it still offered a sense of the mood that day:

> Today, the seventeenth of May, is the day on which the great organization known as the Korean National Association has formed a local Mérida branch. The representatives dispatched from each hacienda gather like clouds, like the various delegates who gathered at the Continental Congress in Washington, like the various representatives who gathered during the time of the French Revolution. How admirable, the establishment of the local Mérida branch! Though in days past we may have been scattered amongst the natives of this land with no organization, today we are the citizens of a civilized nation with our own organization, so why should we not celebrate twice and dance and make merry a hundred times? Let the prosperity of our National Association be an opportunity for the swift restoration of our native land.

Jo Jangyun's excitement was especially evident in the passage about American independence and the French Revolution, though he knew little about them. When the speech reached its climax, the young people who had been waiting impatiently beneath the platform lit fireworks. The fireworks, though lit hastily, emblazoned the sky above Mérida. Thus ended four years of bond slavery.

# 60

THE CONTRACTS MAY HAVE EXPIRED, but almost no one tried to return to Korea. Such was the destiny of those who owned no land. Whether because they didn't have the money to travel, or they had married Mayan women, or there was no way for them to make a living if they returned, they settled down in the Yucatán one by one.

Jo Jangyun founded his military school in Mérida and called it Sungmu ("revering the military") School. The soldiers of the Korean Empire from Pyongyang played pivotal roles at the school. Most of them had converted to the Baptist Church; they all tattooed their wrists with ink. They secured funds for the school through a credit union. On November 17, 1909, four years after the signing of the Protectorate Treaty, which bound Korea to Japan, they held a demonstration of traditional martial arts, during which Jo Jangyun declared the Protectorate Treaty null and void.

The next day, the 110 students of Sungmu School, organized into two platoons, all dressed in uniforms of white hats, white shirts, and black pants, wrapped themselves in black and red sashes, and paraded through the city streets. At Jo Jangyun's command, standard-bearers carrying the Korean and the Mexican flags took the lead, followed by buglers and a military band, then young people in straight ranks, and behind them the old and infirm. When the procession passed before city hall, the governor of the Yucatán came out and waved to them. They could not have felt more joy at their liberation. Dressed in clean clothes and marching down the central streets of Mérida, streets of which they had only dreamt, they were filled with pride.

Following this, a play was staged. Workers from the haciendas dressed up as Korean soldiers and Japanese soldiers and acted out a mock battle, a war skit in which they imitated even trumpets and cannonades. The Korean soldiers captured all of the Japanese soldiers alive, forcefully concluded a peace treaty, then received compensation for war damages. They cheered and shouted, "We won! We won!" Those who had been upset at briefly becoming Japanese soldiers were determined not to be outdone, and shouted even louder, "Long live Korea! Long live Korea!," celebrating their own scripted defeat.

# 61

ON AUGUST 16, 1910, the Korean Empire, which had clung to life like a plant to a rock, disappeared into history. Japan annexed it, and Resident General Terauchi Hisaichi was appointed Governor General. Suicides in protest of the annexation swept the nation. Resistance leaders like Yi Geunju and Kim Dohyeon, government officials like Yi Mando and Jang Taesu, and scholars like Hwang Hyeon, among others, ended their lives in a variety of ways.

The immigrants in Mexico had known little of affairs in their homeland, and so were shocked to hear that they no longer had a nation to which they could return. They took out the small pieces of paper that they had treasured as most precious. They had waited a month in Jemulpo harbor for these passports to be issued, and now, long since yellowed from the dry climate and their lives of wandering, they were useless.

# 62

BACK IN JANUARY 1910, an epidemic had raged across the Yucatán. Five people fell dead, including two newborns. Bang Hwajung and Hwang Sayong left Mérida and returned to the United States. As soon as Hwang Sayong reached Los Angeles, he was elected president of the Korean National Association of North America. In addition to his other responsibilities, he began to examine ways to solve the problems of the immigrants in Mexico at one stroke.

In September, Hwang Sayong left for Hawaii. He spent nine months touring the islands. He told the Koreans there of the horrible situation in the Yucatán and how much better off they were. Together they conceived a bold project to move all of the Yucatán Koreans to Hawaii in one group. They met with the Sugar Planters' Association and stated their intentions, and the plantation owners, who were suffering from a shortage of labor, willingly agreed. They volunteered to petition the U.S. government for permission for the workers to enter the country. The plantation owners and the Koreans drew up a plan to move one hundred people as soon as their entry was cleared. In the face of great travel expenses, the Koreans of Hawaii and the mainland demonstrated an amazing spirit of sacrifice, shouldering the entire burden and immediately soliciting contributions. In Hawaii they collected $5,441, and on the mainland they collected $536.

When most of the preparations were complete, the Korean National Association sent a letter to the Mérida branch inviting four representatives to Hawaii. Jo Jangyun, Kim Seokcheol, and two others headed for San Francisco. The four of them were not a little excited at the idea of treading the soil of the United States, a country they had only heard about. Kim Seokcheol, who had converted to Christianity not long before, kept mentioning the story of Moses, comparing their journey to the Exodus of the children of Israel from Egypt. The four felt a strong connection to the hot desert climate, the hard labor, the epidemics, the oppression, and the suffering described in the Bible. They also believed that God had finally forgiven their sins and begun the great work of their salvation. Bang Hwajung and Hwang Sayong were compared to the Old Testament prophets. Hawaii was the Promised Land flowing with milk and honey. According to Hwang Sayong, the climate in Hawaii was mild and the water abundant, so there was no thirst, and not only were the wages high but the cities were prosperous, and there were many opportunities for education.

# 63

Don Carlos Menem got off the train with his travel bag and walked into the station compound at Puebla. His servant José followed him with his luggage. A police officer approached Menem and saluted him, then he tapped the leather bag that José carried. "Let's have a look." José waited for Menem's instructions. When Menem nodded, José put the bag on a desk and opened it. Inside were Menem's neatly folded clothes and some books. "What books are these?" The policeman flipped through the pages. Menem stroked his mustache and answered, "Herodotus and Rousseau." The policeman nodded and stepped back. "Thank you for your cooperation."

Compared to the calm Menem, José was a little nervous. In

the station there seemed to be more policemen than passengers. As they walked beyond the barrier, José whispered to Menem, "I think they are on to us. It will be dangerous." Menem did not reply, and stood in front of the station, waiting for someone from Aquiles Serdán's household who was supposed to meet them. Anxious minutes passed, but no one appeared. "What should we do?" asked José. Menem took out his pocket watch. Already thirty minutes. This could not be. "Go see if there is a clean hotel near here, and if there is, bring a porter back with you." José ran off.

Menem had received Serdán's memo a week earlier, about two weeks after Francisco Madero had called for an armed rebellion while he was in San Antonio, Texas, and one week before he was supposed to rebel, on November 20. Both a passionate supporter of Madero and a friend of Menem, Aquiles Serdán had secretly returned to his base of operations in Puebla to prepare for the insurrection, and he had sent a memo to Menem urging him to join the cause. In the memo it was written that five hundred liberalists would gather at his house, a surprising number. Yet no one had come out to the train station.

A short while later, José returned with an old, bent porter. With one bag hoisted on his back and the other bag in his hand, the porter led the way to the hotel. José offered to carry a bag, but the porter refused his help. The hotel was small and cozy. The owner, who was in the lobby, seemed surprised at Menem's splendid appearance. "Sir, I see that you have come far." Menem nodded and discreetly asked the owner, "Has something happened here? There were police all over the station." The owner threw up his hands and began to talk. "You don't know? This morning the police chief raided Serdán's house. The two have always been bitter enemies, you know. He held out the search warrant and Serdán opened fire right then and there. Anyway, Serdán was a bit hasty. Even a fool could see he was assembling his forces, bringing in weapons every time the front gate opened. I hear that he disguised himself as a widow, but his costume was so poor that everyone knew. They all just pretended not to know. After all, he's an aristocrat and a wealthy man."

Menem took his room key and asked with feigned lack of interest, "So what happened?" The owner shook his head. "It was horrible. The police and the state army stormed the place and shot everyone dead. Serdán's entire family was massacred, including his younger brother Máximo, and the weapons that were piled in the storehouse were seized. The same went for the liberalists who had already arrived. So, anyway, will you be taking a meal?" Menem waved his hand. "I'm not very hungry. I think I will just go up and rest."

The next morning, there was a brief report in the newspaper on the slaughter at Serdán's house. Menem's hair stood on end. He called José, told him to pack his bags, and hurried to leave Puebla. "Where will you go, master?" José asked. "To San Antonio." José, his face white with fear, said, "Why would you go there? Is that not where Madero is?" "Tomorrow the history of Mexico will change, and I can't very well confine myself to the middle of nowhere in the Yucatán, can I? Return to the hacienda if you don't want to go." José looked as if he were about to cry, but he did not leave. They bought railway tickets for Mexico City, where they had to change trains to get to San Antonio.

When they had almost reached San Antonio, after an anxious two-day journey, the train suddenly stopped. They heard gunfire. A few armed troops came over a hill and met a counterattack by soldiers in uniform who were waiting for them. "Master, I have never seen such a ridiculous troop. Ah, they soon turn tail and run!" José chattered on, leaning out the window. Menem watched them as well. These might have been Madero's troops, coming from the northern border. "Pull your head back in! Do you want to get shot?" Menem grabbed José by the scruff of the neck and yanked him in. A passing attendant confirmed for him that Madero's troops had been defeated by the federal army and were now fleeing. The day of the uprising had finally come, but Madero's troops disappointed him. Menem wondered if he should just turn around right here, but he had gone this far so he collapsed into his seat. He stayed there until the train reached San Antonio.

Madero was anxiously considering strategy with his supporters at the Hutchinson Hotel. Menem sat at a distance and watched him. There was an air about Madero that only the noble-minded possessed. When he had finished his meeting and came out to the lobby for tea, Menem approached and greeted him. "We have met before, President Madero. I am Don Carlos Menem, from Mérida." Madero waved a hand. "I am not president. And I am sorry, but I do not remember you." Menem clutched at Madero as he turned away. "I am a friend of Aquiles Serdán. I have come straight from Puebla." Madero's expression changed. "Señor Menem, you have come a long way. Have some tea with me." Menem sat down and told him about the battle he had seen from the train. Madero laughed as if it were nothing. "My uncle's troops were supposed to come from Mexico, but they did not arrive. Thus my troops returned. But the mood elsewhere is intense. Especially in Chihuahua, the flame of revolution is blazing like wildfire. Wait and see. We will not forget Serdán's death. We have heard the news as well. It was truly horrible. So, what was it like there?"

Menem had originally intended to tell the truth. But a completely different story sprang from the mouth of this descendant of a French swindler. With tears streaming down, he related to Madero the great massacre that had taken place at the house as if he had seen it with his own eyes. Menem himself had fought heroically, but most of his comrades died gallantly in battle due to the snare laid by the cowardly police chief. He was so violently choked with tears when he related the deaths of Aquiles Serdán and his brother Máximo that Madero could only pat him on the shoulder. Before he knew it, Madero's staff and supporters had gathered around to hear of the great massacre at Serdán's house. Menem gradually grew more excited and continued his dramatic monologue.

"That's enough," Madero said with grief in his voice, cutting him off. He waved everyone away. Then he spoke quietly to Menem. "Do you believe in telepathy?" Menem hesitated for a moment at this unexpected question. "Well, I have heard of it." The presidential candidate Madero stared into space as he spoke: "I believe in it. The gods relay their messages to humanity through telepathy. This is what all of the revelations received by the prophets were, including those of Moses. Not long ago, an American named Bell invented the telephone, but that is far too limited a means of communication, nothing more than communication between two people. But telepathy is different. It is slowly being proven scientifically as well. If we want something strongly, we can convey it to someone, sometimes to many people. You may not believe this, but yesterday I received a telepathic message from Serdán." Madero put his hand on his chest. "It was such a heartbreaking thing. When I was young, a fortuneteller once revealed to me that I would be the president of Mexico. And to this day I have not doubted that even once. And now that revelation has become a telepathic message and is spreading all over Mexico. If that is not revolution, then what is?"

This talk of telepathy, coming from the lips of an intellectual who had studied for five years in Versailles and Paris and then studied agriculture in Berkeley in the United States before returning to Mexico, aroused misgivings in Menem's heart concerning the course of the revolution. A few days later, Menem returned to the Yucatán.

# 64

KIM IJEONG, WHO HAD been living in secret in the state of Chihuahua, was following the path that Bang Hwajung and Hwang Sayong had shown him and attempting to cross the border when he came under fire from Mexican government troops and United States border guards. He received a slight wound in one arm, and he gave up on the border crossing for the time being and stayed in Mexico. The little money he had was dwindling. He was not even aware that the Mexican Revolution was under way. But when he encountered troops led by the union leader Cástulo Herrera, holding rifles and marching along the ridge toward Temosachic, he immediately understood what was going on. The revolutionaries treated his wound and invited him to join them. Buoyed by the passion of revolution, they put into practice the spirit of fraternity and solidarity, two early virtues of the struggle. The members of the revolutionary army were truly diverse. Hacienda laborers, university students, shop clerks, repairmen, mule sellers, beggars, miners, cowboys, deserters, lawyers, and American mercenaries were all mixed together.

Yet Ijeong rejected their invitation in a roundabout way. Going to the United States was his first priority. Ijeong was of a mind to earn money in Chihuahua and attempt another border crossing. He parted with the fighters and waited for a train. But the train never arrived. The entire state of Chihuahua was seething with the zeal of revolution. He rode on mules and in carriages and made his way to the city of Chihuahua. But the revolutionaries foiled even that plan. They commandeered trains in order to transport weapons and troops.

The new revolutionary leader he chanced upon was Pascual Orozco. Orozco had been a merchant in western Chihuahua, where he had driven mules and transported ore. His greatest enemies had been the bandits of the countryside, who were after his cargo. He had grown up fighting the bandits, and for him battle was a way of life. Orozco had no great hatred for Díaz, nor did he have any affection for Madero. He was only enraged at the tyranny of the Terrazas family, who held power in Chihuahua. He gradually built up his own force, taking the city of Guerrero, a vital rail junction, and brought in revolutionary leaders like Pancho Villa, and he rose to become the greatest power in northern Mexico.

Ijeong stayed in Orozco's camp for several days. Those of the revolutionaries who were peasants knew of life on a henequen hacienda. "Sugar cane, cotton, it's all the same. The only thing different is the length of the hacendados' beards," the peasants said. "You say you're going to the United States? That won't change anything. The wealthy live off the fat of the land, and the immigrants work in sugar cane plantations or orange groves until their necks break." Still, Ijeong did not abandon his dream of going to the United States.

A few days later, federal troops attacked Orozco's soldiers. Armed with heavy weapons, they pounded the undisciplined revolutionary rabble. Ijeong fled with the insurgents along a ridge just below the skyline. One of them gave him a weapon, and Ijeong fired a gun for the first time in his life. The feeling was similar to when he had held the knives in Yoshida's galley. The excitement that emanated from the cold and functional metal spread throughout his body like a drug. When he loaded a bullet and pulled the trigger, it felt as if all of the old bitterness that had built up in his body was expelled in that one shot. His bullet pierced the thigh of a federal soldier and kicked up a cloud of dust as it buried itself in the ground. Red blood mixed with the dust.

The battle ended, and Orozco's men had taken a large number of casualties. But Ijeong did not leave the troop. And he held his gun when he slept. A few days later, Ijeong's troop received orders: they were to launch a surprise attack on a sizable contingent of returning federal soldiers. That was the Battle of Malpaso Canyon, which would long be remembered in the history of the Mexican Revolution. On that day, the revolutionaries caught the forces led by Colonel Martín Luis Guzmán unawares and took many spoils of war.

Ijeong captured a federal soldier who was trying to flee. In his pocket was some rotten corn. He pleaded for his life. Ijeong could not understand him. As soon as he returned with the soldier, the revolutionaries stripped him naked and made him sing. His penis shriveled as he sang his lungs out. Then the revolutionaries let him go. At that point, there was still some humor left in the revolution.

News of the victory at Malpaso Canyon excited anti-Díaz revolutionaries around the nation. The first victory in battle that Ijeong had ever experienced paralyzed his reasoning. He forgot about the United States and about Yeonsu. He even forgot about all the contempt and suffering at countless haciendas. In victory in battle there was genuine happiness. And he liked the atmosphere in the revolutionary army as well. It was similar to what he had tasted in Yoshida's galley. A world of only men. A world where he was exempt from all obligations. They were filthy and noisy, but among them there was peace.

The old and rough peasant soldiers asked Ijeong about the country he had left behind.

"There are brave men like you there as well, of course," Ijeong said. The revolutionaries asked, "Who do they fight?" "They fight the Japanese army." "Why do they fight them?" "Because they took away everything. Japan annexed the whole country." The Mexican revolutionaries shared his rage as they thought of how the United States had swallowed up New Mexico and Texas in the north of Mexico. But they soon lost interest in talk of a distant Asian country, and a country that no longer existed at that.

# 65

AT TEN O'CLOCK on the night of May 21, 1911, Díaz finally raised his hands in surrender. The gist of the peace accord signed by the revolutionaries and the federal army was as follows: Díaz would resign from office by the end of May. The government would issue compensation for the damage caused by the revolution. And new presidential elections would be held. On May 24, an excited crowd swarmed the presidential palace. The machine guns on the roof spit fire. At two-thirty in the morning on May 26, the weary, sick, old dictator left the palace, where he had resided for decades, and boarded a special train bound for Veracruz. In Veracruz he boarded the German ship *Ipiranga* and spoke to his devoted servant General Victoriano Huerta, who had come to see him off, uttering the famous words that would be on everyone's lips throughout the Mexican Revolution:

"Madero has unleashed a tiger. Let us see how he deals with this tiger. After much suffering, he will ultimately come to see that the only way to rule this country is my way."

## 66

JO JANGYUN'S PARTY arrived at the port of San Francisco. They followed the pontoon bridge into the harbor and were asked a simple question by the immigration inspector: "What is your business in the United States?" He looked a little nervously at Jo Jangyun's darkened face and massive frame. Jo Jangyun boldly replied that they were on their way to Hawaii as members of the Korean National Association. The immigration officer, who spoke Spanish, asked them again in Spanish. Jo Jangyun revealed that they were representatives of a group of immigrants and were entering the country in order to settle in Hawaii. The officer glanced at the faces of Jo Jangyun and the other three, went into an office, and then came out again. An official took the four of them into an empty room and had them sit down. They stayed there for six hours. The official informed the government of their reason for entering the country and waited for instructions. The U.S. Bureau of Immigration concluded that they could not allow the four to enter for the purpose of working. Contrary to what Jo Jangyun had expected, the Hawaii Sugar Planters' Association had not received permission in advance from the Bureau of Immigration.

Jo Jangyun's party was confined in the bureau's holding facility for forty-three days. During that time, the Sugar Planters' Association and the Korean National Association repeatedly requested permission for their entry from the relevant authorities and anxiously awaited the outcome. In the end, the four men were put on a ship called the *Lucky Mountain* and forcibly deported. The Koreans of Mérida were also paying close attention to events as they unfolded. Yet when the effort stalled and ended in deportation, the bold project that had been seen as the Exodus of the twentieth century vanished. Thanks to Jo Jangyun's party, the Bureau of Immigration had thought that the Korean immigrants in Mexico were going to flood en masse into the United States, and they had enough of a headache as it was with the friction between Chinese and white laborers.

A total of $547.82 was paid for their stay and boat fare. Bearing the guilt of not only having spent their brethren's money in vain but also of having everything go wrong, the representatives quietly returned to Mérida. But Mérida was not quiet. The wind of revolution had reached it as well.

# 67

A YEAR PASSED. Francisco Madero was now president. The United States did not like him, and the political situation was chaotic. Coup attempts were made, and Madero was not able to keep these under control. Completely naïve, he entrusted the suppression of these coups to General Huerta, who had followed Díaz to the end. Huerta positioned competent generals in the wrong places and ordered incompetent generals to make reckless attacks, causing pointless casualties. In Mexico City he bombarded the residential area where the diplomatic legations were concentrated, killing more than five thousand civilians. Two skillful shots were fired, one hitting the door of the Ciudadela fortress, where the rebel troops were hiding, the other hitting the main gate of the presidential palace. The capital became a living hell. Bodies were scattered everywhere. The corpses that the survivors did manage to retrieve were brought to a park, doused with kerosene, and set on fire. A stench and smoke hung over the city streets. Despite having five times as many troops as the rebels, Huerta stalled for time. He was waiting for grievances against the irresolute Madero to be raised. He entertained Madero's younger brother and confidant, Gustavo, and offered him cognac. Then he took a phone call, said he had forgotten his pistol, and asked if he could borrow Gustavo's for a moment. Naïvely, Gustavo handed Huerta the pistol that he carried at his waist. When Huerta left, a group of soldiers rushed in and arrested Gustavo. At around the same time, another group of soldiers told President Madero that he was under arrest by order of General Huerta. Huerta's lightning coup ended its first act with the execution by firing squad of President Madero. Just as Díaz had said, the tiger was on the rampage, and there didn't appear to be anyone who could tame it.

# 68

THE FLAME OF revolution continued to burn. Venustiano Carranza, the governor of Coahuila, drove out Huerta, and the bandit-turned-revolutionary-leader Pancho Villa won a series of victories over the federal troops and was becoming something of a legend. The thirty-year-old Emiliano Zapata was also using guerrilla warfare to harass Mexico City and trip up the federal troops. Álvaro Obregón, who would later turn the tide of the revolution and become president himself, led his Mayo Indian troops to victory after victory as well, and he was being called an ever-victorious general. Heroes emerged to test their strength against one another as if they had been waiting for just this opportunity, this Mexican version of China's Warring States period. Industry and commerce were hurtling downhill like a car without brakes. It was Huerta's fate to follow in Díaz's footsteps and board a German transport at Veracruz.

On August 15, 1914, Obregón's army at last triumphantly entered Mexico City. The brave Yaqui Indian troops beat their drums and marched proudly at the head of the ranks. Yet Pancho Villa did not recognize Carranza, and Emiliano Zapata also could not allow control of the government to fall into the hands of Carranza, a large landowner. Carranza and Obregón felt the pressure from the pincer attack of the two star players of the revolution and retreated to Veracruz. Clever and meticulous, Obregón took all of the important civilians with him when he withdrew. Personnel vital to the maintenance of rail and communications networks came first. He took as many of the clergy with him as possible. This was not because he liked priests, but because he wanted to drag them from their luxurious cathedrals and force them to witness the tragic plight of the people. Before his departure, Obregón ordered physical examinations of the clergy. Of the 180 priests, 49 of them — 27 percent — were suffering from venereal diseases.

An advance element of Zapata's peasant troops marched into Mexico City on November 26. It was a quiet entrance, with no sound of victorious trumpets and no showy parade. Zapata's troops met little resistance as they seized the agencies necessary for maintaining order, such as the police station. Pancho Villa, who advanced from the north, entered Mexico City on December 4. The former bandit and the former peasant had much in common, such as the fact that they both had so little education that they were nearly illiterate. Yet they were both geniuses of guerrilla warfare, and they were both very popular with the people, and their first meeting began with stammered words of mutual respect. These two shy, rustic leaders denounced Carranza's craftiness and congratulated each other on their accomplishments. Two days later, the northern troops and the southern troops held a large-scale joint victory parade.

Among the northern troops marching down the Paseo de la Reforma was an Asian soldier, drawing the attention of the crowd. It was Kim Ijeong. As part of Pancho Villa's ever-victorious División del Norte, Ijeong had finally entered the center of Mexico. After three years of revolution, he was twenty-five years old. Pancho Villa's army was loved and welcomed by the people wherever it went, and Ijeong received similar treatment as part of that army. There was nothing wrong with being that sort of revolutionary. It was an existence that crossed back and forth between life and death. On occasion he longed for women, and at these times he thought of Yeonsu, but now that he had joined the insurgency he was not free to move about as he pleased.

Unlike Emiliano Zapata, Pancho Villa began a reign of terror as soon as he entered Mexico City. The capital was quickly plunged into chaos as arrests and executions were carried out according to a list that had been drawn up in advance. Blood begat blood. The soldiers had to learn how to murder without question, like Mafia hit men. Day after day they held pistols to the chests of those who could not fight back and pulled the trigger. It was like drawing faces on pieces of wood and using them for target practice. Ijeong, too, pulled the trigger without thinking. Every time he did so, something in his heart collapsed a little. The landowners must die, he thought. He believed that the hacienda system, which filled only the bellies of the large landowners, had to be abolished immediately. The same went for the filthy slavery system under which people were bought and sold. Strangely, though, the ruling class was not easily caught. After Ijeong had shot a number of men, he found out that they were petty farmers and poor people no different from him. It didn't matter whom they supported; they were drafted and joined the war, sometimes on Huerta's side, sometimes on Villa's side, and sometimes on Obregón's side. Ijeong blindfolded them and put a bullet in their heart. Orders were orders.

Yet Ijeong loved Villa. Villa, who had beaten to death a foreman who was raping his younger sister and then fled the hacienda to become a bandit. Like Zapata, he was illiterate and impulsive in all he did. By his very nature, he hated nations, institutions, and laws. He was not an anarchist, but ultimately he acted like one. He had no interest in founding a nation. That was precisely what made Villa so attractive. He hated the landowners and the learned, and put that hatred into practice. He had crossed the line once and killed hundreds of Chinese for no reason, but people still loved this impulsive and whimsical man.

Ijeong sometimes wrote in a journal: "Can a nation disappear forever? What if it can? Since the start of the revolution it has been just as if there was no nation in Mexico. Everyone prints their own currency and kills those who use different money. Butchery leads to butchery. The powerful are all advancing on Mexico City. Here is both the start and end of this long revolution. Tens of thousands have already died. Has all this happened because of the former nation, or because of a lack of a nation? We had the Korean Empire, but we were not happy. And now it is the same with Mexico. From somewhere comes the stench of blood. The stronger nations, Japan and the United States, start wars and support civil wars in order to rule the weaker nations."

Miguel, a Mexican soldier with whom Ijeong was close, was a curious anarchist. Chewing on cheap cigars like gum, he always said things like this: "Nations are truly the root of all evil. Yet the nations do not disappear. If we drive out those caudillos and accomplish the revolution, other caudillos will seize control of the government. So what can we do? We can only shoot them all to death. If the revolution is to continue, that is the only way. A permanent revolution, that's what it is."

"Then will you shoot Villa if he becomes president?" Miguel flashed a smile at Ijeong's question. "That is my belief. Politics and convictions are different." In contrast to the young Marxists who served as staff officers under Zapata, those who followed Villa had more diverse backgrounds and views. Among them were anarchists who had come from Russia and Spain, and romantic Trotskyites from Germany. Ijeong was confused. What was clear, though, was that none of the nations that Ijeong had passed through, not even Villa's camp, was the ultimate form of government he desired.

One day, Pancho Villa and Emiliano Zapata invited diplomats to the presidential palace. The great powers, including the United States, Germany, Great Britain, and France, were summoned by the revolutionary leaders. Some attended, some did not, using illness or a holiday as an excuse. Ijeong stood guard outside the palace with the other soldiers. The revolutionary troops were a little timid before the splendor of the capital. The guerrillas in their old uniforms looked shabby before the vast Zócalo. When cars carrying the diplomats began to stream into the presidential palace, Ijeong watched them with indifference. One of the cars, a new model Ford, stopped. The passenger door opened and a man stepped out, then the car went on to the palace.

It was Yoshida. Dressed in a formal swallow-tailed coat, he approached hesitantly and held his hand out to Ijeong. Ijeong shifted his rifle from his right hand to his left and shook his hand. "It's been a long time. I never thought I would see you here," Yoshida said. He glanced at Ijeong's uniform and comrades. "You're a Villista." Ijeong's comrades stared at him with wonder as he spoke in Japanese. "Did you know that Villa killed some two hundred Chinese in Torreón for no reason at all?" Ijeong nodded. "And yet you are a Villista." Ijeong spoke in Spanish. He could not talk about Villa in Japanese. "Sometimes he just goes out of his head. There is no reason for him to dislike the Chinese. He is just hotheaded, and that's what is so attractive about him. But what are you doing here?"

"I went to the Japanese consulate and turned myself in. The consul said that he was sorry, but he had no way to arrest and take me into custody. He asked me if I would like to work for him, so I settled down there." Yoshida held his arms out and smiled. "What do you think? Not bad, eh?" Then he lowered his voice. "We do not think Villa and Zapata will last long. Consider this carefully."

Ijeong nodded expressionlessly. "That does not matter to me. After all, I am an outsider." "You mean a mercenary?" Ijeong shook his head. "I volunteered, but my situation is no different. It is good to see you." Yoshida's face clouded over. "We probably won't see each other again, will we?" Ijeong moved his rifle from his left hand back to his right hand. Their replacements were coming. Ijeong signaled to his men to withdraw. "Probably not, but who knows what might happen?" Yoshida grabbed Ijeong as he turned to go. "Oh, by the way, you're Japanese now, too. As such, your actions should be reported to us. You probably knew this, but all of the Koreans living in Mexico became Japanese citizens in 1910. So if you need a passport, if you are treated unfairly – anything – come to the Japanese embassy. It is the legation's duty to protect our citizens abroad."

"I did not know. But I never agreed to become Japanese." Yoshida laughed. "Since when does an individual choose his nation? I'm sorry, but our nation chooses us." Yoshida clapped Ijeong on the shoulder and went into the presidential palace.

# 69

IGNACIO VELÁSQUEZ had a dream. A white, winged horse flew down from the heavens through the clouds. The heavenly horse was so dazzlingly beautiful that it looked like it belonged to God. On it rode a young man he assumed to be an angel, and he was smiling at Ignacio. The angel spoke to Ignacio, who had bowed down and was praying. "Can you give your life for the Lord?" Ignacio was overcome with emotion and bowed to the floor. "Of course. If the Lord desires it, how could I cling to this petty life? Give me the order. The army of the Lord will march forth."

When Ignacio woke from his dream, his sheets were soaked with sweat. It was no ordinary dream. He went out to his prayer room and knelt down. "Lord, just say the word. I offer up this body to you." He tended to some business on the hacienda and read the newspaper that had been brought to him by an overseer. The state of affairs in Mexico was critical. Things had been changing so fast since Porfirio Díaz was ousted that no one could see what was coming. "Pitiful atheists!" Ignacio ground his teeth. They had not stopped at overthrowing the leader but had begun to attack the landowning class, the Church, and the clergy. Ignacio mustered the hacienda's soldiers. Among them marched Choe Seongil in smart leather boots. Ignacio told his men that the moment of the decisive battle was approaching. Not all of the overseers and foremen sympathized with Ignacio. Some of them were already leaning toward the revolutionaries. What was so wrong with tearing down the landowning class and the Church? But Ignacio trusted steadfastly in their loyalty. At least one of them would faithfully live up to his expectations: Choe Seongil, the thief of Jemulpo, who had transformed himself into Ignacio's most fanatical henchman. Whenever he appeared on the hacienda, all of the laborers grew nervous. His nickname was the Executioner. He overturned altars to the ancestors and took the whip to those who attended Baptist services.

There were hardly any Koreans left at Buena Vista hacienda. Many of those who had left when their contracts expired were unable to find jobs elsewhere and returned to the haciendas, but not to Buena Vista. Because Ignacio and Choe Seongil were still there, the freed laborers avoided the place. Some of them left for the sugar plantations of Cuba, others for big cities like Mexico City, Veracruz, and Coatzacoalcos. Choe Chuntaek and the whalers from Pohang settled in a fishing village near Coatzacoalcos. They borrowed nets and boats and caught fish, and the women took the fish they caught and sold them at the market.

Among those who left for Veracruz was the Stone Buddha, Bak Jeonghun. After he had gained his freedom, he remained on the hacienda for three years and saved his money, then went off to Mérida. Jo Jangyun had asked him to stay with him there and help with the branch office, but Bak Jeonghun chose to go it alone: "I don't think I'm the type of person who gets along with a large number of people." As soon as he arrived in Veracruz he went into a barbershop near the piers to ask for a job. An old Negro barber tilted his head. "Where are you from?" "I've come from Mérida." "Have you ever cut hair before?" "No. But I am good with knives and scissors." The barber took hold of Bak Jeonghun's hands and looked at them carefully. "You've done hard work on the haciendas, I see. But why do you want to learn to be a barber?" Bak Jeonghun had his reasons. Cutting hair was something you could do without talking. The life he dreamed of was one where he quietly clipped with his scissors, went home, ate dinner, and went to sleep. He said that he didn't need much compensation, he only wanted to learn the work. The old Negro, who was from Cuba, willingly took him in. Thus began Bak Jeonghun's life as a barber. In only three months, he learned everything the barber could teach him. He was especially good at shaving, and he soon had regular customers of his own. The people of the port knew him as the mute Chinese. He ate and slept in the back of the barbershop and took care of the cleaning and odd jobs.

He received his first monthly wages on the first day of his fifth month on the job. As soon as the workday ended he walked outside and down the street. He had been eyeing a Chinese restaurant there, and he pushed aside the curtain, went inside, and sat down.

A woman came out to take his order. She spoke clumsy Chinese, but her scent reached him first. Bak Jeonghun lifted his head and looked at her. Her face was familiar. The woman did not recognize Bak Jeonghun, but she sensed something in his look. He remembered who she was from her aristocratic profile. The girl who had sat quietly in a corner of the *Ilford* a long time ago.

Yeonsu was the first to speak. "Have you come from Mérida?" she said in Korean. Bak Jeonghun nodded. Yeonsu glanced back at the owner before speaking again. "Where do you live?" Bak Jeonghun told her about the barbershop. She lowered her voice and asked, "Have you heard anything from Mérida?" "I worked on the hacienda until 1913. Then a few months ago I came here. That is all. There was talk of everyone leaving for Hawaii, but that came to nothing, and after that everyone scattered to the wind." Yeonsu's face grew red and she wiped the table with a cloth. As she did so, she kept glancing around at the owner. Bak Jeonghun realized that she could not talk freely. Yeonsu lowered her voice and asked, "Do you know a man by the name of Kim Ijeong? He worked in the galley on the *Ilford* and he was briefly at Yazche hacienda . . ." Of course Bak Jeonghun remembered the young boy whom Jo Jangyun had named. "He was sold to Chenché hacienda, where I was, and went on strike with us. On the day the strike ended, he borrowed some money from my friend Jo Jangyun and ran off to the north. We wondered about him from time to time. Ah, now that I think about it, the two representatives from the United States, Bang Hwajung and Hwang Sayong, I think they said that they saw him in the state of Chihuahua. He was about to cross the border, so he is probably in the United States now." Yeonsu's face grew dark. "I am embarrassed to ask, but my father, the one called Jongdo . . ." Bak Jeonghun shook his head. "I don't know. Ah, you had a younger brother, didn't you? I heard that he is doing well. I heard that he worked as an interpreter and these days has been put in charge of management, bringing laborers to the haciendas and receiving a commission. He is probably still in the Yucatán."

Bak Jeonghun ordered his food and offered her some. She looked back toward the owner. The fat owner nodded. Bak Jeonghun ordered far too much food for two people to eat so that she could sit as long as possible. Yeonsu realized that this man was quiet and prudent, and she was drawn to him. No, that's not it, she thought. I am just happy to see a Korean after so long. She got up and went to the kitchen. Bak Jeonghun sat alone and snacked on pieces of duck as he emptied a bottle of Chinese millet liquor. And for the first time in his life, he decided to speak up. He pretended to make his way to the bathroom and stood in Yeonsu's path as she came out of the kitchen. It was a narrow hallway. "Are you being confined here?" Yeonsu nodded. Not long away from the henequen hacienda, Bak Jeonghun grasped the whole situation in an instant. He spoke. "Since I lost my wife to illness, I have never given thought to another woman. But seeing you makes me think that all my resolution was for nothing. I want to live with you. I have become quite a skilled barber, so I can earn enough to feed you."

She was torn between the young man whom she loved so much, but for whom there was almost no chance of returning, and the gentle retired soldier who stood across from her. The Chinese owner was beside her before she knew it. He could not understand Korean, but with his merchant's intuition he immediately understood. He grabbed Yeonsu's arm and dragged her back to the kitchen.

# 70

THE YUCATÁN GOVERNOR, Salvador Alvarado, who had supported President Carranza and General Obregón, received information that the armies of Villa and Zapata were attempting to seize the henequen fields, to appropriate them for military expenses. In a place where various forms of currency were circulated indiscriminately, henequen was truly green gold. All Villa's and Zapata's men had to do was get the crop to the port of Progreso and American importers would pay them in cash. The governor did not hesitate to order the henequen fields near Mérida and Progreso to be burned, including Ignacio Velásquez's Buena Vista hacienda. Government troops came and doused its fields in kerosene and set them on fire. The fire caught the west wind and spread through the whole hacienda. With this, the first of the shaman's prophecies came to pass: "When the wind blows from the west, the sun will be hidden even at midday." Just as the prophecy said, the black smoke that rose from the henequen fields darkened the land, turning the sun red. Hundreds of henequen fields were reduced to black ash, and the laborers became jobless.

The American hacendados and henequen importers, who had lost their haciendas and all their property, petitioned Washington to intervene in the Mexican Revolution. An American fleet was dispatched near Veracruz.

# 71

ONE MONTH LATER, Bak Jeonghun received a few months' pay in advance from José the barber. Then he walked into Yeonsu's Chinese restaurant and negotiated with the owner. The owner took one look at Bak Jeonghun's face and knew that he was determined. Not only that, he sensed that things would go terribly wrong if he ignored him. He was a Chinese merchant who lived and died by material gain. Bak Jeonghun handed him 150 pesos and took Yeonsu.

"I don't believe it," she said, on the verge of tears. "What might have happened to me if you hadn't come?"

With that, a new life began for Yi Yeonsu. She moved her belongings to the barbershop. José played the guitar to celebrate their new start. It was passionate music that would loosen up even the stiffest person. The shop regulars flooded in, drinking and singing and dancing. Yeonsu was intoxicated for the first time in her life and threw herself into Bak Jeonghun's arms.

It is only natural that things that are not used for a long time should atrophy. Bak Jeonghun's body was duller than his spirit; it did not react at all to the flesh of a woman. So their first night together was uneventful, and Bak Jeonghun was upset. But Yeonsu did not blame him. She thought that perhaps it was better that way. Her own body was not exactly unresponsive, but her feelings were not yet urgent. "It's all right," Yeonsu consoled him as she held him close. "It's probably because of the alcohol," he said. The former ace marksman drank some strong liquor and fell asleep.

All in all, they lived happily. Yeonsu's life before that had been so horrible that she found joy in ordinary things. She delighted in the freedom to go about as she pleased, as when she went on evening walks with Bak Jeonghun. Yet there was still a problem that Yeonsu needed to resolve. She waited and waited, until one day she opened her mouth. "Do you think we could go get my child?"

"Ah, that's right, you said you had a child, didn't you? Then we must get him. But we'll have to pay to take him with us." Yeonsu bit her lip. "Don't worry," Bak Jeonghun said. "I'll get paid two months from now. Then we'll go to Mérida."

Not long after that, a man in a military uniform entered the barbershop and plopped himself down in an empty chair. His subordinates hurried in behind him. The man had a stylish black mustache and said that he wanted a shave and haircut. Bak Jeonghun tied the cloth around his neck, picked up his scissors, and began to cut the man's hair. When he had finished trimming his hair and shaving him, Bak Jeonghun politely bowed his head. His customer smiled when he looked in the mirror. He said that he was very pleased with the haircut. One of his men paid the bill. After the soldiers left, José approached Bak Jeonghun with wide eyes. "That was General Obregón, President Carranza's right hand. He may have retreated here to Veracruz, but you wait and see. He will return to Mexico City soon. A thief like Pancho Villa cannot defeat Obregón."

From that time on, Bak Jeonghun was Obregón's personal barber. The general showered him with money printed by the Carranza administration. Each of the revolutionary armies issued their own currency, and each faction prohibited the use of pesos issued by others in the areas they controlled, so people were not able to buy goods even if they stuffed their pockets with various types of currency. A murderous inflation ensued. Yet Bak Jeonghun diligently saved Obregón's money. Eventually he went to the Chinese restaurant where Yeonsu had been confined and exchanged the bills for the 150 pesos he had paid for her. The restaurant owner did not resist Obregón's barber. He even tried to refuse the money, saying that he did not need to give him the currency from Obregón's camp. But Bak Jeonghun threw Obregón's pesos in the owner's face and returned to the barbershop.

One day, when Bak Jeonghun was passing a firing range, Obregón asked him, "Didn't you say that you were once a soldier?" When Bak Jeonghun said that he was, Obregón promptly took an American rifle from a soldier standing nearby and tossed it to him. "Shoot for me." Bak Jeonghun declined, saying that it had been a long time since he had fired a gun, but Obregón persisted. Bak Jeonghun shot ten rounds from the prone position and hit the target one hundred meters away with eight rounds. He was given ten more rounds at Obregón's command, and he fired all ten into the center of the target. Obregón helped him up. "You don't have to worry about being a barber anymore." Obregón was fond of this taciturn Asian. He had always maintained friendly relations with the native peoples, such as the Yaqui Indians, so the barber's nationality was of no concern to him. Furthermore, the man had no interests in Mexico, so there was little worry that he would betray him, and he could not understand complicated conversations in Spanish. Bak Jeonghun said to Obregón, "I have a young wife, so it will be difficult for me to go to battle." Obregón smiled as he spoke. "It won't take long. Villa and Zapata are both amateurs at war. They may be laughing in Mexico City now, but they won't last. You will soon be able to return and go eat Chinese food with your young wife."

# 72

CHOE SEONGIL AND Ignacio Velásquez knelt at the entrance of the cathedral in Mérida, dipped their fingers in holy water, and crossed themselves. Inside the cathedral were Jesuit priests, students, and those of like mind to Ignacio. With their weapons in hand, their expressions were so grim as to be comic. The bishop of Mérida blessed them, calling them crusaders who fought against atheists. The Mass was performed hastily, as if they were pressed for time. "Amen, amen, amen." A nervous tension blanketed the cathedral. As soon as the bishop who had officiated the Mass said, "Go and spread the Gospel," he retreated to the vestry and fled through the rear door.

Some of those in the sanctuary kept watch through the loopholes in the wall on what was going on outside, and when they grew fatigued from the tension and yawned, torches began to appear one by one from afar. As the torches passed by city hall and the park, they suddenly increased in number and speed. "They're coming!" The sound of shouting in the cathedral echoed like the hymns of a choir. The cathedral was as noisy as a market, with the sound of guns being loaded and pews being piled into barricades. Choe Seongil went up to the belfry and looked down. The square in front of the cathedral was a sea of torches. Gunfire could already be heard. "Punish the landowners! Seize the Church's property!" The torches flooded in with the shouting of slogans. Ignacio Velásquez's gun spit fire. The fortress-like cathedral, built on the former site of a Mayan shrine, did not fall easily.

It was then that Choe Seongil realized that those like Ignacio were the minority. He had lived only on Buena Vista hacienda, so he had thought that most Mexicans were secretly fanatics like the hacendado. But that was not the case. They were put on the defensive.

Choe Seongil came down from the belfry and saw the cross above the altar. Jesus barely managed to hold up his body as he hung there, his face twisted in agony. Ignacio was cooling down the heated barrel of his long rifle with a wet towel as he fired. Having fought through all sorts of hardships, Choe Seongil had a foreboding that neither guns nor anything else would be able to stop those rushing torches. He went down to the crypt. Light and air came in through a slanting hole where the ceiling met the wall. He shoved his body into the vent, which was barely large enough for a person to fit through. When he had wriggled all the way through like a maggot, he came face to face with a steel grate. He shook it, but it did not open. Gunfire still rang outside. He only barely managed to crawl back down the way he had come.

The cries outside the cathedral gradually grew louder. He returned to the sanctuary. Ignacio was praying behind a fortification of sandbags. Choe Seongil sat down next to him. His mind was a flurry of thoughts. When they had entered the church, he had not imagined that the situation might turn so grave. They were completely surrounded by the mob. There was nowhere to run. The thief from Jemulpo grabbed a gun. Then he looked down at Ignacio. He had never been able to understand his God, but it was his God that had driven off the old man that had sat on his shoulders. Though Choe Seongil did not believe in God, he did believe in miracles, like the way his epilepsy attacks had disappeared when he'd met Ignacio. That blasted old man, who had appeared suddenly, choked him, mumbled nonsensical words, and brought him to strange places, had tucked his tail between his legs at a few drops of holy water from the fat Ignacio and that mangy priest.

Choe Seongil looked down again at the sea of torches surging outside the cathedral. There was no way out. He grasped the butt of his rifle. He pointed it at those who were thronging in to destroy the happiest time of his life and he pulled the trigger. In that moment he was an overseer in a leather vest and a soldier of the Lord and the adopted son of a fanatical hacendado. Ignacio and Jesus, not that mob, had given him his whip, his boots, and his sombrero. Ignacio finished his prayer, approached Choe Seongil, and gave him a bandolier. "Those cowards, if they take just a few rounds, they'll run off screaming for the Blessed Mother and for Jesus. Don't worry. If they break through the cathedral door, just keep shooting."

Choe Seongil prayed in earnest for the first time. "Jesus, in truth I do not know you. But this has happened because of you, so please help me."

Boom! "Raaaaah!" A log that played the part of a battering ram shattered the front door of the cathedral and hundreds of people poured in like water through a ruptured dam. The landowner crusaders pulled their triggers as one. But those in the rear knew nothing of the carnage taking place in front and continued to push forward. No matter how many they shot down, it was no use. Like David's *Sabine Women,* the crowds climbed over the bodies and stormed into the church. The only difference was that there were no bare-breasted women. The brown-skinned crusaders retreated to the higher ground of the altar and choir and fired their guns. But the attacking crowd was much faster.

The looting began as soon as the barricade fell. The people carried out sacred relics and treasures, candlesticks and vestments. The riflemen who had defended the cathedral were being dragged out. The mob struck them on the head with clubs. Choe Seongil's gun felled three more of them, but it was meaningless. He threw away his gun and fled toward the belfry. But the mob had already climbed up ladders and was entering the belfry through the top. They struck Choe Seongil in the chest as he ran up the spiral stairs, and he tumbled back down. He immediately lost consciousness.

Time passed. That acute pain and illusion that he had forgotten so long ago returned to him. The shapeless darkness spoke: "I am the one who died in your stead." Choe Seongil waved his hands and shouted, "No! Who dies in someone else's stead? Who on earth are you? Who are you?" The shape choked Choe Seongil. "I am the Jesus of those you killed." Choe Seongil struggled. "What is my sin? I killed them because they deserved to die. And you choked me on the *Ilford,* before I killed them. Ah, please take your hand away! I cannot breathe!" The shape said, "My time and your time are different. There is no before or after for sin. Your sin is not acknowledging your sin."

He opened his eyes and found himself in the square. His shoulder joints hurt so badly it felt as if his arms were being torn out. The tops of his feet burned as if someone were searing them with a hot iron. He looked around. It was amazing. He was floating in the air.

Am I already dead? But he was not. People were gazing up at him from below. He looked to his side and saw Ignacio Velásquez lying on the ground, tied to a cross. A bald man smiled and drove a nail into Ignacio's palm. Only then did Choe Seongil realize why his shoulder joints hurt so much. He was hanging on a cross with his arms spread out. Gravity kept pulling his body downward. The blood that flowed from his palms soaked his armpits. His feet, which were pierced by a large nail, hurt so badly it felt as if millipedes were gnawing their way into them. Choe Seongil shouted urgently, "Look here! I do not believe in Jesus and I am not even Mexican! I am a Korean! I am a bystander! Save me, please!" A man approached, pointed at him, and said, "You beat us and raped us and killed us. You must die." Sweat trickled into his eyes. Choe Seongil recognized him: he was a Mayan laborer from Buena Vista hacienda.

The hammering ended with a clamor, and dozens of people pulled on ropes to hoist Ignacio's cross upright. They tried several times but lost their balance, and Ignacio slammed to the ground. He screamed like an animal and cried. He desperately prayed the Hail Mary. But no one could understand him.

Seeing Ignacio like that, Choe Seongil thanked God that he had lost consciousness. Gunfire rang out from afar. The reinforcements of Governor Alvarado were entering the square from the north. The mob, having finished their looting and executions, fled into the twisted alleys of the market to the south. Someone approached Choe Seongil and aimed a gun at his head. Choe Seongil closed his eyes. "Hurry, hurry!" he pleaded. The conclusion was not as long as he thought it would be. With a bang, everything ended. Choe Seongil enjoyed a feeling of peace that he had never before experienced. There was no pain and no rage. There was only the feeling that a long and tedious journey had finally come to an end. Suddenly his spirit, floating high in the sky, was looking down on the chaos of the square before the cathedral. Like a close-up in a film, he saw Ignacio Velásquez's end as well. Someone swung a sword at him as he lay on the ground, still nailed to the cross. He was being sliced up like a fish on a cutting board.

With this, the shaman's second prophecy was fulfilled. "When the flames move and the sound of thunder is heard, death will come quick. Death!"

# 73

PANCHO VILLA WAS chewing on a chicken leg and staring at a map. His staff officers stood around him, leaning over the map. Something bothered him about the fact that the army of Obregón, who had been driven away to Veracruz, had skirted around Mexico City and entered Querétaro. The region of Jalisco, including Guadalajara, was strategically vital to Villa's northern division and Zapata's southern division. Obregón's intentions were clear: he was trying to divide them. Villa set up his corps headquarters in the city of Irapuato, on the border of Jalisco. In accordance with Villa's orders, Ijeong stopped the slaughter in Mexico City and moved to the military headquarters. Villa's troops and Obregón's troops faced each other at a distance of seventy miles.

Pancho Villa liked to scare his enemies out of their wits with a thunderous cavalry charge, and this tactic was also well suited to his character. He had to lure the enemy out onto the plains in order to effect the charge, but the foolish enemy commander Obregón had crawled down onto the plains of his own accord. Villa's confidence soared and his troops' morale was high. For his part, Obregón devoted all his energy to acquiring cannons and machine guns. Unlike Villa, Obregón knew well the lessons of the Great War that had broken out in Europe not long before. He could not overlook the power of Villa's lightning charges, but he could apply methods used on the battlefields of France and Belgium: if one dug deep trenches and laid down barbed wire before them and fired machine guns from behind them, the cavalry charge that was Villa's forte could be neutralized. So the plains of Celaya, which Villa had thought were to his advantage, were perfectly suited to Obregón's plans as well. Irrigation ditches for wheat farming stretched out left and right on the flat ground, and if these were dug a little deeper and a bulwark raised in front, they would be ideal for use as military trenches. Obregón mobilized fifteen thousand troops, dug his trenches, set up fifteen cannons and about one hundred of the latest machine guns, and waited for the decisive battle.

The Villista general Felipe Ángeles counseled against a great battle. "Obregón is luring us. If we simply cut off his supplies and stall for time, he will surrender. Their supply lines are growing longer now. It would be to our advantage to cut off his supplies with Zapata's troops and wait for our chance. The enemy is the one who wants a quick battle and a quick conclusion." In the end, his words were correct, but they were not the right words to convince a man like Villa. Villa, the former bandit, was a thug to the bone. In the world of thugs, cowardice was even more hated than death. Thus Ángeles's advice only strengthened Villa's determination. He had led a mere eight thugs across the Rio Grande and had ultimately become a general who led tens of thousands of troops. Why should he do now what he had not done when he led only eight? Villa also knew that Zapata's troops were nothing more than a disorderly rabble that had no skill in regular warfare. He had entrusted the storming of Veracruz to Zapata's troops, but they had not been able to advance a single step. He thought of himself as the only person able to turn the tide of the revolution back in their favor.

Before daybreak on April 6, 1915, Ijeong was cleaning his gun with the soldiers. Miguel approached and offered him a cigarette. Ijeong lit it and said, "Villa's probably going to give the order to attack soon, isn't he?" Miguel nodded. "I saw the cavalry saddling their horses." Ijeong blew out smoke and asked Miguel, "You really think a permanent revolution is possible?" Miguel looked at Ijeong for some time, to try to judge his thoughts. "Look here, politics is all a dream. Democracy, communism, anarchism, it's all the same. They were all created so we could shoot at each other." Miguel lifted his gun. "This comes first, and words come later. Of course I believe that. Even if I didn't believe it, that's the only way. I was seventeen when I first killed a man. Back then I was with Zapata's troops. And now I serve under Villa. Yet nothing has changed for me."

When the sun rose, Villa gave the order for his infantry units to advance. He did not use his cavalry, his strength, because he had seen the long trenches and barbed wire stretched out across Obregón's encampment and the gleaming barrels of the machine guns. Even Villa knew what that meant. Because machine guns had a shorter range and were less accurate than rifles, Villa's troops had the upper hand early in the battle. They pushed Obregón's forces from the city of Celaya and entered it. Ijeong's regiment formed the vanguard. A member of the regiment took the belfry of Celaya's cathedral and went up and rang the bell excitedly. When the clear, rich sound of the bell reached the battlefield, the morale of Villa's troops rose.

Yet Ijeong's rhythm was severely disturbed by the sudden sound of the bell. It was as if it had stirred up some sediment that had lain quietly inside him. Only then did he realize, paradoxically, that he owed that quiet, that indifference, to war. Thanks to war, he had been able to hide and hold back all the desires and conflicts inside.

Thanks to the rigorous tension demanded by shooting, maneuvering, and commanding, he was free from the past he had left behind. The place where no one would reproach him for this was the battlefield. But the piercing, bright bell of Celaya shook him. Beneath that belfry, as bullets flew back and forth, he remembered the flame-shaped arch of Chunchucmil hacienda and Yeonsu's warm body. He remembered his trembling hands when he pulled the trigger for his first murder and his second murder. Had Miguel not approached and touched him, he might have stood there, lost in thought, for some time. "Hey, Kim," Miguel said, "something's not right. I think Obregón is going to counterattack soon. He retreated a little too quickly."

Bak Jeonghun stood next to Obregón and watched the progress of the battle with him. They had also heard the bell of Celaya. Obregón was not particularly disturbed by it, and he reinforced his troops and ordered them to push forward. He arranged the machine gunners all along the line and suppressed Villa's riflemen. Obregón had the upper hand in numbers as well. Even Obregón's own unit, of which Bak Jeonghun was a part, participated in the battle and showered Villa's troops with bullets. It had been a long time since Bak Jeonghun had participated in a real battle. This weighed far less on his mind than aiming his rifle at the guerrillas of his own country as a soldier in the strange army of a small and weak nation, and an army commanded in turn by Japan and Russia at that. He did not care whether it was Obregón or Villa. Yet judging by Obregón's character, he felt that it would not be such a bad thing for him to become the leader of Mexico. With the curious philosophical attitude common to mercenaries, he calmly joined the battle. Bak and Obregón's unit advanced to the bell tower of Celaya. Bak aimed at the Villista in the belfry who was ringing the bell. That soldier determined their morale, so he had to be taken out quickly. Bak's bullet struck the bell. Ping! A sharp report rang out. The soldier dropped flat. The moment he lifted his head to locate the enemy, the second bullet pierced his forehead. Blood splattered on the white walls of the belfry. At that, Ijeong's regiment abandoned the belfry and retreated. Bak Jeonghun climbed to the third story of a building in the center of Celaya and aimed his gun at the retreating file of Villa's troops. Into his field of vision came a familiar face, a Korean face, though it was covered by a beard. Ijeong. The boy had become a young man. Bak Jeonghun did not pull the trigger and waited for the regiment to pass.

The offensive and defensive skirmishes between Obregón's and Villa's troops continued throughout the night. The battle left the streets of Celaya and ended on the evening of the next day, April 7. Villa's troops had retreated all the way to their headquarters in Irapuato and regrouped. It was a day of humiliation for Villa. But Obregón was not happy. His goal had been not merely to defeat Villa's army but to annihilate it. If he did not cut their throats this time, there was no doubt that Villa, who was skilled in both guerrilla and regular warfare, would continue to hound him.

In order to break through the slow tide of battle, Villa resolved to sweep the enemy away with one of his cavalry charges. With reinforcements arriving from Jalisco and Michoacán, Villa's forces totaled 30,000 men. His cavalry was intact and he outnumbered his enemy two to one. He thought that he could simply go around the barbed wire. On April 13, Pancho Villa ordered his cavalry to charge. The northern cavalry, a legend of the Mexican Revolution, galloped out at once to the sound of trumpets. But the horses hesitated before the barbed wire, and at that moment Obregón's machine guns shot forth flame. Bak Jeonghun's rifle repeatedly spit fire from his position in the rear. Obregón steadily racked up points as horses without their riders and riders without their horses ran pell-mell before the barbed wire. On the other side, Villa committed the error of ordering the waiting second and third lines to attack. Obregón's troops toppled Villa's pride without budging from their trenches. This reckless charge continued all day. Between 3,000 and 3,500 cavalry were lost.

On the fifteenth, Obregón ordered General Cesáreo Castro's 7,000-strong cavalry, which he had not used even in his direst moment, to go around Villa's flank and attack from behind. Villa's remaining infantry fell futilely before Castro's cavalry, which galloped in like a storm. Ijeong heard the sound of 7,000 mounted men thundering toward him. It sounded as if a giant had taken hold of the mountains and shaken them, to tear them out by their roots. Already most of the infantry had lost their will to fight and begun to flee at the roar and the shaking of the earth. The cavalry seemed to come down from on high like the armies of heaven, rampaging across the battlefield, bringing their swords down on the heads and shoulders of the infantry. Ijeong ran toward Villa's headquarters. He thought it would hold out the longest. His judgment was correct. Obregón's cavalry met significant resistance in its attempt to penetrate the center. Loyal troops risked their lives to defend Villa. Ijeong was ultimately able to join Villa's file as it fled to the south.

The Villistas, who had been invincible legends, were devastated by the cavalry tactics that had been their forte. Villa ordered retreat after retreat. Obregón pursued him to the very end. Villa's lands fell one by one into Obregón's hands. Villa did take one of Obregón's arms in battle on June 3, but he lost everything in return. Villa, the commander of the División del Norte, was on his way back to being a bandit.

"I want to return to Veracruz. I think it is time to eat Chinese food again," Bak Jeonghun said as he tied a cloth from Obregón's neck over the stump of his left arm, which was wrapped in a bandage.

Obregón laughed heartily and nodded. Then he had an aide bring him a wooden box. It was filled with crude bills printed with President Carranza's face. "Take this. Your wife will like it." Bak Jeonghun declined, but Obregón was adamant. "If you ever come to Veracruz," Bak said, "I will cut your hair for free." Obregón smiled; his hair cascaded down over his ears and forehead. "If you ever want to be a soldier, come see me." "But I couldn't even protect your arm." Obregón grabbed Bak Jeonghun's arm with his right hand. "But we still won, didn't we?"

Bak Jeonghun took the box with the bills inside and returned to Veracruz. José was comfortably cutting people's hair, as always. He held his arms out wide and embraced Bak, who glanced toward the back of the barbershop. There was no sign of anyone. "Has my wife gone somewhere?" José shook his head with a grave expression on his face. "She's not here." Bak Jeonghun looked glum. "Did someone come for her?" The old barber smiled brightly. "I got you! She went to the market and will be back soon." His mind now at ease, Bak went into his living quarters and unpacked his things. He could smell his wife's scent. It was the scent that his fellow soldiers had long ago called the smell of roe deer blood. He dropped into bed and fell asleep.

When he opened his eyes Yeonsu was looking down at him. A few days later, they packed for a trip and left for Mérida. José prepared a lunch for them.

# 74

BAK JEONGHUN and Yi Yeonsu arrived at the arched entrance to Yazche hacienda. A guard whom they didn't recognize stopped them. Yeonsu asked if there were any Koreans on the hacienda. The guard said that there were. When they said that they had come to see the Koreans, the guard asked them to follow him. They walked to the office next to the storehouse, where the paymasters worked. It was a familiar place. One of the paymasters vaguely remembered Yeonsu. He told her that only a few Koreans remained, that most of them had left. After a while, the paymaster also remembered her father, who had refused to work to the very end, and her lethargic mother.

Yi Jongdo had taken his son with him and left on the day their contract expired, but the paymaster didn't know where they had gone. Yeonsu hesitantly asked what had happened to his wife. The paymaster spoke with an overseer and flipped through a notebook similar to an account book, and then he scratched his head and laughed uncomfortably. Yeonsu squeezed the handkerchief she held in her hand. "What is it?" she asked. "We have a different hacendado now," the paymaster said, "and fortunately this place was not burned. So we can still grow henequen here, and with the price soaring because of the revolution, we have had a good number of buyers." He deftly flipped through the account book and spoke again. "Hmm, the interpreter paid for your release, I see." She asked, "What happened to my mother?" The paymaster flashed a smile. "She's fine. You may find it hard to believe, but not long before your contracts expired she married a Mayan overseer. She's living at another hacienda nearby. Shall I contact her?" Yeonsu lifted her hand to cut him off. "No, that's all right." "She's living quite happily," the overseer said. Was this the same woman who had refused to speak to her daughter when she became the concubine of an interpreter? It was not that Yeonsu could not understand her mother, whose actions were not unreasonable. Maybe it was better this way. There was no hope of going back to Korea, her husband was incompetent, her daughter had been corrupted, and her son had left. The long years suddenly felt like a mischievous lie.

Yeonsu finally brought up the reason she had come. "There was a woman named Maria." The overseer frowned. "There are a lot of women named Maria." "She lived with the interpreter, Gwon Yongjun. She will have a child with her." Another overseer stepped in and said that Maria had gone out to work, that she would return in a few hours. "Can we go to Maria's house?" The men shook their heads and said that they couldn't allow that; the new hacendado didn't like that sort of thing. Yeonsu sat down with Bak Jeonghun and drank the tea that they offered. How big is he now? He was born in 1906, so he would be nine already. Why did I not risk my life to escape from that Chinese? But even if I had gotten here, I wouldn't have had the money to take the child with me. She was shaken by guilt.

When a few hours had passed, they heard the sound of people approaching. A handsome boy who looked just like Ijeong was walking with a Mayan woman toward the storehouse. She had more wrinkles, but it was clearly Maria. The boy bashfully lingered a few steps back as Maria held her arms out wide and the two women embraced and cried. Maria pointed to the child, who had ducked behind her. He spoke neither Spanish nor Korean, but Mayan. Yeonsu spoke to the child, first in Korean and then in Spanish, but the only thing he understood was "Mama." Maria slowly wagged her head as if to say that she had had no other choice. It was she herself who had done wrong, not Maria, thought Yeonsu, but she could not hold back tears of resentment. That spark of resentment flared into rage at her mother, Lady Yun, who had married a Mayan and left the hacienda. I will never forgive her for the rest of my life. If only she had taken care of him, we would at least be able to speak to each other!

The overseer brought over a guard who had been passing by. He spoke both Spanish and Mayan and acted as an interpreter. Maria asked Yeonsu why she had waited so long to come. Yeonsu told her that she had had no choice. And that she was thankful. Then Yeonsu asked if she could take the child with her. Maria made a strange face. She said something to the child in Mayan and he ran off. Maria spoke for some time to the guard who was interpreting. The guard nodded his head and listened until she finished, then he told Yeonsu what she had said. "She says that the child is her child." Yeonsu could not believe her ears. She grabbed Maria's arm. Maria turned away from her. Yeonsu screamed, "That's impossible!" She argued with the overseer, who flipped through the account book and said, "It says here that the child is Maria's." The child ran back to Maria, who pressed her lips together. Moisture glistened in the corners of her eyes. It was not that Yeonsu couldn't understand her position. But still.

Bak Jeonghun, who had been standing quietly behind them, stepped forward. He approached Yeonsu, who was in a state of panic, and whispered something into her ear. Yeonsu opened her eyes wide, as if she had just come to her senses. Maria had a bad feeling about her look and took a few steps backward, holding the child tightly to her. Yeonsu approached the overseer and spoke.

"How much is he?"

The overseer glanced at Maria and held up ten fingers. "It's because of the inflation." He scratched his head. Bak Jeonghun took out two 50-peso notes with Carranza's face printed on them and handed them to the overseer. At that moment Maria grabbed the child and ran away. An overseer on horseback chased her down and lashed at her with his whip. Yeonsu shouted, "No! Stop it!" Maria collapsed and the overseer took the child and gave him to Bak Jeonghun. Yeonsu ran to Maria and lifted her up. Maria shook her off and collapsed to the ground, raising her hands to the heavens and pouring out curses in Mayan. When Bak Jeonghun approached her, took out 100 pesos more and handed them to her, Maria grinned like one gone mad. Then she folded up the bills and put them in her mouth. The overseer and the paymaster came running, but Maria did not open her mouth. She stubbornly chewed and swallowed the bills. When the furious overseer kicked Maria, Bak Jeonghun struck him in the face with his fist and then took a pistol from his pocket and aimed it at them. The overseer and the paymaster raised their hands. Bak Jeonghun took the child and Yeonsu and left the hacienda.

They went to Mérida. The child thought of this quiet man as his father and stuck close to him. They slept at the splendid Grand Hotel near the cathedral. They could not talk with the child at all, yet he was quickly captivated by the warmth Bak Jeonghun showed him. Furthermore, in the child's eyes Bak Jeonghun was a very rich man, a man who ate in the finest hotel and restaurant in Mérida. Having never before left Yazche hacienda, the child enjoyed the magnificent night streets of Mérida so much that he did not sleep. And he stuffed himself with food until he thought his stomach would burst. But Yeonsu did not eat a thing.

Bak Jeonghun left the woman and child at the hotel and went to the branch office of the Korean National Association, not far away, to visit his fellow soldiers Jo Jangyun, Kim Seokcheol, Seo Gijung, and others. For the first time in ages, he drank with men who were glad to see him and got very drunk. And he spoke frankly in his native tongue of everything that had happened to him. He returned to the hotel well after midnight and fell asleep. When dawn came, he took the woman and child and left for Veracruz.

# 75

NOTHING HAD CHANGED in the port of Progreso — the stretches of fine white sand like swimming beaches, the piers that stretched out into the ocean, the large ships floating far off, and the small ships shuttling among the wharves. Ijeong thought of when he had first arrived here ten years before. During that time he had become a member of Villa's army and killed countless people. His words grew fewer and his wounds grew greater. He looked at his hands. They were softer than they had been in the henequen fields, but his right hand was thick with calluses where he had held his gun.

Just as he had done on that day ten years ago, Ijeong boarded a train at Progreso station. The train cut across the charred black henequen fields and let him off in Mérida only thirty minutes later. The mood in Mérida was chilly due to Governor Alvarado's arson. He took another train there for Yazche hacienda. Unexpectedly, when he finally came to stand before the gate, he felt no emotion at all. He only felt serene. Perhaps it was because he had no more than a vague hope that she might be there. He walked into the hacienda. The old paymaster sat in the office, and he laughed when he saw Ijeong. "What is it this time?" Ijeong asked back, "This time?" "It's only that we're being visited by a Korean a day these days. Have you come for a child as well?" Ijeong shook his head. "A child? No. I came for a woman." Ijeong described Yeonsu — her age, appearance, family relations, and so on. The paymaster stared at Ijeong as he might at a curious animal, then shrugged. "She was here last

week. She came with some man and took a child with her." Ijeong
furrowed his brow. "What on earth are you talking about?" The paymaster said no more. There was nothing more to say. Ijeong returned to Mérida and saw Jo Jangyun for the first time in seven
years. Jo Jangyun stared in surprise at Ijeong, now a dashing young
man. He embraced him and tousled his hair. "So you're alive. We
thought you had gone to the United States." Ijeong stroked his
beard. "I almost did."

Jo Jangyun and Kim Ijeong stayed up all night, talking about everything that had happened since they had last met. Ijeong heard
about Veracruz, Bak Jeonghun, Yi Yeonsu, and the child. He buried
his head in his knees. "A lot has happened. I'd better go to Veracruz
and pay her a visit."

Jo Jangyun said, "Don't go. You can trust him. I heard that he
was Obregón's barber. And even if he weren't, he is not a man who
would starve his own wife and child. Forget the child whose face
you've never seen. Bak Jeonghun will raise him well."

# 76

IJEONG STAYED IN Mérida for a few days. Going to Veracruz, as
Jo Jangyun had said, didn't seem like a good idea. Yet since he had
heard the bell of Celaya, whenever he closed his eyes he saw Yeonsu's face. Maybe he just longed for someone to comfort his body,
worn out from war and revolution. That was something he could
never get from Jo Jangyun and the others. He envied Bak Jeonghun
his good fortune.

I'll just go see her. With no certainty that she would be happy to
see him, he boarded a ship for Veracruz. When he arrived, he went

to the address that Jo Jangyun had given him and found the barbershop. He loitered out front as customers went in and out and food sellers went up and down the street carrying round baskets. People got their hair cut, got shaved, and ate tortillas. He couldn't see Bak Jeonghun, let alone Yeonsu. From afar he heard the cathedral bell. The school annexed to the cathedral must have let out, for he heard the sounds of children chattering as they rushed out. A short while later, a child pushed aside the barbershop curtain and went in. His face was that of an Asian. The child went into the courtyard next to the shop and splashed in the water. Not long after, when the shadows grew long, a woman stepped out of the shop. Ijeong knew this woman, who turned in the direction of the market. She was dressed like a Mexican, but from the way she walked he had no doubt it was Yeonsu. The baby fat was gone from her cheeks and the line of her chin was sharper, but it was definitely her. Yeonsu spoke in Korean, "Seop! I told you not to do that, didn't I?" The child mumbled something in Mayan and went back into the barbershop. Even though she was scolding the child, her face brightened with happiness.

When Yeonsu's shadow had disappeared, Ijeong went into the barbershop. José paused in cutting a customer's hair to greet him. He seemed a little nervous at the arrival of a strange face. Only Ijeong himself was unaware that there was an irreversible darkness in his face, the face of a man who had been through war and committed meaningless murder. Ijeong sat down in a barber's chair. A man who had been putting charcoal into a stove to boil shaving water took off his gloves, brushed off his hands, and approached Ijeong. It was only after he had tied the cloth around Ijeong's neck out of habit that his eyes met Ijeong's in the mirror. Bak Jeonghun spoke in Spanish.

"How would you like it cut?" When it came to cutting hair, at least, he had never spoken Korean. He had used Spanish from the moment he had begun to learn the trade. Ijeong answered in Spanish. "Short, please." Bak Jeonghun sprinkled a little water on his hair and wordlessly began to cut. The child came running in from the courtyard and watched his father work, but he soon lost interest and went back out to the courtyard. Ijeong said nothing. Neither did Bak Jeonghun. Only José watched out of the corner of his eye as a strange silence fell between the two Asians. Tension hung in the air. Ijeong noticed the portrait of Obregón that hung on the wall. He started speaking in Spanish. "The revolution appears to be almost over."

"That's what they say. General Obregón, he certainly is something, isn't he?"

At that old José interrupted. "He was Obregón's barber, you know. He fought in the Battle of Celaya."

Ijeong closed his eyes. "Ah, is that so? I was there too."

The scissors snipped thin air. José stole a glance at Bak Jeonghun's scissors. It was the glance of a skilled barber. Then Bak Jeonghun suddenly spoke in Korean.

"Which side were you on?"

"Villa's side."

"Many died."

"It is always like that in war."

"They say that they are hunting down Villa's people these days."

"Who knows when the situation might change again?" Ijeong said. "So why were you on Obregón's side?"

"He came here and took me with him."

"Is that all?"

Bak Jeonghun stopped cutting and lathered Ijeong's face.

"I have no interest in those sorts of things. I just want to live here quietly with my wife and child. What about you? Did you really follow Villa because you liked him?"

"Yes. I was hot-blooded."

Bak Jeonghun held the razor blade to Ijeong's left cheek and gently brought it upward.

"And now?"

Ijeong hesitated for a moment.

"In truth, I still am."

Bak Jeonghun pointed to the child playing outside.

"He is your son. But if it's OK with you — well, no, even if it's not OK with you, there isn't much choice — I would like to raise him. Until your blood cools."

The razor blade passed beneath his ear.

"I will not take him with me. I am in no position to raise a child."

"If you are not going to take him with you, it would be better if you left now."

Ijeong raised an eyebrow.

"His mother will be returning shortly."

Bak Jeonghun stopped shaving and brushed bits of hair from Ijeong's neck. Ijeong tried to pay him, but Obregón's barber would not accept the money.

"I will raise the child well. If something should happen with General Obregón, and something happens to me, please take care of my wife and the child. And take care of yourself. No matter what we might do, this is a revolution of a nation not our own. Whichever way it may go, it is best to leave it up to them."

Ijeong went outside. The sky was still bright but the sun could not be seen. Bak Jeonghun kept a gentle watch by the barbershop entrance, like a hunting dog pretending to look the other way. His eyes were smiling but his posture was full of tension. Ijeong turned his steps toward the piers. From afar he could see Yeonsu returning from the market. Bak Jeonghun, his face expressionless, greeted her and led her into the barbershop. Ijeong returned to Mérida. The bell of Celaya was once again ringing in his ears.

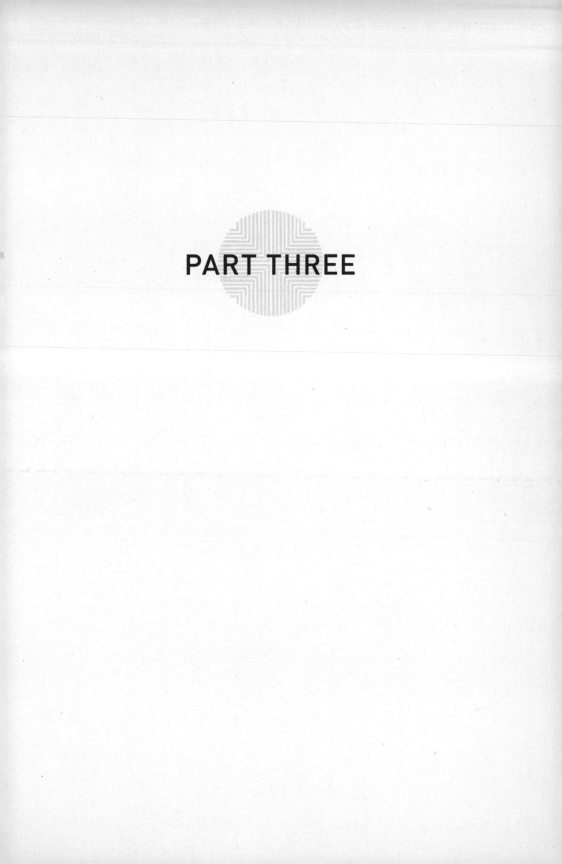

PART THREE

# 77

THE STORIES CONCERNING what happened later in Guatemala vary widely, especially those about the nation that was founded there. Most of the men died in the jungle, but even those who came back alive did not fully understand the origins of that strange nation. There are many cases where a nation's beginnings are shrouded in mist compared to its decline. The following is the leading version of what occurred during those few years in Tikal.

One day, a man led a crowd to the Mérida branch office of the Korean National Association. He was a Mayan, and he said that his name was Mario. His features were unusual. His eyes were sharp and fierce, but his expression was gentle. Mario told Jo Jangyun and Kim Seokcheol an interesting story.

The southern part of the Yucatán Peninsula belonged to Guatemala, and its border faced the Mexican state of Campeche. If you crossed the border and entered Guatemala, you would find a vast jungle there. The Mayan civilization had blossomed long ago in this primitive forest, but now it was nothing more than a tropical rain forest. Before the imperialists had drawn lines on the map, the Mayans had built small nations across the entire peninsula, and these nations repeatedly rose and fell. Some thought that the physi-

cal characteristics of the Yucatán made the emergence of a central-
ized nation impossible. This was because there was abundant water
and produce throughout the region, and no great rivers flowed like
in China, so there was no pressing need for the emergence of a uni-
fied state.

Mario said that his people were fighting against the forces of
President Manuel Estrada Cabrera in the southern Yucatán, in the
northern jungles of Guatemala. A dictator who had come to power
in 1898, President Cabrera was so brutal that Porfirio Díaz could
not begin to compare with him in atrocities. Díaz had at least con-
tributed to the modernization of Mexico, but Cabrera did such pre-
posterous things as designate his birthday and his mother's birthday
as national holidays while he drove the whole of Guatemala into a
quagmire of abject poverty, all for the sake of large American agricultural companies. He was without a doubt the common enemy of
the Guatemalan people. Not only that, but Cabrera's Guatemala,
unlike mestizo-centered Mexico, relied on a ruling system centered
around whites. This meant cruel treatment of mixed bloods and
Mayans. The Mayans, who made up a solid majority of the population, were faced with the severe oppression and discrimination of
the Cabrera regime, and this naturally led to an uprising of Mayans
around the nation.

In particular, the area of Tikal in northern Guatemala was far-
thest from the capital, Guatemala City, and devoid of a transporta-
tion network that would allow access by road, by water, or by air,
and so was ideal for executing a guerrilla war. The problem, however, was force of arms.

"I have heard that there are many former soldiers among the
Koreans of the Yucatán. We need able-bodied men who have abundant combat experience and can handle weapons," Mario said to
the group of men around him. "In return, we will pay you three mil-

lion American dollars. Cabrera has stashed away vast sums of cash, so if the revolution succeeds, a large amount of money will fall into the hands of the revolutionaries. Right now people are outraged at Cabrera's rule and public opinion has turned against him. He will definitely not last long."

Their mouths dropped open at the huge sum. Three million dollars. Not three million pesos, but three million dollars. That was enough for everyone who participated in the war to turn their lives around and still have some left over. They could contribute not only to the operating funds of the Sungmu School and the Korean School, but also to the overseas independence movement. Considering that the total amount used in planning the group move to Hawaii was five thousand dollars, three million was an almost incomprehensible sum to them. Jo Jangyun asked if they could first send a few dozen men and then later recruit and dispatch more. Mario said that would be fine.

Jo Jangyun called an emergency meeting of the Mérida branch. All of the young Koreans who had lost their jobs when the henequen haciendas went up in smoke were interested. The flame of revolution had already swept through the Yucatán as well, so the young people were fascinated by unlimited violence, and the rumors of Ijeong, who had served as a member of Villa's army, also stimulated them. Stories of Ijeong swelled far beyond reality; he was becoming something of a legend among the Koreans. But Ijeong had lived a rather calm and quiet life since his return, and Mario's words had not changed that. He was not particularly interested in Guatemala. Jo Jangyun tried to persuade him.

"You must go. You have abundant combat experience and speak Spanish well."

"I don't want to go this time. After all, this is someone else's revolution, is it not?"

"Yes, that's true. But with three million dollars, we can use that money not only for our own finances but also as capital for the overseas independence movement, so you can't just think of it as someone else's problem."

"I'm sorry, but I have no interest in that either."

Ijeong stubbornly rejected Jo Jangyun's and Kim Seokcheol's overtures. Finally, Jo Jangyun erupted in anger. "How can you live your life thinking only of yourself! Are you planning on idling your time away and eating up the association's food?"

He was like a father to him; he had given him his name. And eventually Ijeong gave in. He no longer wished to involve himself in the revolutionary wars of other countries, but he had no choice. He had no way of making a living right then. He went to Mérida and gathered information on the situation in Guatemala. Guatemala was practically in a state of anarchy. Both Mexico and the United States wondered when Cabrera's regime, with no authority and no validity, would fall. Only the sum of three million dollars was in doubt.

Yet the Mérida branch office resolved to join the war. Forty-two men, most of them students of the Sungmu School, volunteered as the first wave of mercenaries. Among them, of course, were the veteran fighters Jo Jangyun, Kim Seokcheol, and Kim Ijeong, but a large number were in their late teens and had been children when they had left Korea. The person Ijeong was most glad to see was Dolseok. He was startled at seeing Ijeong for the first time in seven years and patted his face. "You've become an entirely different person!" Dolseok had married a Mayan woman on the hacienda but had been unable to take his wife and children out with him. So he went back to the hacienda, raised a ruckus, and was thrown in jail. He managed to be released when Hwang Sayong and Bang Hwajung had come, but had spent the following years in and out of prison. "Why?" Ijeong asked. Dolseok held up his hands and said, "Light fingers."

Seo Gijung, who had joined the military at the same time as Jo Jangyun and whose wish had been to go back to Korea and buy land, also came to Mérida. He had wandered around the state of Campeche selling ironware, but had ultimately failed. The last person to arrive was the palace eunuch Kim Okseon. Now in his late forties, he was the oldest of the volunteers. He pleaded to be allowed to join them, saying that this was his last chance in life, and no one could dissuade him. His dream was to open an inn and restaurant in Mérida upon returning from Guatemala. In his restaurant he would play the guitar, which he had recently learned, for his customers. He had first laid a hand on this instrument in the Yucatán, but like a true palace musician he had quickly learned to play it and boasted his own musical style. He tuned his guitar so that it was slightly off-key, and this curious dissonance evoked forlorn feelings in the listener. It was neither a minor key of the West nor a minor key of Korea but Kim Okseon's unique key, and when the folksongs of the Yucatán and Korea were sung to his music, they were truly beautiful.

Ijeong tried to stop him from going. "It is a jungle there, filled with bugs and wild animals. War is not for people with soft hands like you. And you have never fired a gun." But Kim Okseon was adamant. "Everyone tried to stop me when I said I was going to Mexico. But look at me now. I easily survived in those brutal henequen fields and made a living even during the turmoil of the revolution. Please, take me with you. If I do not go this time, I will not have another chance to earn such a large sum of money. The henequen trade is finished."

A few days later, some men sent from the Guatemala revolutionaries arrived and drew up a contract. In the contract it said that the

Koreans would always obey the orders of their commanding officers and serve faithfully until the day the Cabrera government fell, and that they would be paid three million dollars as soon as the revolutionary army entered Guatemala City and removed the dictator. The forty-three of them signed their own contracts, and a separate contract, to be signed by the commander of the revolutionary army and the president of the Mérida Korean National Association, was drawn up and signed by Mario and Jo Jangyun. When the signing was over and they were about to embark on their grand undertaking, one more person arrived. It was Bak Gwangsu. He had been making a living repairing pot bottoms, and he sometimes visited Mérida to read people's fortunes and on rare occasions perform a shamanic ritual. He was thin as a rail but his face had a healthy color. Someone told him that the hacendado Ignacio had been nailed to a cross and died at the cathedral, and Bak Gwangsu answered that he knew. "I heard the shaman died as well," someone else interjected.

In July 1916, forty-four Korean mercenaries, among them former soldiers, a palace eunuch, a thief, a guerrilla, laborers, orphans, and an apostate priest, followed their Guatemalan guides across the border of Yucatán, through Campcche, and across the Mexico-Guatemala border. With no boundary markers whatsoever in this jungle region, they were unaware for some time that they were already in Guatemala. It was only about 250 miles in a straight line from Mérida to their destination in the Tikal region, but the way was rough.

Their first camp in the jungle hinted at just how rough the road ahead of them would be. Everything there was different from the Yucatán. The humidity was intense and the insects that attacked them were incomparably more vicious than those on the haciendas. Leeches sucked their blood, and mosquitoes bit them through their clothes. There were also bugs that burrowed into flesh, so even if you pulled them out their heads would remain. The Mayan guides adeptly swung their machetes to make a camp. Here, too, the Koreans had to learn everything over again.

The guides pointed at a tall tree. "We communicate with the gods through that tree." The tree was called ceiba. Its trunk was white and its branches, which rose high enough to compete with the clouds, were surrealistically red, like the abode of gods. They prayed briefly before the ceiba tree, then broke off nearby vines and made ropes to tie up hamacas. In the jungle there was a unique way of living. Huge snakes slept calmly above their heads; monkeys made forays against them.

The Koreans finally reached the revolutionaries' base of operations in Tikal, in the El Petén department. Tikal contained the grandest ruins of the Mayan civilization in Guatemala, but everything, including the massive pyramids, was covered in lush trees and earth and looked like small hills rising from the flatlands. Not a single one of the Koreans who arrived there after the arduous journey knew that this was a historic ruin. Some of them wondered at the strange stonework or headless stone statues scattered throughout the jungle, but they didn't take those thoughts any further. Kim Ijeong and Jo Jangyun immediately realized that the lay of the land was such that it could be easily defended. The pyramids, which had been built a thousand years ago, were natural fortresses and lookout towers that allowed a view for dozens of miles in all directions. At the tops of the pyramids were shrines where the priests had dwelled and performed their sacrifices, and these were sturdy enough to be used as bunkers.

Trees that had been growing for a long time rose as if to pierce the sun, and red parrots squawked noisily as they flew between them. The jungle was so dark that fires had to be lit in the middle of the day. The jungle was not quiet. Frogs croaked from all directions, keeping the men up at night. On nights like that, snakes swallowed snakes and frogs ate frogs.

On the day they arrived at Tikal, Jo Jangyun summoned all the men and spoke in a lighthearted voice. "Seeing how we met no resistance on our way here, this place is without a doubt an ownerless land. There is something that I have been thinking about for many years: founding a nation here. When we get our money from them, those who want to go back will go back, but let the rest of us stay here and build a nation. We will call it New Korea, and we will choose a president as they do in the United States. Then let us tell Japan, the United States, and Korea of this, proclaiming to the peoples of the world that our nation is still alive. You saw on the way here that there are many insects and animals in this place, yet it also abounds with trees and fruit, and fertile land and water are abundant, so it is the best place for an industrious people like ourselves to live." The memory of the failed exodus was still fresh in his mind. "This place is just as good as Hawaii. Even if we were to go to Hawaii, we would have to work for others on the sugar plantations, but here we are free. We can stand boldly as an independent nation. We will call all our brethren scattered through the United States and Mexico to live here, farming and trading. Where else is the old remnant kingdom of Balhae? This is Balhae right here."

Yet his idea failed to arouse any real sympathy. They all nodded out of courtesy, but they had decided to return to the Yucatán once they got their money. Nevertheless, Jo Jangyun's grand scheme continued. "In the new nation, everyone will be equal, and it will be a republic. Mayans who want to may join us and live with us, but they will be ruled by us."

"Why is that?" Kim Ijeong asked. Jo Jangyun replied in an incredulous tone, "Are you saying that we should be ruled by them?" "Why do you think that one side must necessarily rule the other?"

Bak Gwangsu, who had been quiet up until then, said, "Why, you ask? Because he's worried that we'll become extinct. We are the minority and the Mayans are beyond number. He is worried that if we mingle with them, we will ultimately disappear. But we're all going to die anyway."

Someone spit and cut off Bak Gwangsu. "This shaman fellow is saying cursed things, damn it!"

Jo Jangyun worked diligently to create the framework for the nation. He built a slightly larger hut to use as a headquarters and wrote everyone's name on a piece of paper and tied it up. Kim Ijeong was placed in charge of military affairs. He inspected weapons and explored the lay of the land with the Mayan commander, Mario. He taught marksmanship and formations to the untrained soldiers.

Not long after, sporadic battles broke out. The Mayan guerrillas attacked the government base at Lake Petén Itzá. On the counterattack, government troops rounded the lake and struck directly at the guerrilla camp on the outskirts of Tikal. Most of the Koreans followed them into battle, yet the government forces were far more spirited than they had expected. Kim Ijeong attacked the Guatemalan troops' rear, using guerrilla tactics he had learned under Pancho Villa's command. The troops fell back to Lake Petén Itzá for fear that their retreat would be cut off. In the midst of the chaos, some of the government troops passed by the pyramid where Jo Jangyun and others were positioned, and showered them with a hail of bullets.

Jo Jangyun was cowed by the bullets that came flying in. The upper part of the pyramid was riddled like a honeycomb by the Guatemalans' bullets. Fortunately, those troops retreated, but Jo Jangyun realized that this guerrilla war was not going to end as easily as Mario had said it would. With the exception of Kim Ijeong and a few others, the guerrillas were mere children with no combat experience, and Kim Seokcheol and Seo Gijung were retired soldiers who hadn't held guns in over a decade. Furthermore, the army of the Korean Empire had not been trained for a guerrilla war in the jungle. After a few more battles, Jo Jangyun was forced to admit that the Korean mercenaries with whom he would be fighting were nothing more than a ragged rabble. And it also occurred to him that the three million dollars they were supposed to receive from the Mayans was totally unrealistic.

The next morning, Ijeong rose from his bed and realized that everything was too quiet. Something was missing from the camp. He went outside and silently counted the Koreans one by one. He called to Dolseok, who was passing by, and asked him if he knew the whereabouts of Jo Jangyun and Kim Seokcheol. Dolseok didn't know where they were either. Ijeong rang the bell and gathered the Koreans. As he had suspected, no one knew where the two were. Upon searching they discovered that their belongings were gone as well. Later, at the muddy edge of the camp, Ijeong found two sets of footprints that disappeared into the jungle.

The night before, Jo Jangyun had gotten up and gone outside. He still had much to do. Staying alive was his first priority. He could not die here. He had to prepare for an assault on mainland Korea and had to carry out the overseas independence movement. No matter how much he wanted to deny it, the provincial government in the jungle had been a wild dream. He unburdened himself in private to Kim Seokcheol. "Even if we were to truly found a nation here, who would recognize us?" Kim Seokcheol agreed. "It was a childish idea. This jungle will kill off even the healthy, and when the government troops besiege us, we will be killed like dogs." Jo Jangyun beat his chest as he spoke. "Then shall we convince everyone to go back?" Kim Seokcheol shook his head. "What about the money we've already received? The revolutionaries will come to Mérida and shoot us all dead. Let us two go back and report to the

Korean National Association, then return after we get instructions. For everyone to die here would truly be to die in vain."

They left the camp before the day grew light. Their steps were even more cautious at the thought that the Mayans might execute them if they were caught, in accordance with the contract. And so the two leaders who had dragged everyone into the jungle headed north that night and ran for their lives.

It was as if some fate were slowly approaching Ijeong with a wide grin. Come on, come. Ijeong sucked forcefully on a cigarette. The anger of those left behind was tremendous. "We thought they were our leaders, and look what they've gotten us into!" someone shouted. "Let us pursue them now and shoot them dead!" But no one was as shocked and bitter as Ijeong. After Villa had been routed, the reason he had returned to Mérida, and the reason he had gotten involved in all this, was Jo Jangyun.

Nevertheless, Ijeong calmly appeased them. "I will be responsible for the contract with the Mayans. It might be upsetting that they left, but maybe it's better this way. Now, if we get the three million dollars, it will all be ours. Forget the political games of the esteemed men of the Mérida branch office or the Korean National Association. That money belongs to the forty of us left here. Those who survive will get everything." They all nodded. Ijeong said, "If you agree to this, let us make our thumbprints. And from now on, traitors will be punished. Only then will we all be able to get back alive." They fell over themselves to sign their names on a piece of white paper and make their thumbprints. Then Ijeong drew blood from his finger and wrote "Deserters will be killed" at the bottom.

Despite this fervent declaration, that night more men attempted to escape. Ijeong heard the sentry yell, got out of bed, picked up his gun, and ran into the jungle. There were two deserters; it was difficult to get through the jungle alone. After a chase, the two were caught and dragged back to camp. One of those caught was Jo Jangyun's comrade Seo Gijung. The other was eighteen-year-old Bak Beomseok. Seo Gijung looked at Ijeong and laughed obsequiously. "We weren't running away. We were going to come back." As for Bak Beomseok, he was trembling like a leaf. Tears and mucus ran together as he knelt down and hung his head to the ground.

Ijeong took from his pocket the document covered with red thumbprints and showed it to the two of them. Then he marched them to a reservoir near the pyramids. There were a lot of bogs before the reservoir. Up until then, many of the Koreans had thought he was just bluffing, to raise morale. But Ijeong aimed directly at the back of Seo Gijung's head and fired his pistol. Seo Gijung, who had sensed his death and struggled at the last moment, dropped with one shot. Eighteen-year-old Bak Beomseok met the same fate. But he was more composed than Seo Gijung. With no Buddhist temple nearby, he left only these words and then closed his eyes: "I pray only that my karma will end here." This time as well, Ijeong mercilessly pulled the trigger.

From that day on, there were no more deserters. The only way out would be to kill Ijeong first. Battles were infrequent. The government troops withdrew to the southern highlands before a pincer attack by the guerrillas. Under the command of the Mayan officers, Ijeong's men ambushed the retreating troops and won a small victory.

Three months went by. Tranquil days passed without casualties, with the exception of a twenty-year-old man who died of fever. Ijeong sat at the top of one of two small, twin pyramids, deep in thought. Perhaps Jo Jangyun's scheme had not been absurd after all. Was Pancho Villa so special? He beat a foreman to death and became a bandit, then took advantage of a period of revolution to become a general, and in the end triumphantly entered Mexico City.

Of course, Obregón drove him off, but even Obregón had been a typical greenhorn at first. And yet was not Guatemala in a far more severe state of anarchy than Mexico? Given the situation, founding a nation would not be so difficult. The Mayans could have their nation and we could have our own small but powerful nation, centered here at Tikal, where we could be self-sufficient. We are outsiders anyway. There is no possibility that we could ever grow like Obregón.

During the next battle, Ijeong indirectly presented his scheme to a Mayan revolutionary commander. "If Cabrera is ousted, you will drive out the white people and start your own nation, no?" The commander said that they would. "Then you too will go to Antigua or Guatemala City, those hospitable highlands, the land of eternal spring?" Again he said that they would. "Then there would be no problem if we founded a small nation around Tikal?" He laughed heartily and said that the Koreans could found a slightly bigger nation if they wanted. He mentioned Belize, to the north, and said that it was a country brought into being by black slaves from Africa. "Similar to your plight, yes?" Ijeong said, "This is very important to us, as our nation across the Pacific Ocean has disappeared." The revolutionary commander nodded as if it were of little importance. Ijeong could see in his face that he wondered what a few dozen people could possibly do.

Then the commander sternly appended a condition: "Except that Tikal will not do. You can stay here for a while in order to help us. But this place is holy ground. By Lake Petén Itzá to the south or in the jungle regions farther north is fine, but not Tikal."

When he returned, Ijeong gathered the remaining soldiers and told them of his plan. There were those who opposed it. Of course there were those who laughed at it as well. No one readily agreed with Ijeong's idea.

"We are nothing more than mercenaries. If their revolution suc-ceeds, we will simply get our money and go back." "Go back? To where? Do we have someplace to go back to?" "Whatever the case, we can't live in this jungle." "Why not? Here there are no hacienda-dos and no governors, only us and the Mayans." "The Mayans may need us now, but if the revolution succeeds, they will chase us out. This land is sacred to them." "It doesn't have to be here. There are lots of good places in the north of Guatemala." "Fine, let's say there are. What does it matter if we have a nation or not?"

Ijeong appeared to think for a moment. Then he grinned. "If it doesn't matter whether we have a nation or not, then does that mean we can have one? If that's true, then we can make a nation, can't we?"

A brief silence fell. "We may all die tomorrow. Is there anyone here who wants to die as a cursed Japanese or Chinese? I don't," Ijeong said. "Then wouldn't it be better to have no nationality?" Dolseok asked. Ijeong shook his head. "The dead cannot choose to have no nation. We will all die as the citizens of a nation. We need our own country. Even if we cannot die as citizens of the country we created, at least we can avoid dying as Japanese or Chinese. We need a country in order to have no nationality."

Ijeong's logic was difficult to grasp. In any case, it was not his logic that convinced them; it was his passion. And that passion was a curious thing. It was not a passion to become something, but a pas-sion to not become something.

And one month later, they founded the smallest nation in his-tory in the temple square of Tikal. The name of the nation was New Korea. The only nation names they knew were Korea and Joseon, so they didn't have much choice. The Mayan revolutionary com-mander sent them a bull as a present. Ijeong sent him his thanks and reassured him that they might have begun here, but they planned to move south to Lake Petén Itzá soon. As a shaman, Bak Gwangsu quietly and humbly performed the sacrifice to celebrate the birth of a new nation, and Kim Okseon went up to the highest place and played his flute. When the ritual ended, Ijeong spoke. "This country is a new country with no division between noble and common, high and low. Now, in this place, we are responsible for its fate. Let us tell Mexico and Korea, letting them join in the establishment of this new country." But almost no one took this declaration of the founding of New Korea seriously.

Their country survived for over a year in the jungle of Tikal. New Korea prohibited desertion and thievery first of all. A month later, some of the soldiers married Mayan maidens. Their country then prohibited child marriage and the keeping of concubines. As time went on, intermarriage with the Mayans increased. The Mayan guerrillas paid them no mind. The wedding ceremonies were a compromise between the Mayan style and the Korean style. Two days before the wedding, the groom would ride a horse to the Mayan village and perform a wedding ceremony in their fashion. They slathered mud on the groom's head and sang songs. They sometimes pretended to seriously threaten to kill the groom, and at other times they fed him a strange potion that made him hallucinate. Yet when the day of the wedding came, they congratulated the bride and groom and sent them off to Tikal with the playing of drums. When the bride arrived in Tikal, they performed a simple wedding ceremony in the Korean style. There was no splendid bridal headpiece or rooster with its legs bound; instead, the couple bowed to each other, shared a cup of liquor, went into the new paja prepared for them, and spent their first night together.

Dolseok found a partner. She was a sixteen-year-old girl who had lost both her parents to the government troops. The couple could not communicate with each other, but they looked happy. Once they went to bed, the sound of ecstatic moaning was heard outside until morning. There were no secrets in the pajas.

Ijeong did not seek a partner. There were those who said that he was trying to set an example, but Ijeong generally spent his time patrolling the area and thinking about places where they could strike out and places where they could draw back. Along with a Mayan guide who could speak Spanish, Ijeong traveled around Tikal, realizing for the first time that this was no ordinary place. The guide said, "This is sacred ground. Look." Stone tombs could be seen wherever he pointed. He grabbed a vine and pulled. At that, a pile of earth crumbled to reveal a stone building. According to the guide, around 700 A.D. a new king, Ah Cacau, appeared. This strong ruler, whose name meant Lord Cocoa, began to build great stone structures here. He was buried in what is called Temple I. Until the year 900, when the Mayan Empire in the area began to collapse for unknown reasons, Tikal enjoyed an age of prosperity. But long before that, countless new arrivals founded kingdoms in Tikal. This happened repeatedly, beginning around 700 B.C., and it was said that the population reached 100,000 by the sixth century A.D. Those in power immediately recognized Tikal's strategic value, even though it was covered by the jungle.

Like the two humps of a camel, the tall Temple I and Temple II stood facing each other; if an army could occupy them first, the enemy would be hard-pressed to pass between them. And around them were many hills, buried ruins that were useful for ambushes and retreats. Past Temple I and Temple II there was a small reservoir on the left, and farther along, Temple III formed yet another steep hill, functioning as a defensive line. If the guerrillas could not repel the enemy there, they could retreat to Temple IV, some six hundred feet away, make their last stand there, and then flee along a narrow path that ran to the northeast.

The reign of the mini-nation of New Korea was unexpectedly long. President Cabrera had his hands full dealing with the problems cropping up near the capital and had no time to pay attention to the northern jungle. Ijeong chose people to be in charge of the supply of goods and to enforce the law. He could lead battles, so he did not appoint anyone else for that. The tranquil days continued. The new year came. The Mayans and the New Koreans had a tug of war in the village square with a rope of twisted henequen fibers. At first Ijeong and his people won, but at the end the Mayans won. They held a festival and enjoyed the days. They even played a mock cavalry battle. Three men formed the horse, one rode on top, and two teams fought against each other. Ijeong and his people won at this. The women divided into sides and cheered on the men. They played the Korean yut game using people as playing pieces, and they also held Mayan-style wrestling matches.

Mario said that the Mayan-mestizo joint revolutionary army in the central region was now threatening the capital. He was glad, saying that the moment of Cabrera's fate was at hand. The government troops who had taken up positions around Lake Petén Itzá were building high wooden barricades, devoting their energies to defense. For the time being, there seemed to be little chance of fierce fighting breaking out. Ijeong asked Mario, "Why are we not advancing south? Isn't that why you hired us?" Mario said, "This is our last base of operations, so we can't leave Tikal empty. And because this place is sacred ground, if we do not defend it, the Mayans will collapse."

One night, after much thought, Ijeong wrote a letter to Bak Jeonghun in Veracruz. "Myself and a few dozen of our people are now at Tikal in Guatemala. We have founded a small country here. It is called New Korea. Here in the jungle, local produce abounds and we lack nothing. It is hotter than the Yucatán, but it rains a lot.

Here, no one exploits anyone else. We sleep with guns in our arms, but our hearts are at ease. Please convey this message to your wife. That I am well. And that I am healthy. And that I wish with all my heart that she will always live happily with you. Please tell her this."

He addressed the envelope but did not mail it. Yet when he left his hut the next day to meet with Mario, the person who had been placed in charge of collecting and sending the mail inadvertently picked up his letter and sent it along with a Mayan mule train that was leaving for Campeche. Ijeong returned and discovered that the letter had been sent, but he was not too upset about it. Even if Yeonsu read it, she would not come here, nor would she abandon Bak Jeonghun and her child.

He also wrote a letter to Yoshida at the Japanese embassy. "Please convey this letter to the ambassador. The Korean people have not had a nation since Japan forcibly occupied the Korean Empire, but in September 1916, in Tikal, Guatemala, on the other side of the world, we finally founded a new nation. Please inform your nation of this. We expect that you will recognize our small country, just as you recognized the revolutionary government of Mexico."

Ijeong showed the letter to all who could read. Then he read it aloud. Two letters, one in Korean and one in Chinese, were sent to Mexico with the mules. But Ijeong was subdued. He had not sent the letter because he really desired international recognition. Rather, it was because he knew all too well that it would be difficult for this nation to last long. Just as Bak Gwangsu had said, this hot and humid jungle, like a blast furnace, would melt everything in the end. People, contracts, races, nations, even sadness and rage. Thus Ijeong believed that there needed to be an official record of what they did in the jungle, if only for a short time. Japan's Ministry of Foreign Affairs was the most suited to this task. They would have to take an interest in the ghost of the nation they had annexed.

Another half year passed. President Estrada Cabrera, who had easily defended his government from attacks by demonstrators and revolutionaries, was now determined to wipe out the Mayan guerrillas who were active in the northern lowland jungle. The United States supported his decision and provided capital and weapons. Tens of thousands of punitive troops assembled south of Lake Petén Itzá. The government troops divided into three brigades and began an operation to mop up the guerrillas in the jungle as one would catch fish in a well with a net.

Of course, the Mayan revolutionaries knew of every movement of Cabrera's troops; they had informants scattered around the jungle. But even though they had detailed information, there was nothing they could do in the face of a massive army. A few revolutionary units launched sporadic surprise attacks on government troop camps, but the troops returned fire with machine guns. A few days later, as soon as the sun rose, the army's attack began. The guerrillas resisted here and there, but they could not withstand the assault and continued to retreat before Cabrera's forces, which captured one region after another like falling dominoes. Ijeong's men agonized over whether to abandon Tikal or to stand and fight against the government there. But at the last moment, Ijeong decided to retreat. "We head north." Mario's Mayan troops were also retreating in that direction. Ijeong's squad had hesitated, and now it was too late; even their Mayan guide had followed his own tribe in retreat. Ijeong set fire to the camp and fled north. But the government troops already held the north.

To the east, then. A government battalion followed close behind Ijeong's troops as they changed direction. Ijeong ordered a few of his men to lie in ambush and continued his retreat, but the ambushers did not wait for the enemy to draw close and hastily rejoined the ranks. It became clear once more that they were a ragged rabble.

There were only about a dozen or so trustworthy soldiers. After their escape had been cut off several times and they had lost three men, Ijeong returned to Tikal's Temple I, where they had started. After leaving a few men in ambush in an unexpected place to distract the government troops, he remained at Temple I with twenty of his men and positioned the rest at Temple II, planning to ambush the troops as they passed between them. Ijeong lost two more men in the process.

When the Guatemalan forces heard gunfire from the small twin pyramids near the central square, they suspected an ambush and headed for Temple I. They speedily climbed Temple I and Temple II, intending to occupy favorable positions before the guerrillas did. But the Koreans were already entrenched there. Ijeong waited until the last moment, when the enemy was nearly at the summit, and then all opened fire at once. The temples, which had been built at a steep angle to exalt the glory of the gods, were slippery now that they were covered with earth. Most of the government troops fell to the bullets that poured from the heavens, and the rest of them moved hastily to avoid the gunfire and tumbled back down, injuring themselves. The guerrillas scored a similar victory at Temple II. The government troops retreated to the area around the temple square and re-formed their lines. Ijeong took eight men and pursued them, showing them that they still had the will to fight. At that, the frightened troops dropped their ammunition and supplies and withdrew to the outskirts of Tikal.

A few days later, Cabrera's forces attempted a bolder attack. They set up machine guns on the tops of buildings that were about the same height as Temples I and II and poured bullets into the Koreans' position. The infantry used ropes to climb up under cover of the machine guns. Ijeong's men cut the ropes and fired their rifles, but it was not enough. Ijeong decided to retreat to Temple IV, around which there were no other buildings. Ijeong's troops slid down the western face of the Temples I and II, and the thirty-odd men that remained of New Korea's fighting force fled toward Temple IV, two hundred yards from their present location. A few of them remained behind in the trees to hinder the pursuers and cover the guerrillas' escape. Sweat poured into their eyes and soaked their clothes. Some were bleeding from wounds on their arms and legs. They all followed Ijeong's orders and climbed up the steep face of Temple IV. The older Bak Gwangsu and Kim Okseon fell behind. Their comrades tied ropes around their waists and pulled the two up. Bak Gwangsu put his gun down and sat in front of the small shrine at the top. He looked at the sky and said, "Hey, Mr. Palace Eunuch. Why don't you play the flute for us?" Sweat fell onto the hot barrels of their rifles and hissed as steam rose up. Kim Okseon laughed and said, "Hold on just a little longer. They said that Cabrera would be overthrown, did they not?" Then he took out his flute. Ijeong listened to the clear sound of the flute on top of Temple IV, some two hundred feet above the jungle floor, as he pulled up a German machine gun they had seized from the government army a few days before. The soldiers, hearing the music, were gripped by nostalgia.

When the men gazed around them from the summit of the pyramid, the jungle looked like a vast green blanket. From the side, this pyramid, which was said to have been built in 741, looked like a giant, swollen termite mound, and the slope on all four sides was treacherously steep. Unlike the other Mayan pyramids, which had been built on great isolated plains, the pyramids of Tikal, rising from the tangled jungle, felt like a completely different world. Those who had sweated buckets climbing up here desperately prayed that the Guatemalan troops would pass by them and follow the main force of Mayan revolutionaries that had retreated to the north. Ijeong commanded four soldiers to fire their guns into the air as they fled north in order to lure the government army toward the northern ruins.

But the government troops were not fooled. They also saw that Temple IV was a point of strategic importance. Their main force approached and surrounded the temple and a fierce battle broke out. In accordance with their usual practice of not fighting at night, when the sun set they withdrew while maintaining their perimeter. In the morning, though, they would rush in again and renew the battle. The mercenaries were running out of ammunition. The government troops changed their strategy and settled in for a siege. As darkness fell, Ijeong decided that they would take advantage of the cloudy weather to break through the perimeter. Ammunition was one thing, but there was no water on Temple IV. Dolseok's squad returned from the north and attacked the army's rear, and Ijeong's men rolled down the temple's steep north face like a slide. The government troops fired at once into the darkness. Ijeong ran as if mad. The sound of flying bullets rang, zing zing, in his ears.

He finally arrived at their destination, the reservoir. Five men were already there. Dolseok and four of his men, who had helped them on the fringe, were gasping for breath. Bullets flew in every direction. At that moment something cold ran down Ijeong's chest. And the clamor of gunfire drew closer.

"It's the enemy!" They all splashed through water up to their knees and spread out in all directions. As he ran, Ijeong felt his neck and found that blood flowed from where he had been grazed by a bullet. It didn't appear to be a serious wound. The government troops scattered and chased them. Dolseok, who had gone ahead, screamed to them, "This way!" Where Dolseok pointed was a small hill about three times the height of a man. At the bottom was a small hole, the entrance of another Mayan structure from long ago — it might have been the tomb of a great personage. The surviv-

ing eleven men went inside one by one, and the last one in cam-
ouflaged the entrance with vines. The stench of blood and sweat
mixed powerfully with the smell of mold. They held their breath
as they pointed the muzzles of their rifles toward the entrance and
waited for the troops to pass by.

A short while later, Kim Okseon, who had been late in fleeing, appeared before them, gasping and dragging his gun. Dolseok
started to bolt out, but Ijeong stopped him. At that moment, a government soldier's bullet passed through Kim Okseon's heart. This
soldier came up, aimed at Kim Okseon's head, and calmly fired a
few more rounds. Thus ended the life of the last palace eunuch musician of the Korean Empire. The Guatemalans left his body and
maintained their formation, continuing forward. As soon as the government troops had gone, three vultures descended on Kim Okseon's body in a noisy flurry of wings. One of them pecked at the eunuch's chest. Blood spurted up and soaked its beak.

Ijeong left one guard behind and commanded the rest of them
to head down to the basement of the ruined building. There might
be an exit there. When they went down they found an unexpectedly broad space. But it was a dead end. They all relaxed a bit and
took some rest in that place, their faces gloomy. "We're all going to
die, aren't we?" said a young mercenary. Ijeong was bothered by the
blood that flowed from his neck. Dolseok tore some cotton cloth
that he had and wrapped it around Ijeong's neck like a bandage.
The bleeding stopped but it still hurt terribly. Ijeong found a chair
sculpted in the form of a jaguar. The jaguar's back formed the back
of the chair, and the head acted as the legs. The place was filled
with intricate stone sculptures and graven hieroglyphs, which were
nothing more than meaningless fragments of stone to them. Ijeong
thought about the numerous kingdoms that had been founded in
Tikal. He grew melancholy. They had all fallen.

Dawn broke and the sun rose above the trees. Ijeong and his men waited there for night to fall. When darkness came he went outside and looked around. His throat was so dry. He didn't sense any sign of the government troops, only the thick jungle undergrowth. Ambush was not the enemy's specialty, so he eliminated that possibility. They headed east first, quietly advancing step by step. After they had walked about half a mile in this way, they gradually began to relax. They concluded that the army had withdrawn to its quarters. Ijeong warned them several times to stay alert, but he could not completely stem the excitement of the young people who had escaped death. Suddenly, several monkeys screeched and swung from tree to tree. Something was out there. The monkeys fled from Ijeong's right to his left. His men, who were as used to life in the jungle as anyone, ran in the direction the monkeys were fleeing. Pow, pow. The bullets flew faster than sound and brought down the soldiers. The sound of gunfire was like popping corn. Ijeong blamed himself for leaving their hiding place after only a day. Vines ruthlessly scratched at his face as he ran. He cast off the bandage that had been wrapped around his neck. There was no end to the sound of bullets zipping past his ears. When he reached the two low, twin pyramids to the north, there were only three men beside him. Ijeong caught his breath and reloaded his rifle. But before they could regroup, they were completely surrounded by soldiers who had come down from the twin pyramids.

Ijeong threw aside his gun and raised his hands. An army officer ordered his soldiers to bind the four of them. Then he walked ahead of them. When they reached the swamp he told them to stop. The government soldiers fired their guns one after the other from behind, enjoying it. Ijeong was the last to fall. His knees, face, and stomach were driven into the swamp.

Bak Gwangsu never escaped from Temple IV. He had always

liked that place. He watched the sun set from the top. When the popcorn sound of gunfire from the north face and over by the reservoir stopped and the government troops confirmed the results of the battle, a few soldiers tied ropes and climbed up to the summit of Temple IV. They were startled to see Bak Gwangsu sitting there, free from harm. He sat as quietly as a corpse. When they realized he had no intention of attacking them, they prodded his body with their military boots. Bak Gwangsu held out both hands and stood up like a tumbling doll in an attempt to not fall over, and he smiled brightly. The soldiers smiled too, and then aimed at his head and pulled their triggers. His body fell into the shrine. The soldiers searched the dead man's clothing. In his chest pocket they discovered an old and faded certificate that looked as if it might rip at the slightest touch. On this document, Chinese characters reading "Born on Wi Island, Jeolla province, 28 years old, Bak Gwangsu," and the official seal of the Korean Empire glimmered faintly. Yet there was no one who could decipher these characters.

# EPILOGUE

A dozen of the mercenaries barely succeeded in escaping from Tikal. They first made their way to Mérida, then scattered throughout Mexico.

Jo Jangyun and Kim Seokcheol returned to Mérida and reported the results of the Korean expedition to Guatemala. They claimed that the Mayans had deceived them. Jo Jangyun remained in Mérida and resumed serving as the leader of the Koreans. Kim Seokcheol participated in the excavation and restoration of Mayan ruins at Chichén Itzá, near Cancún.

Gwon Yongjun stayed in the San Francisco area and became an opium addict. After his money ran out, he was reduced to working as a day laborer. When Japan attacked Pearl Harbor in 1941, he was mistaken for a Japanese and arrested. He died of lung cancer in an internment camp.

Don Carlos Menem lost much of his fortune, including his henequen hacienda, during the turmoil of the revolution. He ran for governor of the Yucatán several times, but lost to Governor Salvador Alvarado. In his final years he entered a local monastery and donated what little remained of his estate to the Church.

In Mérida, Yi Jongdo heard that a massive anti-Japanese demonstration had taken place in Korea shortly after Gojong died, in 1919. Erroneously believing that the Japanese would leave and the dynasty would be restored, Yi Jongdo refused to sleep and gave himself over to writing a memorial to the throne, hoping to offer political advice to the new emperor. Before completing his work, he suffered a fatal stroke. Upon his death, Yi Jinu burned all of his father's belongings.

Yi Jinu worked as a manager and interpreter on haciendas in the Yucatán until the 1920s. He married and had two children. When the henequen trade withered, he crossed over to Cuba and earned a lot of money doing similar work on the sugar plantations there. Later he entered the clothing business. He had a large house in Havana and headed several firms, but when the Batista government fell and Castro came to power, he fled to Florida without so much as a handkerchief to his name, and died there.

The Guatemalan dictator Manuel Estrada Cabrera was overthrown during the revolution of 1920 and fled abroad. Just before that, Mario, the guerrilla leader, was killed in the jungle by a bullet from another guerrilla's gun.

In the autumn of 1917, Bak Jeonghun received a letter addressed to him from the state of Campeche. It was Ijeong's letter, which had been sent a year earlier. At nearly the same time, Kim Jeongseon, a Baptist evangelist in Guatemala City, visited him. Kim Jeongseon told him the news of Ijeong and the others. When he left, Bak

Jeonghun asked his wife to go with him down to the piers. He strad-
dled a log bench and spoke.

"News has come. They say your friend died in Guatemala."

Yeonsu showed no emotion when he told her this. Then Bak
Jeonghun gave her the letter. When she had read it, she wept.

"So he came here."

Bak Jeonghun nodded.

"I cut his hair and shaved him."

Yeonsu nibbled at her fingernails. And she did not cry again.
Three years later, Bak Jeonghun had a sudden heart attack while
cutting hair, and he died. Yi Yeonsu began a lending business with
Bak Jeonghun's money. In only a few years she became so rich that
no one in Veracruz could look down on her. She then went up to
Mexico City and bought a few bars that also served as theaters and
hired dancers. She grew to be a prominent figure of the amusement
district, doing no work for charity, relying on no religion at all, and
devoting herself only to raking in money. The police and the civil
authorities tried a number of times to bring her up on charges of
promoting prostitution, but they failed. She died in Mexico City at
the age of seventy-five. All her property was inherited by her son,
Bak Seop.

The main industry of the Yucatán Peninsula today is tourism. Mil-
lions of visitors swarm to the Mayan ruins every year. The henequen
haciendas have almost all disappeared, turned into wasteland, but
a few of them have been transformed into museums that welcome
tourists.

Only in 1956 did research and exploration of the jungle-covered
Mayan ruins of Tikal begin in earnest. The University of Pennsylva-
nia and the Guatemalan government undertook research and resto-

ration projects. In 1991, the Guatemalan and Spanish governments decided to restore Temple I and Temple IV, which were covered by earth and trees, to their original forms. Research teams found a few skeletons at the summits of the temples and nearby, and these were sent to museums. But no traces were unearthed of the group of mercenaries who had passed through that place, or of the small, insignificant country they had founded.

## AUTHOR'S NOTE

This novel began with a conversation between two passengers on a flight from Los Angeles to Seoul: a researcher on the history of Korean emigration and a Korean-American film director. The researcher had only just met the film director on that flight, yet he told him a story that was a little hard to believe. He said that at the turn of the twentieth century, more than a thousand Koreans boarded a ship, crossed the Atlantic, and arrived in Mexico, and some of them formed a small nation in the jungles of Central America. I heard this story later, from the film director. At the time I paid little attention to it, but the story stayed with me, buried in a corner of my mind. It sounded too strange to have been made up, and for this reason I suspected there might be some truth to it. Still uncertain, I went to the library to look for historical materials. I stumbled upon an article from 1916 in the *New Korea* in San Francisco. This newspaper, published by Korean immigrants living in the Bay Area, reported that some of the Koreans who had been "sold" to the Mexican henequen haciendas had fought as mercenaries in the Guatemalan civil war, and that they had founded a nation in the jungle but were soon wiped out. My curiosity was piqued.

I made up my mind to write this novel and began to research the story in earnest. It was not easy. Sources were scarce, and those that I could find were vague. To add to the difficulty, as soon as the emigrants left Jemulpo, Korea was reduced to a colony of Japan. They were completely forgotten. Only a few brief newspaper articles depicted the emigrant laborers who were leaving for the unknown land of Mexico. The Koreans on the British ship *Ilford* were a varied group. According to the records, discharged soldiers, members of the royal family, Catholic priests, palace eunuchs, shamans, and women and children of all ages boarded the ship. Aristocrats, commoners, even freed slaves were thrown together. Some of the passengers kept journals. Through these journals I discovered that there were two deaths and one birth during the voyage, and that when the emigrants arrived in Mexico they were scattered among various haciendas, and almost none of them succeeded in ever returning home.

In the spring of 2003, I traveled to Mérida, in the Yucatan, and began gathering information. I found a handful of descendants of the immigrants, but none of them spoke Korean. Yet they did know the word "kimchi" and ate something similar to it. I crossed the border into Guatemala and, after visiting Tikal and the surrounding area, settled in the city of Antigua to write my novel. Later, I returned to Seoul and finished the writing there.

Why did I call the novel *Black Flower*? Black is a color created by combining all the other colors. Similarly, everything is mixed together in this novel — religion, race, status, and gender — and what emerges is something completely different. The feudal order of Korea collapses in an instant. But there is no such thing as a black flower; it exists only in the imagination. In the same way, the place that the characters in the novel hoped to go to is a utopia that does not exist in reality. They arrive in the wrong place and live out their lives there.

While I was writing, I thought of myself as a sort of shaman. The desires of those who had left for a distant place and been completely forgotten came to me like letters in bottles cast into the sea, and I believed that the emigrants directed me to write their stories. It was only when I finally believed this that I was able to begin — and finish — the work. So it is only fitting that I dedicate *Black Flower* to the 1,033 people who left Jemulpo Harbor in 1905.